THIS HOE GOT ROACHES IN HER CRIB

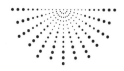

QUAN MILLZ

QUAN MILLZ PRESENTS

A NOTE TO READERS

This is a work of satirical fiction that could be described as a dark comedy combined with social commentary. In no way do the descriptions of the characters reflect my personal feelings or beliefs in regards to those of African descent, particularly Black women. The stereotypes employed in the book are deliberate in that I attempt to cast a light on the state of contemporary urban pulp fiction.

Enjoy,
QUAN MILLZ

CHAPTER ONE

"*A*LL THESE FUCKIN' ROACHES AND SHIT! AHHHHH! GOD MOTHAFUCKIN' DAMN IT!!" Fredquisha's murderous gaze was laser-focused onto five black-brownish roaches.

All ranging in sizes.

"Ughh! And a bitch ain't got time for this shit today! I'm hungry and a bitch need to get her pussy ate," the agitated section 8 strag continued to nag.

The biggest roach – Daddy Roach Sr. – embarked on a dangerous journey to lead his family to a mecca of stale food. His wings lightly flapped. He used his long, wise antennas to lead his loyal wife of thirty-two days, their two well-trained teenage sons and their precious baby daughter towards the distant smell of decaying Domino's pepperoni and sausage pizza crust hiding away in a dark corner of Fredquisha's messy apartment living room.

Every third Friday of the month when them food stamps hit her EBT card, Fredquisha usually treated her three kids to greasy pizza, saucy buffalo wings, and cinnasticks. The pizza fiesta was sort of like a food stamp renewal day of celebration. Truth be told though, the pizza was also a way to get them muhfuckin' kids temporarily off her flabby, tatted back.

Fredquisha hated to have to spend her weekends watching her "bad ass" kids, especially when she needed to get ate out and dicked down by some local ChiRaq savage. Only God knows why she was so annoyed watching them…ain't like the bitch had a job where her weekends were invaluable, deserving precious relief from a hard week of work. Every day was a fucking weekend for this hoe.

ANYWAYS…

This particular crust Daddy Roach Sr. scented had been nestled away for weeks. Shit – possibly months, out of the purview of other vermin living in the grimy apartment.

Had Fredquisha's mama taught her the importance of admiring cleanliness as a virtue, the months-old crust would've been a non-issue. Perhaps then Fredquisha would've not been staring down the critter family peacefully pilgrimaging along the hallway's dusty white cracking baseboard.

"I swear to GOD! These mothafuckin' kids keepin' my house nasty as SHIT! They gettin' on my last damn nerves and I got shit to do today! They really gon' make me go off on they mothafuckin' asses!" Fredquisha griped under her dry, morning blunt-infused breath.

Fredquisha – better known as 'MooMoo' in the streets – positioned herself in close proximity to the migrant roach family. A bitch was ready to go to war against the critter enemies invading her living room.

Her eyes turned to homicidal slits. A butterfly of anxiety flapped its wing in her growling empty stomach. Fredquisha knew roaches were hard to motherfuckin' kill. If she was going to be victorious in offing this sneaky fuck nigga roach and his family, she needed to smite hard, so she could crush their organs, killing them on instant impact.

Fredquisha raised her right foot, leaned down and then pulled off her Wal-Mart black flip-flop. Now armed and dangerous with the $2.99 plastic flip-flop in her hand, she slowly and carefully hovered her weapon of choice over Daddy Roach Sr. His long antennas wavered side to side, unaware of Fredquisha's looming death plot.

Raised in Chicago's notorious Cabrini Green housing project high rises 'til the age of twenty, Fredquisha had no trace of fear for roaches in her body. No fear of white mice. No fear of daddy long leg spiders. Not even a trace of fear for Norwegian brown rats. Once a major problem in Chicago's slums.

Ducking and dodging at the sound of rapid gunfire was the most valuable tool any young nigga growing up in Chicago's fucked up and ultra-violent housing projects had to learn quickly. And then the next valuable housing project survival skill young niggas had to acquire was the art of killing roaches.

Fear of stray bullets aside, any child regardless of socioeconomic status starts off with an innate fear of insects, bugs and other creepy, monstrous creatures. Nonetheless, young project niggas are taught to cultivate Japanese samurai warrior-like fearlessness when it comes to living with roaches. Why? There's a 99.9999 percent chance these kids are going to be roommates with bugs until the day they leave their piss-smelling public housing residencies.

Therefore, from a tender age, young Cabrini kids got initiated into a gang of hardened roach murderers, learning how to gangbang on those muhfuckas when they encroached their set [living room, bedroom, kitchen, etc.]. So, with all that being said you already know a ghetto bitch like Fredquisha was a certified roach hitta. *Concentrate, bitch. You got it,* Fredquisha thought to herself. *Kill these fuck niggas...*

SMACK!

Daddy Roach Sr. went on to be with the Lord.

The front of his obituary read:

3

Homegoing Celebration For The Late Daddy Roach Sr.
Sunrise May 2018- Sunset June 2018
Rev. Dr. Lucious Roachson, III presiding...
Mama Roach, shocked and grieving, tried to flee for cover. Her three kids trailed her, but this lethal Fredquisha hoe obviously wasn't going to let them get away. They had to mothafuckin' die too and be buried next to their daddy!

"Where the fuck ya'll think ya'll goin, huh?" Fredquisha shrieked with retribution colored in her vicious words.

SMACK! SMACK! SMACK! SMACK!

Gruesome genocidal sight. An entire family wiped out.

But this was just the beginning of a growing problem...

Daddy Roach Sr. had 1,861 brothers, sisters, nieces, nephews, uncles, aunts and other relatives lurking in the cut, ready to get to that pizza crust and other discarded trash scattered throughout the cluttered and disgusting apartment.

An unclouded Saturday morning. The first weekend in June. Chicago's South Side. The neighborhood: the infamous Englewood. A ten-unit apartment building owned by Mr. Nathaniel "Nate" Garrison, a retired, 67-year-old postal worker, stood on the corner of 63rd Street and Halsted Avenue.

Twelve years ago, after giving the United States Postal Service thirty hard, sweaty years of carrier service, the Chi-town Bronzeville native decided to dab into real estate per the advice of his younger brother Louis. The younger brother had owned some low-income rental properties throughout the predominantly black south and west sides of the city, and big bro Nate wanted to get a slice of the apparently rich and decadent rental property income pie.

Nate was hesitant at first given. He was the more fiscally

conservative sibling and didn't want to fuck up his retirement coins. Nate, divorced now for nearly ten years, father of four kids, and grandfather to nine, eventually caved in and gave rental property investing a shot.

Flash forward a decade and two years later...It turned out that buying an apartment building in the heart of the gradually depopulated Englewood ghetto and filling it with section 8 voucher recipients was a guaranteed government-subsidized goldmine. Good ass passive income that diversified his diverse retirement funds.

Nate's $65,657 yearly pension, untapped 401k, $1300 monthly social security check and rental property income afforded him the opportunity to take his quarterly trips to the Dominican Republic. There he'd sipped on margaritas and dined on young, chocolate prostitute pussy he'd often procure from Punta Cana's white sand beaches.

His penchant for foreign coochie explained his lack of addressing the growing issues plaguing the apartment building that housed roughly twenty-three tenants. Nate was very hands-off when it came to his property management, often times paying Glen, his functional crackhead ex-brother in law, to do spotty, erratic building maintenance. The decade of ownership devolved Nate into a prototypical Chicago slumlord.

This is the exact reason why on this beautiful and sunny Saturday morning, Ms. Fredquisha Pierce, a tenant who had been in the building now for some three years, was manifestly heated – and not by the sun, but by the sight of the roach family she just massacred with no remorse.

This was a problem from time to time she tried to get Mr. Garrison to fix. She'd contact him every so often through e-mail or phone call. Some days later, toothless crackhead Glen would arrive, chit chat, spray the house, lay out some traps and then take off, not to be seen or heard from for months.

Nonetheless, at the end of the day, the former Cabrini Green resident just grew immune to the infestation. Roaches were... just roaches. A minor nuisance really. Not a problem she felt compelled to bitch and complain to the City of Chicago's Housing Authority (CHA) in a letter or phone call. Crazy thing was, CHA had a dedicated hotline she could've easily dialed to address the pest issue.

Even crazier – Fredquisha was a section 8 voucher holder and these types of issues would get any landlord in trouble big mothafuckin' time. So much so Nate's despondent slumlord ass could end up getting banned from the Section 8 program and could face serious fines. And not just fines from the federal government, but even the State of Illinois and the City of Chicago.

However, the unemployed and welfare system abusing Fredquisha didn't want to rock the boat and snitch on Mr. Garrison. Why? She was constantly late paying her percentage of the rent that Section 8 didn't cover to Mr. Garrison. Nevertheless, unlike other landlords, he didn't give a fuck so long as he was getting that steady check from the 'gubment'.

Rather than clean up the crushed roach corpses slimed onto the bottom of the wall and baseboard, the uneasy and rushed single mother of three furiously made her way back into the kitchen in search of her half-smoked, peach-flavored Philly blunt. Fredquisha picked the blunt up off of one of her dirty kitchen countertops and wedged it in between her crusty, plump purple lips. She whisked out a lighter from her left pocket and lit the blunt up. She took three long puffs. Exhaled. Waited a few moments to let the weed calm her jittery nerves. The THC high overtook her portly body. Fredquisha then opened the palm of her left hand and then hawked up the biggest ball of gooey, frothy spit into her palm. She put the lit end of the blunt out into the viscous pool of saliva and then stuffed it in her pocket for later. Nasty bitch.

Her breath a bit tart, Fredquisha now needed the refreshing taste of menthol in her mouth. Why she just didn't go brush her teeth instead? Well, she was gonna handle that later when she went to go take a shower.

The veteran roach assassin rummaged through a drawer near the same filthy, crowded countertop and pulled out her pack of already opened Newports.

"Fuck!" She forgot she was already on her last square. Then she quickly remembered she had a partly smoked cig resting in an ashtray with other butts, an almost overflowing mound of ash in the middle. The half-smoked square was cooling the fuck out like it was relaxing in a crowded Carnival cruise jacuzzi.

Fredquisha, slowly getting angry again, dashed into the semi-smoky living room and hastily located the ashtray sitting on top of a brown coffee table. Once Ms. Pierce spotted the cigarette she smoked last night, she leaned down, pulled it out of the crowded ashtray and then slapped it in between her cracking, dark violet lips. She lit it up with a blue BIC lighter in her hand. She took as many quick puffs as she could to finish the cigarette. Once the cig was no longer smokable, she put it out in the ashtray. She blew out a steady stream of smoke from her nostrils like a medieval dragon.

With a trail of lingering Newport smoke following her, Fredquisha marched through the dusty, smoky, and dimly lit hallway of her apartment. Her heavy feet thumped on the filthy beige carpet as another roach ran for its life, out of Fredquisha's sight. Lucky muhfucka. He better thank the roach Lord!

Disregarding the chit-chat and laughs she heard coming from her two sons' bedroom, Fredquisha stormed her way towards her youngest child's bedroom.

She pulled out her cell phone from her back pocket, glanced down in her hand and saw 9:43 AM splattered across the partly cracked iPhone screen. The phone's neon pink cover encrusted with sequins and glitter evidently didn't do shit to protect the screen from cracking some months ago. She had dropped it at a Hooter's out in suburban Lansing while she was on a date with some low key dope boy.

The agitated mother bit her lip. Fredquisha shook her head out of frustration of feeling like time wasn't on her side anymore. Grumbling, she slipped the phone back into her back pocket. Waves of infuriation once again swept over her. She was mad as fuck that she just wasted four minutes killing some roaches.

Without even bothering to knock, she barged right into her daughter's bedroom. Her daughter was sitting on the floor Indian style, using a couple of off-brand broke crayons to doodle in some cheap Dollar Store coloring book. The young girl quickly looked up at her obviously angered guardian. The young daughter knew her mother was livid as her body language projected, "lil girl, I'm finna whoop yo ass!" Fredquisha, with her eyes now widened in rage, gawked her young daughter straight into her unassuming, juvenile brown doe eyes.

"UMMM, MYYAH! WHAT THE FUCK IS YOU DOIN?!?"

The young girl, Myyah, was frozen and silent for a moment before she carefully answered, "Colorin'...'cuz I'm done cleanin'..."

Fredquisha looked around with her scrunched her yellow face up. Her vicious eyes widened with more irritation as she saw a pair of pink socks on the floor.

"YOU AIN'T DONE YET! YO ROOM STILL LOOK A MESS!" Fredquisha roared, and then continued to shout, "LIS-TEN! YOU BETTER HURRY UP AND CLEAN MY SHIT UP, LIL HOE. IN TWO SECONDS, I'M FINNA SMACK THA FUCK OUT CHO UGLY ASS!" Fredquisha then screamed out a list of things she thought Myyah still needed to tidy up before she was scheduled to go over her grandmother's house for the rest of the weekend.

"Ok," Myyah responded once Fredquisha gave her another four chores she needed to complete.

Fredquisha then growled at six-year-old Myyah, "DAMN! You know you just like yo stupid ass, hardheaded ass daddy! That's why he locked the fuck up now!" As the mother kept screaming threats of violence towards her now terrified daughter, Myyah jumped up from the floor and jumpstarted her "cleaning".

Poor Myyah, tremoring at the sound of her mother's hostile tone, nippily tried to do her best to finish tidying up her room – the smallest in the entire apartment. It was actually not a bedroom, rather a large utility closet that Fredquisha converted into a bedroom. Here was the kicker – Myyah's room was in actuality the cleanest in the entire 'three-bedroom' apartment. Aside from her mother, Myyah also lived with her two older half-brothers.

Fredquisha stood by Myyah's bedroom door, now holding her arms by her crusty, blackened elbows. She rapidly tapped her foot against the beige carpeted floor – obviously in much need of a vacuum. Hell, truth be told, it needed to be professionally cleaned.

Regardless of the trillions of THC molecules running a marathon within Fredquisha's blood vessels, Fredquisha's anger was getting gradually explosive, especially with Myyah. Fredquisha had places to go, people to see, and ultimately some dicks to suck later tonight if her plans went smoothly.

Fredquisha, 34, once a vixen back in her day, was now a tired ass looking hoe who stood at about 5'5 and weighed a solid 213 pounds. She thought she was around 175, but she hadn't been to her general family physician, Dr. Patrice in while. Her doctor was down the block at the free Women's Health clinic. But Fredquisha only made a visit when she had a bad yeast infection, STI, or when she'd get a long-lasting, turbulent case of bacterial vaginosis.

Known once for her small waist, Fredquisha was now in possession of a plump, undefined midriff. Remnants of what was once a thick ass now resembled two steroid-injected brown potatoes lumped together. A set of double-d cup drooping titties hung from her chest. With no bra on, it was visible from the shirt covering her chest that she had both nipples pierced.

The biggest black satin bonnet cap crowned Fredquisha's head this morning, matching the slightly torn up black wife beater wrapped around her chest and torso. A big Celtic cross tattoo was etched into her unshaven right arm. A spread of angel wings was tatted across her upper chest. Some faded blue denim Bermuda shorts she bought some years ago from the Rainbow store not too far away tightly snugged her cellulite-ridden legs.

Under the sour-smelling bonnet were seven cornrows braided into the ratchet mother's skull. Yesterday Myyah's disability check (Fredquisha had the girl diagnosed with ADHD to get them social security-federal government coins) came in the mail, and rather use the funds towards good use like tutoring or afterschool care, a bitch was about to go get her hair, nails, and feet done.

Tonight was the night Fredquisha swore up and down she was gonna snag her a baller at DASH, some upscale black night-club in the South Loop (South Downtown). Paulette, Fredquisha's hairdresser (really just her bestie who knew how to do hair), had this bomb ass ultra-long, middle part lacefront that she was gonna glue onto the bitch's head and have her ass looking like she was straight from Bangladesh or some shit.

With time slipping away and the feeling of anxiety giving her a slight migraine, Fredquisha temporarily turned her attention away from Myyah and then shot her head down into the room across the hall. "Ay, Quimani and Zy'meer! Ya'll need to hurry the fuck up and be ready in five minutes! Yo grandmama gon be here soon and so will Myyah's! I got shit to do and you bad ass kids already fuckin' with my mothafuckin' weekend plans! HURRY THE FUCK UP NOW!"

"Ok, mama..." the two boys barked from the other side of their bedroom door.

Not saying a word, the slender brown-skinned daughter continued to scuttle her room, trying to figure out what else she could do to make the room look tidier. Still feeling her mother's vicious presence burning in the back of her head, Myyah quickly scanned the room with her innocent eyes looking to see if she did a good job. She felt she was done and did her best to follow her mother's irrational instructions.

Since her father, Austin, was locked up and serving a two-year sentence in Cook County Jail for a probation violation, Myyah lived in the oppressive terror of her mother. Myyah living with Fredquisha went completely against Austin's wishes. Before getting locked up, he tried hard to convince a judge to hand over custody of Myyah to his mother, Mrs. Watkins.

Austin thought Fredquisha was reckless, filthy, irresponsible and unfit to be a parent. Was he lying though? Hrrrm. Nevertheless – of course, this was HIS 'perception' and the courts have a different perception. So, unfortunately for Austin, his quest to get his mother awarded custody of Myyah fell on deaf ears.

Like most of these nonchalant, non-caring family courts that seem to always side with the mother (even without doing faithful due diligence), Judge Kathleen Steinberg, right before Austin was sentenced and locked up, threw the gauntlet at him. The Judge refused to hand over custody to Austin's mother. Her reasoning was that the courts couldn't trust the family of a man who was a reputed gang member and gun trafficker.

Also, there were no official reports of abuse filed with DCFS that made Fredquisha out to be an incapable parent. If anything, the judge ended up siding with the "struggling single mother". The judge didn't just stop there though. Not only did she deny Austin's motion to hand off full custody to his mother, but she also rescinded his shared custody agreement with Fredquisha and gave the abusive mother full custody, virtually eliminating his legal visitation rights. Courts wouldn't even consider court-supervised visitation. Making Austin out to be a ruthless criminal, the judge even considered a protective order against the father, and it was enforced until the day he went to jail and would remain in effect until he got out and went back to court for another hearing.

Truth be told, Austin, while he was sincere and had a good heart to do right by his daughter, fucked up and didn't do his research. See, that day in court Fredquisha was the one who ended up truly playing her cards right. She had Jocelyn, her section 8 caseworker, vouch for her and her "motherly" qualities. She had 'good' references from the daycare she used to work at in Pullman.

Austin wanted the judge to consider possible testimony from Myyah herself, however, the judge refused. Said she couldn't truly honor testimony coming from five-and-half-year-old for two reasons: Myyah was diagnosed with ADHD, so Judge Steinberg said that any 'negative' testimony coming from a 'mentally challenged' child couldn't be trusted. And (2) Myyah, well, she was five-and-a-half at the time, and age plays a huge role in the credibility of testimony.

Absolutely devastating...But this wasn't a fringe case unfamiliar to a lot of men. This was an everyday occurrence in so many family courts in America.

Now, one would assume that a woman who wanted full custody of her child obviously had an unshakable and unbreakable bond with her growing daughter. But this simply and obviously wasn't the case at all between Fredquisha and Myyah. Fredquisha simply wanted to get her claws on the child for the sake of extracting government benefits and a yearly tax write off.

Nothing else.

Now, Fredquisha did do the bare minimum to provide for her daughter's basic necessities. However, she obviously showed more love and support towards her two oldest sons. Quimani, 12, and Zy'meer, 10, always had the freshest and latest shit. Jordans. PlayStations. Cell phones. You name it, those two young bad nigga boys had it.

Myyah on the other hand...Well, her mother would barely buy her anything. All her toys came from the Dollar Star. Bitch wouldn't even buy her own daughter toys at least from Wal-Mart or Five Below. While her boys stayed with the freshest linens copped from the malls out in the 'burbs or department stores on Michigan Avenue, Myyah had hand-me-downs, donated clothes or clothes bought from the Salvation Army... and that was if Fredquisha felt like spending some extra money on the girl.

So, where did all of this antipathy for her six-year-old daughter come from? Before getting locked up, Austin and Fredquisha were in an off-and-on, turbulent relationship. Although he truly had no long-term plans to wife her, he still paraded her around as his main. However, as their tumultuous relationship unraveled, Austin ended up leaving Fredquisha and this set off a cascade of events that ultimately led to there ~~their~~ being a deep and dangerous rift between Fredquisha and Austin.

Fredquisha, being a bitter and spiteful ratchet bitch, made no qualms either to take her disdain for Austin out on his progeny. Twisted at it may seem, Myyah was Fredquisha's punching bag in every sense of the word while Austin was locked up. Frequent ass whoopings. Starvation. Grounding. Emotional Abuse. Verbal Abuse. You name it, Fredquisha specialized in it and made it known to Myyah every day she wasn't well liked.

It was sickening that a woman could birth such an innocent child into the world, and rather than take their frustration out on the father, she'd turn her frustration onto her very own innocent and precious daughter who simply just wanted to enjoy her semblance of a childhood. Tears...

"AHHH!" Myyah screamed as her eyes spotted the biggest brown roach crawling one of the walls in her bedroom. Myyah instantly dashed towards the corner and had an expression of trepidation buried into the small features of her brown face.

"WHAT YOU SCREAM FOR, HOE!?!?" Fredquisha rasped with a screwed-up face.

"It's a roach, mommy!"

As Fredquisha pulled the half-smoked blunt out of her pocket and lit it up in front of the child, she huffed, "Bitch – a roach?", rolling her eyes and shaking her head. But Fredquisha, hearing her daughter call her "mommy" suddenly got her very inflamed. "...AND WHAT I TOLD YOU ABOUT CALLING ME MOMMY?!? CALL ME FREDQUISHA! GOT IT?!?"

Myyah jumped again, "Yes, ma'am..."

The panicked girl froze for a moment, still looking at her mother with full fear. But not fear rooted in respect. Fear rooted in a pending ass beating. "There's a roach on the wall, Fredquisha..." Myyah slowly answered pointing at the roach, the sound of dread defining her response.

Fredquisha rolled her eyes again as she blew out a steady, heavy stream of smoke from her wide nostrils and huffed, "Ughh, really lil bitch? That's just a damn roach! Fuck you scared for, pussy hoe??! Go get yo shoe and go kill it. NOW!"

"But I'm scared, Fredqui—"

"DON'T MAKE ME ASK YOU AGAIN OR ELSE!" Fredquisha interrupted.

Instantly cutting off Myyah's plea, Fredquisha ambled deeper into the room and towered over her visibly shaken daughter. "Now I said go get cho shoe and go kill it NOW!"

Silent and quivering, a tear ran out of Myyah's right eye as she looked up at her so-called mother. "I'm scare—"

SLAP!

Without hesitation, Fredquisha's right hand went across Myyah's face. "I SAID KILL IT! IN FACT, GO KILL IT WIT CHO HAND! FUCK THE SHOE!"

Not wanting to jumpstart a Saturday session of physical brutality, Myyah listened to her mother's stern instructions as she fought back tears. She carefully paced herself to the wall where the roach was located. In Chicago, roaches often looked like Rice Krispies with tiny legs. However, last year, after coming back from a quick getaway in Florida, Fredquisha somehow managed to bring some down south roach eggs in her luggage back with her.

When she and a few of her besties went down to Miami for spring break, they stayed at an AirBnB, and that was where Fredquisha believed the infestation started. She fucked up and left partly opened packages of Little Debbie Nutty bars in her suitcase and more than likely some 3-0-5 mama roaches smelled the sweet chocolate peanut butter crisp buffet from a mile away. At least that was the story Fredquisha told herself to justify where the big ass, non-local roaches originated. Who knows if that was the truth, but Fredquisha refused to do anything serious about the growing roach problem in her apartment other than call up Glen to spray.

Myyah, now only a foot away from the roach, climbed on her bed and cautiously moved her hand closer to the wall.

"Girl...If you don't kill that muhfuckin' roach, I'm finna kill yo muhfuckin' ass..." Fredquisha warned with widened, intimi-dating eyes. Myyah had listened too because she knew her "mother's" word was bond when it came to ass beatings.

The young, petrified girl raised her hand and hovered it about an inch away from the roach.

"Myyah! If you don't stop fuckin' around and kill that roach! Bitchhhh! I SWEAR! I'm gonna go across yo nappy head!"

Myyah's hand trembled. She couldn't do it. The roach was literally almost the size of her palm and had the thickest wings. Wings were so long and thick, that muhfuckin' roach was offering first class tickets to fly other critters to Dubai and shit. The roach's long antennas moved from side to side almost as if it could detect looming death...You better run Forrest, run Forrest, RUN!

Fredquisha once again quickly spat in her hand and put the blunt out. She looked around the room and saw a VIBE magazine on top of the girl's dresser. Myyah obviously didn't read VIBE. Fredquisha forgot and left it there one night when she cussed the girl out for not cleaning up the bathroom right. Fredquisha quickly rolled the magazine up into a makeshift pipe and lunged towards the girl. She then raised the VIBE magazine pipe in her hand and pulled it back in the air, ready to go across Myyah's skull. "KILL IT, GODDAMN IT!"

SMACK!

Myyah's hand crushed the bug in her hands; the roach's exterior crunched in her small palm. Gut gooey white-yellowish roach gut slime splashed all over. Myyah would've vomited, but she had nothing in her stomach to throw up. No food was in the house other than an old loaf of bread, an expired package of off-brand Wal-Mart deli ham and some watery yellow mustard.

Fredquisha leaned in and grabbed Myyah off the bed, "Now go wipe yo goddamn hands! Get some paper towel and clean that mess up! I'm givin' yo ass a minute!" Fredquisha then swiped the magazine against the girl's back and bottom. "Wastin' my damn time!" Fredquisha continued to grumble as she made her way out of the bedroom.

Buzz. Buzz. Buzz.

Fredquisha's iPhone nestled in her back pocket vibrated. She threw the magazine back onto the dresser, picked the blunt up and put in her mouth and then whipped out her phone. She saw a text come in from 'Mama'.

"I'm downstairs" Fredquisha's mother, Evelyn, texted. The ratchet matriarch agreed to babysit her grandchildren this weekend. Mrs. Watkins, Austin's mother, was minutes away from picking up Myyah to babysit her as well but hadn't texted Fredquisha yet.

"QUIMANI AND ZY'MEER! HURRUP! YO GRANNY HERE! GET YO SHIT AND LEAVE!" Fredquisha barked in front of the boys' bedroom door.

Suddenly the door opened and the two boys, decked out in some fly gear from the Nike store, hugged their mother and then flashed down the hallway and out the front door. Fredquisha smiled, feeling overcome with joy as she watched her two boys exit the house. She wasn't just joyful she was going to have some time to herself. She felt a sense of rapture and pride that her boys were growing fast, becoming the young men she'd always envisioned. Real street niggas. Dope boys. Just like their fathers.

Myyah, after washing her hands, made her way back into her bedroom and began to clean up the roach murder scene on the wall with some water-drenched paper towel. Fredquisha's disposition quickly went back to insane as she looked her daughter up and down as if she was some unknown, wayward stranger.

"If you make any mention to yo grandma of what happened today, remember, you gon get it when you get home, you understand me, lil girl?"

"Yes ma'am," Myyah carefully replied as she wiped the wall.

"When you get done, bring yo muhfuckin' ass and your clothes' bag to the living room and sit there and wait for your grandmammy to come here. Do not mess with my television either. I'm finne go take a shit then shower. Do not come in my room for nothin'. Don't run your tiny hands through my fridge either. Let yo granny feed yo ass. She should be here in fifteen more minutes. You understand me?"

"Yes, ma'am..." Myyah once again responded.

"Good..." Fredquisha spun on her flip-flops and strode her way towards her bedroom. The sound of her flops popping filled the hallway.

CHAPTER TWO

*A*fter getting her weekend belongings together and following her mother's well-defined set of instructions, Myyah sat quiet and attentive in the living room, anxiously awaiting the arrival of her grandmother. Any other normal child would've been watching cartoons on a carefree Saturday morning, but Myyah was an exception. The girl wasn't even allowed to watch Saturday morning cartoons. Barely could watch TV throughout the week either.

Fredquisha thought the moment baby girl started watching the Disney channel she'd get hooked to wanting to go to Disney World. And the last thing Fredquisha had on her agenda was to take the daughter she truly didn't want to some amusement park all the way in Florida. Nonetheless, you already know she'd take her sons in a heartbeat. But shit, even then Fredquisha was too selfish to even go that far and take her sons out the state on a nice Disney vacation. She'd let their daddies do that. If a bitch was going out of town, it was for her own enjoyment.

With the TV off, all Myyah could hear was the scrambling of roaches fluttering their wings mixed in with the echoing of crackhead voices outside on the already busy street. Clucks looking for an early morning high.

Despite being birthed by an insane and abusive bitch, Myyah was such an adoring, beautiful young lady. She favored her father Austin, although she was a tad lighter due to her mother's yellow complexion. Despite having 3B hair grade, Myyah's hair was a complete, untangled mess this morning and was in bad need of a new hairdo.

No cooked breakfast was in the girl's stomach, and as time ticked away, her stomach growls increased in intensity.

Myyah could hear from a distance her mother was still in the shower. Under any other circumstances, she would've sat still and obeyed, but the growls rumbling in the acidic pits of her stomach were becoming painful. She couldn't go on any longer. If she was going to subdue her hunger pain, she only had some few minutes left to quickly make herself something to eat.

Baby girl slightly slid her body off the couch, but just as she inched herself off of it, she somewhat slid herself back in place. She knew if her mother caught her combing through the fridge without her permission would lead to an automatic, immediate ass whooping.

She sat for a few more seconds, contemplating what she should do. With the stomach pains increasingly surpassing her threshold of tolerance, an emboldened Myyah, quiet as she could be, got up from the couch and sauntered into the kitchen.

Although she was too short to look into the sink, roaches raved and rioted amongst mountains of pans, plates, cereal bowls and utensils sedentary in the sink. Trillions of bacteria and viruses were living out their best days on them mold-covered dishes.

Fredquisha nor her two oldest sons hadn't done the kitchen in days, so the roaches were having a fest going after remnants of food rotting away in the sink. Thank the heavenly Lord baby girl didn't need to get anything out of the sink; otherwise, she probably would've come down with a horrible strep throat infection.

Myyah opened the refrigerator and looked around to see if she could possibly make herself a small ham and cheese sandwich. Her eyes latched onto the package of ham and then a loaf of bread sitting in the fridge.

KNOCK! KNOCK! KNOCK!

Myyah's slightly underweight body jumped at the sound of someone knocking at the front door. Not wanting to look like she was doing the opposite of what Fredquisha told her to do, Myyah suddenly slammed the fridge's door and then dashed back into the living room and sat on the couch, pretending as if she hadn't made a move.

The knocks on the door were more than likely coming from Myyah's grandmother, Mrs. Watkins.

"Damn, girl! Go get the door," Fredquisha growled as she made her way into the living room, frantically rubbing her head with a pink towel. A Newport cig drooped from her lips.

Fredquisha quickly slipped her black satin bonnet back on and took a puff from her cigarette. After taking a shower, Fredquisha opted this time to put on a maroon 2000 Pierce Family Reunion t-shirt. With a big oak tree spread across the faded t-shirt, the slogan, "A Family That Prays Together Stays Together", was written in cursive under it. Pretty ironic this ratchet bitch would be wearing such a shirt given that she didn't give two shits about trying to keep any semblance of "family".

Fredquisha was the type of hoe that didn't want a real lasting sense of peace with Austin nor his family. Yeah, granted, her and Austin weren't together anymore, but at least for the sake of Myyah's happiness and welfare one would think that Fredquisha would want to keep good relations with her child's father's family. Nope.

Myyah quickly got up from the dirty, stained brown cotton couch and opened the door. "Grandma!" Myyah exclaimed as she lunged at her 61-year-old grandmother and gave her the tightest embrace.

"Girl, I ain't seen you in forever! Oh, how I missed you so much! You ready for this weekend! You know your daddy miss you so much and he can't wait to see you!" Mrs. Watkins smiled and exclaimed as she held her grandbaby.

"I missed you too, granny!" shy Myyah shouted, somewhat fighting back tears. She was so glad to see her grandmother.

As Mrs. Watkins stepped closer into the house, she scanned the living room and quickly muzzled her face with her right hand. She looked back down at Myyah, trying to playfully ignore the wretchedness of the living room. If she thought that the living room's space was bad, she needed to see the rest of the mothafuckin' apartment. The house horribly reeked. The smell tearing apart her nostrils was almost inexpressible. An aromatic mélange of fishy pussy, cheap alcohol, cigarettes, roach spray, fried chicken, piss, booty cheese, must, hair grease, old hair weave, unwashed clothes, rotting food and pickle juice over-whelmed Mrs. Watkins' nasal cavity. It was the fragrance of abject squalor and ratchetry. The irony though was that Mrs. Watkins could tell Fredquisha attempted to mask the conglom-erate of disgusting smells with some cheap Dollar Store 'Zesty Mountain Spring' air freshener.

As Mrs. Watkins' continued to look around and absorb the nastiness of the apartment, her eyes even burned a bit. Her skin even itched a tingled. Maybe her reaction was a bit psychoso-matic, but any decent person stepping into the apartment prob-ably would've had the same reaction.

The last time Mrs. Watkins saw her granddaughter was about a good seven months ago. Although Fredquisha had full custody over Myyah, occasionally she would allow Mrs. Watkins to talk to Myyah over the phone or let her stay with her over a weekend. Of course, this was only done when it was of utmost convenience to Fredquisha.

Even with all of the bullshit and tension present between Austin and Fredquisha, Mrs. Watkins always tried her best to be cordial with the psycho mother for the sake of Myyah's welfare. Although there had been times when the grandmother wanted to fuck Fredquisha up like she was some random, disrespectful street bitch who tried to snatch her purse (when in truth she was), Mrs. Watkins didn't have it in her to stoop to guttersnipe-level. Doing so could've potentially ruined any chance her son had at regaining some visitation rights once he got out.

Mrs. Watkins always offered her assistance and monetary help to make sure Fredquisha was taking good care of her granddaughter. Even despite living all the way out in Matteson, the far southeast suburbs of Chicago, Mrs. Watkins had no problem driving into the city to get her granddaughter for the weekends.

One would think that any opportunity Fredquisha had to get rid of the girl she would take it. Oh, and then add in some cash too?!? But nope – MooMoo didn't want to take the risk of having Myyah tell her grandmother something that might lead to some sort of child welfare investigation from the city or the State. Then, Fredquisha always wanted to feign she was on some Ms. Independent shit. But bitch – you dependent on the state?!? The fuck?!? ANYWAYS...

However, this weekend, after seven months of not seeing the girl, Fredquisha finally allowed Myyah to go stay with her grandmother for a few days. Although it did take a deep talk with Dr. Sterling for Fredquisha to do so, her permission came with a stern warning to her daughter. Throughout the week Fredquisha kept telling Myyah that if she fucked up and revealed any details about their living situation and how she was being treated, she'd whip her ass, maybe even kill her.

"Damn, child, yo mama ain't been feeding you or somethin'?" Mrs. Watkins jokingly remarked, but a degree of

23

concern was laced in her voice as she gazed Myyah up and down. The grandmother noticed Myyah looked a bit underweight.

Myyah didn't respond. *"Don't be tellin' yo grandma shit, or I'll take you out this world."* That's all grandbaby could hear her mother say as she thought up of a possible response to her grandmother's question. Rather than say something, she just opted to continue to hold her granny tightly. Didn't want to let her go.

Fredquisha, standing some short feet away, formed a slight grimace on her face. She was ready to beat Myyah's little ass if she gave Mrs. Watkins any inclination that she wasn't feeding her. Hrrrm, yeah, she was feeding her alright. Vienna sausages. Canned beans. Off-brand cocoa puffs with milk beyond its expiration date, on the verge of curdling. Mind you, her sons were eating like young Saudi Arabian royalty – McDonald's, gyros, pizza puffs, chicken wings, ice cream, candy, Mexican food, etc. Even when this Fredquisha bitch got her stamps and treated her kids to pizza, Myyah was only allowed to have half of one slice and one buffalo drumette. No ranch sauce either. The rest of the greasy Friday pizza mini-buffet was devoured by her two chubby, spoiled sons.

Mrs. Watkins then looked up at Fredquisha with a flat, somewhat angered face as she ran her hands through Myyah's uncombed hair. She grumbled, "Hey, Fredquisha...You got her stuff ready?"

"Yeah, go get your bag, baby girl..." Fredquisha commanded Myyah. Crazy she would call her baby girl. It was obvious she was putting on a show for Mrs. Watkins. Under any other circumstance Fredquisha would've been calling the girl an expletive like hoe or bitch, but now that her grandmother was here, she had to at least pretend to be endearing.

Myyah let go of Mrs. Watkins and then made her way back into the dusty living room, picked up a small black garbage bag near the coffee table and then strolled over back to her grandmother.

Mrs. Watkins saw the garbage bag in Myyah's hand, her face flying to a state of complete shock and confusion. "This is her clothes and what not? Are you kidding me? You ain't got this girl an overnight bag or a suitcase?"

Fredquisha rolled her eyes and exhaled. "Mrs. Watkins, I can't afford any of that right now! I'm on a strict income! Look, the garbage bag will be just fine. Besides, don't she got some clothes at your house and shit?" Fredquisha spat as she puffed on her Newport.

"Yeah, I do...But, seeing how she looks like she lost some weight, I don't know if she will fit any of them clothes..."

"Well, like I said, that's all I got, so I'm sure ya'll will figure it out...Anyways, I'll see ya'll tomorrow. I gotta get goin' 'cuz I got my hair appointment soon."

"You know, Fredquisha, if you need help or needed me to buy stuff, you could've always called me or said something...," Mrs. Watkins chirped as she held Myyah.

"Mrs. Watkins, please, I got it! I know what I'm doin'. I don't need you questioning my parenting skills or nothin' like that. Besides, if your hardheaded son wasn't in jail, maybe he could contribute..."

Mrs. Watkins' mouth dropped and shook her head. "Hey, don't bring my son up into this! I know he ain't perfect and made PLENTY of mistakes. He knows that too as he sits up in that jail. But you know damn well I'm here to give you help if you need it. You got my granddaughter out here lookin' all raggedy and shit," Mrs. Watkins spat as she looked around the filthy apartment.

Her disturbed pupils once again scanned the baseboards running along the apartment floors and noticed thick, gray crud layering them. A tell-tell sign they hadn't been cleaned in ages. Empty Domino's pizza boxes were scattered all over the living room floor. Empty bottles of vodka and Hennessy lined the adjacent kitchen countertop. Mrs. Watkins then looked up at the ceiling and saw a group of big, thuggish roaches running a train on some THOT roach in the corner. Her thick roach pussy juice splashed all over the place.

"...And look at this place! This place is absolutely filthy! Fredquisha, how in the hell are you raising three kids here? This makes no damn sense! You got these babies livin' with roaches!"

"Mrs. Watkins! Please, just leave! Please! You doin' the most right now!" Fredquisha barked, shaking her head, shooing Mrs. Watkins and Myyah away. "You lucky I'm even lettin' her ass go with you!"

Mrs. Watkins shook her head and huffed, not even bothering to patronize that last rude ass comment. "Come on, baby girl. Let's go..."

Knowing Fredquisha was a manipulative scalawag, Mrs. Watkins grabbed her granddaughter by her hand and scurried them out the apartment and into the parking lot where her Nissan Murano sat idle. Jonah, Mrs. Watkins' youngest son, and also Myyah's uncle, sat in the front passenger seat waiting for the two ladies to arrive.

Mrs. Watkins approached the left passenger side of the truck. She was glad she contained her words moments ago since she knew if she gave any lip back to Fredquisha suddenly her ass would use that as ammunition to stop Myyah from spending the weekend with her. Mrs. Watkins opened the back passenger door, helped Myyah in and then threw her bag of clothes in the back.

"Hey, Uncle Jonah!" Myyah smiled as she reached in to give Uncle Jonah a hug.

Jonah scanned his niece up and down and too noticed Myyah's bodily changes. "Myyah! Girl, you gettin' so big but you lookin' so skinny. Yo mama ain't feeding you or something?"

Myyah didn't say anything. She just shrugged her shoulders. *"Remember, lil bitch, I'll fuck you up if you run yo mouf..."*

"I know right! I said the same damn thing back in that apartment," Mrs. Watkins commented hearing Jonah's observation about Myyah's visible weight loss. "Anyways, we gonna go to Golden Corral on our way back home and get you some real food in your stomach! You hungry, baby girl?" Mrs. Watkins asked as she helped Myyah secure herself in the seat and then proceeded to help her fasten her seatbelt.

"Yes, ma'am!" Myyah innocently answered with a huge smile running across her face.

"Good then...We gotta get some good food in yo stomach before your dance tonight!" Ms. Watkins closed Myyah's door and then opened her door, got in and fastened her seat belt. The family took off and made their way back to the suburbs.

This particular weekend there were two reasons why Fredquisha reluctantly agreed to let Myyah go over her grandmother's house. One – Fredquisha just wanted to have this weekend to herself, kids free. Destined to meet someone new and get some rich trap boy dick, Fredquisha didn't wanna have to deal with any distractions coming from her kids.

Secondly, this weekend, Chicago's Cook County Jail was hosting a daddy-daughter dance for inmates. At the request of Dr. Tameika Sterling, Austin's jail-based social worker, she wanted Myyah to attend the daddy-daughter dance.

The 5th Annual Daddy Daughter Dance was hosted in the first week of June. The County Chief Sherriff started the widely successful program to help inmates keep their bonds strong with their children. The dance essentially served as inspiration and motivation for inmates to stay on good behavior, and ultimately get out of jail, get their lives right and never come back. It was the perfect way to reduce recidivism given that the program had been piloted in other cities and was shown to be a success.

Austin, initially pessimistic that Fredquisha would even agree and let Myyah attend this year, was super-elated when he found out through Dr. Sterling that Fredquisha granted Myyah permission to come. Myyah was excited too since she had not seen her father since he was locked up.

When it came to making weekend plans, Fredquisha usually had no issues sending her sons over to her mother's place. However, when it came to Myyah, she didn't want her around her own family and refused to let her mother spend time or money on the girl. If her mother was gonna spend money on her children, she wanted all dollars to go towards her sons, not Myyah. This bitch was so twisted. If and when Fredquisha got a sitter for the girl, usually it would've been one of her besties like Paulette or Shauntanae.

Now finally free from her children, Fredquisha was in full carnival mode. She slammed her apartment front door, locked it and made her way into her kitchen.

Rummaging through her virtually empty fridge, Fredquisha pulled out a brand new chilled bottle of Tito's vodka and some orange juice. But baby lemme tell you…Looking around even more, this kitchen was an absolute fucking disaster. Dishes had been in the sink for weeks. A couple of juvenile roaches danced around an adjacent countertop like they were at an 8th grade prom. The linoleum flooring was sticky from constant spills of grape drink, soda, and other sugary liquids. Over to the left at an adjacent countertop sat several opened containers of fried chicken bones covered in ketchup-stained wax paper. If one were to look closely, mice pebble shit was scattered all over the floors as well. Aside from the growing roach problem, mice were another growing issue. But Fredquisha was unbothered. Glen, the crackhead maintenance man, told her to get a cat to deal with the mouse problem. But Fredquisha hated animals despite living with an array of vermin.

Fredquisha closed the fridge and then walked into her living room. But damn, God knows what lay behind the stove and fridge. Fungus. Mold. More mice shit. A roach kingdom. A roach galaxy. Who knows?!?

Any respectable landlord wouldn't tolerate this absolute filth. But Mr. Garrison didn't want to piss off tenants and lose them. This part of Englewood that Fredquisha lived in was perhaps one of the most dangerous sections in the entire city of Chicago, perhaps even Illinois. With shootings happening damn near every night, no one in their right mind dared to want to willingly live in the area. Nonetheless, Fredquisha didn't mind. She was born and raised in this neck of the woods and to her, the area was just the set. She reasoned no one would fuck with her since she knew all the guys in the area.

Fredquisha sat down on the couch, turned on her television and tuned into a rerun of Judge Mathis. She cracked the bottle of vodka open and took a swig. Then she opened up the carton of orange juice and poured it into a mug she had sitting on her coffee table. God knows how long that mug had been sitting there, but Fredquisha used the mug usually for her homemade cocktails.

After she made herself a cocktail, she took slow slips. This bitch obviously lied about needing to get somewhere. Paulette's ass was gonna come over some hours later and glue that raggedy weave into her head in less than an hour. Fredquisha needed her kids out because she had her an 11 AM dick appointment coming up soon.

Buzz. Buzz. Buzz.

Fredquisha's phone vibrated. There the dick was. Ready to get jumped on.

She whipped her phone out her right pocket and saw a text message coming from Deontae, one of her "guys".

Deontae: WYOF (What you on fam?)

Fredquisha began typing back, "Shit, nothin'...Waiting for you. Where u at?"

Buzz.

Deontae: "About 20 min away. I got one of my guys wit me."

Fredquisha typed back: "Ok…So glad these kids is gone. I need some dick and more weed ASAP!"

Buzz.

Deontae: "I got you – OMW"

Fredquisha responded: "Who buddy?"

Buzz.

Deontae: "One of the guys from the block. He fammo. Good peoples. He ain't on bullshit…"

Fredquisha asked: "He down for whatever?"

Buzz.

Deontae: "Yeah"

Fredquisha agreed: "Ok. Hit my line when you get here."

Buzz.

Deontae: "Bet"

CHAPTER THREE

*B*ass heavy lyrics to the deceased infamous Lil JoJo, a local Chicago drill rapper, thundered from the black 2005 Chevy Monte Carlo strolling up Halsted Avenue. Sunlight reflected off illegal tints plastering across all windows of the car. As bass thumped in the trunk, its vibrating, war-like sound mixed in with the car's V6 exhaust. The tints were the perfect way for Deontae to hide and immerse himself in the thick cloud of weed smoke filling his whip.

"So, where we goin' again?" Marvin, one of his guys', asked as they strolled up the street, headed to Fredquisha's apartment about five blocks north.

Deontae pulled the fat Blackwood blunt out of his mouth and passed it to fam. He blew out a dense plume of smoke from his nostrils, his eyes glued to the light traffic on the two-way street. "Man, I know this thick, yella bitch that stay up in Engle-wood that wanna let the team hit in exchange for some weed and pills…"

Cough! Cough! Some fire ass dro was playing the drums inside of Marvin's lungs. He covered his mouth and tried to contain his cough.

"Damn! she down to do two dinos in the AM?" Marvin asked as he finally got some oxygen in his lungs. "Shorty sound like a super-THOT!"

Deontae chuckled, "Hell yeah she is. I smashed plenty of times. I told her you was wit me." Marvin passed the blunt back to Deontae. He took a few tokes from the blunt and turned down the music slightly.

Deontae turned his face towards Marvin and asked, "So, you down, nigga?"

"Hell mothafuckin' yeah you know I'm down, my nigga. Shit, some AM pussy? Shit better be schmackin' like some muhfuckin' Kellogg's frosted flakes – GREEEEEAAAAT!"

Deontae busted out laughing. "My nigga you's a goofball for real for real." The weed-pull pusher paused for a moment. He rubbed his fresh, wavy fade and wiped his mouth. A tad on the chubby side, Deontae was light brown and was decked out in typical dope boy attire. Long white tee. True Religions. Red Jordans on his feet. No belt on of course, so the moment he got out the car his pants were going to be sagging. Marvin was wearing a similar outfit. His Jordans though were turquoise.

"Ok, well, just as a warnin' tho, shorty's crib might be a wreck. She kind of nasty with it, but that pussy fiyah though," Deontae confessed.

Marvin let out a nervous chuckle. "Niggggaa, what!?! We finna fuck a bitch who got roaches and shit in her crib?"

"Yeah man, but, shit, I'm tellin' you, that pussy is schmackin' and the bitch will slurp on a dick and drink nut like it's a muhfuckin' vanilla bean Frappuccino from Starbucks...Venti size. That's the tallest, my nigga!"

"Broooo, yooo, you nasty as fuck," Marvin laughed, choking on the weed smoke. "I'mma have to do an assessment on this bih's crib before I decide if I wanna fuck or not..." Marvin snickered again and shook his head. The slightly chubby tanned buddy wondered if his dude was playing games with him and just trying to deter him from getting some ass, but he was down for whatever. If the bitch was offering some ass, he was up for the task.

As the Monte Carlo made came up to the intersection of 63rd and Halsted, Deontae spotted shorty's building, then parked on the empty side street. Deontae checked to see if any parking meters lined the street. Nope. Good 'cuz he owed the city $300 in parking tickets and one more, a big ass yellow boot was going on one of the Monte Carlo's tires. He chucked the engine off, took the keys out the ignition and stuffed them into his pocket.

"Aiight, so like I said don't get freaked out and shit 'cuz the hoe a lil filthy with it. But she gon suck them balls, might even lick yo ass!"

"Nahhhh, she can suck on them balls, but the ass is completely off limits…"

"We'll see…"

Marvin produced a scowl on his face and hung his mouth open in disgust. "Nigga…You gay."

Deontae smacked his teeth. "Fuck nigga, get out of my car so we can get this pussy and then bounce so we can get somethin' to eat!" Deontae jokingly shoved Marvin.

Fredquisha's weed man opened up his front console, looked down and whipped out a bottle of some cheap, big ass green bottle of Curve cologne he copped from the Wal-Mart on 87th not too long ago. He doused himself in a million sprays and then handed it to Marvin who followed suit. The two young Gangster Disciples gang members hopped out the all-black Monte Carlo, wiped themselves free of blunt ash and made their way up to the front door of the apartment complex.

Deontae pulled out his phone and shot Fredquisha a text alerting her that they'd arrived and were downstairs at the front door. Less than thirty seconds later the front apartment door buzzed. "Wal-lah! Magic!" Deontae smiled. He checked his pockets one last time just to make sure he brought his stash of OG kush weed and XTC pills with him. Once he felt he had everything there, he pushed the front door open and led himself and Marvin through.

The duo made their way up to the second floor of the apartment building. They trekked down the cigarette-smelly hallway to Apartment 3B. Arrived.

Knock. Knock. Knock.

Fredquisha jumped at the sound of the three thuds pounding her door. She quickly pulled herself up from the couch, rushed through the cluttered living room and made her way to the front door of her apartment. She swung the door open, and there stood Deontae with a huge grin daubed across his face along with the more nonchalant, slightly nervous looking Marvin.

"Wassup, lil mama! Got you kids out for the muhfuckin' weekend and shit, I see!"

"Shit, you already know! Couldn't wait to get their asses out! They be so damn irra!" ('irra' was a Chicago's nigga way of saying irritating).

Deontae was a local, small time dope boy from Roseland neighborhood. Standing at around 5'11, Deontae although on the chubbier side, had this semi-linebacker build to him. Marvin was built similarly.

"Come on in...Place a bit messy, but fuck it, ya'll ain't gon be here that long anyways." Fredquisha led the two gentlemen in and then slammed and locked her door.

Marvin's eyes widened at the filth splattered across the entire apartment, and almost wanted to instantaneously throw up at the portfolio of disgusting smells punching him in his mouth, even his mouth. Ain't it funny how sometimes you can smell shit (no pun intended) through your mouth?

Silent, Marvin's eyes peered into the kitchen and saw the

sink overflowing with dishes. "The fuckkk???" he thought to himself, completely blown the fuck away. He truly thought Deontae was fucking with him about the condition of Fredquisha's apartment, but he obviously wasn't joking. This bitch needed Inyanla Van Zant to come and give her a reality check into the depth of her filth.

Marvin looked down and instantly snapped. "Ahhhhhh!"

Stomp! Stomp!

A roach ran across his shoe and he screamed, quickly trying to kill it.

Deontae looked at Marvin, slightly embarrassed. "Bro, chill the fuck out, it's just a fuckin' roach. You scared of roaches, pussy nigga?"

"Man, fuck you.

That roach was the size of a cat. Lil nigga tried to run up in my pants and shit!"

"Boy, bye!" Fredquisha lightly roared and rolled her eyes. "Where is you from anyways? Ain't you from the hood too?"

"Man, I'm from the South Side. 71st and Jeffrey. But…"

"But what? You ain't seen a roach before? Nigga, you a lie!"

"I mean, I seen a roach before. Just not a thousand," Marvin joked.

"ANYWAYS…" Fredquisha, slightly annoyed, rolled her eyes and huffed. But just that quickly, she changed her disposition, smiled and stuck her tongue out. "So, what ya'll on this weekend?" Fredquisha asked.

"Shiiit. Nothin'. Same shit, different day…." Deontae replied.

"I bet…"

"Anyways, ya'll want something to drink? I got some Vodka. I also got some Hennessy in the cabinet."

"Nah, I'm good," Marvin quickly replied.

Deontae smacked his teeth. "Lemme get some of that Henny…Go get the henny, nigga," Deontae instructed Marvin.

"I said I'm good bro…"

"I know you said you good, but I ain't. Go get it so I can roll up this loud, fuck nigga. Yo, Fredquisha, which cabinet it in?" Deontae, sensing Marvin's disgust with the condition of the apartment, was lowkey fucking with him. He wanted to throw his ass deeper into the filth by exposing him to the abomination that was lurking in the kitchen.

"In the right cabinet next to the sink...There's some cups there too," Fredquisha replied.

"Aiight, bro, stop playin' and go get it..." Deontae grinned, then grabbed Fredquisha by her upper arm and danced her into the living room, and then sat on the couch together. He whipped out his big ass Ziploc bag of weed, a pack of grape-flavored Dutches and his lighter.

Marvin cautiously strolled into the kitchen. "Man, this is some fuckity fuck shit, for real for real," he thought to himself as he entered the kitchen. Complete filthy madness smacked his dark brown pupils. Roaches galore. Taking cautious, deliberate steps, he laser-focused his eyes into the cabinet that apparently contained the bottle of Hennessy.

Once Marvin arrived at the cabinet, tuning out the nastiness that defined the entire kitchen, he opened the cabinet. "Fuck!" he griped, quickly closing the cabinet. He saw four roaches chillaxing near a glass. He closed his eyes, took a deep breath and then slowly opened the cabinet again. Trying to ignore the roaches, he quickly pulled the bottle down and then made dashed back into the living room.

Although Marvin would give Fredquisha 4.3 on a scale of one through ten, her ass truthfully deserved a -17.8 for living in this nasty, fucked up apartment. Hopefully this Fredquisha bitch would get high sooner rather than later so he can fuck and then bounce.

Marvin entered the living room and then sat on an adjacent love seat as Fredquisha and Deontae looked enthralled with one another. "You rolled up yet?" Marvin asked.

"Yeah, fuck nigga. Just waitin' for yo scared ass…"

"Mann, just light that shit up bro," Marvin responded. Slight frown scrunched his face as he scratched his arms. Psychosomatic.

CHAPTER FOUR

*D*eontae picked the freshly rolled blunt resting on the coffee table up and handed it to Fredquisha. "You wanna do the honors?" Deontae asked Fredquisha if she wanted to light up the blunt and be the first to take some hits.

"Sure," she smiled and grabbed the blunt out of Deontae's hand.

Fredquisha wedged the blunt in between her tight, dark and dry violet lips. Despite taking a shower, she didn't bother to brush her teeth yet. Let alone put on some balm to heal the desiccation and cracking present on her long, plump lips. Only God knows what this bitch's breath smelled like...then again, Deontae, maybe even Marvin was about to find out in a few minutes. Eww.

Deontae handed her his black BIC lighter and then she proceeded to light up the blunt. Three hard pulls she took then blew two streams of dank smoke from her nostrils. The filthy living room began to reek of marijuana, however, the THC fragrance didn't have the muscle and potency to overpower the vile stench present throughout the apartment.

MooMoo handed the blunt to Deontae. He followed suit, taking three long, hard tokes from the blunt.

Cough. Cough.

He pounded his chest; a scrunched scowl came across his face. He leaned over to Marvin and passed him the blunt.

Marvin leaned in a bit and took the blunt of Deontae's hand and proceeded to take his pulls. Once he blew smoke from his mouth, he passed the blunt back to Deontae who then passed the blunt to Fredquisha. This was ritual for habitual weed smokers. Three tokes. *Pass.* Three Tokes. *Pass.* Three Tokes. *Pass.* The circle of blunt life.

As the fat Dutch blunt went around the room, Marvin began to relax a bit and get acclimated to the grime and pong emanating throughout Fredquisha's apartment. Despite hearing the faint sounds of busy roaches scrambling throughout the apartment, Marvin just sat back and enjoyed the intense weed high taking over his body. "Fuck it," he told himself. "I'm just here for the pussy anyways," he thought. He leaned over to the coffee table where the bottle of Hennessy was at. "You got any clean cups?" Marvin asked Fredquisha as he gripped the bottle and looked around the immediate area.

"Boy, just swig that shit…" Fredquisha responded.

"You sure?" Marvin politely asked.

"Nigggaaaa…" Deontae responded with a tilted head.

"Aiight, cool then…" Marvin nervously chuckled, opened up the bottle of Henny and then took a swig. "Ahhhh!" he groaned and slapped his chest. The biting, dark liquor swam down his esophagus and then down into the pits of his hungry, growling, empty stomach.

A nigga was fuckin' hungry. Deontae and Marvin should've stopped at a Micky D's and gotten some sausage biscuits along with some hash browns. Maybe even pancakes. But slidin' in some pussy this morning was first on the agenda. The grub could wait. Especially now that McDonald's was serving break-fast all day long. The one thing Marvin wanted to eat now was that nasty bitch's coochie.

Marvin watched idly to see what the next move was gonna be. At any minute he expected Deontae to commence the sucking and fucking. With the TV lowly blaring in the background playing a rerun of Paternity Court, Marvin observed Deontae coolly slide his hand down Fredquisha's stomach and then into her shorts.

Fredquisha felt Deontae make his move. He slowly slipped his hand down into her shorts and then gently rubbed her increasingly wet, moist pussy lips. Then he twiddled her fat, pulsating clit. Despite the orgy of nasty smells circulating throughout the apartment, Fredquisha's pussy must was hot and rank enough to perforate up to Deontae's nostrils. It wasn't so much a bad smell though. Just heavy – a sign to Deontae that Fredquisha's coochie was hot and ready for some dicks to slide in and tear them pink walls down.

Fredquisha lightly moaned with her eyes closed. She then opened them and gawked at Marvin who looked ready to get his meat slurped on. "What you waitin' on? Let me suck that dick…" Fredquisha commanded.

Marvin got up from his seat and made his way over to the couch. He quickly pulled his shirt up and then unbuttoned his pants. He pulled down his pants and boxers in one swift motion, immediately exposing his hardened, seven-and-a-half-inch penis to both Fredquisha and Deontae.

Now, any person might think some potentially bisexual shit was about to go down, but this was a common 'thing' for a lot of homeboys to do. Find some hood rat THOT bitch who was willing to do multiple dinos all at one time. Dino was a Chicago nigga's way of saying dick.

With his right hand still in Fredquisha's hot pussy pocket, Deontae used his left to unbutton his pants and then slide down his boxers to get his dick ready to be sucked or fucked on. He was debating if he was gonna let the hoe slurp on his nine-inch meat first before he dipped in the pussy or if he was gonna tag the pussy was some strokes and then let the abusive mama hoe slob on his shit. Either way, a nigga was gonna bust a fat ass nut this late morning and then slide back to his first baby mama's crib to get some pussy from her. Later that night he had a date scheduled with some strag he met at a Pep Boy's out in Dolton.

Without hesitation Marvin stuffed his dick into Fredquisha's mouth. As she tickled his balls and rubbed his taint with one hand, she stroked his meat with the other. "Hold up, let me take my pants off," Fredquisha said as she temporarily took the dick out of her mouth and then stood up from the couch to take her shorts off.

Taking her shorts and panties off in one swift motion, she then laid back down on the putrid, stained brown couch and spread her legs, revealing a semi-hairy cooch. Although somewhere down the line Fredquisha had some white in her blood, them pussy hairs was definitely 100 percent Kunta Kinte African. With the immediate area smelling like hot, musty puss, Deontae fathomed if her coiled, bushy pussy hair was responsible for the intense odor. It didn't matter though. Deontae loved the smell of pussy. So long as a bitch didn't smell like the kitchen of a Joe's Crab Shack, Deontae was good as fuck. He was gonna get his nut.

In fact, before Deontae was destined to stretch them pussy walls out, he had to get a taste of the cooch. He further spread her legs open and then pulled her into the middle of the couch as Marvin hovered over her, still getting his dick sucked. Although Deontae couldn't see it – his eyes were laser focused on the bushy pussy meat sopped with creamy juices –an audience of perverted roaches lurked from a distance, watching the threesome action go down.

Some of the roaches conversed among themselves,

distracted from their mission to find food crumbs. Some had their eyes wide opened, delighted in the fuck fest about to go down. However, a few of them critters yawned. They had seen her get it in several times before. What was happening now was like a bad Ebony amateur vid on PornHub, so they took off in search of some fried chicken bones or some leftover, stale French fries rotting under the sofa.

Deontae leaned in and buried his chubby face into Fredquisha's pussy and began to ferociously eat the scalawag out. Disregarding the taco meat bush cutting up his upper lip, Deontae sucked on the woman's clit as he slid a finger in and out of her loose coochie. Easily locating her g-spot, he massaged the bumpy love spot until he could tell she was climaxing by the shivering of her jiggly, cellulite-covered thighs.

"Fuckkk, keep doin' that shit, keep eatin' that pussy," Fredquisha moaned and mumbled as she delighted in Deontae's tongue dipping in and out of her twat hole.

With Marvin's dick still in her hands and mouth, Marvin was ready to get in on the pussy action. He took his dick out of Fredquisha's mouth, slapped her on the cheek a couple of times to wipe some of the drool off his heavy rod. He bounced over to Deontae, looking to switch places. His turn...although he wasn't gonna taste the bitch's pussy right after his guy did so. That would've some ultra-gay shit to him.

Deontae stood up and then floated over to Fredquisha. He hovered over her as she grabbed his hard, salami roll-like veiny dick meat and instantly began to devour it in her mouth. She sucked on it as if she were a hungry redneck trucker smacking on some almost expired gas station beef jerky. "Yesss, fuck! Gobble that shit, you nasty bitch!" Deontae barked.

Marvin eyed the pussy with his glassy pupils, ready to use his dick as a weapon to inflict maximum damage on her wolf pussy. Pulling Fredquisha's lumpy legs closer to himself, Marvin parted her pussy lips with his dick and entered into her gooey canal. Despite having some loose pussy, Fredquisha was able to snap and lock him in good. The tightening around his dick made Marvin up his stroke game.

Once terrified by the army of roaches surrounding him in the filthy apartment, the now roach-oblivious Marvin succumbed the bliss of Fredquisha's pussy walls massaging his dickhead, taking him away from the ratchet wretchedness of the apartment. This disgusting fuck boy continued to slide in and out of her, pounding her as her stomach fat waggled like a pan of freshly made jello. Shit, even though Bill Cosby was a now convicted pussy fanatic predator, if his old, perverted ass saw this apartment, he wouldn't dare try to drug this Fredquisha heaux to get some of that cooch no matter how juicy and or tight it was. Old fuck nigga would've had his ass at home trying to get it in with wifey.

Nevertheless, both these niggas fucking Fredquisha were foul as fuck for so many reasons. First, they were messing with a bitch who obviously had a serious problem with cleanliness. Who in their right mind would mess with a woman who, on top of having a clear roach problem, kept her house looking like a dumpster? Then, even worse, this bitch had the audacity to raise her kids among this dismal sordidness! But fuck all of that! Why weren't these fools wearing protection? Did they just assume Fredquisha was on the pill? Had her tubes tied? Had her uterus scraped a million times from abortion after abortion, rendering her incapable from having future children?

Obviously, none of these issues mattered to both Marvin or Deontae. Although Marvin was initially disgusted with Fredquisha's living conditions, at the end of the day, that still didn't demotivate and stop him from tagging some random THOT he didn't know. Pussy is pussy – regardless of its station in life. This was the way how so many Chicago hood niggas carried themselves – recklessly fucking these no good, disgusting nigga hoes, giving them the gas and ammunition they very much desired to keep their ratchetry alive and bourgeoning.

CHAPTER FIVE

*C*rispy gusts of Lake Michigan wind danced in delight amidst the blazing sunny backdrop as Saturday progressed into the mid-afternoon. With barely a cloud in sight, this was typical for the start of June in the Chi.

Cook County Jail was metropolitan Chicago's central jail complex located on 2700 California Avenue in the city's predominantly Mexican Southwest Side. Located on nearly 100 acres, in actuality it was the largest single jail site in the whole entire mothafuckin' US. It temporarily housed Chi-town's accused criminals as they awaited trial for various crimes. Gang members, dope dealers, domestic abusers, rapists, car jackers, drug traffickers and others called County their second home given the frequency of how often they came in and out of the place.

The jail, colloquially known as "County", was temporary shelter before inmates were tried in a court and shipped off to some state prison miles away from the city. Most inmates only spent a month or two here before they were sentenced and sent away. However, some were held here indefinitely, serving out long, prison-like sentences thanks to a complicated, jammed up court system filled with corruption, red tape and other administrative inefficiencies.

Nonetheless, despite the negativity that often characterized the jail, today about fifty inmates, all participants in the Daddy-Daughter Dance program, crowded their mostly young black and brown selves into the small auditorium located inside of one of the jail's low security centers.

One participant was Austin DeVaughn Watkins, Myyah's biological father. He, along with other inmates, were preparing for the dance later tonight by setting up round tables, chairs and other decorations inside the auditorium.

Decked out in an orange jail-issued uniform, Austin worked diligently side by side with another inmate, DeMario, arranging the round tables and foldable chairs around the makeshift dance floor. If one were to take a cursory glance around the auditorium, most of the inmates had hardened looks that matched their turbulent lives of crime and violence. Some had faded tatts scribbled all over their faces. Some had flashy gold grills permanently engraved into their mouths. Others had dark circles burned around their eyes – the revealing sign of stress and turmoil they'd experienced living that murderous ChiRaq street life.

Austin, however, wasn't like the rest of the inmates. He was somewhat modelesque and to many looked like he definitely didn't belong inside the jail, but more on a NYC fashion runway. Standing at around six feet tall, he was in possession of smooth dark brown skin that paired well with his had suave brownish gray eyes. Well-kept twists ran down to the middle of his back. A lightly shaven facial beard adorned his chiseled face. Built like a running back for the Chicago Bears, had Austin not messed around in the streets as a teenager, he had a high chance of being on someone's football team, getting ready for the upcoming pre-season.

Austin spent most of his childhood and teenage years growing up in the heart of Chatham, a predominantly black middle-class neighborhood on Chicago's South Side. There he earned the nickname "MC" or "Morris", as everyone said he resembled Morris Chestnut.

Austin, recently turning 35, came from a decent, working-middle class family. His father, Gary Sr., who died some years ago from colon cancer, was a retired city streets and sanitation worker and his mother, Delores (most people always called her Mrs. Watkins), was a retired special education teacher. Despite growing up with church-going black parents who did their best at rearing their kids to be outstanding citizens, Austin was their only child out of four who somehow managed to get sucked into Chicago street life.

Austin was the second oldest in his family. His oldest sister, Kelly, was an executive director of an education nonprofit. His younger brother, Gary Jr., worked as an IT administrator for the City of Chicago. His other younger brother, Jonah, was currently finishing up his master's in creative writing from Columbia College.

Austin up until his junior year of high school always had his ambitions set on going to school to study architecture. However, when he turned sixteen, he got involved with a local gang and started committing petty crimes. Shoplifting, selling nickel bags of weed and coke was his start to his trouble. Eventually he became a jack boy. His specialty – robbing affluent white snobs on the city's North Side and Downtown.

As he got older and into his twenties, Austin ramped up his involvement in the streets and became the gun plug, selling all types of illegal handguns, semiautomatics and rifles to affiliated gang members across the metro. No bullshit, he did have a solid, good (yet turbulent at times) run...up until about six years ago. The ATF's local office in Chicago set up a private task force to go after illegal gun trafficking in the city. One of Austin's "homeboys", Boonk, got snatched up by the Jakes. After rounds of torture, a confession (snitching) and a plea deal led the ATF straight to Austin. The jack boy-turned-gun trafficker got caught up in a major sting, and after being faced with multiple charges, Austin was looking at damn near life in federal prison. Even with this being his first major offense, that didn't matter to the federal prosecutors looking to squash Chicago's growing gang violence problem. To the white boys in suits, Austin hustled tools of death that were linked to Chi-town's growing murder rate.

For the average nigga who got caught up in the game, by this point, they would've accepted their fate and began to mentally adjust to life in prison. Gary, Sr. couldn't see one of his own go down like this and he became hell bent on trying to save his son and see him redeemed. Furthermore, he couldn't fathom seeing his son spend the rest of his life behind bars, especially since Austin had a daughter who he needed to rear. So, after much praying and deliberation, the Watkins patriarch dipped into his retirement savings and used damn near $100,000 to hire Attorney Alton Jones, one of the best criminal defense lawyers in the Midwest to save his son from them crackers. Guess you could say Alton Jones was Chicago's version of Johnny Cochran.

After lengthy back-and-forth talks with the federal prosecutors, Austin, on behalf of Mr. Jones', negotiated a plea deal. A deal that essentially allowed Austin to walk away with just six years of probation. There is a God, Gary, Sr., thought when his son got out of jail. Three months later though, Gary, Sr., passed away. Then, it wasn't even a full year later that Austin found himself back in legal trouble.

On a cold and rainy night, Austin got pulled over for a broken headlight. One thing led to another, the cops found a bag of weed and immediately took him to jail for violating his probation. Because Austin's crime was simply a petty drug possession misdemeanor, rather than ship him off to federal prison, the Feds decided to keep him detained in County for a minimum of two years. Although two years seemed like nothing considering just two years prior Austin was facing more than sixty behind bars, those two years still felt like a life spent in eternal hell.

Austin's scheduled release date was in a month – July 1st. With less than a month left before getting released, Austin was doing his best to ensure he'd never come back to jail ever again. Lesson fucking learned.

One of the first things Austin had plans on doing after getting out of jail was going to college to get his bachelor's degree. Before his father died, Austin made a promise that he would clean himself up, get his act together and go back to school to get his bachelor's like the rest of his siblings did. It was the ultimate dream Gary Sr. wanted for all of his kids – to be college educated since he never had the opportunity to do so.

Wanting to fulfil that promise to his father, when Austin first got locked up he worked studiously hard to obtain his GED and also enrolled in a carpentry program. Inmates were encouraged to pick up a trade and Austin always loved doing craft projects as a teenager. It was something him and his father bonded over before he got sucked into them unforgiving ChiRaq streets.

The sound of clinks from metal chairs and foldable tables mixed in with the faint, peaceful conversations inmates were having with one another. "Man, I can't wait until I finally get out this muhfucka...," Austin moaned as he set up some brown metal seats around a round gray table. "Shit feels like an eternity..."

"Why you even in here in the first place?" the short, portly and older light-skinned DeMario asked, shaking his bald head.

"Man, probation violation. Jakes pulled me over for a broken headlight and found a bag of loud in my front console. Dumb shit – I know…" Austin shook his head as he continued placing chairs around tables other inmates were slowly setting up.

"Yeah, well, I been in here for damn near seven years…I know them two years felt like centuries…Can't wait until I leave this muhfucka too. Leave that street shit finally the fuck alone," DeMario uttered.

"What you in for?" Austin asked DeMario.

"Man, they got me on a possession with the intent to distribute. I'm a third time offender so they slapped me with a ten-year minimum…"

"Damn, they ain't send you down state…"

"Nah, prison overpopulated and because I'm a low-level, non-violent offender, County keepin' my ass…"

"Damn, well, at least you not all the way down in the boon-docks…Probably easy for your peoples to see you and shit, ya feel me?"

"Yeah, true…especially my baby moms and my girl…Man, I miss them so much that's why I can't wait until tonight, so I can have some sense of what home feels like, you know?"

"Yeah, bro…I understand trust me. Well, maybe not the baby moms part. My BM be on straight bullshit," Austin groaned, shaking his head. His trivial scowl then immediately turned into a smile once he thought about Myyah. "But my baby girl, Myyah…I miss her ass every fuckin' day."

"Yeah, I know bruh, keep thinkin' about her. It'll make you wanna stay your ass out for real this time. I regret every single day of my life doing dumb shit."

As the two men continued to talk and work at the same time, Dr. Sterling, the lead jail social worker, made her way into the auditorium with another corrections officer to her side. Dr. Sterling was medium height and build and had of locks with conch shells at the end of them. Decked out in full professional attire – a black suit, white blouse and some cheap pumps – if one had blurry vision, it would be easy to mistake Dr. Sterling for Lauryn Hill. The forty-something-year-old Dr. Sterling had her PhD in Clinical Psychology from the University of Chicago and had been working in prison mental health services for the last decade or so. "Hey, DeMario...I need to talk to you for a second," Dr. Sterling yelled from the front entrance of the auditorium.

Her prominently audible and serious-sounding yell of DeMario's name echoed throughout the auditorium, immediately catching everyone's attention. All the inmates suddenly stopped what they were doing and turned their attention towards Dr. Sterling. "Damn, why she yellin' my name like that for?" DeMario muttered as he put the seat in his hand down on the ground and slowly made his way towards the unassuming social worker.

Seconds later everyone returned back to what they were doing. Some inmates were lining the walls of the auditorium with high-end mauve and white linens, along with glittery ribbon decorations to make the entire place look regal and welcoming.

Dr. Sterling pulled DeMario off to the side as a corrections officer stood on guard.

"NOOO! NOOOOOOO! NOT MY BABY! NOOO! PLEASE NO!!!!" DeMario screamed. Austin, along with the rest of the inmates, suddenly threw their gaze at a screaming and emotionally disheveled DeMario. "Come on, brotha, it's gonna be alright. I got you," Officer Thompkins, the tall and built black corrections officer said, trying to keep DeMario from collapsing to the ground. "LORD! WHY! TAKE ME INSTEAD, GOD! PLEASE NOT MY BABY!"

Everyone completely paused what they were doing and gawked at DeMario's emotional breakdown. Austin had no idea what was going on with DeMario but based on DeMario's flustered behavior and erratic cries it was quite obvious something happened to his daughter.

A few other corrections officers, two tall white, young looking dudes, entered the auditorium and helped escort a semi-limp DeMario out of the auditorium. Dr. Sterling, still standing idle next to the entrance of the auditorium, pursed her lips and shook her head in disbelief as she held her arms by her elbows.

Curious as he was, Austin stopped what he was doing and slowly trekked over to Dr. Sterling. "Hey, Dr. Sterling. I hate to be nosey, but what happened to my brother?"

Dr. Sterling exhaled… "Early this morning his fiancée and his daughter were unfortunately caught in crossfire of a shootout that happened on Lake Shore Drive."

"Well, is she ok, is everything gonna be alright?" Austin asked, although his street intuition informed him based on DeMario's breakdown she probably didn't make it.

"Unfortunately…no. But his fiancée is in critical condition."

Austin, a bit disturbed from hearing the news, covered his mouth with his right hand and shook his head in shock and disbelief. "Man, I'm so sorry to hear that. That's some crazy ass shit to have happened today. She was supposed to be here, right?"

"Yes…That was his only daughter…"

"Fuckkkkk," Austin continued shaking his head as he lowered it.

"Count your blessings, Austin…When your daughter gets here, you need to love on her as much you can because you never know what life will have in store for you."

Austin couldn't say anything in response. He just nodded in affirmation to her statement and walked away. It was completely fucked up for something like that to happen on what was supposed to be splendidly happy and beautiful early evening, Austin thought as he continued to assemble chairs around tables.

"Ay yo, what happened, bro?" Hector, another inmate asked. Hector was your typical Mexican clicked up gang member who was serving a four-year sentence for possession.

"Man, some niggas shot up DeMario's fiancée and his daughter this morning on the e-way. Baby girl didn't make it. His BM is fighting for her life…"

"Man, the game dun fuckin' changed. Muhfuckas is straight murkin' people on the highway now? Ain't no more respect for the rules and regulations." Hector, a bonafide Latin Disciples member, was referring to the norms and ways of old school gang affiliation.

"Shit, you ain't lyin homie…" Austin responded.

Later that afternoon after getting done setting up the auditorium, Austin made his way back to his cell to get ready for the evening. The dance was scheduled to start around 6:30 PM promptly. After taking a shower and shaving, he put on a suit that his mother bought for him on clearance from Macy's in Downtown. Looking classy and dapper in a black Tom Ford suit, the time had arrived for Austin to make his way back to the auditorium.

One of the corrections officers who was assigned to be a supervisor of the inmates for the night went by and got Austin and other inmates out of their cells and escorted them down to the auditorium. Butterflies of anxiety flapped their wings inside of Austin's stomach as he anxiously awaited the arrival of Myyah. Not seeing or talking to her in years had really taken a serious emotional toll on him and he didn't know how he was going to respond to seeing her.

After getting down to the auditorium, there was still some

time before the start of the entire dance. 5:58 tick tocked on Austin's watch as he helped Dr. Sterling set up a photo booth inside the auditorium. One of Dr. Sterling's best friends, Monique, was an event planner and a photographer who was going to take pictures of inmates and their family. She was also going to help people operate the photo booth. Dr. Sterling wanted to ensure inmates had colorful, graphic reminders of the event to keep them motivated and on task to stay committed to transforming their lives for the better. There's nothing more powerful than seeing a visual representation of your intimate bond with your own flesh and blood, and Dr. Sterling wanted to make sure inmates knew exactly what they were missing being locked up inside the heavily guarded jail.

"I think this is good to go now, Dr. Sterling," Austin said as he finished assembling the photo booth. "Damn, you did that pretty quickly. See, Austin, you are one talented brother. You got them good hands. You need to open up your own construction business or somethin' when you get out!" Dr. Sterling commented, amazed that Austin was able to put the photo booth together in no time. Monique would've did it but given that her assistant had to call out at the last minute, she was scrambling to set up lighting around another photo set in the auditorium.

"Is DeMario gonna be alright?" Austin probed, expressing concern his fellow inmate was going to mentally break. Austin knew he wouldn't be able to handle that type of devastating news himself. The last thing he could do was fathom his baby dying in such a horrid and unexpected manner.

"Well, it's too early to say. We got him in the psych ward now and sedated because he threatened to kill himself..." Dr. Sterling tightened her plump, red lips and put her hand on Austin's shoulder in a non-flirtatious manner (she was a lesbian), "That's why Austin I want you to really do your best not to get caught up anymore in that bullshit once you get out in the streets. A lot of people are rooting for you, including your daughter. I just know once she walks through those doors, she is going to bawl...And so are you."

Austin nervously chuckled since Dr. Sterling was right. "Thank you, Dr. Sterling. I'm gonna do my best when I get out," Austin assured as he gazed around the auditorium and glanced all of his inmate brothers dressed up, looking like they were about to go eat at a five-star French restaurant in Downtown.

This entire day had been somewhat nerve-wrecking for Austin. He didn't know what flood of emotions were going to overwhelm him once his daughter walked through those auditorium double doors. From time to time when his mother would visit him she'd did her best to relay over how Myyah was doing. However, she couldn't report much since Fredquisha barely let her visit Myyah or stay with her, let alone talk to her over the phone.

"Well, it's about that time Austin..." Dr. Sterling noted as time got closer to 6:30.

"Yup..." Austin replied and turned his attention towards the front entrance of the auditorium. In about fifteen minutes or so, daughters of the inmates were going to be escorted into the auditorium with their guardians. Tonight, Mrs. Watkins was going to be there with Myyah.

Austin took a deep breath and strolled over to a table where a big fruit punch bowl sat out along with a platter of some mini-sandwiches, chips and other snacks. Austin picked up a red plastic cup and then scooped up some ice and some drink from bowl, needing to take a quick sip of something to drink before the start of the dance.

With the lighting in the auditorium retrofitted to resemble a prom, the entire auditorium glowed with soft pink lighting that matched the princess-like linens and faux diamond sparkling decorations that the inmates worked on all day.

As Austin kept taking small sips from the cup, he kept seeing flashes of Myyah enter his head. He didn't know exactly how she was going to look. In two years, going from four to six years old can make any child look visibly different. Just thinking of all the time he lost not seeing his baby was slowly pulling at his delicate heart strings and right then and there, as the DJ put on Luther Vandross' "Dance With My Father", Austin came to the full realization that he was totally failing as a father.

CHAPTER SIX

*a*fter picking Myyah up from Fredquisha's old, grubby and crowded apartment, the Watkins clan hopped on the I-57 expressway and jetted back to the tranquil and spacious suburbs. Myyah was just so unbelievably relieved to be out of her mother's disgusting apartment and away from her unrelenting tyranny. As Mrs. Watkins zipped down the somewhat empty highway in her Murano, Myyah happily stared out of her tinted passenger window, taking in the vast and green suburban scenery. It was a far contrast from her everyday gritty and dangerous Englewood reality.

Aside from the trauma she experienced living with her trifling mother, Myyah's neighborhood was completely horrid. Englewood wasn't even one of the biggest neighborhoods in the city – it was a section only three square miles on Chicago's mid-South Side. Yet hyper-poverty, extreme gang violence, drugs, prostitution, murder, domestic abuse and other ills that typically plagued inner cities defined life for residents in the area.

Frequent streams of gunshots, sobbing mothers, crackhead fights and roaring bass heavy trap music was the soundtrack to life in Englewood. Irrespective of Chicago's brutal weather, armies of dope boys and gang members roamed the streets, aimlessly living life, setting themselves up to be future murder statistics. Nearly fifty percent of the residents in the area lived at or below the poverty rate. If one were to take a drive around the area, one would notice that virtually every other house was abandoned, marked with red X signs on their molded wooden doors. Tall, uncut shrubbery gated off many of these run-down houses and flats; dereliction their sole occupant. The Chicago Fire Department years ago started this program called the Chicago Red X Program that was designed to place red X placards on vacant houses and buildings, alerting first responders and firefighters that essentially these marked properties were beyond fucked up. Enter at your own risk. Shit, truth be told, the entire neighborhood needed a big red X on it. Dwell there at your own risk.

Sad as it may seem, just generations ago Englewood was once a bourgeoning black community filled with prosperous middle class black families pursuing the American dream. Nonetheless, like so many other black communities across the United States, Englewood went through major decline in the 70s and 80s, and now the area was a living nightmare of urban desolation and decay.

Myyah always told herself she needed to do her best to make the best grades in school so she could become a doctor and live far away from the roach-infested ghetto her mother seemed so cool and content rearing her in. Myyah's imagined future of stability and prosperity kept her motivated despite being surrounded with so much negativity and destruction.

As the Watkins family got close to home, as promised, Mrs. Watkins stopped at a local Golden Corral to get Myyah something to eat for lunch. Although Dr. Sterling did inform Mrs. Watkins days earlier that some light refreshments were going to be served at the dance later tonight, Mrs. Watkins didn't want to risk having Myyah go into the dance hungry. Besides that, the noticeable weight loss on the girl had Mrs. Watkins maddened as it was more than evident Fredquisha wasn't providing adequate meals for the girl.

Honestly, what else would it be? Why would a growing girl her age be so small and not bigger? Although she had no verifiable proof, these were burning questions scorching Mrs. Watkins' conscience as she commanded her vehicle's steering wheel, her right foot heavy on the gas going ten miles above the posted 60 MPH speed limit. Not wanting to breakdown and go on a rampage about Myyah's possible malnourishment, Mrs. Watkins had to fight her inkling to pick up her cell phone, call Fredquisha and cuss her the fuck out. If she was fifteen years younger, Mrs. Watkins would've owned the passionate energy to beat the fuck out of the abusive bitch, but her fighting days were long over. And truth be told, the last thing she needed to do right now was get herself involved in some petty, back-and-forth argument with Fredquisha's neglectful ass. Besides, Mrs. Watkins was fully aware Fredquisha was the type of manipulative bitch who would then threaten to cut Austin and his family off from ever seeing Myyah again given the law was on her side with that ill-conceived custody order. All the grandmother could do was just try to calm herself and just focus on tonight. For right now, it was just important to get something heavy in calories into Myyah's small stomach.

Once the family got inside the restaurant and got assigned a table, the trio made their rounds around the buffet. "What would you like, Myyah? You can get anything you want!" Mrs. Watkins announced. With so much to choose from, Myyah didn't even know where to start.

"I can have anything, grandma?" Myyah politely asked.

"YES! Anything, baby doll!" Mrs. Watkins smiled.

"Can I have some fried chicken and green beans? Dem is my

favorite. Fredquisha don't let me have chicken when she gets it for my brothers. She says I can't eat it 'cuz I'm not old enough yet…"

"Really? Chicken? Girl, you can have all the chicken you want! What part you want? A breast? Thigh? Wing? I bet you love drumsticks!" Mrs. Watkins was a bit taken aback though hearing Myyah call her mother by her first name.

Myyah smiled, revealing a mouth containing some slightly rotting teeth. A few others were missing. Again, tell-tell signs Fredquisha wasn't even keeping up with the girl's dental health. "Yes I do, granny! Can I have three of them?!?"

"Yes! Come on. Let's get you some mashed potatoes, macaroni and some corn bread too!"

After Mrs. Watkins went around the buffet and fixed Myyah's plate along with hers, they made their way back to the table. Jonah was already sitting down waiting for the two women to arrive. He didn't want to start eating without them given his mother always wanted to say grace before eating.

"Sorry about that, son," Mrs. Watkins apologized as she pulled out a chair for Myyah and then pulled out hers. Myyah sat down and almost began to dig into her plate. "No, no, no, baby girl! We gotta say grace first!" Mrs. Watkins innocently chastised her grandbaby, but in an enlightening manner. "We gotta make sure we bless our food, so it can be healthy for our bodies!"

"Yes, ma'am!" Myyah had a grin on her face that projected slight embarrassment. Of course, back at home, blessing one's meal wasn't a requirement. Hell, Fredquisha hadn't even bothered to teach the girl about God, religion, or even prayers. Basic bedtime ones at that.

"Jonah, go ahead and pray…And Myyah, say it along with us so you can learn how to pray and bless your food, ok?"

Myyah nodded her head, "Ok…"

Jonah and then Mrs. Watkins lowered their heads, clasped

their praying hands together and closed their eyes. Myyah somewhat followed their cue and quickly mimicked what they did. Jonah then began to pray -- "Thank you heavenly father God for this food we are about to receive. And we pray that it will nutritious and healthy for our bodies. In Jesus' name we pray...Amen!"

Although Myyah tried to closely follow along, she stumbled on some of her words. However, Mrs. Watkins nor Jonah judged her given it was an honest and fruitful attempt by the young girl. It was quite unfortunate she had a mother who didn't teach her shit about how to pray, let alone teach her basic manners at the dining table.

"Ok...NOW we can eat... Dig in girl, I know you're hungry! All skinny and what not! What does your mother feed you?" Mrs. Watkins sarcastically questioned and snickered. She was trying to use innocent humor as a means of extracting info on what Fredquisha was feeding (or not feeding) her granddaughter.

"We eat a lot of hot dogs and beans. Fredquisha said we can't really afford a lot of food because we don't have that much money...," Myyah revealed.

Mrs. Watkins eyes turned to angered slits hearing Myyah call her mother by her first name again. Brief, awkward silence all of sudden became the fourth person at the table. Jonah nervously beamed at his mother. She then gawked back at him, giving him the same curious yet agitated look. Without saying anything, their frozen body language let each other know they were essentially thinking the same thing.

Myyah observed the slight pouts on her grandmother and uncle's face and quickly muzzled her mouth with her tiny, soft brown hands, "Oops, I should've never said anything. Fredquisha said I shouldn't be telling everyone our business...," Myyah apologized, desiring to somewhat downplay, even possibly retract the potentially embarrassing revelation.

"It's ok, sweetheart. Don't worry. I'm not gonna tell her anything, so don't you worry. Just go ahead and enjoy your lunch so we can head back and try on that special dress your dad and I bought for you tonight, ok?"

Myyah's slight concern dithered away as she produced a huge smile. "Yes, ma'am!"

As the awkward tense moment disappeared, the three returned to having light conversation while they diligently ate their food. Myyah was still hungry and wanted more chicken and some sides. Under any other circumstance Mrs. Watkins would've made commentary about the girl's gluttonous eating habits, but assuming her granddaughter was somewhat being starved and needed as much as she could eat, Mrs. Watkins didn't even mind if Myyah wanted a third or fourth plate. After round two, and everyone was visibly full, they left the restaurant and headed home.

About twenty minutes later, the family pulled into the vast driveway of the Watkins residence. Mrs. Watkins, along with Jonah, lived all the way out in far southeastern Matteson, a suburb about a good forty miles away from Downtown Chicago. Jonah, 25, decided to stay home rather than live in the city while he pursued his master's degree at a school in Downtown. Rather than drown himself in unnecessary student loan debt to rent some over-priced studio apartment near his college in South Loop, he opted to just stay home out in the suburbs with his mother and not have the worry of rent and utility bills boggling his mind. Besides, after he got done with school he had plans on relocating to Los Angeles to pursue a career in screenwriting. He needed to save up as much money possible. While he wasn't at school, Jonah worked as a part-time bartender at a restaurant in neighboring Orland Park. From time to time he'd drive for Uber and Lyft.

After retiring, Gary Sr. and Delores sold their longtime Chatham residence and upgraded to a big, six-bedroom suburban McMansion in the heart of an upscale gated community. It had always been a lifelong desire of the Watkins to save up and buy a huge and gaudy palace-like house in the 'burbs, away from the hustle and bustle of the city. Although they originally had plans on relocating somewhere down south like Georgia or North Carolina, the couple opted to stay in Illinois to be close to their children and grandchildren.

Gary Sr. always envisioned having a home with a big backyard with enough space to host cookouts for his entire immediate and extended family during the summer. He coveted having enough space to set up a pool for his grandchildren, especially since three of his grandchildren had birthdays during June and July. Also, he wanted a big enough house to have large Christmas parties where he could show off the wet bar and entertainment lair he made out of the vast basement. Gary Sr. was truly a family man, and what he wanted more than anything was just to have a place big enough so that his four children and their families could come over and crash anytime they wanted. However, now that he was gone, and Austin was locked up in jail, Mrs. Watkins hoped one day, once Austin got his life together, he along with Myyah and his future wife and other children would join the rest of the family in celebrating birthdays, Memorial Day weekends, fourth of Julys, Labor days, Thanksgivings, and Christmases, etc. Mrs. Watkins knew her son wasn't a perfect individual and made his fair share of mistakes, but now that he was less than a month away from getting released, she wanted to work hard to ensure her husband's vision came to pass.

Once the family got out of the SUV and made their way into the house, Myyah stormed straight down the vast foyer and right to the luxurious living room. She jumped on the massive Italian black leather sectional couch and grabbed the remote control to the 80-inch flatscreen hi-def TV in the center of the room. It had been months since Myyah had the opportunity to watch television, especially the cartoons she liked. The last time Myyah had been over here, she was so enraptured with watching cartoons, she spent hours in front of the television as if she hadn't seen something so entertaining before in her life.

"Hey, baby girl, before you get sucked up in that tube, let's go try on this dress! I know you're gonna like it so much! It took us a long time to find it!"

"What does it look like, granny?" Myyah asked as she flipped through channels, trying her best to quickly locate the Disney channel.

Mrs. Watkins smile, "It's a surprise! Come and let's go check it out!"

"Ok!" Myyah threw the long black remote back onto the couch and followed her grandmother upstairs to a guest room that contained mostly clothes and toys specifically for the girl. Since Mrs. Watkins barely saw this one grandchild of hers, she specifically designated a room to be Myyah's when she was allowed to come over.

Mrs. Watkins opened the bedroom door and allowed Myyah to walk in first. Within seconds the girl's big doe brown eyes widened once they attached to a Princess Tiana Dress inspired from Disney's "Princess and the Frog".

Myyah had a fanatical obsession of the movie and always envisioned herself being just like Princess Tiana. The last time Myyah came over to her grandmother's house, she watched the movie at least ten times. Her grandmother gave her a copy of the DVD so she could watch it at home, but once she got back to Fredquisha's house, "mommy dearest" took it away, and inevitably sold it at a local electronics store to get weed money.

The dress was absolutely splendid! Mrs. Watkins and Austin knew once Myyah saw the dress she would become exceedingly euphoric, and indeed she was. She began to bawl; heavy Amazon waterfall tears fell out of her adorable eyes and down her bony brown cheeks. The dress consisted of pale yellows and soft greens. Made out of light yellow organza with detailed light green organza overlay, the dress had a sparkly and bedazzling pewter colored flower with hanging green leaves running along the waist. The dress looked just like the one Princess Tiana wore in the animated movie. Mrs. Watkins searched for the dress for ages at the local malls until one day one of her church members, Sister Betsy, recommended she order the dress off Etsy. Her recommendation definitely worked out. Mrs. Watkins didn't hesitate dropping $400 for the dress along with getting a matching three hoop petticoat and shoes.

Myyah ran her hands across the dress just to confirm it was real. Once she gripped the fabric and rubbed it in between her finger tips, she let go, spun on her feet and then lunged at her grandmother and held her tightly. She buried her head into her granny's stomach and sobbed out of pure happiness.

"Ohh, why are you crying baby girl? Don't cry! You're gonna make me cry!" Mrs. Watkins exclaimed, tripping over her words as a million emotions flooded her body. Fighting to hold back her own flood of tears, Mrs. Watkins held onto Myyah and rubbed her back, consoling her.

"Here, let's try it on and try to make some adjustments if we need to, ok?"

"Ok-k-k," Myyah stuttered, wiping her face and sniffling her nose. "Th-thhh-thank you so much, granny. This is the prettiest dress I've ever seen in my life!"

Mrs. Watkins was so damn conflicted. Seeing Myyah's reaction was priceless. It was an incredible bonding moment she was sharing with a granddaughter she barely got to see. But it was also bitter and painful evidence indicting Fredquisha of the crime of being a selfish, greedy and non-caring parent who obviously didn't bother to shower her only daughter with gifts. Granted, without a doubt Myyah was head over heels obsessed with Princess Tiana and that explained her reaction to seeing the beautiful dress. But what young girl honestly has that type of breakdown over clothing? Mrs. Watkins speculated. The only type of girl to do so is one who is neglected and in turn becomes overwhelmingly thankful for little things like getting new clothes. Something so many children her age took for granted. Now, truth be told, Mrs. Watkins didn't need to spend $400 on the dress. She could've easily bought one for $50, but given the special occasion tonight, Mrs. Watkins wanted to go all out for her grandbaby, and even more importantly, her father. Mrs. Watkins just knew once Austin saw Myyah in the dress it was going to be a transformative moment – a moment of spiritual motivation and self-realization. All the push Austin needed to get his shit together, so he can do right for his one and only daughter. But the other scorching conflict sizzling in Mrs. Watkins' mind was her absolute disdain of Fredquisha and how much she wanted to fuck that bitch up the next time she saw her. Mrs. Watkins had to play it cool though for Myyah's sake and for Austin's sanity.

As Myyah and Mrs. Watkins' emotions simmered, the grandmother helped the girl take her clothes off so she could try on the dress. When Mrs. Watkins first saw Myyah and the amount of weight she lost, at first, she was concerned the dress was no longer going to fit, but once Myyah tried the dress on, its fit turned out perfect.

"I have one last surprise!" Mrs. Watkins beamed.

"What's that, granny?" Myyah was staring at herself in the mirror, admiring the dress.

Mrs. Watkins walked over to a small closet in the room, opened it up and reached up to pull down a shoebox. She opened it up and pulled out something wrapped in pink and lavender tissue paper. She laid the gift down on the bed for Myyah to unwrap. "Here, come open this up," Mrs. Watkins said.

Myyah turned around and walked over to the bed. She slowly unwrapped the gift and instantly her mouth dropped. It was a replica of Princess Tiana's crown. "OH MY GOD! GRANNY! YOU ARE THE BEST GRANDMA EVER!" Myyah shrieked and cried once again. "I get to wear a crown too!"

"Yes, my princess. You get to wear this crown. You're cute little angel self is going to look so gorgeous for your daddy tonight!"

CHAPTER SEVEN

"You got your seatbelt on, baby doll?" Mrs. Watkins asked as she chucked up the engine to her Murano.

"Yes, granny!" Myyah grinned and responded.

"Good! Always remember to put your seatbelt on when you get in a car. It's a lot of crazy drivers out here and you never know what can happen," Mrs. Watkins explained, looking back in the rear-view mirror as she adorned her granddaughter.

Grandma put the SUV into reverse, slowly backed out of her driveway and took off into the glowing orange and amethyst sunset that filled the skies.

Despite the daddy-daughter dance not being some luxury Gold Coast high-end gala or ball, Mrs. Watkins was dressed as if she was going to party with hifalutin white folk and other Windy City power brokers. Tonight, she decided to wear a black one shoulder jumpsuit that she recently bought from Macy's. The grandmother would've opted to wearing something more casual, but after the dance, Mrs. Watkins was actually going to head out later tonight and go stepping at the Dating Game, a small lounge located right off Stony Island Avenue on the South Side of the city. Jonah had agreed to babysit Myyah after he got off his shift. In fact, after the end of the dance, he was going to drive into the city and then pick up Myyah and take her back home.

Mrs. Watkins, despite being in her 60s, was in remarkable shape. They say black don't crack, and Mrs. Watkins was the living embodiment of that timeless adage. One could easily mistake her for being in her mid-40s. Guess you can thank her youthful appearance to yoga, Zumba and cycling classes four to five times a week at her local LA Fitness on top of her semi-vegetarian diet.

Standing at around 5'5 and weighing no more than 125 pounds, Mrs. Watkins eerily resembled a younger Lena Horne. She had short and wavy black hair with streaks of gray. Although she wasn't super-light skinned like the famed and legendary black actress, her hue was Creole red due in part to her Louisiana ancestry.

"Girl, you look so beautiful! We're gonna take so many pictures tonight! Wow! Your father is going to be happy to see you. Are you happy to go see your daddy!"

"Yes! I miss him a lot!" Myyah exclaimed. She then asked, "Does he miss me a lot?"

"Of course! He talks about you all the time. He can't wait until he gets out so he can be with you every day!"

Myyah grinned as she dangled her small feet. "Granny – why is daddy in jail?"

Mrs. Watkins suddenly froze and didn't know exactly how to come up with the right answer. She had to seriously think of how to carefully word her response so that way she wouldn't put negative thoughts about her father into the girl's head. God knows Fredquisha was probably already using every opportunity she had to denigrate the man, so Mrs. Watkins wanted to make sure the answer she gave her grandbaby would be truthful yet respectful.

"Well, baby girl, he just made some bad choices. But he's not going to do them anymore because he cares about you so much and he wants to make sure he's there for you all the time."

"Was he a bad guy? Did he shoot a gun or something?"

"I wouldn't say he was a bad guy. He just hung around bad people and got influenced to sometimes do bad things. But listen, don't worry about that. Your daddy ain't gon' do bad stuff no more, ok?"

"Ok..." Myyah then turned her head and looked out her passenger window, once again admiring the backdrop of the suburban scenery as the sun glowed among the tangerine and lilac cloud streaks filling the skies.

Mrs. Watkins turned on her radio and tuned into a local jazz station. The soulful Al Jarreau sung his famous "We're In This Love Together" ballad. Hopping back onto the I-57 expressway, Mrs. Watkins put her foot on the gas in order to make it to the event on time. 5:15 PM tick tocked on the car clock, and it was going to take about a good 35 minutes to get to the jail if Mrs. Watkins went at least five above the posted speed limit.

Dr. Sterling told all guardians they needed to get to the jail by 6 PM if they wanted to attend the event, otherwise, they were going to be unfortunately turned away. Mrs. Watkins would've left her house earlier, however, she got caught up and lost track of time because she essentially had to give her grand-daughter a complete makeover. Myyah's hair was a tangled mess, and Fredquisha didn't even do her part in agreeing to get the girl's hair done for tonight. Mrs. Watkins meant to ask Fredquisha earlier about why she didn't get Myyah's hair done, but after she confronted her about the condition of her apart-ment and got rushed out, the question slipped her mind.

About fifteen minutes passed. Mrs. Watkins was now getting on the Dan Ryan expressway. Now in Chicago's city limits, she had to slow down her speed given there was much more traffic. Some more minutes passed and suddenly traffic came to a complete halt.

"Oh, hell…We got some traffic. Damn it!" Mrs. Watkins shook her head. "Oops, I'm sorry, baby doll. I didn't mean to curse. Don't say that word," the grandmother quickly apologized.

"It's ok…" Myyah replied. She then asked, "Are we going to be late?"

"No, we should be fine. I just think there is some construction going on…," Mrs. Watkins explained as she tried to peer out her windshield to see what was holding up traffic. It had to be construction because she saw some orange cones lining the sides of the expressway and from a distance saw flashing white construction lights emanating from distant MAC trucks.

Now in a complete jam, the Murano sat idle.

BOOM!

"AHHHHHHH!!" Myyah and Mrs. Watkins' screams filled the SUV. The Murano violently jolted forward after a black Honda Accord crashed into its bumper.

Mrs. Watkins for a moment closed her eyes and almost saw her life flash before her. "Oh MY GOD! This idiot just hit me!" Mrs. Watkins barked as Myyah's sudden cries filled the car. The girl had no idea what happened, and she too blanked out for a moment. Mrs. Watkins then looked in her rear-view mirror and saw the Accord literally hunching her vehicle's tail. She exhaled and then quickly turned in her seat and stared at Myyah to see if she was alright. "You ok, Myyah?!?"

Myyah couldn't produce words, just sustained, loud cries with her doe eyes now squinted in shock and fear.

"Shhh, shhh, it's ok, baby girl! This guy just hit us from the back," Mrs. Watkins tried to quickly console the girl, reaching back and rubbing her legs. "It's gonna be alright. See, this is why I told you we need to put our seatbelts on…" Pretty ironic she gave that life lesson just less than thirty minutes ago, and now here both women were caught up in an accident that could've been potentially worse had not any of them been wearing their seatbelts.

Myyah slowly quieted her cries. Mrs. Watkins then unfastened her own seatbelt and got out of the truck. She looked at the back of her truck and saw that it was completely smashed in. Had the Accord been going any faster, there was a real possibility Myyah would've definitely been hurt, if not outright killed!

Mrs. Watkins gasped and clutched her mouth in surprise. Was her Murano even drivable now? she wondered. She then turned her gaze over to the Accord and saw that its front was completely fucked up as well. The grandmother peered into the windshield. It was completely whited out from the exploded airbag. Mrs. Watkins lunged over to the driver's side door and looked into the window. A young, dark-skinned girl, who looked no older than 25, was squeezed between her seat and the exploded driver's air bag.

"Oh shit! Can you not get out?" Mrs. Watkins nervously asked. She looked around to see if any other drivers may have stopped to help them.

"I think...I think I can!" the young woman responded.

A white pickup truck slowly strolled passed the accident and then stopped. A white man, who looked fortyish with a jet-black Elvis hairdo, hopped out of his truck and darted over to Mrs. Watkins.

"Is everything alright, ma'am?" the white man asked as he pulled out his cell phone. "Did you call 9-11 yet?"

"NO! OH MY GOD! I think she might be stuck in here! Can you call them?!?" Mrs. Watkins, flustered, opened the driver's side door, leaned in, and attempted her best to pull the semi-portly woman out. Once she got out, the young girl frantically looked around as she rubbed her neck. "Oh My God! I'm sooo sorry, miss! I had dropped my phone for a second, and before you know it, when I looked up I hit you!"

Mrs. Watkins deeply inhaled and then let a stressful breath out and grabbed her forehead.

"Why, God? Why?!? I was supposed to be taking my grand-daughter to a daddy-daughter dance and now I think I'm gonna miss it!"

The young, chubby girl clutched her mouth with her hands and apologized, "I'm soooo sorry! I really am! I feel so bad now," she wept as a tear escaped her right eye.

Mrs. Watkins shook her head as she lowered it. "It's ok…At least we are alive…At least we are alive…"

The Caucasian good Samaritan got off the phone and walked over to the two women.

"The police are going to be here any moment now. Are you two women ok? Anyone in pain? Sometimes adrenaline can flood your body and make everything seem alright…"

"I'm fine…But I need to go check on my granddaughter and tell her what happened. She's still inside my car," Mrs. Watkins said.

"I think I'm fine, my neck just feels a bit tight," the younger woman responded as she massaged the right corner of her neck.

Mrs. Watkins walked over to the right back passenger side of the Murano, opened up the door and nervously grinned at Myyah. "You ok, baby doll?"

"Yes, granny. Am I still going to be able to the dance?"

Mrs. Watkins took a deep inhale again and then exhaled. She pursed her lips and hung her head to the side. Myyah looked at her grandmother, her silence gave her the answer she was looking for.

CHAPTER EIGHT

"**You** ou ready, bro?" Jaheyim, another black inmate standing next to Austin, asked as 6:29 tick tocked on Austin's watch. "Yeah, man, just a bit nervous. Ain't seen my baby girl in two years, broski!"

"Yeah, I feel you...Same predicament."

Beyonce's "Daddy" lowly blared from the fat black speakers set up in the auditorium. Officer Thompson, a fifteen-year veteran corrections officer inside the facility, had always volunteered for the annual dance, and tonight was no exception. Dr. Sterling knew he had a DJ business outside of working for the jail and asked him years ago if he would love to donate his services to the program. Without hesitation he agreed to do the event for free given he truly wanted to see the men inside the jail maintain strong relationships with their young children.

All of the inmate-fathers lined up in one single line as they faced the double door entrance of the auditorium. All the men, looking dapper, had huge smiles plastered across their faces. It didn't matter that all of them were locked up behind bars. Tonight, they were going to get a taste of freedom.

The doors opened, and suddenly a line of girls, all ranging in ages, colors and ethnic backgrounds, began to make their way inside the auditorium.

"Daddy!" That's all you heard come out of the jubilant mouths of the young girls once their eyes located their fathers. Austin stood idle, hoping at any moment he'd see Myyah. As more girls poured into the auditorium, Austin scanned the group wondering where Myyah was. Then mothers, grand-mothers, aunts, even some uncles and grandfathers made their way inside. Austin still didn't see Myyah or his mother.

"Hrrrm," Austin mumbled to himself, growing increasingly concerned something may have happened to Myyah and his mother. Somewhat shivering in fear, he just remembered what happened earlier to DeMario and God forbid something similar happened to Mrs. Watkins and Myyah.

Moments later, Austin then observed Dr. Sterling make her way back into the auditorium. She scanned the room and saw him as well, they both instantly locked their eyes onto one another. She beckoned him over near the corner, away from the group of girls and fathers, so they could have some privacy. Trillions of butterflies formed in the pits of Austin's stomach as he just knew something bad had to have happened. Fighting back tears, he nervously sauntered over to Dr. Sterling.

"Hey, Austin...I got some bad news," Dr. Sterling revealed.

"Please, don't tell me—"

Dr. Sterling interrupted him and said, "No, it's not anything serious like earlier. But unfortunately, I just got a call from your mother, Mrs. Watkins. They got into a car accident on the freeway and they won't be able to make it." She took a deep breath, exhaled then continued, "I'm sooo sorry, Austin. I know you were really looking forward to this."

Austin tremored at hearing the news. "Wait, was it a bad accident? Are they ok?"

"Yeah! They're fine! She said some young lady hit her as she was making her way north on the Dan Ryan. The young woman had to go to the hospital, but they had to get their car towed back to the suburbs, and you know according to detention center policies, we can't admit visitors in after a certain time for security reasons. I'm so sorry, Austin. I know this is devastating..."

Austin's eyes turned to weltering slits and his body grew tense. Silent, he didn't know what else to say. He was looking forward to this now for months and unexpectedly the opportunity to see his daughter was taken away. Not wanting to display full-on anger or agitation in front of everyone, Austin produced an uneasy smirk and muttered, "Well, at least they are alright. Besides, I'm getting out at the end of the month anyways, so I'll get to see her then."

"Yes...Of course! Don't let this deter you Austin." Dr. Sterling patted Austin on his back and then strolled off to go introduce herself to the girls and their parents.

Austin, now completely devastated, walked over to an empty round table and sat down. He watched the rest of the inmates reunite with their daughters and family members. Austin balled up his right fist and punched himself about four times in his thigh, fighting back tears of rage. He needed to leave. This wasn't what he planned for at all and he felt cheated.

He got up, and not wanting to make a scene, he excused himself to the bathroom in the auditorium. Once inside, he found the first stall, threw himself inside, sat on the toilet and began to uncontrollably bawl. Aside from his father's funeral, this was the second time in his life he cried and sobbed like a newborn. As salty tears escaped his eyes, all he could visualize were imagined flashes of Myyah wearing that Princess Tiana dress and the crown he wanted to get his baby girl so badly.

Some moments passed and suddenly the door to the bathroom flung open. Officer Clayton, a supervising detention center guard, who volunteered to help with the event tonight, strolled inside to use the urinal. Austin, not wanting to be embarrassed by his crying, abruptly paused his emotional breakdown and wiped his face. He got up from the toilet seat, exited the stall and made his way to a sink.

Officer Clayton, himself a black man as well but in his 50s, looking like a zesty Judge Joe Brown, flushed the urinal and strolled over to the sink. "You alright, Watkins?"

"Yeah…Yeah, I'm good, sir. Just got some really bad allergies. You know how it gets during these Chi-town summers," Austin lied. However, his limp and gray body language was telling a different, somber truth.

"Oh yeah, I got'em bad too…How's your daughter? I know she's having a blast out there."

"Yeah…umm, she couldn't make it." Austin couldn't even give the man eye contact as he said those words. "Dr. Sterling just told me they got into a lil accident on the e-way. But it's all good though. I'm just glad they're ok and everyone else out there got a chance to see their peoples, you feel me?"

Officer Clayton went silent and scanned Austin up and down. He looked into his reddened, glassy eyes and said "Oh, man, I'm so sorry to hear that, Jenkins. You sure you alright, bruh?"

Austin tried to play it off by coolly nodding his head, "Yeah, yeah, I'm fine, sir. Just you know, like I said, these allergies are killing me. I think I should head back to my cell to get my medicine."

"Alright, well, I can take you back if you like? I gotta head on outta here anyways."

"Oh ok, I appreciate that then…"

The two men then exited the bathroom and slowly meandered their way through the crowd as inmates danced with their daughters to the melodies blaring from the speakers.

Austin, numb and confused, couldn't even look at his other inmate-brothers enjoy their time with their daughters. Although he didn't want to come off as envious and selfish, he felt like he rightfully deserved to have the same sense of happiness everyone else seemed to be relishing. But then he quickly reminded himself of what happened to DeMario earlier and how that could've easily been his situation. Putting himself in DeMario's shoes, he erased his envy and hoped the inmates and their families would have a good ass time.

Back in his cell, Austin took off the suit jacket and neatly hung it up. He didn't have the energy to take off the rest of his outfit. He just laid in his cell bed, stared up at the ceiling and kept thinking about his plans once he got out. He was going to fight hard, very hard, to be there in every second of Myyah's life until the day he died. And that bitch Fredquisha wasn't going to be able to stop him. He closed his eyes and drifted off to sleep.

CHAPTER NINE

redquisha, and two of her ride-or-die besties, Tykeisha and Antoinette, bobbed their weave-covered heads to a catchy Cardi B song. MooMoo was did the fuck up tonight from head to toe. She was in full south side hood chick mode. Her lace front ran down her back, damn near touching her ass. She was rocking a gold, v-neck see through mini-dress that hugged every lump and bump in her thighs, ass and midsection. However tonight, to conceal her true bad-bodied figure, Fredquisha had her corset tightly wrapped around her midsection to stop the combination of belly fat and stretch marked skin from being revealed to the world at large. With no bra on, it was somewhat possible with a naked eye to see her pierced nipples. Matching gold stiletto pumps were on her feet. Now, from a cursory glance, one would assume Fredquisha was a paid boss bitch who ran her own hair shop or nail salon. But Fredquisha's ass was unemployed and living off Illinois' tax payers.

Fredquisha knew Tykeisha and Antoinette from the neighborhood. The trio went to the same middle and high school and had been besties since then.

Tykeisha, short, fat, and black, but didn't mind wearing loud, bold neon-colored lace fronts. With a huge gap in between her two front teeth, she almost looked comedic with this purple lace front bob she had on her head. Bitch looked like she was straight out of BeBe's Kids.

Antoinette on the other hand, was just a shade lighter than Tykeisha, but was much slimmer. Antoinette was a home health aide and was currently going back to school to get her RN license. Despite Fredquisha asserting herself as the de facto leader of the trio given years ago she truly was a standout sexy hoe, Antoinette now was the sexiest and resembled Tiarra, Scrapp DeLeon's baby mama, from Love & Hip Hop Atlanta.

As she sipped on her Mai Tai, Fredquisha scanned the dark and somewhat smoky nightclub. Tonight, B-Kilo, a local rapper from the West Side was performing, so you already know the club was filled with hood niggas from every section of the city. B-Kilo had two number one singles in the country and was on the verge of signing with Cash Money Records. So, while the crowd tonight was definitely on the hood side, without a doubt there were plenty of men in the room who had cash out the wazoo. This was the very motivation for why Fredquisha was trying to set her eyes on a baller she could possibly snatch up, bring back home and hopefully secure a future bag.

Earlier in the day, after getting some weed and some quick, bomb ass dick from Deontae and Marvin, Fredquisha wasted no time on preparing for this very hour. The outfit was bought last week with some child support she was getting from Quimani's father. Oh, and by the way, Quimani and Zy'meer had different fathers.

Quimani's father, Mark, better known in the streets as "Marco Polo" was the same age as Fredquisha and worked full-time at a payday loan company up on the North Side. However, the job was just a front – a way for him to get easy access to social security numbers and sell them on the dark web, the internet's "black market". Mark was an established credit card finesser and a lot of people came to him to get "working capital" to start up their own hustles. Mark was also linked to Chicago's local rap scene. So many local rap artists and producers in the Chi at one point in time came to Mark to "crack" cards so they can get come up on some quick loot and use the funds to invest in their music careers. In actuality, Fredquisha wondered if she was going to run into his ass tonight since he ran in the same circles as B-Kilo.

Zy'meer's father on the other hand was a well-known dope boy out in the South Suburbs who pushed everything from heroin, coke, weed, xannies, ecstasy, lean, etc. Kevon, better known in the streets as "Gooch", was the definition of a mobile "street pharmacy". You name it, he had it. Although he wasn't on kingpin-level, he was close, but didn't want to let his operation get too big. So obviously due to Gooch's "occupation", Fredquisha didn't get him on child support because he still fucked around in the streets. She had arranged with him to not get him cast into the "CHSUP" system so long as he gave her a good "five hunned" a month in cash.

"Bitch, its so many fine ass niggas in here tonight!" Antoinette chirped as she sipped on chilled Hennessey and coke.

"Hell yeah, in fact I see this one sexy ass nigga I'm finna go talk to right now to see what the fuck he's on," Fredquisha said as she attached her manipulative pupils onto this tall, slender light skinned nigga with long dreads.

Fredquisha had an addiction to street niggas that somewhat resembled athletes. In fact, all of the men Fredquisha ever fucked with were dope boys who could pass for professional football or basketball players – hence the reason why she hooked up with Austin.

Buddy who she was gawking at had some skinny chocolate bitch all up on him, but Fredquisha, being the aggressive bully bitch she was, was going to dead that flirtatious shit. Pretty bold given that she didn't know who that bitch was. For all she knew, that could've been his main bitch, side bitch, or just simply someone who he was pursuing. But to Fredquisha, none of that mattered. Once she devoured eye candy with her devious stare, the nigga was all hers. She didn't believe in sharing.

"Antoinette, listen hoe, you need to go over there and 'accidentally' spill that motherfuckin' drink all over that silly ass hoe over there and then let me get my hands on that nigga..."

"Bitch, who you talkin' about? Antoinette asked as she looked around to see exactly who Fredquisha was referring to in the club.

"Look straight ahead and then turn slightly left. You see that tall, yellow nigga over there with the long dreads? Then see skinny, fake ass Azealia Banks lookin' ass bitch all over him.? That's the bitch I'm talking about." Fredquisha's eyes turned to evil slits, all types of ratchet machinations ran through her one-dimensional mind.

"Hahah, G, you're funny as hell, but I'm down to ride for my bestie," Antoinette smiled, shaking her head.

"Good...And Tykeisha, I need you to be look out and security in case a bitch might try to fight."

"Baby, you didn't even need to ask. You know I got you, boo!" Tykeisha stuck her pierced tongue out and proceeded to take a sip of her drink.

Fredquisha quickly ran her champagne-colored acrylic finger nails through her lace front. She then cracked her knuckles, neck and even popped her back in case she had to fight a bitch, maybe even a few bitches.

"Ya'll ready?"

"Yup!" Both besties replied together.

The ratchet bestie trio carefully strolled over to the light skinned dude and the skinny chocolate bitch. Fredquisha kind of went off to the side and hid behind some niggas just posted around, making fake light conversation. Tykeisha stood off next to MooMoo.

Antoinette, strategic as she could be, then lightly and obliviously walked passed the "couple". She pretended to have tripped over her heel and then thrusted the drink all over the brown girl, "OOOOPS! I'm so sorry! I'm so sorry, ma'am," she lied.

"Ughhhh! You bitch! You did that shit on purpose! Bitch, I already know how you ghetto hoes get down!" Fake ass Azealia Banks, although stunned, was pissed and ready to beat a bitch's ass for getting the drink spilled on her.

Sensing the potential threat facing Antoinette, both Fredquisha and Tykeisha stormed over to the chick and scanned the enraged woman up and down. "Bitch, who the fuck you callin 'ghetto hoes'?!?" Tykeisha barked, only inches away from the chick's face.

"BITCH! YOU AND YO UGLY ASS MAMMY!"

"I'll beat cho mothafuckin' skinny ass, you crack hoe lookin' ass tramp! You want these hands, hoe?!?" Fredquisha interjected and stood nose to nose with the enraged woman.

"Ay, ladies, come on now! Calm that shit down!"

"You know what, I'm not gonna stoop to these basic ass, trashy hoes' level. Bye, nigga. Have at it! This nasty, fat bitch look like she probably got roaches in her crib anyways…" The mad as fuck chick then walked off and sashayed her wet self to the nearest women's bathroom to clean herself up. But then suddenly she spun on her feet and dashed up to Fredquisha and her besties. Light skinned buddy with dreads tried to hold the girl back from putting her hands on Fredquisha, "Ay, shorty! Cut it out, bro! It ain't that serious"

"Nigga, get yo fuckin' hands off me! All I'm gonna say is bitch, don't let me catch you in the streets!"

Fredquisha scrunched her face up and rolled her eyes and neck, "Whatever, skinny bitch. You ain't with the shits like that!"

"We'll see bitch! Don't let me find out about yo punk ass,

heaux!" The enraged, slender woman then walked off to the bathroom.

"Anyways...So, what's your name?" Fredquisha asked as she gently rubbed the dude's shoulder and smiled. Tykeisha and Antoinette, realizing the mission was accomplished, walked away to go find some other sexy paid dicks in the club.

"Quantrell – but my niggas call me 'Trel'," he responded and smiled as he took a sip from his drink. Some brown liquor of course. Niggas loved that dark.

CHAPTER TEN

*A*bsolute pitch darkness defined the late morning suburban starry skies. A tad cloudy. A gust or two ruffled wide oak trees lining the complex gated community the Watkins lived in now for some years. The full moon shown its glory, giving graceful light to the forest-like Matteson suburban enclave. Most gated communities in the far-east suburb virtually had no street lighting, so moonlight was the only source of evening luminosity.

12:45 AM flashed on the dashboard of Jonah's car as he navigated his way through the upscale neighborhood. Once the younger brother spotted his residence, he pulled into the dimly lit driveway of Mrs. Watkins house, his eyes now glued to Mrs. Watkins' damaged Murano. Jonah turned off the engine, opened his door and got out of his navy blue Mazda6. A recent purchase he made to drive for Lyft and Uber, and also have reliable transportation once he moved out to Los Angeles with this longtime girlfriend.

Jonah, standing at around 5'9, looked like a shorter, slender version of Austin. The only difference was a lightly shaven jet-black beard wrapped around his face and he had a fresh low wavy fade on top of his head. Jonah worked as a part-time bartender, and at times a server, at Natalya's Vineyard, a French restaurant and local winery in the neighboring Orland Park.

Austin shook and sank his head once he fully gawked and analyzed the entirety of the damage done to his mother's Murano. The crossover-SUV damn near looked totaled, but Mrs. Watkins wasn't going to know the full extent of the damage until Monday or Tuesday when a GEICO claims adjuster was scheduled to come out to do an assessment of the damage.

After the accident Mrs. Watkins and Myyah had to wait about a good hour before a tow truck came and got the family and took them back to the burbs. Obviously missing the dance, Myyah was completely devastated and spent the rest of the night crying, eventually sobbing herself to deep sleep.

After Jonah was scheduled to get off work, he was supposed to head into the city to go pick Myyah up from the dance and take her back home in the 'burbs to babysit while his mother went out for the rest of the evening. But after the car accident his mother promptly called him and told him what happened. Little bro was a bit emotional about the entire ordeal given he truly wanted Myyah to go visit her father. Rather than come straight home, Jonah then opted to stay a few more hours at the restaurant to get some extra hours and tips.

Jonah made his way up to the front door of the brick McMansion and opened the door. He solemnly walked in through the foyer and quickly noticed his mother on the couch in the living room, still awake and watching a rerun of Family Matters.

"Hey, mama…"

"Hey…," Mrs. Watkins responded.

Jonah exhaled… "She still upset?"

Earlier Mrs. Watkins had texted him and told him how

Myyah was such an emotional wreck from not being able to go to the dance.

"Well, she's sleeping now," Mrs. Watkins exhaled. "I just put her to bed not too long ago."

Jonah made his way into the living room. He could tell from his mother's stiff and gray body language that she too had been crying. He peered into mama's eyes and noticed they were bit glassy, even slightly reddened. Jonah sat down next to her, lightly grabbed her and held her.

"It's ok, mama...Austin's gonna get out soon anyways, and hopefully he'll get to dance with her for the rest of her life..."

"I know, but still...We spent so much time and effort planning all of this. And all it took was for one accident. One silly ass girl on the expressway to mess it all up," Mrs. Watkins cried, wiping the tears that slowly ran down her cheeks.

Jonah didn't respond. He just nodded his head, continuing to console his mother.

The two sat in silence in the dark living room. The colorful light emanating from the TV illuminated the room. Some ten minutes later, Jonah closed his eyes. Mrs. Watkins followed suit.

About an hour passed.

Ding! Dong!

Jonah abruptly opened his eyes at the sound of the doorbell. Red and blue police lights flickering from outside seeped into the living room's windows, bouncing off the walls in the entire den and living room.

"Whoa, what's going on?" Jonah asked as he released his mother from his embrace. Mrs. Watkins slowly opened her eyes and saw the police lights dancing on the walls as well.

"Why are the police here?"

Jonah strolled over to the window, looked outside and saw a Cook County Sheriff's car. His heart beats picked up in intensity as he then dashed to the front door and quickly unlocked it and swung it open. "Good evening, or morning…Is everything alright, sir?" Jonah asked the man who he assumed was a Sheriff.

"Is Mrs. Delores Watkins, mother of Austin Watkins, home, sir?"

"Yes…"

Jonah turned his attention towards his mother who was slowly walking his way to the front door. "Mama!"

"What's going on, officer?"

"Good evening, ma'am. I'm Officer Clayton. I'm a supervising detention center supervisor. It's about Austin…"

CHAPTER ELEVEN

HOURS EARLIER BACK AT COOK COUNTY JAIL...

*O*fficer Clayton sensed Austin wasn't being forthcoming when they were in the bathroom together. Allergies his ass. Knowing Austin's background, Officer Clayton walked out the bathroom torn and conflicted. On one hand, the detention center obviously had serious visitation enforcement policies. But on the other hand, he didn't want the inmate to become potentially suicidal over not seeing his daughter.

After he escorted Austin to his cell, he was supposed to have gone straight home. But his called his boss, Director Miller, the deputy director of corrections, and explained the situation that apparently happened to Mrs. Watkins and her granddaughter. Although the detention center has very strict policies, Director Miller tonight made an exception.

Clink. Clink. Clink.

Officer Clayton lightly tapped on Austin's cell door. He slowly opened his depressed brown eyes and wiped them, trying to adjust his vision to see who was trying to get his attention. He stood up and walked over to the door and peered out the tiny window and saw Officer Clayton's beady eyes and Joe Brown mustache.

The rattling of keys could be heard, and then the door to the cell opened up. "Hey Watkins, go put your suit back on, get that crust off your face and come with me…"

Austin scrunched his face up on confusion. "Why, what for?"

Officer Clayton leered. "Look, just do as I say, boy," Clayton commanded in a warm, brotherly tone.

Austin didn't know if he was dreaming or if he was fully awake, but without hesitation he quickly followed Officer Clayton's instructions. He lunged over to his sink, slapped chlorine-reeked cold water on his face and dried it off with a towel. Then he put the suit back on, jetted out the cell and then trailed the somewhat fatherly guard.

Austin looked down at his watch and saw it was almost ten minutes before 3 AM. Although he had a partial inkling as to what was going on, he didn't want to ask any more questions. He just followed the guard-supervisor to wherever he was taking him. A smile from the east coast to the west stretched across Austin's dark chocolate chiseled face.

"Baby girl! Wake up! We gotta go!" Mrs. Watkins shook her granddaughter awake.

Myyah opened her still sob-filled glassy eyes and gazed at her grandmother. "What's happening, grandma?" Myyah asked, confused.

"We get to go see your daddy!" Mrs. Watkins' eyes widened with overwhelming happiness.

"For real?!? We can see him now?!?"

"YES!" Mrs. Watkins screeched. "Come on! Let's get this dress back on!"

Without even continuing to question her grandmother, Myyah got up from the bed and walked over to the closet. Her grandmother quickly helped her put the dress back on. Mrs. Watkins then quickly pulled Myyah into the bathroom, quickly washed the girls' face and then the both of them jetted downstairs. Jonah, wide awake and thrilled, followed the women. The family then hopped into Officer Clayton's Crown Vic and sped off into the city.

Nervous and excited, Myyah held her hands, eyes glued to the highway as Officer Clayton commanded the steering wheel. Jonah was in the front fiddling with one of his DSLR cameras. Mrs. Watkins had her arms wrapped around Myyah's shoulders.

"Am I dreaming, granny?!?" Myyah excitedly asked.

"No, baby girl! This isn't a dream at all! This is real!"

CHAPTER TWELVE

*A*ustin and Officer Clayton trekked down the hallway of the bright detention center. Emotions began to over-take Austin. His heart beat raced like a champion horse at the Kentucky Derby. As the two men got close proximity to the auditorium, Austin was on the verge of collapsing and breaking down right then and there.

Officer Clayton had called up Dr. Sterling after the close of the event and informed her that he had permission from Director Miller to extend visitation hours, and that he wanted her to keep the dance floor open and all the decorations intact so that Austin could have a chance to dance with his daughter. Dr. Sterling, elated, agreed without a hesitation. So did the DJ.

As Austin and Officer Clayton approached the doors of the auditorium, the fatherly detention center supervisor paused and turned directly into Austin. The inmate was fighting his hardest to hold his salty tears back.

"Now, listen Watkins, I didn't have to do this, but I knew you were bullshitting me back in that bathroom. Man to man, I've been in your shoes. I lost my daughter Christina two years ago to leukemia. I think about her every god damn day of my life.

You have a chance bro to do right by that little girl in there. Go in there, love all over her, hold her, kiss her, tell her you love her a million times…And after you get out of here, I better not see or hear about your ass in here ever again. Got it?"

Austin, hearing Officer Clayton's words, tore him down. Officer Clayton now seemingly looked a tad frazzled and wracked with grief, but despite almost breaking down himself and crying over his deceased daughter, he wiped a few tears that trickled out of the corners of his eyes, leaned in and gave Austin a tight, brotherly hug. "You got this, young man. Do right by that girl. Be there in every moment of her life…You never know what tomorrow brings."

"Ok-k," Austin stuttered.

Officer Clayton released Austin. The detention center supervisor then turned his attention back to the double doors of the auditorium. Soft, flowery vibrations of Luther Vandross' "Dance With My Father" poured through the door. Clayton opened the doors, and instantaneously Austin's passion-filled eyes enclosed onto his family, most importantly, his daughter he hadn't seen in two long, hard years.

Myyah's eyes zoomed right into solemn Austin. "DAD-DDYYYY!" she wailed as she took off running towards her father. Austin, doing the same, met his daughter halfway into the dance floor.

Austin quickly collapsed to his knees with his arms wide open. Myyah flew into his embrace and Austin held her tightly as their sobs filled the surrounding area.

"Oh my God! My baby girl! You gon' always be my baby!" Austin cried as he looked Myyah into her face and gave her kisses all up and down her cheeks and skinny neck. "Look at you, you've gotten so big!"

Myyah couldn't respond. She was so overawed with jubilation at the sight of her father, that words wouldn't even make sense at this point. Despite being six, there was nothing like the growing bond a daughter had with her a father, especially in this instance. The love a girl has for her grandmother, uncles, aunts and others is one thing. But the love a daughter has for father – indescribable and unfathomable.

When a man lives up to the expectation of fatherhood, protecting and guiding his kith and kin, daughters stand in admiration of their kingly qualities. And given that Myyah was living in such tumultuous conditions with a woman who didn't even deserve the title "mother", Austin at this point was Myyah's only true source of parental love and protection. Unfortunately given Austin made bad choices in life that resulted in him losing split custody and going to jail, Austin couldn't be there to protect his only daughter.

Dr. Sterling, smiling, used a paper towel she had her pocket to wipe tears from her face. She clasped her hands together and mumbled, "This is healing. This is God…"

Mrs. Watkins and Jonah, both overwhelmed, trembling with elation, soaked in oceanic tears, strolled over to Austin and Myyah. "I'm so sorry about earlier, son!" Mrs. Watkins muttered and smiled.

Austin picked a still crying Myyah up and then went in to hug his mother, "Thank you, mama! Thank you so much! You just don't even understand."

"I know! Don't even say much! Enjoy this time with Myyah!"

Austin then turned his attention towards Jonah, "Waddup, lil bro!"

"Ahah, nothin, just got some bad allergies, that's all!" Jonah laughed as he wiped tears from his face and went in to give his big brother a huge hug.

"Yeah, I know. All that pollen and dust in the air got me out here lookin' crazy as hell!" Austin responded, chuckling.

As the Luther Vandross' song continued to play, Austin took Myyah off his shoulders and stood her up. "You ready to dance, princess? You look so beautiful in that dress!"

"Yessss, daddy! I wanna dance all day, all night, forever, with you! I never wanna leave!"

"Me either, princess, me either!"

Mrs. Watkins and Jonah strolled off to let Austin and Myyah dance together to the tune.

Dr. Sterling and Officer Clayton stood off to the side and observed the beautiful reunion between father and daughter.

Officer Clayton pulled out his phone and stared at a background picture of his deceased daughter, Moriah, who died from leukemia at the age of 28. He couldn't hold it in anymore. His manly, weeping cries quickly caught Dr. Sterling's attention.

"Awww, Officer Clayton, it's gonna be alright. Shhh, shh, don't cry," she consoled.

"If...If I could just have one more dance with my daughter. I'd do anything, anything in the world to get it," he muttered and wiped his face of tears. He quickly gathered himself, wiped his face and muted his sniffling. "Sorry about that, Doc. Been two long years."

"Time heals everything," Dr. Sterling responded.

"Well, if it does then my heart has years more to recover."

CHAPTER THIRTEEN

HOURS EARLIER...

"OOOH SHIT, BITCH! THAT'S MY SHIT! CRUCIAL CONFLICT!" Antoinette screamed as the throwback 90s west side Chi-town classic "Hay" rumbled from the speakers inside the still crowed hip hop club.

Suddenly a flood of ratchet chicks started throwing their hands up the air, swaying side to side, twerking as the Crucial Conflict Mary Jane melody vibrated the walls of the club.

"She crazy as hell," Fredquisha remarked in response to Antoinette's shout. Still posted up next to Trel, the two were still chopping it up, long after the confrontation with brown skinned bitch earlier.

Most clubs in Chicago closed at 3 AM. "What time is it anyways? I'm finna bounce pretty soon," Trel said as he whipped out his phone from his pocket and glanced down at the time on his iPhone 8. "Shit, damn, it's almost 1."

"Damn, you just gon' up and leave a bitch like that?" Fredquisha sassed and smiled. She trying to give his ass a hint.

"I mean, you wanna bounce with me too?" Trel smilingly asked, licking his lips, scanning the woman up and down.

"Well, lemme go check in with my girls! I gotta go pee too. Drinkin' all damn night got my bladder 'bout to explode," Fredquisha quipped and as she twiddled with the end of her cheap lace front, looking all fake bashful and shit.

"Ok. Just meet me outside. I'm gonna get us an Uber. So, we gon head back to your place then?" Trel probed.

"My place? Why not your place?" Fredquisha lightly spat back, a tad confused. She didn't feel comfortable bringing Trel over given the nastiness of her apartment. First impression is the best impression, and the last thing she needed was to have Trel come over and end up getting turned off by the horrid messiness and squalor of her apartment.

"Well, we can't crash at my crib 'cuz my baby mama and my kids over there..."

"Baby mama?!?! NIGGA! You ain't tell me you had a baby mama?!? The fuck?!?!" Fredquisha suddenly got fucking pissed and rolled her eyes, huffing. This nigga had her all the way fucked up. She'd be damned if she shared a nigga with another bitch, especially a bitch who was already classified as the main.

Trel smacked his teeth responded with, "Man, it ain't even like that. She just stayin' there until she get her own place. We ain't even fuckin' like that."

Fredquisha, now silent, thought about it for a second. She scanned Trel up and down. Every time she looked deep into this nigga's face, her pussy moistened. Trel reminded her of Dave East with long dreads. Nigga was so fuckin' sexy and fine, and she couldn't wait until she to get her purple, blunt-stained lips wrapped around his big dick.

If Trel was being completely truthful about his situation with his BM, Fredquisha wouldn't mind going along for the ride with her new bae. However, if it turned out he was lying, well, who knows. But a bitch like Fredquisha still might try to mess up Trel's "situation" and position herself to be the main bitch in the nigga's life.

"Fine, whatever," she succumbed. "I'll meet you downstairs..." Fredquisha said as she went over to Antoinette and Tykeisha, grabbed them and led them to the bathroom.

Inside, the three women huddled around a sink. "Bitch, I'm finna take his ass home," Fredquisha said as she rummaged her purse, looking for e-pills she bartered for pussy earlier from Deontae. Once she located her small manila, folded up envelope of pills, she opened it up, took a pill out and popped one on her tongue.

"BITCH! Ain't you pregnant?!?" Tykeisha spat and scrunched her face up when saw her bestie pop an e-pill in her mouth.

Fredquisha was now staring at herself in the mirror, sucking on the e-pill, trying to get her make up together before she was about to head back downstairs to meet up with Trel. She smacked her teeth and screwed her face up at Tykeisha's statement.

"And?" Fredquisha rolled her neck. "I'm still deciding if I wanna keep this little muhfucka or not. Shit, I already got three. Four is just doin' the most. I can't be out here getting my life boggled down with these bad ass kids."

Tykeisha's mouth flung open. "Hoe, it don't even matter! If you do keep it, you puttin' dope all up in that baby. Baby gon come out retarded."

"And, so what? If it do, that's just some more SSI money. I can always use some extra funds. Shit, bitch, I'm tryna buy a Benz next year. Hot pink too. Match the color of this fire ass pussy I'm finna throw on this nigga."

Tykeisha and Antoinette busted out laughing. Truth be told, Tykeisha wasn't THAT alarmed and judgmental at Fredquisha ingesting the drug. She just was shocked that Fredquisha would be that bold and fearless to pop some XTC knowing damn well she was eight weeks into a pregnancy supposedly. "Let me get one then," Tykeisha asked with her hand out.

"Here, bitch..." Fredquisha opened her purse and then opened the envelope of e-pills. Tykeisha stuck her fingers in the package and then placed the pill under her tongue. "ANYWAYS – you better take care of that situation quick then if you trying to snatch this nigga up. What he do? Sell dope? Rap?" Antoinette asked as she then went to adjust her dress in the mirror.

"Bitch, he said he into real estate. He just came out 'cuz apparently B-Kilo his TiTi's second cousin or some shit like that," Fredquisha explained as she attempted to seal the right fake eye-lash back onto her eyelid. "Gosh, these shits are so damn cheap!" she commented, infuriated that the eye lash was somewhat slipping off.

"We'll see though. For right now, I just wanna see with this dick do. I'll report back to ya'll in the AM." Fredquisha then quickly thought that she told Mrs. Watkins Myyah needed to be back in the afternoon. But now that her "Mission: Get New Dick" was on the verge of being accomplished, she wondered if she just call up and tell Mrs. Watkins that she could keep Myyah until Monday.

School in Chicago was on the verge of letting out for the summer and Monday was a teacher's work day. Students didn't have to be back until Tuesday. School was scheduled to end the following week. If "Dave East with dreads" bae was going to end up being a promising situation, lots of changes around her house were going to be needed.

"Aiiight darlings, I'm finna bounce. Hit my line tomorrow!" Fredquisha closed her purse, hugged her besties and then made her way downstairs to meet up with Trel.

He was standing on the corner of the well-lit city street with his phone in his hand, checking the ETA of the Uber driver he just ordered not too long ago. "Sorry 'bout that. It was so crowded in there," Fredquisha apologized as she walked up to

Trel and smiled. "No worries, buddy ain't gon be here anyways for another four minutes." Fredquisha grinned, "Cool."

Ding! Trel looked at his phone and then looked down the street. He saw what appeared to be the white Ford Fusion belonging to Amadou, his 4.8-star rated Uber driver. "Finally," Trel said and pointed to the Uber driver.

The Ford Fusion pulled up to the curb of the street and its doors unlocked. Trel opened the right back passenger door for Fredquisha to get in. "Thank you!" she replied and wiggled her way into the car. Trel went to the other side and hopped in.

"How are you all tonight? Amadou the driver asked and smiled in the rear-view mirror. "By the way, you forgot to put in your address, sir…"

"Yeah, I know. I'm fine, but umm what's your address?" Trel asked Fredquisha.

"Well, I was thinkin' instead of my place, maybe we can go to a hotel."

"Hotel? You got a reservation?" Trel asked.

"Nah, but nigga, don't worry about it. Mr. Uber Driver, can you take us to the Marriot down in Hyde Park? It's off Lake Shore and 53rd street."

"Ok, ma'am…" Amadou responded. He quickly pulled up the Uber driver's app on his phone and typed in the Marriot's address. Once Google Maps got loaded and he had his directions, Amadou took off.

"One of my girls work at the hotel," Fredquisha lied. She was going to quickly order her a room on her phone and use up some of Myyah's SSI money to get a room.

"Well, since you got us with the room, you wanna stop and get somethin' to eat first? White Palace right around the corner," Trel asked as he put his arm around Fredquisha. Feeling his muscular forearm grace her neck sent a bolt of electricity down into panties, making her pussy even more wet. #winning.

"Yeah…That's cool. I'm hungry as fuck anyways," Fredquisha said. Bitch was always hungry.

Trel leaned forward into the front of the car. "Ay, yo bro. Stop at the White Palace off Roosevelt."

"Ok, sir," the thirtyish, semi-musty African Uber driver replied as he took a hard right, going against the GPS' directions. Some minutes later, the Ford Fusion carrying the new 'couple' arrived at the 24/7. The goal was to grab something greasy to soak up the alcohol fermenting in their stomachs and then head to the hotel in Hyde Park, a neighborhood right off the Lake on the South Side.

"Just give us fifteen, bro. I got you with a big tip," Trel said and handed Amadou a $20 bill so he could wait for them to get their carryout.

The couple hopped out of the car, made their way inside the restaurant and ordered their take out. A good twenty minutes later they headed back out the restaurant, hopped back into the car and then sped off to the hotel about a good fifteen minutes away.

On their way, the two not giving a fuck, started making out in the back seat. Fredquisha grazed her hand along Trel's thigh and felt his hardening meat. Her pussy of course was glowing in excitement. This nigga had to be packing at least nine, if not ten, she thought.

"Man, I'm so fuckin' hard right now. My BM ain't sucked a nigga up in ages," Trel chuckled, confessing his sex life with this children's mother was in the midst of drought. As he planted kisses up and down her neck, he slid his hand in between Fredquisha's thighs and rubbed her musty, unshaven fat pussy meat popping through her thong.

Fredquisha licked and kissed the side of Trel's tatted up neck, sending blood down to his groin at a million miles an hour. MooMoo then went to do the unthinkable; she unzipped his pants and leisurely whipped out his tanned erect dick leaking with precum.

Trel's eyes flew wide open as he was a bit terrified. He flung his gaze to the front of the car to see if Amadou was creepily observing what was happening in the back seat. "Shit, you gon get us banned from Uber!" Trel whispered.

Placing her index finger over his long lips, Fredquisha suppressed Trel's agitation. "Shhhh," she cut his mounting apprehension. Without hesitation she buried her head down into his lap and fed her mouth his hard dick. She was gonna show bae what that mouth do. Hoe is life.

CHAPTER FOURTEEN

*A*fter getting back from the dance, Mrs. Watkins woke up early that same Sunday morning and prepared a huge country breakfast for Myyah and Jonah. Despite only having about a good three hours of sleep in her body, Mrs. Watkins wanted to spend as much time as she could with her granddaughter before she was scheduled to head back to her mother's.

Mrs. Watkins whipped up some eggs, bacon, grits, French toast, hash browns and sausage. Grandma wanted to feed the girl as much as she could before she went back to her crazy ass, noncaring mother. On any other Sunday Mrs. Watkins would've gladly gone straight to early morning church service, but given she rarely had opportunities to see Myyah she decided to skip service and take her granddaughter to a local park that had a big swimming pool and water slides.

"Good mornin', grandma!" Myyah surprisingly greeted her granny as she made her way into the kitchen and watched her finish cooking breakfast.

Mrs. Watkins turned on her slipper-covered feet and

produced the biggest grin at the girl. "Baby girl! I didn't expect you to be up so soon! Aren't you still tired?"

"No, not really...Sometimes I don't sleep much back home 'cuz I be afraid of the bugs in the house."

"Oh no, well...I'm afraid of bugs too. They won't bother you though."

"I know, but sometimes they crawl on me and give me nightmares."

"Crawl on you?" Mrs. Watkins screwed her face up in slight disgust.

"Yes," Myyah confessed and then quickly muzzled her mouth.

"Oh no, baby doll, it's ok, I'm not gonna tell your mother." Mrs. Watkins sensed that Myyah once again told something she wasn't supposed to be saying. She quickly tried to change the subject to qualm the girl's fear. "Anyways, how was that bed? Was it comfortable enough for you?" Mrs. Watkins asked as she chopped up cubes of butter and put them in the pot of grits she had cooking at a low temperature on her stove.

"Yes, ma'am. I got really good sleep. The best sleep ever. The bed in Fredquisha's house is kind of bad. It hurts my back all the time..."

Mrs. Watkins raised her brow and looked strangely at her granddaughter. "Why are you calling your mother by her first name?"

With her hands behind her back, Myyah swayed side to side, a bit timid to say anything that might get her in trouble with her mother. "She said I have to call her that 'cuz its more respectful," Myyah explained.

"So, you don't her mama or mother?" Mrs. Watkins asked.

"No...I have to call her Fredquisha..."

Mrs. Watkins blood boiled like the grits on the stove just thinking what type of psychological abuse Fredquisha was possibly subjecting Myyah to on a daily basis. Given that Mrs.

Watkins rarely saw Myyah, she never had enough time to probe deeply and ask Myyah what was really going on at home and if her mother was treating her well.

The rare times when Fredquisha did allow Myyah to see her grandmother, the wench only agreed to let her visit her in a public space like a mall or a Chuck E. Cheese. Hearing Myyah refer to her own mother by her first name was the first red flag raised by Fredquisha. Truth be told, there were other red flags long before this morning, but those red flags were seen from a far distance and could easily be illusive and imaginary. Well, no not really, and Mrs. Watkins knew something serious was going on over at Fredquisha's house, but she never had enough ample evidence to prove Fredquisha was being abusive or negligent.

"Ok, well, I guess. Anyways, you don't call me by my first name. You call me grandma, or granny, ok?"

"Ok, granny," Myyah smiled, lunged at her grandmother and hugged her.

"So when does my daddy get out of jail again, granny?"

"At the end of this month! He was sooo happy to get a chance to see you! He missed you so much."

"I was excited to see him too! Can I live with him when he leaves?"

Mrs. Watkins froze. She didn't know how to answer that question. She would've easily said yes, but given the precarious custody situation, she had to figure out a way to be truthful yet hopeful. "I don't know, baby girl. We will have to talk to your mother about it soon."

"Ok," Myyah responded.

"Why do you wanna live with your daddy?"

Myyah looked at her grandmother and her eyes began to water. "I just miss him, and Fredquisha won't let me see him. I ask to see him all the time and she tells me no."

Mrs. Watkins took a huge deep breath, ready to explode. Myyah scrunched her face up. She wiped her eyes as tears almost escaped her eye ducts. "And, she just say mean things to me."

"Mean things like what?" Mrs. Watkins tone became abruptly serious.

"She says I am ugly and dumb."

"WHAT?!?"

Myyah quickly muzzled her mouth and then attempted to run off and hide. Mrs. Watkins panicked and tried to grab the girl, "Wait, Myyah, come back here! Tell me! What is your mother doing to you?"

Mrs. Watkins caught up with Myyah in the living room, grabbed her and turned her around. She got down on one knee and looked the sobbing girl in her eyes. Myyah couldn't look her grandmother straight in the face and tell her the truth about the wide scale abuse and torture her mother had been subjecting her to now for years.

"Please, baby girl, if your mother is hurting you or saying mean things to you, we need to know so that way we can fix this! If you tell me the truth it means that you can stay here with me and your daddy!" With tears of fear running down her face, Mrs. Watkins tried her best now to assure her granddaughter she had nothing to fear in confessing the abuse.

"She hurts me every day!" Myyah screamed.

"Oh My God! Don't worry. I'm going to save you from that woman. Ok?" Mrs. Watkins screeched as she wiped Myyah's tear-covered face.

After Myyah's melancholic confession and breakdown, her grandmother took her back into the kitchen and continued to probe her as she simultaneously prepared breakfast. Fuck the park. Mrs. Watkins now had to scramble against precious time to save her abused granddaughter from the fucked up trifling 'mother'.

Jonah eventually came downstairs and into the kitchen. After Mrs. Watkins got Myyah situated with watching a Disney movie, she took her son to the side to tell him what Myyah relayed to her about the abuse that had been going on in Fredquisha's apartment. Mrs. Watkins almost had to hold Jonah back from taking off into his car to go confront Fredquisha. She told him if they were going to save Myyah, they needed to go through the appropriate legal channels. The last thing she wanted to do was break the law and further dig herself along with Myyah and Austin into a deeper hole.

The morning shifted into the afternoon, and Mrs. Watkins was literally walking on pins and needles. She needed to come up with a very quick plan on how she was going to liberate Myyah from the abusive clutches of Fredquisha.

12: 45 PM splashed across the microwave clock in the kitchen. Mrs. Watkins sat in her dining room table, contemplating her next move. Time was no longer on her side. At any moment she needed to begin to get Myyah's belongings ready. The original plan was to go straight to the park right after breakfast, but now with this new-found revelation, Mrs. Watkins needed to shift gears and get a solution to this dark problem facing her granddaughter. Then the idea hit her – she was going to call up Alton Jones, Austin's former criminal attorney, and see what could be done.

Despite it being Sunday, she pulled out her cell phone and then went into her contact's list and pulled up Alton's name. And just when she was about to hit dial…

Ring. Ring. Ring.

"FREDQUISHA" popped up on her cell phone. The sadistic mother was calling her. Why? Mrs. Watkins wondered. She told Fredquisha she was going to drop Myyah off by 5 PM. It wasn't even one yet. Why was she checking in. Mrs. Watkins took a deep, hard breath through her nostrils and swiped right.

"Hey, Fredquisha…" Mrs. Watkins whispered. She didn't want Myyah to hear she was on the phone with her mother.

※

Fredquisha yawned and stretched... "Hey, Mrs. Watkins, I was callin' 'cuz I know I said you had to drop Myyah off at 5 PM..." MooMoo smiled and then looked at Trel sleeping like a baby in the hotel bed, "But I was wondering since you barely get to see her if you wanted her to stay with you until tomorrow night. She gotta be back to school by Tuesday."

Mrs. Watkins jumped at the sound of hearing Fredquisha offer Myyah to stay longer. "YEAH! Sure thing! I mean, are you sure? This isn't some trap or game you trying to play, is it?" Mrs. Watkins was taken completely off guard.

"No, no game. I just had a late night last night and then I still got other stuff to do. I got a job interview tomorrow down at Wal-Mart that I need to prepare for anyways," Fredquisha lied. Well, lied about the job interview down at Wal-Mart. She was being completely truthful about her "long" night with Trel.

"Well, ok, if you say so, I can definitely keep her until tomorrow..."

"Alrighty then, well, I guess I'll see you tomorrow then."

"Ok, Fredquisha..."

"See ya'll later—"

Mrs. Watkins suddenly interrupted before Fredquisha was about to get off the phone and asked, "Hey Fredquisha, if you ever want Myyah to stay with us for much longer because you just need more time to yourself, we are more than willing to help out. I know you and Austin have had your troubles and you still raising your two other cute boys. I know Myyah can be a handful."

Fredquisha, naked and scratching her hairy, sperm-crusted cooch, rolled her eyes. She mumbled, "Mrs. Watkins. Thanks for the help, but I got it. Trust me. Maybe I can see about sending her more often."

"Ok, Fredquisha. Anyways, enjoy the rest of your day and I'll tell your daughter you said hello and that you miss her,"

"Bye, Mrs. Watkins." Fredquisha hung up and threw the phone back into her bag sitting on top of the hotel room's dresser.

MooMoo jiggled her way back over to the bed, hopped in and snuggled up next to Trel. "Sorry about that, you ready for round eight?"

"Damn, girl, yo pussy ain't sore?" Trel jokingly growled as he wiped his mouth.

"Baby, this pussy has short recovery time. Come on!"

"Myyah! Baby girl! I got some good news! Fredquisha is gonna let you stay for another day."

"Did you tell her what I told you?" Myyah asked, looking scared.

"No, baby girl. Not at all. But we are gonna fix this, ok?"

"Ok..."

"Anyways, let's go get ready to go to the park! And afterwards we can go get some funnel cake! Have you had funnel cake before?"

"No, what's that?"

"It's fried dough. It's like one big waffle with ice cream, chocolate syrup, whip cream, with a cherry on top!"

"That sounds good!"

Myyah got up from the couch. She and Mrs. Watkins headed upstairs so she could get changed out of her clothes and into appropriate swimwear for the park. Once the two women got ready, Mrs. Watkins called for a Lyft ride to the park. The two women spent the rest of the day relishing in fun, trying their best to oblivious to all of the madness going on in Myyah's life.

CHAPTER FIFTEEN

*E*arly Monday morning. The melodic singing of birds chirping outside could be faintly heard as the sun rose to devour the suburban Chicago skies.

7:23 AM blinked on the oven's clock. After making a big pot of coffee, Mrs. Watkins wasted in no time in trying to strategize on how she was going to liberate her granddaughter from Fredquisha. She sat down at her desk inside of her office, took three gulps from her big mug of Ethiopian fair trade black coffee, and pulled out a yellow legal pad and a black ink pen. Once she got situated and comfortable to jot down notes, websites, phone numbers, etc., she pulled out her phone and called Attorney Alton Jones.

Now, any other person would've moved quickly to call the Illinois Department of Children and Family Services. But that wasn't the route that Mrs. Watkins wanted to take just yet. She figured there had to be some sort of legal maneuver she could use in order to fight the custody agreement. There had to be, she assumed. She also wondered if perhaps she called 911 and had Myyah recount her testimony to the police, that would trigger some sort of immediate investigation which then in turn perhaps Mrs. Watkins could get a protective order against the mother and fight the custody agreement. Instant victory.

Nevertheless, Mrs. Watkins quickly realized even if all that went through, she nor Austin were Myyah's legal guardians and the judge would have no plausible grounds to award custody of Myyah over to her. There was the very REAL possibility that if the police and ultimately the courts took Myyah out of Fredquisha's custody, they would then default to hand over custody to Myyah's maternal grandmother – Fredquisha's mother – not Mrs. Watkins. That definitely was not a desired outcome either.

Calling up Alton was the first thing Mrs. Watkins wanted to do just to get some quick legal advice. Although the call was probably a crapshoot, it was at least worth a try.

Ring. Ring. Ring. Ring.

"Good Morning, Alton Jones," the family friend and powerhouse attorney answered the phone.

Mrs. Watkins quickly cleared her throat. "Hey, Mr. Jones, this is Delores. Austin's mother."

"Oh, hey Delores. Why are you calling me this early? Something happened again to Austin?"

"No, it's actually not about Austin. It's about his daughter.... Myyah."

"The six or seven-year-old girl of his?"

"Six – she'll be seven in a few more months… But yes, her."

"What seems to be the issue."

"Well, I have her staying with me right now for the weekend. Her mother barely lets me see her because of this crazy ass custody agreement. Myyah just told me yesterday that her mother hits her and calls her all types of crazy names. She told me she wants to li—"

Alton interrupted, "Wait, wait, wait Delores. You know I respect you and I'm always there for you and your family, but first, family law is definitely out of my wheelhouse of experience." He continued, "Secondly, I'm just gonna be completely honest with you. I know exactly where you're going with this, and before you attempt to make any moves to fight to get the girl in your custody, just know you're going to need more than Myyah's 'word' to make a judge bust a move and hand over custody."

"I know, Alton. Listen, I know. But she was crying and sobbing yesterday. Telling me these crazy stories of how she calls her all types of hoes and bitches. How she sometimes starves her!"

"Wow...She said all of this?"

"Yes! I am not making this up! I don't think she would make this up either! And then when I went to go pick her up on Friday, I had a chance to see her mother's place! It was absolutely filthy! I mean the bitch had trash splattered all over the fucking place. Roaches were climbing on the walls and shit! I mean, excuse my language..."

Alton grumbled, "It's alright, listen...I'm sorry if I was about to cut you off and sound short, it's just that I get a lot of these calls and I'm already ready with a script. You won't believe how many calls I get from baby mamas, grandmas, even some baby daddies who have nothing more than mere allegations. And a lot of times it's just people trying to get revenge on their ex-spouses or family members they aren't currently getting along with..."

"Look, I understand all that completely, but I need to act fast, Alton. I just didn't know who else to call or what else to do first."

"Well, hell, first have you tried to report her to DCFS? I mean, that's the first place I would call. If Myyah doesn't have any visible marks on her body that can signal assault or trauma, it's her word versus her mother's. You'd need witnesses. Up until this point it doesn't sound like you have any of that. Do you?"

Mrs. Watkins exhaled, "No, I don't."

"See there…I am not trying to be pessimistic or anything, but you are dealing with the government here. Even if the good Lord Jesus came down from the sky right now and told DCFS and a family judge they need to hand over custody, you still need documentation. Document. Document. Document. Try to get as much evidence you can before you try to move in on the woman."

Mrs. Watkins rolled her eyes, "I understand,"

"Good, well, anyways…Normally I would've billed for this call, but seeing as how you all are a family friend and what not and a case like this I wouldn't even take up, I'll let you all slide. Other than that, if you need a family lawyer, one of my cousins, Stacy Perkins up on the North Side in the city handles complex cases like this all the time. I'll text you her info. Sounds great?"

"That'll work, sir. I really appreciate it…"

"No worries. I'll text you. I'll send you that info once I get out of this trial."

"Thank you."

"Have a good day, Delores."

"You too, Alton…"

Mrs. Watkins hung up the phone. "Motherfucker," she grumbled, rolling her eyes and shaking her head.

The only thing Delores could do next, and per the recommendation of Alton, was call DCFS.

She was conflicted. As a former special education teacher, she knew could've easily called DCFS and had a caseworker sent out to Fredquisha's apartment, but she also was very much aware of DCFS's reputation as moving at the speed of molasses dripping from a tall redwood tree.

Hell, by the time DCFS sent a caseworker out to Fredquisha's house there a real possibility that Myyah would endure more rounds of abuse and torture. With nothing else to do or lose, Mrs. Watkins then stormed to the DCFS website and called the 1-800 child abuse hotline.

Rapidly tapping her fingers against her desk, breathing hard, gazing off into the computer screen, her phone kept ringing and ringing. Finally, the DCFS prompt kicked in.

"Thank you for calling the Illinois Department of Children and Family Services' 24/7 child abuse hotline. To speak with a live representative in regard to a possible child abuse incident, press 1. To speak with a representative about a preexisting case, press 2. For all other inquiries, please remaining on the line."

Mrs. Watkins quickly dialed "1". Ring. Ring. Ring. Ring.

"Thank you for calling the Illinois Department of Children and Family Services' Child Abuse Hotline, this is Cheryl, are you call in to report a new case of child abuse?"

"Yes, I am."

"Ok, ma'am. And what is the name of the child?"

"Her name is Myyah Chennelle Watkins."

"How old is she?"

"She's 6."

"And who are you in relationship to her?"

"I am her paternal grandmother."

"What is the child's name?"

"Fredquisha Pierce."

"How old is she? I believe around my son's age. 35"

"And what's your son's name?"

"Austin Watkins."

"And he's the established biological father?"

"Yes, I believe so…"

"Ok, and where is he currently?"

"He's…" Mrs. Watkins took a deep breath and exhaled, "He's currently incarcerated."

"Ok, and I am assuming the mother has full custody?"

"Yes, ma'am…"

"Ok, so where does Myyah live? She lives with her mother in the city or in the suburbs?"

"She lives in the City of Chicago."

"Do you know the mother's address?"

"Yes, it's 6310 S Halsted Avenue, Apartment 3B, Chicago, Illinois."

"Got it."

"Ok, so I am going to ask you a series of questions. Half of those questions will require a numerical response on a scale of 1-5, with 1 being 'not likely' and 5 being 'very likely'. Afterwards, a senior case manager with the department will evaluate your responses and from there determine if a home visit is necessary, is that ok?"

"Yes...that's fine."

Mrs. Watkins and Cheryl, the phone case manager, went back and forth. Mrs. Watkins tried her best to answer the questions truthfully based on what Myyah told her yesterday. Her nerves on fire, Mrs. Watkins hoped that the information would lead to some sort of immediate child services investigation. But overwrought with doubt and pessimism, Mrs. Watkins just knew it was going to be days, possibly weeks before something happened.

"Alright, ma'am, well that concludes all the questions I have. As mentioned before a child services caseworker will evaluation the questionnaire and from there make a determination as to whether or not a home visit is required. If you don't have any other questions, I will conclude the call now. Do you have any last questions?"

"How long do you think it'll take before someone comes out?"

"Well, that will depend on the severity of the abuse and what a caseworker thinks may warrant an immediate home visit and possible referral to the Chicago Police Department for further investigation. It could be a day, it could be a week. Nonetheless, if you feel like the child's life is in danger, police call 9-11 immediately, ok?"

"Ok, ma'am. Thank you so much."

"You're welcome. Have a wonderful day…"

"You too."

Mrs. Watkins hung up the phone. Still rapidly tapping her well-manicured fingers against her desk, she glanced down at the computer screen and saw that it was almost 8 AM. Myyah was still sleep. Grandma knew she had to take her grand-daughter back to her mother's apartment tonight. Still with the day to figure out a plan, Mrs. Watkins then glanced down at her phone again. She was tempted to do what she felt deep down in her intuition was the best thing to do.

She picked her phone back up and dialed 911.

CHAPTER SIXTEEN

"*M*rs. Watkins...Detective Jackson will see you now," one of the Matteson police station officers caught Mrs. Watkins' attention. Sitting by herself, she was reading some local magazine as she sat in the cold, relatively empty suburban police station.

After calling 911 to go ahead and try to file some sort of child abuse charge against Fredquisha, Mrs. Watkins was informed she needed to bring Myyah and herself down to the station to speak with Det. Lawrence Jackson, a detective assigned to investigate child abuse charges. There, Det. Jackson would conduct an interview with Mrs. Watkins and Myyah to see if the allegations had any merit and then inform them what the next course of action would be.

Mrs. Watkins looked at the short, black female officer and produced an anxious gawp, "Thank you." She stood up and shadowed the officer to Detective Jackson's office.

Moments later Mrs. Watkins along with the female officer arrived at Detective Jackson's office. The detective had spent the last hour and a half along with a child psychologist to help sort through the allegations being levied against Fredquisha in regard to her abuse.

Knock. Knock.

The officer lightly knocked on the Detective's door. "Come on in," Det. Jackson responded. The officer opened the door and escorted Mrs. Watkins in.

"Have a seat Mrs. Watkins. Dr. Nunez, can you take Ms. Myyah here with you while I talk to Mrs. Watkins in private?" Det. Jackson asked the child psychologist and licensed clinical social worker, Dr. Maria Nunez.

Det. Jackson was a 10-year veteran with the Matteson Police Department. After being a beat officer for five years, he then went on to become one of the chief non-homicide detectives in the small suburban police force.

"Yes! Come on baby doll. I have lots of coloring books and candy in my office! You wanna go color?" the chubby and twentyish Dr. Nunez asked Myyah.

"Yes, ma'am!" Myyah innocently responded.

Myyah then twirled her attention towards her grandmother and formed a slightly edgy face.

"Don't worry, baby girl. Grandma just needs to talk to this nice police officer, ok?"

"Ok," she replied and then gave granny a hug.

Once Myyah and Dr. Nunez departed the office, Det. Jackson and Mrs. Watkins had privacy.

Det. Jackson, in his early 40s, looking like a mean Cuba Gooding Jr., took a huge deep breath in, and then exhaled. It was an exhale marked with slight hint of frustration. He scoured over his notes and then gave Mrs. Watkins a look. A look that she just knew he was going to relay some possibly depressing news.

"So, Mrs. Watkins, we definitely have a case here..." he muttered.

"So, what happens next then?" Mrs. Watkins grew tense at

the sound that something could possibly be done to immediately save the girl.

"Well, unfortunately right now…. Nothing."

"Wait, what? You just said we have a case though."

"Yeah, we have a case. But in order for the case to have legs and move to rescue you the girl, here is what needs to happen. First, we have to relay this information over to DCFS. They have investigate these child abuse allegations. These investigations can vary in time. Some move slow. Some very fast. Very fast depending on the severity of the abuse allegations and the evidence they collect." He continued, "Unfortunately in Myyah's case, all we have is her word. The girl doesn't have any substantial markings that show physical violence, trauma, assault or any other types of incriminating evidence that would make a Chicago police officer arrest her mother, Fredquisha."

Mrs. Watkins quickly shook her head in disbelief, "No, no, no. Detective, I get all that. But if the girl is saying that her mother has been hitting her, psychologically abusing her, and doing all types of crazy stuff to her, are we just supposed to sit back and let her suffer like this until some government agency decides to act?"

"Trust me, Mrs. Watkins. I'm there with you – but unfortunately this is the law. I can't circumvent that based on hearsay. And hearsay is all we have right now coming from a six-year-old. We would still need to talk to Fredquisha and get her side of the story. Then we would also have to interview witnesses. Oh, and by the way…This entire case is out of my jurisdiction. I'd then have to refer this over to a detective at the Chicago Police Department."

"So, should I go there now before it's too late?" Mrs. Watkins asked.

"Well, I mean, you can. But even then, they will tell you the same thing. I can always have Dr. Nunez type up a report and give those notes over to CPD. But they are going to do the same thing…And truth be told, they are going to move much slower than us. CPD is overwhelmed with child abuse allegations."

"So, in other words Myyah is fucked. That's what's your telling me."

Det. Jackson lowered his head. "No, I am not saying that at all. But what I am saying is Mrs. Watkins we need to give this time and we can't impulsively act and make her situation worse. I mean, the reality is that you nor her father have any type of shared custody with Fredquisha. In the event the police were to remove the girl from the home, she'd go live with her other grandmother or another designated guardian. I mean, the judge MIGHT consider handing you custody, but for that to happen, you need to lawyer up and get someone who can prove you are a better suited guardian than Fredquisha's family."

"This is…just too much. This girl has been telling me now for the last two days that she doesn't want to go back home, and yet there is nothing we can do to stop her from going into what she says is clearly an abusive situation."

"I know, I'm sorry Mrs. Watkins. But the law is the law. Right now, all we have is hearsay. DCFS needs to conduct an investigation. Then, they will then determine what's the next course of action. In the meantime, my suggestion would be to just to pray, get a good family lawyer and get ready to battle for the girl."

Mrs. Watkins closed her eyes, almost wanting to release tears. She reopened them and noticed Det. Jackson reaching out to shake her hand. She stuck hers out and shook his hand. The both of them stood up in silence. Det. Jackson then led her out of the door and to Dr. Nunez office.

Dr. Nunez had a small office she shared with another investigator. Since she was a per diem child abusive investigator and social worker for the police station, she used the office from time to time in matters similar to Myyah's.

"Oh, hey! Look it's your grandma! All set?" Dr. Nunez

chirped as she turned her attention towards Mrs. Watkins and Det. Jackson.

"Yeah. Like I said Mrs. Watkins, just hold out for now and pray. Here's my card if you need anything," Det. Jackson consoled as he handed Mrs. Watkins his business card.

"Come on, baby girl. We gotta leave now."

"Does this mean I get to stay with you now grandma?"

CHAPTER SEVENTEEN

*O*nce Mrs. Watkins and her granddaughter left the police station without an immediate resolution to their growing quandary, the grandmother-would be-super heroine called for a Lyft to take them back home. They'd arrived twenty maters later. A solemn and depressed Mrs. Watkins walked inside her immaculate, virtually empty and dark house and didn't hesitate in beginning the process of packing up Myyah's belongings.

Jonah was upstairs taking a quick nap and hadn't noticed his mother's arrival. He just got off from a shift at his job. About an hour passed, and as minutes faded into an hour, time drew closer to that moment where they'd have to leave and take Myyah back home. Jonah awakened hoping his mother had some sort of resolution. He made his way to his mother's room where she was packing up some clothes in a small suitcase she bought for Myyah at Wal-Mart.

"So, what's the deal, mama?" Jonah asked

"I gotta take her back. No signs of trauma. No evidence of abuse, at least not yet. We gotta abide by the custody order until DCFS completes their investigation and hopefully refer their findings over to the police. From there, they can arrest Fredquisha, but then Myyah won't come here. She'd have to go stay with Fredquisha's mother or some other relative until we can fight to regain custody."

Jonah lowered his head, "Mama, I'm so sorry…"

"It's cool. We're gonna get her, god damn it. This is such fucking bullshit. This is just so fucked up. God damn inefficient government can't do shit. This is why all of these kids end up dying from abuse," Mrs. Watkins began to cry.

Jonah walked into the room and hugged his mother. "Mama, she ain't gonna die. We're gonna get her, ok? Don't cry. You gon make me cry," Jonah confessed.

"I'm sorry. You're right. I can't cry. We gotta be strong for Myyah," Mrs. Watkins replied as she released her embrace from Jonah and finished packing the carry-on suitcase.

Mrs. Watkins had no other choice unfortunately at this point but to return Myyah back to her mother. Once she had everything ready to go, Mrs. Watkins went into the living room where Myyah was watching "Princess And The Frog".

"Alright, baby girl, we gotta go now."

"Ok," a solemn Myyah responded.

7:34 PM blinked on the dashboard of Jonah's idle car.

"Alright, missy, we got all of your stuff ready to go. Remember, don't tell your mother anything that happened today or what you told me. I am not going to tell her or anyone else. I am going to try my best to get you out of her house and home with me and your daddy, ok?" Mrs. Watkins was helping Myyah into the backseat of Jonah's car.

Jonah, in the front seat, was looking tense and angry, almost as if he was ready to kill Fredquisha once they got to bitch's apartment on 63rd street.

"Ok," Myyah replied, appearing grief-stricken.

"It's gonna be alright, trust me. If your mother tries to hit you or do anything, you call the police or tell someone at your school, ok?"

"Ok..."

"Ok, good."

"And if your brothers hit you too, Myyah, call the police," Jonah interjected.

"Ok, uncle..."

For the entire duration of the car ride, Myyah, depressed and frozen, just peered out of the window, watching the same suburban scenery that once made her happy now make her sad. She was being exiled from heavenly comfort of her grandmother's abode and now was forced to trudge back into the depths of her dark, ghetto, abusive, roach-infested hellish existence with her so-called 'mother'.

Once the Watkins family made their way into the city, billions of butterflies formed in the pits of Myyah's stomach, fluttering their wings, brewing deep-seated anxiety in the abused girl's core. Seeing the gradual transition from idyllic suburban scenery to horrid, derelict city life on the South Side wasn't just gut-wrenching; it was heart breaking.

Although Myyah didn't know that much about God, she did her best last night to pray to her sense of a higher power, pleading for someone to save her. Granny from time to time would tell her God sees, listens and can do any and everything, so Myyah just knew her salvation was on the way since God heard her cries. Saw her pain and suffering at the hands of her mother.

However, now that her granny insisted she had to go back home since her efforts at saving her failed, Myyah doubted if God even loved her.

Jonah pulled off to the side of Fredquisha's building and parked. Sunday evenings seemed relatively peaceful despite being in this part of town. The dusky skies turned orange. The sun began to fade away. So did any sense of contentment Myyah had. It was now gone as her innocent doe eyes attached to the cruddy building.

"Like I said baby girl, we are gonna work to fix this situation and get you out. Please, baby girl, do not do anything or say anything to your mother that might make her go crazy,"

"Grandma, please, don't make me go inside there. I can't. I am just too scared. Please!"

"Baby girl, there's nothing I can do. I can't take you with me!" Mrs. Watkins tried her best to explain, but Myyah was relentless with her begging.

"Granny, please! I'll do anything. Can I just not hide at your place?"

"No, baby girl! You can't hide at my place! Your mother unfortunately has to have you for the time being until we work to solve this entire ordeal for you!"

"Grandma, please, no, NO! Please!" Myyah kept at it, sobbing and weeping. The more her cries thundered in the car, the guiltier Mrs. Watkins felt. She couldn't in good faith just hand over the child to a mother who she knew was completely incapable of raising the girl.

Jonah gawked at his mother, "Mama, we have to take her up there."

"I know, but we can't take her up there crying. Fredquisha will know something is wrong and then she might do something even crazier."

"So, what do you wanna do then?"

Mrs. Watkins exhaled and closed her eyes as a tear escaped her left eye. She shook and lowered her head as she held her mouth with her hand. "I don't know, I don't know what we should do Jonah. I can't send her up there. It's just ain't right.

"I know, but mama, we gotta bring her up there. If we don't,

Fredquisha is gonna call the police and we're gonna get in trouble."

Mrs. Watkins reopened her eyes as she felt her heart beat faster and faster. She scanned the surrounding area, absorbing the backdrop of blight mixed in with roaming crackheads and crazies. This wasn't the type of environment Myyah, let alone any kid, needed to be reared in. Not only was Fredquisha an abomination, but so was this neighborhood.

"Jonah, turn the car back on and let's leave...."

"What?!? Mama, no! We can't do that! I know we don't want Myyah in that house, but mama, we are breaking the law now. This is technically kidnapping."

"Jonah..." Mrs. Watkins turned her head towards her youngest son. "Drive this fucking car...NOW!"

Jonah lowered his head and turned on the engine of the car. He nervously looked around. "Mama, are you sure you wanna do this?"

"Yes, I'm sure...Fuck the law. I'll go to jail before my grand-daughter goes into that hell hole."

Nervous and trembling, Jonah gawked at his emboldened mother. "I would too, mama. I would too. You're right. Fuck that. I'll go to jail too!"

Suddenly Jonah took off into the sunset, barreling down Halsted Avenue, back to Matteson. Myyah's cries diminished. Maybe God does answer prayers, she thought.

CHAPTER EIGHTEEN

EARLIER THAT DAY...2:30 PM.

*O*n Sundays there was a group of inmates who were just returning from their respective religious services. Ironically most inmates didn't bother to attend the small Catholic and Baptist church services hosted every Sunday late morning. Many locked up felt disillusioned with organized religion. Only a few inmates, those who wanted to hold out last hope in Jesus to save them from potentially long prison sentences, attended the Christian services held on site.

Nevertheless, despite the many who didn't bother to show up to hear some secretly gay white priest give some dry lecture or some bucktooth, greasy jheri curl having pastor hoop and holler, the jail actually had a growing Nation of Islam (NOI) and Orthodox Islam Muslim population. Many Black, even some Hispanic inmates gravitated towards Allah and called Muhammad ibn Abdullah their last prophet as they found solace in the desert religion's strict discipline, sense of unity and militancy. Almost kind of like gang culture – Islam had a strong focus on warrior hood. Muslims fought hard for what they believed in and didn't just back down.

The Islamic religion was kind of inspiration for Austin himself. He had been flirting off and on with the idea of becoming a Muslim now for some years, but never took it that serious. He always found himself distracted with street shit. However, now that he was locked up and on the verge of getting released, Austin was attending services every Sunday to give himself the spiritual boost needed to ignite the process of self-transformation.

A sunny, gusty afternoon...One of Austin's buddies, Terrence, better known as 'Bro. Terrence 3X" usually brought Austin to the NOI's study group religious service inside the jail. Bro. Terrence had been locked up now for almost five years, awaiting sentencing in a double homicide. Although he claimed he was innocent, set up by a rival gang for a drug trade gone wrong, Terrence was now facing life in prison for the murder of nineteen-year-old well known rapper and his seventeen-year-old girlfriend.

"As-Salaamu Alaikum, my dear brother. So nice to see you again..."

"Wa 'Alaikum As-Salaam Brother," Terrence said as he returned the greetings of peace back to one of his Muslim brothers. He kissed the short, light skinned, chubby man on each cheek as he shook his hand. "This is my friend by the way, Brother Austin. Austin, this is Minister Shaheed 2X. He used to be an inmate some years ago and moved to Dallas! How's that Texas life treating you, sir?"

"It's treating me fine. So much better than this god-forsaken Chi-town. Brothers killing each other left and right out here!"

Minister Shaheed 2X was an ex-inmate who had at one point in time been in and out of County for petty, non-violent crimes like drug trade. After deciding to get his life right, he joined the

NOI, rose the ranks to becoming a minister, and then eventually moved to Texas where he got married and had two young sons. From time to time when Minister Shaheed came back into Chicago to visit family, he would volunteer on Sundays to assist with the study group's service. Unlike the other inmates wearing orange jumpsuits, Minister Shaheed 2X was rocking an all-black suit, white dress shirt, red bow tie and shiny black shoes.

Austin reached out to shake Minister Shaheed's hand. "As-Salaam Alaikum, brother," Austin nervously smiled. He didn't know if he was saying the Muslim greeting correctly.

Since being locked up, Austin was so close to finally becoming a Muslim and a registered member with the Nation of Islam. However, he was still on the fence given his Christian upbringing. He definitely believed in God, but being out in the streets, seeing so many people killed, made him question the Church, Jesus and the very Christian values his parents instilled him at an early age.

"Well, my brother, I gotta get going. I've been fasting all day. Stay strong, brothers," Minister Shaheed smiled and then walked away.

"He's a good brother. Good role model," Terrence commented as he and Austin began to walk out of the small conference room. As the two made their way towards the exit, Terrence turned his head towards Austin as they finished their light conversation as they walked back to their cells. "... Anyways, like I was saying my brother, Minister Farrakhan be havin' that fire, for real for real. I can get you most of those DVDs from the 90s. Farrakhan was on it real hard back then, bro,"

"Aiight, man, I appreciate it. I'll check those joints out. Just let me know and I'll send you some cash for the DVDs," Austin replied as the two kept pacing themselves down the well-lit hallway.

"Bet. Anyways, I'm finna go chill in the library before dinner. You wanna come?"

"Sure, I ain't got shit else to do. I need to go pick up some more college course catalogues anyways."

"Aiight then…"

The two men then sojourned around the corner to the jail library. Since both Terrence and Austin were locked up in a low-security detention center, inmates were given a lot more latitude as to where they could go. Jail corrections offers weren't as thick in their presence compared to other medium and high-risk security detention centers within the massive county jail complex. This particular detention center that Austin was housed in had security cameras being situated all over the place to record any suspicious activity. Any craziness that went down would then warrant a response from the jail guards.

As soon as Terrence and Austin entered the library, barely filled with inmates, they made their way over to a long aisle of tall bookshelves. Many of the bookshelves were lined with books as old as Abraham Lincoln. While Terrence looked for something to read, Austin scoured up and down the aisle looking for his course catalogues.

A corrections officer, who unbeknownst to the men, had been following them, entered the aisle and slowly crept up behind Terrence.

"My brother, my brother, my brother, look who we have here…the infamous Terrence 3X aka Lil Terry…Still lookin' the same from when you used to hustle 79th and Jeffrey," the tall, slender dark-skinned corrections officer with a shiny bald head growled at Terrence.

The moment Austin heard the menacing words pour out of the correction officer's mouth, he spun his head in the direction of Terrence and the office. His eyes widened with slight anxiety and immediately stood up. He continued to gawk at a now frozen Terry and the threatening officer. He'd never seen the jail guard before.

Looking panicky as hell, Austin's eyes turned to curious slits as he tried to quickly figure out what was going on between Terrence and this officer. The jail guard snickered, scanning both the Muslim brother and his comrade, Austin, up and down.

"Oh, so that's the fuck shit you on, bro?" Terrence replied.

"Yeah, that's the fuck shit I'm on. You fucked up, boy. On fo'nem I'm finna send yo ass straight to the grave, fuck boy," the officer growingly spat back to Terrence. "Fo'nem" was a reference to "Folks and them" – a term heavily used by gang members on the south side to refer to the Folk Nation, which was an alliance of between the Black Disciples, Gangster Disciples, Latin Disciples and a few other lesser known street gangs throughout the Chicago metro.

"Yo, what the fuck is going on, sir?" Austin interjected as he stood there completely confused and worried. How did this particular corrections officer know of Terrence and why was he bringing up street shit inside the jail?

"Don't worry 'bout it. I suggest you dip the fuck out while I take care of this fake ass Muslim unless you wanna get fucked up too," The officer said, looking straight at Austin.

All of sudden the corrections officer whipped out a small shiny hunter's knife. Something that looked like it could bring death in one swipe. Terrence tried to dash off, but before he could the corrections officer grabbed him and shanked him several times in the back.

"AHH! AHHHH!" Terrence cried as he collapsed to the ground.

Austin stood there frozen for a second as the officer continued to dig into Terrence's back. Suddenly he felt the need to intervene, "No! Fuck no!" Austin screamed as he lunged at the officer.

The two men then found themselves locked in an intense battle of life and death. With motionless Terrence slowly losing life, bleeding out on the ground, Austin and the corrections officer meandered their struggle out into the middle of the library's floor. A few other inmates were around to see what was happening, but they ducked and hid, not wanting to intervene.

"YO! WHO THE FUCK ARE YOU?!?" Austin roared, finding himself trying to grab the knife out of the man's bloodied hand.

The corrections officer didn't respond. He just stood there, fighting, trying his best to wrestle for domination and control in the fight. Both men suddenly fell to the ground. As they continued to tussle back and forth, Austin conjured up enough strength to roll the man over. He quickly let the murderous corrupt corrections officer go for a brief moment, threw a few punches into the man's face and the arm that held the knife. Without even thinking Austin grabbed the knife and began to slice away at the man's neck. Blood splattered all over, even on Austin. As the corrections officer clung for his life, spewing out crimson blood from the open wound gaping in the middle of his neck, Austin stood up with the knife in his hand and gawked down at the dying corrections officer.

"WATKINS! PUT THE KNIFE DOWN OR WE WILL SHOOT!" One of two guards standing feet away from Austin screamed towards Austin. Both guards had semi-automatic rifles pointed at the man.

"DROP THE FUCKING KNIFE IN YOUR HAND AND GET DOWN ON YOUR KNEES! NOW!"

Austin, completely shook up and terrified, muttered, "It's not what you think. I was def—"

"WE ARE GOING TO TELL YOU ONE LAST TIME WATKINS! GET DOWN!"

"No, Officer! PLEASE! IT'S NOT WHAT YOU—"

POW! POW! POW!

"Aiight, boys, give granny a hug!" Evelyn, Fredquisha's mama laughed as she went in to give her two grandsons a big hug.

Evelyn looked like a 52-year-old version of Fredquisha, just shorter, fatter and dumpier. Her edges from the sides of her head went missing like some white bitch that went jogging in a forest at 3 AM.

"Mama, can you watch them next week? I got a date on Saturday."

"Bitch, you always got a date. What's the difference this time? I hope he got some real money and ain't some dope dealin' loser that you seemed to be so attracted to."

Fredquisha rolled her eyes. "Bitch, bye. The niggas I fuck with are winnin'. Can't say that about the sorry ass old, fuck niggas you used throw that pussy on back in the day."

"Girl! If that's the case, you got sorry in yo ho ass blood, 'cuz ya daddy was a sorry mothafucka. Anyways, bitch, let me get a cigarette…"

Fredquisha chuckled. Her and her mother were truly besties and despite the somewhat troubling words they were exchanging between one another, they were really joking. Their ratchet talk of men was how they bonded with one another.

Fredquisha, her mama along with her two sons, Quimani and Zy'meer, were standing outside on the corner of the street, just about to go back inside the roach-infested apartment. As ratchet mama rummaged her purse to pull out her pack of Newports to hand her mama Evelyn a square, a silver Nissan Altima zoomed up the street and came to a screeching halt at the corner where the ratchet Pierce family had been standing. Fredquisha gazed into the car and recognized Paulette, one of her besties and her 'hairdresser', and her fifteen-year-old daughter, Quantayzia, in the passenger seat.

All of sudden Paulette hopped out the driver's seat.

"GET OUT BITCH! FUCK IS YOU DOIN'?!? DON'T BE SCARED NOW, HOE!" The enraged hairdresser bestie screamed at her daughter who looked terrified, still sitting in the passenger seat.

"Fuck is goin' on, Paulette?!?" Fredquisha nervously asked as she goggled at her friend damn near drag her daughter out of the passenger seat of the car.

"BITCH! TELL HER WHAT YOU JUST TOLD ME!" Paulette commanded her daughter. Quantayzia looked like she'd seen the ghost of Michael Jackson or some shit. She looked around, huffed and then stared at Fredquisha.

"LIL GIRL, IF YOU DON'T TELL HER WHAT YOU JUST TOLD ME I'M FINNE FUCK YOU UP!"

Quantayzia began to cry. "I'm pregnant..."

"Ok?" Fredquisha was silent and confused. Why was this big news to her?'

"TELL HER BITCH! EVERYTHING! TELL HER WHO THE DADDY IS!"

Quantayzia lowered her head and slowly swayed side from side.

"Quimani..."

"Bitch!?! What?!?! Quimani!" Fredquisha spat back with a scrunched up face.

"YES BITCH! YOUR TWELVE-YEAR-OLD BAD, FAT ASS SON GOT MY DAUGHTER PREGNANT!"

CHAPTER NINETEEN

"*B*ITCH! TELL HER WHAT YOU JUST TOLD ME!" Paulette commanded her daughter.

The way Quantayzia stood there motionless, her mouth partly hung open, you would've thought this little fast ass heffa had seen the ghost of Michael Jackson or some shit. She looked around, panted and nervously glowered at Fredquisha.

Paulette sensed her daughter's trepidation but fuck all that. This fast lil coochie havin' girl better say something before Paulette goes crazy. "LIL GIRL, IF YOU DON'T TELL HER WHAT YOU JUST TOLD ME, I'M FINNA FUCK YOU UP!"

Quantayzia began to cry. "I'm pregnant...," she confessed, somewhat muzzling her mouth with her clammy hands. Red fingernail paint chipping off her fingernails.

"Ok?" Fredquisha was silent and confused. Why was this big news to her?'

"TELL HER, LITTLE BITCH! EVERYTHING! TELL HER WHO THE DADDY IS!"

Quantayzia lowered her head and slowly swayed side from side.

"Quimani..."

"Bitch!?! What?!?! Quimani!" Fredquisha spat back with a scrunched up face.

"YES BITCH! YOUR TWELVE-YEAR-OLD BAD, FAT ASS SON GOT MY DAUGHTER PREGNANT!"

Fredquisha just stood there shocked, immobile, and completely mute. Her eyes couldn't move away from Paulette and Quantayzia. She was attempting her best to process the stream of scandalous information that just blasted her into unreality.

There was just no way in hell she would've thought her oldest son would impregnate his babysitter for so many reasons. First, Quimani was just twelve. What twelve-year-old honestly knew anything about pussy or how to get their little dicks wet? Fredquisha wondered. Then, even if Quimani did have sex with Quantayzia, truth be told it wasn't his fault, it would be the babysitter's fault. She was at least three years older than him and clearly sexually assaulted a minor. Shit, sexually assaulted her son! Just thinking about the fact that this fast ass predatorial young THOT bitch sicked her pussy onto her son enraged Fredquisha second by second. Her blood boiled like hot lava erupting from a volcanic explosion in Indonesia.

"SO, Bitch, what you got to say about it!?!?" Paulette screamed into Fredquisha's frozen face.

"WAIT! WAIT! WAIT! Wait one mothafuckin' minute! I'm gonna need you to stop callin' my daughter a bitch you bulldog lookin' ass bitch!" Evelyn, Fredquisha's mother, spat as she got up in Paulette's face. She had to intervene and defend her daughter from the wild accusations.

Quimani and Zy'meer, looking like guiltless, innocent chubby boys stood off to the side as a possible ratchet fight almost ensued.

"Evelyn, step the fuck away from me 'cuz you just as responsible as Fredquisha is!" Paulette responded, now ready to possibly beat Evelyn's ass as well.

Paulette, a woman who considered herself a BBW boss bitch, was a well-kept redbone who weighed damn near twice the size as Fredquisha. A tad taller, Paulette had a devil red lace front bob crowning her head. Baby blue contacts covered her pupils. The longest fake eyelashes rested on her eyelids. Everywhere Paulette went she had to show the fuck out in case she met a nigga that was going to elevate her to the next level.

Paulette then turned her attention back to a still silent, motionless Fredquisha. The flabbergasted mother and perhaps potential grandmother was still shocked by the salacious allegation.

"First of all Paulette, we need to make sure she even pregnant by Quimani if that's the mothafuckin' case then, if she out here poppin' her lil fishy pussy on these boys, how I know for sure Quimani got her pregnant. Second of all—"

Suddenly Paulette yanked Quantayzia and jutted her in front of Fredquisha. "Look this bitch in her eyes and tell her what else you told me! TELL HER GOD DAMN IT BEFORE I KNOCK YO ASS OUT!"

"We been havin' sex for two years, Ms. Fredquisha...," Quantayzia admitted in a low, terrified pitch.

"WHAT?!?" Fredquisha, shaking her head, quickly spun on her feet and looked Quimani up and down. "QUIMANI! IS THIS TRUE!?!? BOY, TELL ME THIS IS NOT TRUE!"

Quimani looking terrified more than ever, tremored at the sound of his mother's voice. He lightly shrugged his shoulders without saying a word. He just knew he was in some big ass trouble this time.

The eldest boy was on the verge of turning 13, and while Fredquisha may have previously been in denial about the idea of her oldest son being sexually active, all the seemingly blatant warning signs were there. He had a cell phone – but the phone wasn't used for emergencies. He used it to text and call his multiple "friends," many of whom were girls around his age.

Fredquisha would even let him stay up all damn night talking on the phone with his "friends."

It was crazy too 'cuz Quimani always bragged to his mother about having all types of girlfriends at school. Quimani even one time got caught looking at porn on his cell phone, but he lied and told his mama that it was a mistake. Fredquisha simply ignored all the signs that were there, telling herself that her son was acting much more mature than what his age allowed.

Quimani still couldn't say anything. He just looked around at nothing in particular and kept his hands in his pocket. Fredquisha lunged at the boy, grabbed him by his shirt collar and threw him against the apartment building wall.

"YOU BETTA SAY SOMETHIN' BEFORE I KNOCK YO ASS OUT!" Fredquisha roared.

"Yes, we been hunchin'…," he responded.

"BOY! I'M GON FUCK YO ASS UP!"

"Hey! HEY! Fredquisha, let him go! You hurtin' him!" Evelyn shouted, trying to stop her daughter from hitting the boy on the busy street corner.

"Ma! Stay out of my shit! This my son! I can fuck him up if I want to!"

"GIRL! HE JUST 12!" Evelyn then tried to pull Fredquisha off Quimani, but she didn't relent.

"Ma! Go home! I'm gonna talk to you later while I handle this!"

"Girl…"

"MA!"

Evelyn threw her hands up in the air. "Fine, but you dead ass wrong. You need to talk to him before you attempt to beat him…"

"I GOT IT, MA! BYE!"

As soon as Evelyn walked off towards her car, Paulette, still obviously pissed as shit, lunged up onto Fredquisha. "So, ummm, how we can fix this situation?!?!?" Paulette growled as she observed Fredquisha still pinning her son up against the wall.

"We gon need to talk about it later…"

"TALK ABOUT IT LATER?!? We need to talk about this shit now!"

"Paulette! Please, girl! I'm just as pissed off as you are! I'm sorry! I just don't know what else to tell you! But I need to deal with this bad ass boy now!"

Paulette huffed and smacked her teeth. She turned around, grabbed Quantayzia and led her back to the Altima still running. "Come on, let's get the fuck out of here. And, ummm, bitch, you better make sure you call me so we can handle this situation like ASAP!"

Fredquisha rolled her eyes and shook her head. Once Paulette and Quantayzia got in the Altima, the mother and daughter sped off down the street. Fredquisha turned her attention back to her son and got super-close up into his face. "Get cho dumb ass inside the house, you little black fat mothafucka," Fredquisha growled at Quimani.

With tears forming in his partly guilty, partly innocent eyes, ready to pour out onto his cheeks, he anticipated what was about to happen next – a horrid ass whooping from his mother.

Fredquisha let go of the boy and then he and Zy'meer entered the apartment building and cautiously marched up the stairs.

Glen, the crackhead maintenance man, just so happened to be in the building today. Earlier he'd received a call from Albertina, one of the elderly neighbors in the building, that her sink was stopped up and that she needed some last minute assistance. Glen usually would've never made the run, but Albertina offered him a hot plate of food and a wine cooler if he hopped in his Chevy Malibu and stormed down to the building to unclog her sink. Old chitlins and collard green leftovers can create a monstrosity of a clog apparently.

"Hey, Fredquisha, wassup baby doll, you still got that roach problem?" Glen smiled, revealing a mouth with only three teeth. One front tooth, two bottom canines. The rest were smoked away.

Glen could tell something was off with Fredquisha.

"I ain't got time for no chit-chat today, Glen. I'll holla at you later..."

"Aiight, baby doll!" Glen then scanned Quimani and Zy'meer up and down. "Damn, them boys gettin' fat! Ya'll betta slow it down before you get sugar! Fuck around and get yo feet cut off!" the crackhead handyman joked.

"Glen, FUCK OFF! I SAID I ain't time for the bullshit!"

The crackhead screwed his face up and began to walk off, "Well, fuck you too, ole lazy, nasty byeetch," he grumbled under his malt liquor-smelling breath.

Once the Pierce family (well, not Pierce 'cuz Quimani nor Zy'meer had Fredquisha's last name) made it up to the third floor, without hesitation Fredquisha grabbed Quimani by his shirt collar and dragged him down the smoky hallway that reeked of pigs' feet. Albertina's cooking of course. The trio made it to their apartment front door. With one hand still gripped around Quimani's shirt collar, Fredquisha used the other to rummage through her pocket and pulled out her keys. "Zy'meer, open up the goddamn door!" MooMoo threw the keys at Zy'meer. He quickly opened the door and then walked in. Fredquisha pushed Quimani inside the apartment and then slammed the door with her foot. "Zy'meer, lock my mothafuckin' door and then go to my bedroom while I fuck yo brother up!"

Quimani's tears swelled in abundance. "Mama, no, please, plea—"

All of sudden Fredquisha balled her right fists up and threw a blow to the back of the boy's head, interrupting his plea.

BAM!

"Ahhhhhh!" Quimani screeched grabbing his head. "I-I sorry, mama!" he continued to beseech and cry, hoping his mother wouldn't inflict any extreme violence on him. He definitely knew she was capable of it. He'd observed her fuck Myyah and sometimes Zy'meer up on plenty of occasions.

"SHUT UP! All that cryin' ain't gon save yo ass now! Goin' around here dickin' down all these girls! We gon see just how much dick you got in a minute, lil boy!"

"Mama, please, I 'm sorry!'

"NO, YOU AIN'T SORRY! YOU GOT QUANTAYZIA MOTHAFUCKIN' PREGNANT!!! DO YOU KNOW I CAN GET IN TROUBLE NOW, YOU LITTLE FAT, GREASY BLACK NIGGA?!?!"

Without hesitation, Fredquisha began to throw a barrage of punches at Quimani. Zy'meer watched from a distance, almost beginning to cry seeing his brother reel in pain from the relentless blows.

Fredquisha didn't stop with her punches as she dropped every expletive in the book onto Quimani. At each sound of her malicious words, she threw punch after punch into Quimani's chest, face and stomach.

As he loudly wailed out in excruciating pain and released waterworks of distress, Quimani tried his best to collect his apologetic thoughts along with his rapid, asthmatic breathing. Fredquisha still wasn't stopping her violent abuse though, and with every blow she gave her son, she wanted to inflict him into knowing he possibly fucked up her and his life.

Fredquisha halted her punches and saw Zy'meer still standing there off the side. "ZY'MEER! I THOUGHT I TOLD YOU TO GO TO MY ROOM! IF YOU DON'T GO, I'M GONNA FUCK YOU UP TOO!"

Just like that Zy'meer took off crying and went into his mother's bedroom. The only onlookers now were the six or seven roaches off on an adjacent wall, scared and terrified for the boy. They didn't want to see Fredquisha harm him because Quimani was the one son who kept them well fed.

Fredquisha grabbed Quimani again and looked him dead in his eyes. "GO STRAIGHT TO YOUR ROOM AND TAKE ALL YO CLOTHES OFF! INCLUDING YO UNDERWEAR!" Fredquisha commanded, pointing down the dark hallway of the filthy apartment. With his tears mixed in with his salty beads of sweat swimming down his forehead, Quimani slowly trekked down the hallway and then into his room.

Reluctantly following his mother's instructions, he undressed and threw his clothes off to the side. He then sat on his twin-sized mattress, naked and shivering, anxiously waiting for Fredquisha to barge in at any moment.

Meanwhile back in the living room Fredquisha stormed her kitchen. She quickly rummaged through her fridge, pulled out a half-filled bottle of peach Ciroc, twisted the cap off and then chugged the chilled remnants.

"Ahhh!" She gasped for air once the alcohol went down her esophagus and into her stomach. "GOD DAMN IT! All these god damn roaches! You know what! HIS FAT ISS THE REASON I GOT ALL THESE ROACHES! EATING AND NOT CLEANIN' MY PLACE UP! ALWAYS GOT SNACKS AND SHIT IN HIS MOUTH. FAT ASS!"

Obviously now in a state of delusion, Fredquisha rummaged one of the kitchen drawers to locate a pack of cigarettes. "FUCK!" She forgot just that quick she'd run out of cigs at home, but she did have a new pack in her purse. She dashed out of the kitchen, opened up her purse and pulled out a pack of Newports. She slapped a square in her mouth, lit it up, took a few drags, and then searched the apartment for an extension cord. She had an extra one near her television stand and now she was going to convert it into a makeshift whip to teach her son a lesson about not being able to keep his little dick in his pants.

Once she got the brown extension cord whip secured in her hands, she barged down the hallway and then stormed into the boy's room without knocking.

"So how long ya'll two been fuckin', or as you said, 'hunchin', lil boy?" Fredquisha growled as she took a puff from the cigarette.

Quimani didn't respond though as his shivering intensified. With his hands in his laps trying to cover up his exposed genitalia, he looked at his mother, still speechless.

Fredquisha's hazel brown eyes turned to satanic slits as she took the cigarette out of her mouth and blew a stream of thick smoke towards Quimani's face. "So, you just gon sit there? You not gon say anything? You better say somethin' boy or I'm finna fuck you up even more...," Fredquisha warned as she moved closer to her silent and scared son.

Quimani sat on the bed, staring at his insane mother-abuser, tears still running out the corners of his glassy and reddened eyes. His naked, chubby body shivered and jiggled.

"I'm gon ask you one mo mothafuckin' time. Why is you makin' my life difficult, boy?"

"Muhmuh, p—p-ppppplease don hur me, it gon hurt me, please," Quimani stammered and pleaded.

"Nah, nigga, I'm finna put some pain on you since you messin' wit my mind and my pockets!" Suddenly without hesitation, Fredquisha took the cigarette in her hand and injected it into the side of Quimani's neck.

"AHHHH!" Quimani shrieked, feeling the cigarette burn into the flesh on his neck.

SLAP! Fredquisha's hand went across Quimani's face. She quickly bundled the extension cord up in her hand, turning it into a makeshift slave whip and began lashing the boy like he was a thief who got caught emptying out her life savings.

"AH! AHHH! NO, MAMA! NO!!" Quimani cried, doing his

best to utilize his limbs to protect his body from the sharp and quick lashes.

"SHUT UP! SHUT THAT SHIT UP NOW! MAN THE FUCK UP! SINCE YOU WANNA ACT LIKE A MAN, TAKE THIS FUCKIN' PAIN LIKE A MAN!" Fredquisha kept at it, relentlessly striking the boy with the whip.

Given that Quimani was naked, Fredquisha could see his penis, and she quickly noticed that he was urinating all over the bed and floor. "BOY! YOU PISSIN' ALL OVER MY SHIT NOW!?!? OH HELL NAH!" Seeing her son urinate all over the place gave her the incentive to ramp up her attacks. She temporarily stopped her lashes and then quickly scanned the room, looking for another object she could use to exact more pain onto Quimani. With nothing she could immediately use to torture her son, she threw the whip down on the ground, snatched a pillow off his bed and then pinned Quimani into the bed. She took the pillow and began to smother Quimani, "YOU FUCKIN' KIDS MAKE ME SICK! I WISH I WOULD'VE ABORTED YOU LIL FUCK NIGGAS WHEN I HAD THE CHANCE!" Fredquisha growled.

Quimani, fighting darkness and the lack of oxygen, cried, but his anguished screams were completely muffled by the pillow completely covering his face.

"Mama! NO! Let him go!" Zy'meer suddenly busted through the bedroom door. Although he was younger than Quimani, he was just as big, yet more athletic. He balled his fists up, almost looking he was ready to fight his own mother to protect his brother from possible death.

Fredquisha halted her smothering of her eldest and then turned around scanned Zy'meer up and down! "OH, SO WHAT YOU GON DO?!? BEAT MY ASS?!?"

"MAMA! YOU HURTIN' HIM! PLEASE STOP, OR I'M GONNA CALL THE POLICE!"

"BOY! WHO THE FUCK YOU THINK YOU THREATENING!!?!?"

All of sudden Zy'meer stood his ground as Fredquisha stormed towards him. With the whip still in her hand, she tried to swipe the boy, but he ducked and then went under the lash and wrestled his mother down to the ground.

"BOY! YOU GON SHOVE ME DOWN!?!? I'MMA KILL THE BOTH OF YOU!"

"NO YOU NOT!' Zy'meer screamed back as he all of a sudden started delivering blow after blow to his mother's face and torso.

"AHHHHH!" Fredquisha screamed. She totally didn't see Zy'meer's vengeful attack coming, and despite his age, his strength and endurance were overpowering a now tired and lethargic Fredquisha.

The mother, who now found herself on the losing side of the battle, tried her best to muster up the strength to defend herself. But that quickly came to a halt. Because now Quimani, who was no longer afraid of his mother thanks to his brother's intervention, was going to fuck this bitch up...

CHAPTER TWENTY

redquisha somehow managed to escape the unexpected brutality of her two sons, but with the timely intervention of Glen. The crackhead maintenance man somehow or another heard all of the commotion going on from outside the apartment. Before taking off back to his crib on the Westside, he just so happened to be loitering in the alley of the building. He was smoking some of that rock-caine when he heard the screams and yells coming from Fredquisha's apartment.

When Glen stormed into the apartment, he found a naked Quimani and Zy'meer relentlessly kicking and punching Fredquisha to the point where she looked like she was almost on the precipice of passing the fuck out. He stopped the fight, and Ms. Albertina the elderly neighbor, who too heard all the commotion across the hall, called the police.

Within minutes the Jakes showed up...

AN HOUR LATER...

Blue police lights flickering from three Chicago Police Department squad cars illuminated the opaque street corner of 63rd and Halsted. Fredquisha was standing outside, holding ice to the right side of her face, observing her two sons get taken away in the back of one of the police squad cars. A Hispanic-looking officer strolled over to a silently anguished Fredquisha and looked her up and down, partly pitying her.

"So, we're gonna have to go ahead and take the boys to your mother's place. My advice is that they should stay there or with another family friend, maybe even their fathers, for the time being. Unfortunately, because the two boys are minors, we're going to have to report you to DCFS. A case manager will have to conduct a full investigation before your children are allowed to come back to your apartment," the Hispanic officer explained.

Fredquisha lowered her head and damn near busted out crying hearing the potentially deep legal trouble she now found herself in. This shit was just too much to handle, and the last thing she needed was some social worker bitch all up in her shit. Marco and Gooch, Quimani and Zy'meer's fathers, were gonna be pissed as fuck too once they found out what happened, especially since both men were full-on criminals. The last thing those two niggas wanted was to take on full-fledged fatherly responsibilities whilst they managed their illegal street enterprises.

"Ok...," MooMoo huffed. That was the only response she could produce from her swollen lips.

Suddenly MooMoo gasped. SHIT! Where was Myyah?!?

Fredquisha pulled out her phone from her back pocket and glanced at the time. It was damn near 10 PM and the deranged mother quickly realized that Mrs. Watkins hadn't dropped off Myyah.

Fredquisha gawked at her sons in the squad car, almost wanting to break down and sob in front of the officers along with a few distant onlookers. Regardless of the fight, Quimani and Zy'meer were truly her gems and she couldn't imagine that unexpectedly she would find herself caught up in this dilemma of having them potentially stripped away from her.

"Are you going to be alright, ma'am?" The officer asked Fredquisha.

"Yessir...I'm good. I just need to go check up on my daughter. She over her other grandma's house..."

"Ok, well. Like I said, a social worker from DCFS will be in touch. Are you currently under investigation with them?"

"No...Not that I am aware of..."

"OK, well, I'm sure all of this will get resolved. Have a good night..." The officer stuffed a small white notepad into his uniform shirt pocket and then made his way to the squad car carrying the two brothers. Quimani, in particular, kept gazing at his mother with his eyes turned to venomous slits.

Truth be told, Fredquisha's mother, Evelyn, should not have been the one to take the boys in since she herself was on probation for child endangerment. For years Evelyn operated an illegal daycare out of her shitty apartment living room over in neighboring South Shore. About a year ago, one of her client's toddler was supposedly exposed to rat droppings inside the grandmother-sitter's obviously messy apartment. The baby boy ended up coming down with a bad case of Hantavirus Pulmonary Syndrome that damn near killed him. Denisha, Evelyn's client, was obviously enraged as fuck and snitched on her to DCFS, which inevitably resulted in her getting arrested and placed on probation for three years. But damn, didn't Denisha know just from a cursory glance of Evelyn's apartment that it was nasty as shit? This is what happens when you try to have neighbors watch your children for the low.

As soon as the squad car carrying her boys took off,

Fredquisha exhaled and shook her head. She then made her way back into the apartment building. Once she got inside and made her way back into her apartment, she plunged her hand through her purse sitting on the kitchen countertop and pulled out her pack of cigs. With one hand still holding ice against her bruised face, she slapped a square in her mouth, lit it up and took a few puffs as she made her way over to her couch. She pulled out her phone, dialed Mrs. Watkins and waited for the woman to answer...

Ring. Ring. Ring. Ring. Ring. Ring.

Back in Matteson – The Watkins Residence...

Mrs. Watkins and Jonah were anxiously sitting in the living room watching a rerun of Law & Order. Their nerves were wracked with fire and anxiety. Detective Lennie Briscoe, played by the late and great Jerry Orbach, was grilling some crazy ass white bitch about the disappearance of her six-year-old daughter. Mrs. Watkins shook her head at the sound of all those lies pouring from the white bitch's mouth in regard to the whereabouts of her daughter. Grandma just wondered how anyone could be that crude and malicious to their own blood. Once Detective Briscoe had enough of the lies and proceeded to slap handcuffs onto the white lady, Mrs. Watkins visualized seeing Myyah in a similar predicament. But Grandma was so glad now baby girl was peacefully asleep upstairs. She assured Myyah she didn't have to go back to living in ghetto hell with her crazy ass mama in the city. But despite the assurance, Mrs. Watkins was still burning with fear with the possible legal consequences of taking the girl.

Buzz. Buzz. Buzz.

Mrs. Watkins phone vibrated in her lap. Already anticipating a call from Fredquisha, lo and behold, Mrs. Watkins saw her son's trifling baby mama's name flash across her cell phone screen.

"Fredquisha's calling me," Mrs. Watkins exclaimed as she looked up to Jonah who was sitting on an adjacent couch. Mother and son were now edgy more than ever given they'd just technically kidnapped Myyah. "What should I do? The phone keeps ringing…" Mrs. Watkins quickly as Jonah.

"Just answer it and tell that nasty, abusive slut that Myyah isn't going anywhere until DCFS does an investigation!"

Mrs. Watkins quickly swiped the screen of her phone and put it up to her ear, "Yes, Fredquisha," she answered, pretending like nothing was wrong.

"UMMMM! Mrs. Watkins! Where is Myyah? You were supposed to be back here with Myyah!" Fredquisha barked through the phone.

"Yeah. I know that – that is until she told me you've been beating on her and cussing her out. I called DCFS on you and I'm gonna keep her here until the social worker does some sort of investigation on your nasty, despicable ass!"

"BITCH! THAT'S MY DAUGHTER, HOE! YOU CAN'T KEEP HER! FUCK YOU TALKIN' 'BOUT, BITCH?"

"We'll see about that Fredquisha! You ain't gon put your nasty, section 8 paws on my granddaughter again. And just so you know, I've even gone to the police and Myyah gave the police her testimony about your abuse. So good fucking luck with trying to get her back…"

"BITCH! IF YOU DO NOT BRING MY DAUGHTER BACK OVER HERE IN THE NEXT HOUR, HOE I'M FINNA PULL THE FUCK UP!"

"Fredquisha…No. And if you come over here I swear to GOD I will go into my closet and get my husband's gun and show you how much he taught me!"

"YOU OLD ASS RAGGEDY ASS WANNABE BOUJEE ASS BI—"

Mrs. Watkins heard enough and suddenly hung up the phone. She threw it off to the side and held her arms, slightly trembling.

"What she say, ma?"

"Nothin' important. She ain't gon do shit, and if she comes over here, I'm finna blow her brains off her mothafuckin' head. This bitch got me all out of my Christianity fuckin' around with her. Jonah, I swear to God I'mma kill that bitch if she comes over here fuckin' with me and my granddaughter!"

"MA! I don't know about this anymore. We are getting too deep into this. Fredquisha is that type of crazy woman who might come over here with a squad of her delinquent family members!"

"I don't give a fuck, Jonah. I'm from the hood too and the bitch is about to see another side of me!"

Buzz. Buzz. Buzz. Mrs. Watkins vibrated again, and she just assumed it was Fredquisha calling her up. "I bet you that's her ass calling me up!" Mrs. Watkins growled as she grabbed the phone and looked down. To her surprise though it wasn't Fredquisha, it was actually Cheryl, one of her second cousins who lived all the way out in Oak Park, a westside suburb.

Mrs. Watkins quickly changed her disposition, although she was confused as to why Cheryl was calling her this late at night. Did someone in the family die?

The angered grandmother swiped right and answered, "Hey Cheryl, what's going on girl? I haven't heard from you in a while!"

"Chile! I know right, but I got some crazy ass news to tell you!"

"What, what's wrong? Someone died?"

"Nah, hell no. But you remember Aunty Janice's half-brother, Glen?"

"Umm, yeah…. I think I met him years ago at the family reunion. That's the one on crack, right?"

"Hell yeah, he still smokin' that shit. But baby, so I just ran into his ass at Jewel's. You know what he just told me?"

"What?" Mrs. Watkins replied with a screwed up face.

"Baby, why Austin's trifling ass baby mama Fredquisha got into a fight with her two sons. He told me they whooped her ass like a two dollar trick, baby!"

"WAIT!?!? WHAT!?!? I JUST GOT OFF THE PHONE WITH THAT BITCH!?!?"

"Why?"

"It's a long story, but she been abusing Myyah! I got Myyah over my house as we speak!"

"SHIT! Cousin, let me tell you. The cops came and everything. They had to take her two fat ass sons away. Told me they took them over to their other grandmother's house. Fredquisha at home right now lookin' tore the fuck up, you hear me!"

"WAIT! How does Glen even know Fredquisha?!?!"

"Glen does building maintenance work from time to time for Nathaniel. Small world, ain't it?!?"

"What!?!? Jackie's ex-husband?!? Shit! So, this just happened not too long ago then? Like a few hours ago?" Mrs. Watkins replied as she slapped her forehead and looked over at nosey ass Jonah.

"Yes, hunny!"

"I'm finna call this bitch back now. This ain't nothin' but God's divine intervention."

"Aiight, girl! Handle ya business!"

"Aiight, cousin. Thanks for the heads up!"

"Talk to you later…"

"Same here," Mrs. Watkins replied as she hung up the phone. "This bitch ain't gettin' Myyah. We got her ass!"

"What happened?" Jonah inquired.

"WELLLL…. Apparently, them two boys of hers got into a fight with Fredquisha, the cops were called and now it's lookin' like she in some hot shit. That bitch called me knowing her ass in some bullshit. I'm finna call her back and tell her I know the full fuckin' truth now!" Mrs. Watkins was slowly losing her cool, becoming more aggressive, dropping every curse word known to man.

Jonah shook his head and let out a light chuckle.

"Let's see what her ass got to say now," Mrs. Watkins grunted as she quickly went through her phone, pulled up Fredquisha's number in the recent calls list and dialed her right away.

Ring. Ring. Ring. Ring.

Fredquisha manically paced her apartment. Three THOTiana roaches, thinking they were chilling in the 3-0-5, were skinny dipping in a cup of orange juice and vodka sitting on the coffee table in the living room. Despite the putrid smell inside the apartment getting worse minute by minute, Fredquisha was unfazed. All she could think about right now was the precarious situation she had going on with her children. Her two boys just less than three hours ago gave her an intense beat down which resulted in her fucked up face and swollen limbs. They were now temporarily staying with her mother until things got sorted out with a caseworker. Then, Mrs. Watkins was holding Myyah hostage, adamant on not returning the girl until she got a social worker investigating her ass. Fredquisha was on the verge of an epic meltdown, but she wasn't going to let any of this deter her from growing her relationship with sexy ass Trel.

"Pop, lock and drop it! Pop, lock and drop it!" Fredquisha's ringtone on her iPhone went off. Huey's one hit wonder "Pop, Lock and Drop It" was MooMoo's jam back in the day and made it her ringtone.

"ARE YOU OUTSIDE WITH MY DAUGHTER!??!?"

Fredquisha roared, her loud and thunderous voice scaring away the THOT roaches from the vodka pool.

"I heard about ya little situation with your boys. We'll just see about you getting Myyah back after you get your shit together, you nasty hoe. You are OBVIOUSLY not fit to be anyone's mother."

"BITCH! I SWEAR TO GOD IF YOU DON'T BRING MY DAUGHTER BAC—"

Mrs. Watkins interrupted, "Or you gonna do what? Seems like you gon have a caseworker down your back? You really gonna do something to me? Something to Myyah?"

Fredquisha just stood there in her smoky, somewhat dark apartment not able to come up with a quick response. A part of her knew Mrs. Watkins was right. Her hands were tied. In a day or so a social worker was going to be all up in MooMoo's shit and the last thing she needed to do was make her situation even more complicated.

"So, what you got to say now?" Mrs. Watkins continued...

"FINE! FINE! You want her, you can have her! You and Austin! Didn't want her ass anyways! I should've aborted her mothafuckin' ass!" Fredquisha quipped and hung up the phone.

"AHHHH!" Without hesitation, she threw the phone against the wall and on impact, it exploded into several pieces.

All of sudden she quickly regretted doing so given she didn't have another phone she could use and there was a strong possibility Trel was going to be calling her up tonight. "FUCK!" MooMoo then growled realizing the stupidity of her action.

Time was now at hand and MooMoo had to move quickly to figure out what she was going to do to get her semblance of a normal life together. For the first time in months, she conjured up the spirit and discipline to clean up the apartment. Had to. It was time to work overtime to put on a show for the social worker(s).

CHAPTER TWENTY-ONE

*L*ater that Monday night...Chicago's tall, garish skyscrapers illuminated the dark expanse of the wide, partly cloudy skies. The full moon glistened. Earlier today was exceptionally hot and dry; no breezy relief coming from Lake Michigan winds.

Nonetheless, to millions of Chi-town natives, today was yet another day to be in celebration of summer. Tens of thousands of people, many tourists, still jam packed Downtown's vast streets, looking to get in as much fun in the heat of the night. Summers in Chicago liberated people from long, dark months of freezing weather, so now was the time to enjoy everything the Windy City had to offer...

"Welcome aboard Red Line run 905. The next stop is Cermak-Chinatown...," the automated announcement on the southbound Red Line train blared loudly on the relatively empty train car.

Katina Lewis, aka, "Tina", looked down at her partly cracked iPhone 6S screen and glanced at the time. Tina, dark brown-skinned, voluptuous, decked out in green scrubs, long micro-braids running down her back, yawned and wiped her reddened eyes. A symptom of getting less than six hours of sleep seven nights in a row. 11:45 PM flashed across Katina's smartphone. She was still a good thirty minutes away from getting off the EL at 95th street. From there she needed to then transfer to a bus to take her to 115th street. There, she'd get off the bus and walk a block over to her apartment.

Ms. Lewis had been up since 4 AM. She decided to work overtime this week in order to fatten next week's paycheck. Rent was almost due. Light, cable and gas bills needed to be paid. The kids had afterschool program tuition due at the end of the month.

Deontae, the father of her two children, was barely contributing to the household. Said a nigga couldn't get a decent paying gig 'cuz the economy was rough. The other excuse was that he had a record and no company wanted to hire a felon. His rationalizations for not being able to get a normal 9 to 5 were true to an extent. However, Deontae spent most of his time playing video games, pursuing his "music" career or fucking other hoes behind Tina's back.

Despite Deontae being a somewhat notable drug dealer in the wild hunneds (the Roseland neighborhood that starts past 99th street on the South Side), Deontae like most fuck boys always complained about being short on money. There were just so many times Katina was ready to kick Deontae out. Nonetheless, she hoped one day he'd get his act together, stop trapping, eventually get a real job and do right by her and their eight-year-old son and four-year-old daughter.

The hardworking mother unlocked her phone and was just about to call Deontae to let him know she was actually ending her overtime shift early tonight. Earlier she'd informed him she was gonna get off at 2 AM, but she couldn't push herself to work that long tonight. Just as she was about to hit Deontae's line, she mumbled to herself, "Fuck it." Deontae hadn't sent her a message all day long, didn't even bother to call to check up on her during her lunch break. Quite obvious he didn't really care about her, so why should she care about him?

Tina then locked her phone, threw it in her purse and slowly closed her eyelids so she could get in a quick nap. She wasn't afraid of closing her eyes on the train. If someone tried it with her, she had her mace and box cutter ready to fuck someone up. Besides, no one else was in the train car with her except these two old ass Chinese ladies who were probably going to get off at the 35th street stop in Chinatown. In Chicago, the Red Line went as far south as 95th street on the South Side to as far north to Howard up on the North Side, damn near touching the city limits of Evanston. The city was planning one extending the Redline to 130th street so Altgeld Gardens and Riverdale residents could get access to the train. Hell, if the train had already run that far south, Tina wouldn't need to catch a bus.

Ms. Lewis, 27, had been a registered nurse within the pediatric ICU at Northwestern Hospital now for some five years. Katina first started off working as a CNA right after she graduated from high school. She would've gone straight for her RN, but she ended up getting pregnant with her eight-year-old not too long after she graduated from high school. Giving birth to her son somewhat delayed her college dreams. Nevertheless, some years later, she took a leap a faith and enrolled in Olive-Harvey College, a local community college. There she slowly worked to obtain her associate's in nursing so she could work as a registered nurse.

Tina had a vision eventually become a nurse anesthetist. Although right now she didn't have her bachelor's in nursing, once she saved up some more money, she was going to head back to undergrad to get her bachelor's and eventually her master's degree. She wasn't playing either – she'd already been in contact with nursing program advisors at DePaul University and the University of Illinois-Chicago. She had her sight set on becoming an anesthetist because apparently, they started off making over $150,000 a year. Tina couldn't imagine what in the world she would do if she started bringing home that type of money. The salary was going to amount to bringing home more than $5,000 a paycheck after taxes. Right now she was barely bringing home $3500 a month. The more Tina thought about making six figures as an anesthetist, the more she realized the things she could have and do...She'd move her and her two kids out of the desolation of Roseland and buy her a big ass palace in some suburban gated community like Orland Park or Matteson. She'd put her two kids in the best private schools. Pay off all her debts. Buy a new car. There was just so much she could do with making that amount of money while working her dream job.

However, with a fuck boy boyfriend who possessed virtually no real life aspirations, Tina was reaching a boiling point of just finally giving Deontae the deuces. She kind of already had a plan formulated in her head of how she planned on leaving Deontae for good. The apartment she had right now with him was leased in her name, and she had three months left on her current lease. She didn't tell Deontae, but she hadn't renewed the lease. She was going to pinch the shit out of her next four paychecks. From there, she was going to move back in with her mother in Auburn Gresham. She'd already talked to a loan officer at the local Chase bank branch about getting a loan for a condo or a townhouse. She was already making enough money to afford something in the ballpark of a good $180,000. Probably couldn't get anything reasonable in the city, but she figured if she found a job out in the 'burbs, she could then afford a townhouse, shit, maybe even a single family home. Chicago's suburbs were definitely cheaper than the city. Once she moved, her next plan of action was to hit Deontae with child support. Maybe then he'd wake the fuck up, realize he took advantage of a good woman and make better life decisions.

Right now, all Tina needed was just one final nail in the coffin to give her validation she was doing the right thing.

Almost on the cusp of turning 30, Tina realized she'd rather be lonely than to be frustrated and miserable living with bum dick. Although she kind of had the inkling that a lot of niggas weren't on shit, she just knew it was somebody out there for her who would appreciate her for who she was and what she had to offer.

A good thirty minutes passed... "Red Line Run 905. 95th Street is the next stop." The familiar train announcement penetrated Tina's ears and instantly woke her up from her brief nap. She wiped her eyes, stood up, adjusted herself and made her way over to the exit of the train. Once the train came to a complete stop, she strolled off and made her way to the bus terminal to catch the #34 bus. Minutes later, the bus came, and within fifteen minutes Tina arrived at her stop on 115th street. She got off, and then coolly and cautiously strolled up to the apartment building.

"Hrrrm, whose car is that?" Tina mumbled once she noticed a champagne Honda Accord with Indiana tags parked outside her building.

As long as she'd been living here, she'd never seen the car before. Most of the residents in the building and on the block knew each other. And then over 80 percent of the residents were elderly. Most of them drove older cars like Buicks, Lincolns, etc. There were a few young families in her building, but none of them to Tina's knowledge has transportation. They were bus and train bound just like her. Perhaps it was a guest of someone in the building, however, she didn't put too much thought into the car because she was too tired.

She made her way to the front entrance, opened the door with her keys and then made her way upstairs to the fourth floor. Once she'd arrived at her apartment, unit 4E, she opened her front door and walked through the dark living room, and down the hallway towards her bedroom. She didn't even wanna grab anything to drink or eat anything light before bed.

Deep, peaceful, uninterrupted sleep was all she craved right now.

Tina wrapped her hand around her bedroom door and opened it. Before she could even get a foot in the door all sleepiness escaped her thick body. "WHAT THE FUCK! YOU GOT ANOTHER BITCH IN MY HOUSE?!?!?"

CHAPTER TWENTY-TWO

"*O*h fuck! Deontae, wake the fuck up! She's back!"

Some slim-thick yellow bitch suddenly shrieked and jumped at the thunderous sound of Tina's announcement. The manifestly scared side bitch instantly grabbed the bed's maroon sheets to cover herself, then she punched a sleeping Deontae to wake him the fuck up. Scared silly side hoe scurried herself into the corner of the bed. She had to protect herself knowing damn well she definitely fucked up sleeping with another woman's man. Fear enslaved her as her promiscuous eyes landed on Tina's balled up fists.

"YEAH! BITCH! I AM BACK! WHO THE FUCK ARE YOU?!?!"

"I'm just Deontae's friend! He didn't tell me he had a girlfriend!"

"NAH, BITCH! HE GOT A GIRLFRIEND AND A BABY MAMA! AND YOU FUCKIN' HIM IN MY HOUSE WHILE MY KIDS IS SLEEP!"

Deontae slowly awakened and wiped his eyes. Throwing back a bottle of Henny and smoking two blunts had put him into coma-like sleep. "What's going on?" he mumbled and slightly yawned. But once his eyes were fully opened and gawking at Tina standing at the front of the room he yelled, "Oh shit! What you doin' back early?!?"

"FUCK NIGGA! WHO IS THIS BITCH?!?"

Although Tina wanted to know, she actually didn't want any answers. "YOU KNOW WHAT! FUCK IT!" she screamed as she quickly darted out from the door and went back into the dark living room.

All types of anxiety-riddled commotion went on in the master bedroom. The distant sounds of the frantic side hoe doing her best to put her clothes back on her naked body could be heard all the way from the living room. Tina dashed towards the sole utility closet near the front door and searched for her gun. The angered mother quickly located the pistol inside a black combination-lock box. She hastily yet cautiously checked the chamber and then made her way back to the master bedroom.

Light skinned side hoe dashed out of the master bedroom and attempted to make a run from the precarious domestic situation.

"AHHHH!" She screamed and threw her hands up, trying to make a sudden run back into the bedroom once she saw the barrel of the gun aimed right at her forehead.

POW! Tina let the blickie off in the apartment, sending a bullet down the hall and into the upper part of the wall. Luckily behind the wall was cement, so the bullet instantly got lodged, not penetrating over into the next apartment.

"I'm gonna kill these motherfuckers! I work fuckin' seventy hours a week and this fuckin' nigga gon bring a random ass bitch up into my mothafuckin' apartment where my kids are sleepin! Nigga gotta die to-fucking-NIGHT!"

Armed and dangerous, all Tina now saw was crimson red

and she was ready to murder Deontae and the side hoe. She barged into the room and there Deontae with his gun his hand, aimed right at Tina. This nigga thought Tina was overreacting and wasn't going to let her suddenly lose control and end his life, nor the side bitch's.

"Tina put the mothafuckin' gun. You lost your fuckin' mind!" Deontae growled. Gun still cocked in his hand, aimed at his children's mother, this fuck nigga didn't seem to think anything was wrong with the current situation. Well, he knew she'd be inflamed seeing him laid up with some random pussy, but, it didn't warrant her seemingly violent reaction.

"Mommy! Daddy! No!" Both Tina and Deontae's kids were standing near the door, crying and visibly traumatized. Tina, still holding the gun aimed at Deontae, turned around and looked at her frightened and sobbing children.

Now regretful that she put her kids through the traumatic situation, she then turned back around and scanned Deontae up and down. Her hazel eyes turned to hateful slits. She slowly lowered the gun.

"I'm leaving you...You can have this raggedy ass apartment. I'm taking me and my kids to my mama's place. Don't call me. Don't text me. Lose my number. You fuckin' bum. You're such a pathetic excuse of a man and the worst father on the planet. Fucking another woman in my house that you don't even pay rent for while your own innocent children are sleeping. Fucking clown ass nigga." Tina then turned her attention towards side hoe, "...and for you bitch, you can have the whole nigga. His dick is trash anyways..."

Side hoe, shivering, goggled at Deontae and then at Tina, and then back at Deontae. "Can I go now?" she asked biting her fingernails, fear laced in her question.

"Bitch, you can stay. I'm leaving..."

"Nah! NO! You can't go!" shirtless Deontae barked at Tina.

The only thing he had on was a pair of boxers and some flip-flops. "Kylah, get yo shit and get out my house, bitch. I gotta talk to my girl."

Suddenly side piece Kylah gathered her belongings and made a quick dash out of the master bedroom, down the hallway and then stormed out of the apartment. Lucky ass hoe. Hope she learned the lesson not to fuck with another woman's man (although Deontae was worse than New York City street trash).

"Deontae, we ain't got shit to talk about...I'm gone! Kids, go pack up some clothes in your book bags and get all of your stuff. We're leaving your punk ass daddy..."

"Damn! DAMN! Tina, you fuckin' always do this shit to me! You at work all the fuckin' time. We barely have sex. I'm here by myself raising these kids most of the time! What the fuck was I supposed to do?!?!? Keep jackin' my dick?!?" Deontae cried.

Tina ignored Deontae as he just stood there with arms and hand stretched out in confusion. Guess he was hoping Tina would back down from leaving and instantly forgive him. But seeing him snuggled up with some random ass hoe, in HER apartment, in HER bed, everything else in her name, was the last straw. She was done.

Tina rummaged her closet for a travel bag, and then stormed over to her dresser. She threw in as many clothes as she could into the bag because she wasn't determined to come back for a while. Not at least until she had to get the apartment cleaned since she didn't renew the lease.

"COME ON! TALK TO ME, TINA! SHIT" Deontae growled.

"First of all, put your mothafuckin' pistol down."

"Fine!" Deontae threw the gun onto the bed and then got on his knees. "Talk to me, baby! Please! Don't leave me! I swear I won't do it again! I was just horny, and I needed to bust a nut!"

"How you met her?"

"She was just some random ass THOT I met off Tinder. Nobody really important…"

"She knew you had a whole ass 'fiancée'? She knew kids were the apartment?"

"Nah, baby! I swear!" he obviously lied.

"You know I don't believe you, right?"

"Baby! Come on! It's just pussy! It ain't like I love the bitch!"

"Nigga, you got me fucked up. I hope you can get a job quickly 'cuz I ain't paying the rent on this mothafucka. I'm calling up Mr. Miller tomorrow to let him know what went down. Oh, and I didn't renew the lease by the way!"

"FUCKK MAN! YOU HAD THIS SHIT PLANNED!" Deontae snarled. "YO ASS WAS GONNA LEAVE ME ANYWAYS!"

"Yup!" Tina fake smiled as she finished packing her bag. She zipped the bag up and then made dashed across the hall into her children's room. "Ya'll done?"

"Yeah," both her kids said in unison. "Good, let's go. I'm gonna call us an Uber."

"FINE! Get the fuck out! You'll be back! Don't nobody want yo fat, nappy headed ass anyways! And you can't suck dick!"

Tina continued to ignore enraged fuck boy Deontae. By this point in their dysfunctional relationship, the mother had already grown immune and numb to his emotional abuse. From time to time he had a knack for taunting Tina about her weight, hair, and other physical aspects about her that made her feel highly insecure. But now, none of that mattered. He was dead to her. She just walked on unbothered. "I will be puttin' yo ass on child support too, so I hope you get your shit together…"

"Man, ok…I see how it is, fat ass bitch. I got you. I swear to God you gon regret this shit!"

As Tina and her two kids made their way to the front door

of the apartment, she turned on her feet and looked Deontae up and down. "You know, I can't believe I wasted my life thinking you were gonna be someone. You turned out to be worse than the trash sitting outside on the streets right now. The only good thing I got out of you were my two kids. And they don't even really respect your clown ass. So, good luck with life, Deontae... I'm out. And I'm for real about the lease...So unless you can afford to renew it on your own, Mr. Miller is gonna expect your ass out soon."

"But the lease is in your name...You just gon stop paying it?"

"No. I got an emergency rental assistance voucher, but since you aren't on the lease, I'll just go ahead and tell Mr. Miller about our little disagreement tonight. He'll ask you to leave the premises immediately or get your name on the lease. He'll eventually get his coins. But like I said, you're on your own now, childish ass nigga..."

Deontae's eyes turned to vengeful slits. He just shuddered his head up and down. "Ok, then. It's whatever. Don't just be calling me, talkin' about you wanna work on things. Bitch, it's over. Get out!"

"Whatever, nigga. Get a job, fucking bum..." Tina retorted, not even giving him eye contact. As she and her kids trekked downstairs, she pulled out her phone and hailed an Uber. The woman and her two kids walked over to a well-lit street corner and anxiously waited for the arrival of the black Nissan Altima to pick them up and take them to Grandma's house over in Auburn Gresham.

"So, mama, we aren't coming back at all?" Desiree, Tina's daughter asked as she looked up at the still partially angered woman. "Nope. Not at all. We gonna stay with granny for a bit then get our own place far away. Out of the city."

"So, that means we not gonna have to go to the same schools?" Rashad, her son, asked.

"Nope! You're gonna go to a different school too, hopefully!"

"Good, cuz I hated that school anyways..." Rashad replied with a huge smile plastered across his face.

Within five minutes the Uber arrived. The entire family hopped in and sped off into the early morning to Auburn-Gresham. The neighborhood was about a good twenty minutes west of Roseland.

CHAPTER TWENTY-THREE

*B*eep. Beep. Beep. Beep...
Inside the Cook County Jail medical ward, room 450, Austin lay in deep sleep after a given an intense round of a morphine IV drip. The beeping sound of an EKG machine resonated throughout the entire room. Austin was caught up in an apparent mix-up. First responding corrections officers who were on the scene in the library shot Austin thinking he was the perpetrator responsible for the death of Terrence and the unknown corrupt corrections officer. Three rounds of non-lethal rat shots were blasted at Austin's legs and torso, instantly knocking him down to the ground.

After a quick internal investigation, it was discovered that without a doubt that the gang-affiliated jail guard was a crooked corrections officer. Austin was clearly cleared of any wrongdoing, but unfortunately for him, he was shot twice in his legs and one bullet was sent to his stomach. One of the bullets slightly lacerated a section of his colon, hence he needed emergency surgery to prevent major blood loss.

As the morphine began to fade away Austin slowly awakened and opened his eyes...His pupils then latched onto a short, brown-skinned young nurse with a short buzz cut.

"Hey there, looks like you had a rough afternoon a day ago?" The nurse asked with a big smile running across her face. The dimples in her cheeks were a bit flattering to Austin.

Austin reached over and wiped crust out of his eyes with his right hand. Because he was a low-security risk, officers didn't bother to put cuffs his wrists to the railing on the hospital bed.

"Yeah, damn...What happened?" Austin responded to the nurse tending to his IV bag. Being sedated, he somewhat forgot how he even ended up in the jail's hospital ward.

"Unfortunately, you were shot...That Sunday afternoon when you were in the library, one of those jail guards tried to kill another inmate and you intervened...You don't remember?" The nurse smilingly asked.

Austin thought about for a second. "Damn, I do now..." He then rubbed the side of his lower torso. "Ahhh," he moaned out in pain. "Damn, they really shot me though?"

"Yup...But they used small rounds so the wounds wouldn't be lethal. You're gonna be alright though. At least you won't have to spend the rest of your time in the cell. Lucky for you since you get out in a few weeks, you got cleared to stay here until your release. You might need some physical therapy."

"Yeah...Shit, I do...I do get out," Austin said, still somewhat high from the morphine drip still obviously running through his veins. "What's your name?" he asked the nurse.

"Latonya...But you can call me Tonya."

"I'm Austin..."

"I know! Mr. Watkins..." she smiled. "Anyways, I'm gonna go check up on your pain meds and see what we're gonna be feeding you for breakfast. Make yourself comfortable. At 11, the doctor is gonna come check up on you and see how your wounds are healing."

"Ok," Austin responded as he made himself comfortable in the hospital bed.

With nothing on but a green gown, he glanced over at an open window and could see the entire Chicago cityscape glowing among the backdrop of partly cloudy blue skies and morning sunshine. Although he could clearly see he was still confined in a jail as barb wired fences surrounded the entire jail complex, just the idea of being free in a few weeks was exhilarating despite Sunday's 'misunderstanding.' Austin wondered if his mother and other family members were aware of what happened to him, and he didn't get a chance to ask the nurse either. He just sat back, closed his eyes, and continued to enjoy the remaining opioid joy swimming in his blood.

R*ing. Ring. Ring.*
Mrs. Watkins jumped at the sound of her cell phone buzzing. It had been day once since she was in 'temporary' custody of Myyah. Grandma just knew at any moment a barrage of harassing phone calls were going come at her left and right from Fredquisha and her family.

Although Myyah was scheduled to be back in school to finish out this school year, Mrs. Watkins refused to drive the girl back to her school in the city. She knew if she'd done that Fredquisha would be there, ready at the school to pick the girl up and bring her back home. But then again, now that she heard from her cousin that Fredquisha was caught up in a jam with social services and the police over her fight with her boys, Mrs. Watkins assumed Fredquisha wouldn't be that brazen to fight her over Myyah. Fredquisha possibly wouldn't make her current, unsolved legal situation worse, Mrs. Watkins presumed.

9:31 AM bleeped on the kitchen stove. Mrs. Watkins was at her dining room table sipping on her black coffee and reading CNN on her phone when it began to ring. She saw an unknown 773 number, which meant the call was coming from within Chicago's city limits.

"Hello?" Mrs. Watkins answered the phone. Unbeknownst to her, Myyah was slowly making her way downstairs and into the dining room to be with her granny.

"Hey, Mrs. Watkins. This is Officer Washington down at the Cook County Jail."

"Oh, hey!"

"Good morning, ma'am. I'm giving you a call because Austin was wounded in an altercation on Sunday afternoon. He's currently in the hospital recuperating from minor surgery."

"WHAT!?!? Why didn't you all call me or anything!?!?"

"Sorry, ma'am. We would've called you earlier, but we had to conduct a thorough investigation first before we notified you. But like I said, his condition is stable and you can visit him at the jail's hospital if you would like…"

"Ok! Well, I'm coming down right now!"

"No worries. See you soon," the officer responded and then hung up the phone.

"Granny, is there something wrong with daddy?" Myyah asked, standing there appearing solemn as she held onto a brown teddy bear. All that time Mrs. Watkins didn't know baby girl was standing there listening in on the brief conversation from a corner.

Suddenly Mrs. Watkins turned her attention towards her granddaughter. "No, baby girl. He's alright! He's just a bit sick. I'm going to go visit him while you stay here with Uncle Jonah, ok?"

"Ok…"

"Let's make you some breakfast before I go, ok? I'm gonna also talk to your daddy about letting you stay here with us forever..."

"So, I won't have to go back and live with Fredquisha then?"

"I'm hoping so, baby girl...I'm hoping so.

As soon as Mrs. Watkins got Myyah situated with breakfast, she dashed upstairs to go tell Jonah what happened to Austin and that she needed him to babysit Myyah for the morning. Already taking her morning shower, she put on some jeans, tennis shoes and a light jacket, called for an Uber and made her way into the city.

"Watkins! Your mother is here to visit you!" A jail guard knocked on Austin's hospital door, instantly catching his attention as he read a course catalog to one of the colleges he was interested in attending once he got out of jail. Earlier, one of the supervising guards that monitored his cell floor grabbed a few of his course catalogs and other belongings so he could have something to read while he spent the remaining time of his sentence in the jail hospital.

Austin wasn't expecting his mother to come and visit him. He put the course catalog down on the nightstand next to him and then went to adjust the bed with a remote control in his hand.

Mrs. Watkins walked into the room and immediately cried, "Oh My God! My baby! What did they do to you!?!?"

"It's alright, mama, it was just a mishap!" Austin explained with a scrunched up face. He was in some slight pain. "I just took a few bullets to my legs and stomach..."

"JUST A FEW!?!? This is crazy! Just two days ago you were dancing with Myyah and now you're laid in a bed because of a

172

mishap!?!?" she screeched as she made her way closer to the bed and began to rub Austin's face.

"Mama, how did you even find out? Don't cry. I'm gonna be alright!" Austin beamed as he reached in to hug his mother.

"I just got the call not too long ago about what happened! Oh my God! I cannot believe this!" Mrs. Watkins continued to sob.

"Mama, I'm fine. Just relax. Grab a chair and relax. I'm gonna be fine. I just had a little minor surgery. That's all…"

Mrs. Watkins pulled a chair up to Austin's bed. She rummaged her purse for a piece of tissue and wiped tears from her cheeks. "Ok, well at least you are fine. I cannot wait until you get out of this hellhole, Austin. I just cannot wait. It's so much going on with you and Myyah."

"I know. But I only got a few weeks left. They lettin' me stay here until I get released. I guess it's their way of apologizing. At least I ain't got no handcuffs on me," Austin laughed and raised his free hands.

"I guess…" Mrs. Watkins laughed back and rubbed Austin's hand.

"Ohhh, Austin," Mrs. Watkins exhaled and shook her head. "I don't even know if this the right place to even tell you what I need to tell you…"

"What is it?"

"Well, I didn't wanna ruin the night you and Myyah had, especially considering ya'll almost never got the chance to see each other, but Fredquisha…That bitch right there…She ain't right, Austin. She ain't right. That bitch is foul and got your daughter living in some decrepit ass conditions in that apartment."

Austin lowered his head and shook it. He wasn't shocked though; he'd always known Fredquisha didn't know what the definition of cleanliness meant.

"And Myyah told me the other day that Fredquisha had been physically and emotionally abusive to her…"

"What?!?" Austin replied with anger suddenly carved into the features of his dark-brown face.

"Yes...Austin, I always knew she was doing something to that girl, but I couldn't quite put my finger on it. Myyah finally confessed and said that bitch had been hitting and calling her all types of names."

"Mama, please...I can't. I can—"

"Shhhhh. Austin, I know," Mrs. Watkins interrupted. "I got everything under control. I called DCFS and I took Myyah down to the police to file a police report against her. She's staying with me no until everything gets squared away..."

"Wait, what? You went to a judge and got custody?"

Mrs. Watkins quickly looked around and noticed the corrections officer was closely monitoring their conversation from a distance. She leaned in and whispered, "No. I ain't bringing her back to Fredquisha's place until everything gets squared away. To hell with the law. I do not want my granddaughter to be around that wench anymore."

"But mama—"

"Austin, just trust me on this. I got it under control. Fredquisha is going down soon. Just don't worry, ok?" Mrs. Watkins interrupted again.

Austin leaned back in the hospital bed. He closed his eyes and placed his hand over his forehead, slowly shaking it in disbelief.

"Mama, I hope you know what you're doing. Please don't let my daughter get taken away. Fredquisha is a vindictive ass woman. She'll do anything to make sure Myyah stays with her."

"I know, son. I know. But you gotta just have faith and hold out and believe everything is gonna be alright. Can you do that?"

Austin took a deep breath and then exhaled. "I guess."

"Good then...Just relax and get better, ok? Myyah needs you. I need you."

"I know. I'm gonna get better and get out of here ASAP. Just please, don't do anything crazy, ok?"

"Of course…"

"Ma'am, visitation is up," the medium-build white corrections officer standing guard announced.

Mrs. Watkins grabbed Austin's hand and squeezed it. She stood up, leaned over and kissed Austin on his forehead. "I love you, Austin. Myyah loves you too."

"I love you too, mama. Tell Myyah I said I love her and miss her."

"Oh, I will. She misses you too…"

CHAPTER TWENTY-FOUR

*T*uesday afternoon rolled in pretty quickly for Fredquisha as she manically paced her trashy apartment living room. Anxiety laced her muscles. Fear dug in her bones. With a fresh Marlboro square tucked into her plump purple lips, she took long, deep puffs. She would've had a big ass blunt in her mouth, but she'd already smoked her stash and needed to hit up Deontae to re-up.

Visibly angered MooMoo blew smoke from her nostrils and grunted as she kept seeing roaches scurry across the living room floor.

"FUCK! All these goddamn roaches! Fuck this shit! I need to call Mr. Nate to fix this shit immediately!" MooMoo loudly grumbled under breath.

Quimani and Zy'meer was still over at their Grandmother Evelyn's house. Fretful as fuck, Fredquisha was expecting at any moment now a social worker from DCFS or Chicago Housing Authority to show up unannounced. That was at least the stern warning her mother gave her. A typical protocol for social services agencies when child endangerment was a possibility. Shit, truth be told, Evelyn had social services called on her several times decades ago when she was raising her own children, so she already knew what to expect. Evelyn even told Fredquisha she needed to do her best to tidy up the apartment, that way she wouldn't give the social worker any more ammunition to make a case for getting her children taken away from her.

Following her mother's instructions, she attempted as quickly as she could in the best of her abilities to tidy up the apartment. She paced the apartment living room with a black plastic trash bag in her hand, doing her best to stuff it with leftover chicken wing cartons from Harold's Fried Chicken, Pizza Hut and Domino's pizza boxes, empty Corona beer bottles, candy wrappers and other discarded trash. The trash was one thing. Shit was easy to pick up now that Fredquisha had the slight energy and motivation to do so. However, what kept bothering MooMoo more and more was seeing the overabundance of roaches of all sizes slowly take over the apartment.

By this point, the brown-blackish critters were everywhere. Up and down the walls. Crawling on the couches. Scuttling on the living room coffee table. Swarming across the baseboards. Up until now, she was immune to the growing vermin problem, but now that she possibly had social services on her back, she had to do something about the roach issue immediately.

Amidst the backdrop of having to deal with cleaning up the apartment whilst worrying about her boys, another concern for Fredquisha was Myyah. Fredquisha honestly at this point was just willing to give her up and just let Mrs. Watkins take care of her. She didn't even love the girl enough to really care anymore. Sad, but at least slowly she was becoming more and more honest with herself and was willing to put baby girl in better hands.

Hell, there were so many times Fredquisha had thought about letting Mrs. Watkins take permanent custody over her. But of course, the one thing Fredquisha couldn't do was possibly sacrifice the thousands of dollars a month she was receiving to take care of the poor girl. Close to $2500 was at stake and that was enough money for Fredquisha to get her hair did, nails did, buy two to three outfits a week, go on occasional vacations with her besties, even enough money to splurge on drugs and alcohol. It was also enough money for her to go all the way out for her sons. She'd use Myyah's money to buy the boys new clothes, video game systems, and other gifts. But now, with a new baby possibly in her stomach from some random nigga, she could always exploit the newborn to re-up her SSI cash stash.

Buzz. Buzz. Buzz. Fredquisha's phone vibrated in her back pocket. She threw the trash bag down and grabbed the phone out of her pocket. She gawked down and saw that Myyah's school was calling her. "FUCK! She grunted. She needed to come up with an immediate excuse for Myyah's absence.

Fredquisha answered, "Hello?"

"Hey, Ms. Pierce. This is Cassandra down at Daley Elementary. Myyah was absent today and we didn't get a call notifying us. Is she sick or something?"

"Yeah, she been out sick. She got a really bad flu..."

"Ohhhh, I'm so sorry to hear that! OK, well, I hope she gets better. You know this week is the PARCC tests, so there is a possibility she would have to make it up so she can move on to the next grade," the school secretary explained.

"Yeah, ok. She'll be back soon. She ain't gon miss them tests," Fredquisha fibbed.

"Okey-dokey...Take care!" the secretary exclaimed.

"Bye," Fredquisha replied and immediately hung up the phone.

"FUCK!" Fredquisha growled and then threw the phone on the couch. She pulled out her pack of cigs from her left pocket. Immediately taking one out and throwing a fresh square in her mouth, she once again paced the living room, more manic than ever. What in the hell was she going to do now?!? Fuck it, she thought. Myyah needed to bring her ass back, and if Mrs. Watkins was going to put up a fight, she was going to call the police and let them know Mrs. Watkins kidnapped her daughter.

She dashed towards the couch, picked up her phone, unlocked and immediately scrolled through her contacts to find Mrs. Watkins' number.

BOOM! BOOM! BOOM!

"Fuck, fuck, fuck!" Fredquisha was immediately caught off guard by the three loud knocks on her front door. That had to be the social worker. She just knew it.

"Coming!" MooMoo replied towards the knocks as she frantically scanned the living room. There was still so much to clean up. And it seemed as if with the loud knocks on the door, more roaches came out of nowhere looking to greet the unknown guest.

Fredquisha picked the plastic bag up and attempted to quickly fill it with more trash.

BOOM! BOOM! BOOM! "FREDQUISHA! OPEN UP, GIRL! THIS NATE!"

Fredquisha suddenly dropped the bag in her hand and felt sudden relief overcome her. She lunged towards the door and opened it up. She produced a fake smile at Mr. Garrison. "Hey, Mr. Nate. How are you doing? I didn't know you were back in town?"

The landlord, Mr. Garrison, was a somewhat tall yet plump chocolate man with a partly dry, partly greasy gray jheri curl. A black-and-mild was tucked behind his ear. A visibly old beige Kangol hat covered his head, matching his off-brand JC Penny's white polo, Dockers shorts, and beige open-toe sandals. This was the man's typical uniform as he never spent his winters in Chicago; always in the Dominican Republic or at times Panama. In fact, by the dark circles under his eyes and the smell of rum coming from pores, Fredquisha assumed he probably just came back from the Islands not too long ago.

Nate barged right into the living room of the apartment without even bothering to ask if he could come in. His shady eyes slowly skimmed the still dirty apartment. With his hands on his waist, he grumbled and shook his head, "Girl, what you got goin' on over here?!? I get a call from Glen tellin' me you had the police and shit over my damn building 'cuz you and them boys was fightin'!"

"I know, I'm sorry, Mr. Nate. It was just too much going on Sunday and my boys kinda got carried away. They stayin' with their grandma now while I get my apartment cleaned up. Sorry about the mess, you know it's hard raising three kids by myself and shit."

"Lady, you got my shit looking like West Side after the MLK riots. You got me fucked up. I mean, ALL the way fucked up if you think I can let you continue living in here like this. And wassup with all of these goddamn roaches and shit!?!?"

Fredquisha couldn't respond. She didn't have a solid reply to give her landlord. Technically it was his fault though that the roaches were taking over. She'd told Glen on so many occasions about the problem, but they simply refused to call an exterminator to get to the root of the issue.

"Mr. Nate, I told Glen. I mean, he came and laid down traps and shit, but they ain't doin' nothin'!"

"Yeah, they ain't doin' nothin' 'cuz you's a nasty ass...you know what...I'm gon' have to give you a thirty-day notice. I'm gonna have to tell Section 8 about this shit 'cuz you ain't gon mess with my money. Got me ALL the way fucked up."

"No, please, Mr. Nate. Don't do that. I already got them possibly on my back and shit. Please, look. I'll do whatever it takes to get the apartment cleaned up. Shit, I think a social worker might be on their way today!"

"Oh really? What the hell you done did? Glen told me that lil fat older son of yours was naked whompin' yo ass!"

"Mr. Nate, please, I need your help. Don't kick me out. I know I ain't been the best tenant and what not. But if you call section 8, they might take away my voucher. I can't afford no regular ass apartment."

"Hrrrm…" Mr. Nate paused for a moment as he continued to scan the abject grime cluttering the entire apartment. He then slightly turned on his feet, gawked at Fredquisha up and down, and placed his hand on her shoulder. He produced a seductive smile and licked his lips. "I can help you out if you help me out…"

Fredquisha slightly jumped at Nate's seductive touch on her shoulder. She scrunched her face up in minor disgust and surprise. "Whatchu mean help you out?"

"Come on now. Let's not pretend you don't know what I'm talkin' about…And we ain't gotta do it here. We can always get a room down at a Motel on 79th."

All of suddenly Fredquisha slapped Mr. Garrison's hand off her shoulder and balled up her fists. "NIGGA! FUCK THAT! YOU GOT ME FUCKED UP. YOU THINK I'M FINNA FUCK YOU TO STAY IN MY APARTMENT?!?!?"

Mr. Nate snickered and began to walk away back to the front door. "Bitch, I'm callin' Section 8 in the morning. I'mma serve yo nasty ass a 30-day notice tomorrow. I suggest you start lookin' for other places, you ole nasty bad-bodied yella bitch…"

"NIGGA! GET THE FUCK OUT MY PLACE, YOU 'OLE NASTY MOTHAFUCKA! FUCK YOU TALM'BOUT!"

Nate chuckled once again with his hand on the door. "St. Sabina built a brand new beautiful homeless shelter on 87th. Got some new beds in there."

"FUCK YOU!"

Mr. Nate opened the door and coolly strolled out of the

apartment without even bothering to close the door behind him.

Fredquisha lunged at the door and slammed it shut. "NIGGA GOT ME FUCKED UP!"

With her anxiety now higher than the Sears Tower, Fredquisha didn't know what the fuck she was going to do now. The afternoon was still fresh and there was a real possibility the social worker was going to show up at any minute. She couldn't go over her mother's place given she knew her sons still were probably going to be hostile towards her. "Fuck this shit, fuck it!" she said to herself as she dashed towards her coffee table. She grabbed her purse, phone, and keys and then dashed towards the front door. The jig was up. Rather than stay at home, she was just going to have to hide out somewhere and avoid the social worker if she was going to show up today. She needed to hit up one of her besties and chill out, possibly even puff on a blunt to simmer her nerves.

CHAPTER TWENTY-FIVE

$\mathcal{F}$redquisha dashed out of her front door. She speedily scampered down the hallway towards the staircase and saw Mr. Garrison making his way downstairs. Although just moments ago she cursed the shady, perverted man and refused his offer of "assistance" in exchange for some pussy (maybe even head), she was now having second thoughts. She hoped his 'offer' still stood. Deep down in her mind and core, she knew she needed to fix her situation as soon as possible and Mr. Garrison seemed to be the timely solution she needed to save face.

The fear and anxiety of suddenly having her whole entire living situation and lifestyle disrupted now compelled her to rethink Mr. Garrison's offer. Fuck trying to hide out at a bestie's crib for the time being. That was just delaying the inevitable. A social worker was going to show up regardless if Fredquisha tried to hide. And if DCFS wanted to, Evelyn warned Fredquisha that they could get a court order and enter the premises with the police at their side. Not to mention, now with Mrs. Watkins also breathing down her back, holding Myyah hostage for the time being, a bitch needed to make some strategic decisions to ensure her future.

"Wait! Mr. Garrison! Look, wait a minute. Let's talk about this," Fredquisha gasped as she tried to run up and catch up to Mr. Garrison.

The shady landlord looked up and gawked at Fredquisha. "Oh, so you changed your mind, huh?"

Fredquisha didn't say a word. She just tightened her lips and went silent, looking like an innocent little girl. She lightly nodded yes.

Mr. Garrison grinned back, "Come on then, let's go. I got some weed and Hennessy too..."

Creak. Creak...Crea-ka-ka-creaka-creek-creek...That was the rapid knocking sound produced by the headboard of the raggedy motel Fredquisha and Mr. Garrison were now fucking in.

After agreeing to give up some of her juicy crotch in exchange to get her apartment up to code, Mr. Garrison took MooMoo to the White Horse Motel on 79th and Stony Island Avenue. The White Horse was some throwback 1960's two-story motel that was notorious for being the hoe stroll in this neck of the woods.

Mr. Garrison wasn't alone in procuring him some pussy for the night. Most of the rooms in the motel were occupied with Johns pining for the best pussy the South Side of Chicago had to offer.

The motel room was dark and humid. Mr. Garrison was on top of MooMoo, digging her guts out with his old, hardened shaft (thanks to two Viagra pills). By the way the headboard was knocking up against the wall, it was quite obvious he found his spot. You know that nice, juicy nook inside the puss.

Fredquisha's pussy was gooey and tight enough to make Nate amp up his strokes. Each knock the raggedy ass motel's king-sized bed's headboard produced was rhythmic evidence as to just how good the puss was to Mr. Garrison. As for disturbing the neighbors, shit, they were probably getting it in too. No one should've been frightened by the combined sounds of Mr. Garrison's shrieks and the knocks of the headboard. I know my next door neighbor John, the middle-aged white father from Utah, is frightened right now.

"Turn around! Lemme hit it up from the back!" Mr. Garrison growled as he paused in MooMoo's twat.

"Ok…" MooMoo agreed as she got up and then turned on her knees, instantly tooting her jiggly, tatted yellow ass up in the air. Despite being completely turned off by the man, Fredquisha had her cheeks spread wide open so Mr. Garrison could get a clear glimpse of her creamy, lightly shaven pussy.

Fredquisha hoped Mr. Garrison was almost done. She just wanted whatever money and assistance he was going to offer her so she could head back home and get her shit together. Despite Mr. Garrison appearing as if he could handle her juicy ass pussy she was throwing on him, she hoped it wasn't heart attack-inducing.

Old nigga Nate bent over, sniffed her booty hole and then stuck his tongue deep in it. After a few seconds of eating her groceries, he pulled his mouth back and smelled his upper lip. Then he hawked up some spit in his palm and lathered up his dick that was surrounded by a mound of gray pubic hair.

"Ahhhhhhh, shit!" Mr. Garrison moaned, sounding like an elephant dying from thirst. Nigga had no condom on. Nate was old school; condoms were for punks. Besides, Nate figured Fredquisha was healthy given her thickness.

Fredquisha quickly looked over to the right and notice 4:56 PM blipping on the cheap off-brand alarm clock sitting on the nightstand. Nate upped his strokes from the back, and at every pound his torso made against her body, Fredquisha could feel the splash of sweat beads land on her back and ass.

Mr. Garrison sped up his strokes up even more. He threw MooMoo down, instantly collapsing her onto her stomach. His sweaty and heavy body was now completely covering her as he pumped his old dick fervently in between her legs. The creaking of the bed intensified, a sign that the landlord was probably a good fifty-one seconds away from busting a nut. "Ahhh, ahhh," Nate wailed as his breathing got even more hot and rapid. Gusts of his cognac-infused breath ventilated MooMoo's neck and parts of her face. "Ahh, ughh, ohhgh, ughhh!" Nate continued to grunt out loud.

"Come on, baby, fuck this pussy! Cum inside me!" Fredquisha fake moaned and squeezed them twat muscles even harder so this man can hurry the fuck up and get up off her.

You know, truth was, to MooMoo, if Mr. Perkins was about a good thirty years younger, she actually would've been more passionate about this fuck session. Just looking at his features, MooMoo could tell maybe in his day Mr. Garrison was probably a looker. Old nigga reminded her of an older version of a nigga she used to fuck with back in the day. If she was some old bitch looking to get her dry, ancient pussy fucked, Mr. Garrison would definitely get it. Despite the weird situation, the truth was Mr. Garrison's dick wasn't all that bad, to be honest with you. Pretty decent size. Like a good eight and a half inches, especially since that Viagra pill and three Henny's on ice is running a race in his veins. But this situation was just business; nothing more, nothing less.

As Mr. Garrison continued to pump in and out of MooMoo, his dick swelled up and got even harder. Oh yeah, bitch, that big pussy was definitely cooking up some gumbo tonight! Pussy juice was creamy and thick like roux too. Mr. Garrison's eyes turned to squints, beads of his sweat dripped down his forehead and onto MooMoo's back. The headboard pounds against the flowery wallpaper-covered wall harder and faster...

"Ahhh! AHHHH! AHHHH! I'm cumming! AHHH! AHHHHHHH!"

Ladies and gentlemen, mission accomplished! Mr. Garrison came [no pun intended] to save the day. Power of that P. Despite having some loose pussy walls, MooMoo's coochie muscles were flexin' like she was at a bodybuilding competition, destined to come in first place.

"Gahddamn! SHIYYAT!" Mr. Garrison shouted as he slowly pulled out of MooMoo's ass and rolled over to the bed.

MooMoo didn't hesitate. She needed to secure the bag quickly. "Ok, so how you gon help me..."

As Mr. Garrison tried to collect his breath, he rubbed his chest. "You use CashApp?" he asked.

"Hell yeah..."

"Good, I'm finna send you $500. And I'm gon have Glen call up this ole Mexican bitch named Maria. She got a cleanin' service out West. I'mma have her and her brothers come by tonight to help you clean that place up. I can probably get them to deal with the roach problem too. You know them damn Mexican can fix everythang..." Nate then leaned over, picked up his pants and pulled out his cell phone. "What's yo CashApp thang?"

"$BossLadyQuisha"

A bitch finally secured the gold. Not some medal around her neck though. But the help she needed to stop social services from fucking with her shit. Her iPhone 8+ buzzed. That was probably the alert telling her Mr. Garrison sent her the loot.

Fredquisha grabbed her phone off the nightstand and checked to see if she got the money. Yasss, she thought to herself. As she slowly tried to climb her naked, sweaty body out of the bed, Mr. Garrison turned over and grabbed her. "Where the hell you think you goin'?"

"I gotta get the place cleaned...The fuck???"

"Bitch, you think you gave me $500 worth of pussy?"

"Whatchu mean?!?"

"What I mean is, I ain't done yet. You ain't done either. You ain't gon be done until I say I'm done," Nate growled.

Fredquisha lowered her head. She rolled back into the bed and spread her legs, assuming Nate was gonna either stick his dick right back into her or eat her out.

"Nah, you gon come suck on these balls..." Mr. Garrison then smiled, "And then you gon eat my ass!"

"Hell nah! I don't eat no ass! NIGGA WHAT?!??!"

"You want me to take that $500 back? I'll call up the bank and dispute that shit..."

Fredquisha closed her eyes. "Fine..."

"Yeah, see, that's what I thought...Don't act like you ain't ate no ass before...Over there actin' like you got standards and shit. Bitch, you live with roaches."

CHAPTER TWENTY-SIX

TUESDAY EVENING...

"*B*aby, I told you that Deontae was always a no good nigga. But hey, my mama always told me a bought lesson is better than a taught lesson. I'm just so glad you makin' strides to get the hell up out of that apartment and do better for you and my grandchildren."

Mattie, Katina's mother, was casually chastising her daughter in her kitchen as she prepared dinner for her and her grandchildren this Tuesday evening. Spaghetti and meatballs, garden salad, garlic sticks were on the menu. Chocolate ice cream and cake were for dessert.

The two kids were quietly sitting at the dining room inside of Grandma Mattie's bungalow doing their homework. Katina was gathering her belongings in preparation for her long, twelve-hour shift tonight at the hospital.

"I know. I should've been listened to you, but I'm over him now. I'm just over men, period. I'm just gonna do me and worry about my kids for now," Katina replied to her mother's statement as she finished packing her book bag.

"Well, don't give up on men. Shit, you still gonna need a man eventually in your life, if you know what I mean," Mattie turned and smiled at Katina.

Katina knew exactly what her mother meant too by the smirk she had all over her dark brown chubby face. Shit, a vibrator can only do so much for you. Every woman eventually wants to find the right man to be with for the rest of their life. And every woman knows ain't nothing like riding good dick from a good, sexy man who had his shit together. But it seemed like that wasn't the definition of her relationship with Deontae. She didn't even know if that luck would come her way in the near future.

For now though, although she hoped eventually she'd find someone to get with in the near future and start a family, she just wanted to concentrate on her career and her kids. If the right man came her way, she'd give it thought. But being boo'd up wasn't a priority for her anymore.

After Katina finished packing her lunch bag, she made her way over to the dining room table and kissed her two kids on their foreheads. "Ya'll be good with grandma now. I don't wanna hear about no mess when I get back. Remember, this is her house, ok?"

"Girl...My grandchildren ain't gon bother me...Don't get yourself so worked up. You better head out before you're late for your shift."

"Hah, you're funny. Trust me, you don't know my kids like I do. They'll tear your house up!"

"Girl, I KNOW my grandchildren...Right, babies..."

"Yes, granny," both grandkids responded and laughed.

"Anyways, mama. I'll see you tomorrow in the AM. Let me head out before I miss my bus..."

"Girl, take my car. Don't be taking no damn bus and train."

"Mama, nah. I can't do that. Besides, what if ya'll have an emergency. I'm good. If I need to get home quickly, I'll just hail for an Uber or a Lyft."

"Alrighty…If you say so. Go on then so you won't be late!"

Katina smiled and walked over to her mother and gave her a tight hug. "I appreciate it, mama. You're a life saver."

"That's why I'm here…"

Katina quickly made her way out of the dining room and then outside to catch a bus. Despite it being around 7 PM, the sun was still in its full orange splendor, shining its tangerine radiance down onto the city. She hurriedly paced herself down the cracked sidewalk on Ada Street until she got to 83rd. There she waited for a bus to take her to the train station on 79th street.

"Yeah, girl. I just got up and left his ass after I caught his nasty ass in a bed with another bitch. Can you believe that shit? I mean, it's one thing to be fucking another bitch, but it's another to be fucking a bitch in my house while my kids are in their room sleep. Just straight disrespectful…"

Katina was chirping away on her cell phone as she got off the Downtown bus. Not distracted by the light street traffic, she sauntered towards the vast, covered non-emergency entrance of Northwestern Children's Hospital.

By now it was already nearly 9 PM, and the sun no longer glistened the city's skyscrapers. Street lights were the only luminosity present. The moon was covered in a sea of gray clouds. Tonight, the weatherman on Channel 7 said there was going to be some light showers, so the moon nor stars would be visible.

As nonchalant Katina made her way closer and closer to the entrance suddenly she felt someone grab her arm. She quickly turned around and produced a gawk on her face as if she saw the ghost of her deceased father. It was Deontae.

"So you just gonna up and leave and not come back? Come on, stop playin' mothafuckin' games and bring your ass back home!" Deontae growled, his hand still firmly gripped on Katina's.

"Bestie, lemme call you back. This crazy ass nigga showed up to my job!"

"Girl, you alright?" Vanessa, one of her home girls asked.

"Yeah, girl. Lemme call you back..."

"Yeah, get the fuck off the phone and talk to ya nigga..."

Katina quickly hung the phone up and then snatched her arm away from Deontae's grip.

The now agitated nurse and mother screwed her face up in disgust and surprise. "First of all, nigga...Why in the FUCK are you showing up at my job? Are you that fucking crazy? Second of all – what don't you get about us being over?!?!" She continued, "We are done! There is nothing more that I want from you. You can't do shit for me. You can't do shit for my kids. GOOD-BYE. I gotta get to a real job. Something you don't know nothing about."

Deontae looked around his immediate surroundings to see if anybody would notice what he was about to do next. Without hesitation, he pulled out his gloc from his back. He was wearing a black Chicago Bulls jacket to cover up the gun. "Bitch, you think I'm playing with you? You gon bring yo ass home along with my kids or I'm gonna show you how I really feel!"

Tina, almost on the verge of losing her composure, stood her ground and lightly shivered in slight fear. "Oh, so that's the shit you on? You just gon shoot me if I don't follow your commands? Deontae, I thought you were smarter than that..."

Deontae didn't say anything back. His eyes turned to slits. Glancing around once more, he quickly tucked the gun back into his back and slightly shook his head in the affirmative.

"Don't worry, bitch. This shit ain't over. You gon get yours. Do what you gotta do, but trust me, I'mma be back to get what you owe me. Bitch, I held you down when you didn't have shit and when nobody wanted yo fat black ass. But I see what it is. Don't have my kids around no other nigga either or we gon have serious problems, bitch."

Suddenly he turned on his heels and quickly ran away.

Katina closed her eyes and clutched her palpating chest. With her heart ferociously pounding, beating at a million beats per hour, she just knew Deontae was crazy enough to do something stupid. But she couldn't show his ass weakness. She knew if she did and buckled, that was it. He would forever hold her and her kids hostage.

That was the first time ever Deontae had shown that type of potentially violent and dark side to himself, but it came as no surprise to Katina. When niggas quickly realize they've lost something good, they do three things. Fight hard to get it back, let it go and move on, or stop others from having it. In this instance, Deontae was using the fear of murder to stop Katina from moving on. But it didn't work. She was gonna get hers regardless. Deontae sensed that too, which is why he quickly dipped the fuck out. At that very moment, nothing, not even the threat of death could deter a real ass bitch from doing what she had to do to get hers. That was one of the reasons why Deontae was attracted to Katina in the first place. She was gonna be on her grind no matter what situation she found herself in. Nevertheless, Deontae simply couldn't let it go 'cuz he could already sense his life was now destined to be in somewhat shambles. The strong woman who was holding him down for so long was gone.

CHAPTER TWENTY-SEVEN

*W*ednesday morning was slightly more humid than usual. The risen sun was already cooking the city. Rush hour traffic was already roaring throughout the streets. 7:25 tick-tocked on the clock inside of Mr. Garrison's Cadillac DeVille. Jodeci's "Freek'N You" blared from the car's speakers. Fredquisha was sitting in the front passenger seat, staring off into the window. She was trying her best to tune out the 90s throwback jam that Mr. Garrison was whistling to in such a horrid off tune.

With a toothpick slapped in his mouth, the pussy-addicted landlord strolled down Halsted Avenue to drop MooMoo back off at her crib. Some moments later Mr. Garrison pulled into an empty spot on the side street right in front of the entrance of the apartment building. He leaned in, turned the music down and then sat back and yawned. He looked over at MooMoo and scanned her up and down as she sat there silent. She wasn't giving him any eye contact at all.

"Damn, what's wrong wit cha? You hungry or some shit?"

"Nah, I'm good," MooMoo replied solemnly. All she wanted to do by now was run inside the apartment and take a hot bath to get Mr. Garrison's soot off her. The shower back at the Motel didn't do shit given the water couldn't get lukewarm.

"You sure. I can run you by IHOP. I love them red velvet pancakes. Especially with that butter pecan syrup. Them thangs is my shit!"

"Nah, I'm sure I'm good. I got some food in the crib."

"Eww, I know you ain't finna eat nothin' from out of that nasty ass apartment."

"Fuck you, nigga. It ain't that dirty…"

Mr. Garrison rolled his eyes and chuckled, "Bitch, you a lie."

"Man, whatever, BYE!" Suddenly Fredquisha opened the door, but before she could even get her foot out the door Nate instantly grabbed her and yanked her back into her seat. "Where the fuck you think you goin'? Bitch, you ain't dismissed until I say you can go. Remember, I helped you out. Now do you want this breakfast or not?"

"Mr. Garrison. Can I at least check up on my apartment and see if the social workers came by or some shit?"

"They ain't come by…"

"How you know?"

"'Cuz I had Glen on the lookout. He would've told me if they came. Besides he was also there helping to get your nasty ass apartment together…"

"I think you lyin'…I gotta go check up on my shit, bruh." Fredquisha then attempted to step foot outside the car again, but Nate once more aggressively pulled her back into the car.

"I ain't got no reason to lie to you. Like I said, you leave when I say you leave unless you wanna run me back my five-hunned plus what it cost to clean that nasty ass apartment up… You got the cash like that?"

MooMoo sat back in the seat, folded her arms, took a deep breath and then exhaled with her eyes closed. "Fine, man. Come on. You already know I'm under a lot of stress and shit. Why you fuckin' with me?"

"Damn! I'm tryin' to put some food in yo mouth 'cuz I know you hungry and shit. Now stop trippin'. Let's go check on this apartment and then get something to eat!"

"Just something to eat, right? Nothing else, right?"

Mr. Garrison sneered as he fiddled with the toothpick in his mouth. "Yeah. Just something to eat..."

"Promise?"

"Yeah...Promise..."

"Fine..." Fredquisha then opened the front passenger door and made her way out. Mr. Garrison followed suit.

The pair made their way inside the building and upstairs. Once they arrived at the apartment, Fredquisha pulled out her keys, inserted her apartment key into the door, unlocked it and walked through. She instantly flicked on a light switch in the living room and stood in awe. Complete awe. The apartment had been completely cleaned up from top to fucking bottom. The apartment that was once the epitome of filth and wretchedness unexpectedly looked brand spanking new. It was almost as if the apartment had been gutted out and made ready for new tenants to move in.

"GODDAMN! SHIT!" Fredquisha smiled as her devious eyes scanned the entire living room. Not a single piece of trash was found on the floor. Bursts of lavender and ocean breeze incense mixed in with potpourri occupied the entire room, instantly taking even Mr. Garrison by surprise.

Fredquisha moved deep into the apartment and then lunged into the kitchen. Not a single dish was in the sink. All the countertops were completely cleaned. Like a crazed manic, she then opened up every single drawer in the kitchen. All the utensils had been cleaned. Plates, bowls and other Tupperware were cleaned and neatly stacked. She opened the fridge. Every single piece of rotting food had been discarded except an unopened bottle of 1800 tequila.

Fredquisha couldn't believe. Guess she had to see everything in person to believe that Mr. Garrison would keep his word and make the apartment look brand new. There was no longer any doubt or anxiety in her mind that she'd pass any type of section 8 inspection or intense interview from a DCFS caseworker. All she had to do now was wait for the social worker to make his or her unannounced visit and she would be in the clear to get her boys back.

"So, how does it look? You fine with the apartment?" Mr. Garrison asked as he looked around in amazement.

"Hell yeah! Shit, them Mexicans work fast!"

"Hell yeah, they do! That's why I use them for some of my other properties I got out in the 'burbs...Speaking of which..." Mr. Garrison made his way closer to Fredquisha and lightly rubbed her shoulder. "You know, if you ever wanna move out of the ghetto, I got a few places I can show you. You can always transfer your voucher out there..."

"Really?" Fredquisha asked. She never gave much thought to leaving the South Side. Shit, this was all she knew and felt super-comfortable staying where she was at. But given that she was still trying to do her best to snag her a new man, aka, Trel, and that she was on the verge of possibly giving birth, maybe a change wouldn't hurt at all.

"But, what I gotta do to get it? 'Cuz ain't shit free...You already made that point several times last night."

Mr. Garrison chuckled. "We can work something out. Just get the damn DCFS off your back. You call up your section 8 caseworker and tell her your situation. I'll go over my current tenant roster and see what leases are ending. Sounds good?"

"I guess..."

"Ok, well...Let's go get some breakfast then," Mr. Garrison smirked.

"Ok..."

"But before we go," Mr. Garrison licked his lips and then

crawled his hand down to Fredquisha's crotch. "Let me get a quickie..."

"Mr. Nate. Come on now. You said just breakfast and that was it..."

"Yeah, well, I lied...Don't act like you don't want it. You know I beat that pussy up."

"Fine! Come on, dude. You got five minutes!"

"That's all I need!"

CHAPTER TWENTY-EIGHT

BEEP. BEEP. BEEP. BEEP.

*R*ays of sunlight peered through the window curtains of Austin's room, injecting life into his eyes. He slowly opened his eyes and yawned. Still hooked up to the EKG machine to monitor his vitals, the beeping sound still lowly blared in the backdrop. Chitchat from nurses and other patients inside the hospital could be heard from a distance. Austin looked up and saw it was 9:55 AM. Still on a morphine drip to subdue his pain, Austin was getting at least fourteen hours a sleep a day. Under any other circumstance, he would've been up by 6 AM. However with the opioid high slowly dripping through his bloodstream, he couldn't help but stay in a deep sleep since he'd been in the hospital.

The door to Austin's room opened. Nurse Tonya coolly strolled in and produced a big smile on her face. "Oh, I see you're awake now!" she exclaimed as she held a tray of breakfast in her hand.

"Yeah," Austin smirked back. Since he'd been admitted into

the hospital he was finding himself a bit attracted to the woman. "What you got for me this morning?"

"The usual – I got you some pancakes, an apple, turkey sausage, egg whites and a bowl of cheerios. You need those carbs!" Tonya laughed as she made her way closer to the bed.

Austin attempted to sit himself up but was in slight pain.

"Hold on, I got you," Tonya responded as she put the breakfast tray down on an adjacent countertop and went over to help Austin get himself propped up in the bed.

"Thanks," Austin responded and smirked. "So, you got a man?" Damn, he was bold in asking that.

Nurse Tonya jumped in a tad surprise to the question. "Damn, where did that come from?"

"Just asking...You seem like you got a good head on your shoulders. You got a good job. You're nice. Seem honest."

Tonya didn't respond, she just playfully shook her head. "Well, I did. But he's on bullshit like most of you niggas," Tonya responded.

"Damn, what's that supposed to mean? *you niggas*?"

"You know...You men. Black men always be playing games..."

"Men play games regardless of race...Don't make it a black thing."

"Yeah, well. That's all I date anyways. But enough about me. You got a girlfriend? Wife? Significant other?" Tonya made her way over to the countertop where she sat the breakfast tray. She picked it up and meandered back over to Austin and positioned the tray on top of his waist.

"Ehhh, no. Not at all. Been in here for almost two years. My last relationship was kind of crazy. I got a daughter though. Myyah. Her mother is kind of crazy and filthy. I'm trying to get custody of her..."

"Question for you...Why do you men do that?"

"Do what?"

"Blame the baby mother. Call her crazy. Filthy. Like, didn't you know that before you got into a relationship with her?"

"I mean, I wasn't paying attention like that. I was so dumb and out there. Just wanted ass if you want me to be completely honest with you. I didn't think it would ever go that far, but eventually, it did. Now we got a kid together..."

"Typical...You let the allure of sex pull you in and it blinded you to reality? That's the excuse you're gonna give me?"

"Are you judging me? I mean, I am pretty sure you've made pretty bad decisions when it came to being with people."

Tonya paused for a moment and thought about it... "Yeah, you're right. It is what it is though. Sorry if I come off judgmental."

"It's cool though. I get it."

"Anyways, let me check up on my other patients. You enjoy that breakfast and I'll be back to help you start your physical therapy today."

"Bet..."

"Oh and one thing Austin...I'm a lesbian now," Nurse Tonya casually confessed and smiled.

Austin hung his head in shock. "Really?"

"Yes, really. Talk to you later." Tonya made her way out of the room.

Austin shook his head. "Bitches becoming lesbians left and right nowadays."

Austin sat up in his bed and was perusing a course catalog from the University of Illinois-Chicago. Better known as UIC, the university was perhaps the biggest state-based public university inside the City of Chicago. It was Austin's top choice since they had one of the best construction and real estate development bachelor's programs in the Midwest.

Knock. Knock. Knock.

Austin suddenly turned his attention away from the course catalog and towards the door of his room. "Come in," he responded towards the thuds.

Dr. Sterling strolled in with a huge smile on her face. "Austin! I see you are up and at it! Getting your energy back!"

"Hey, Dr. Sterling! I didn't expect to see you!"

"I know! I just came down here to check up on and give you some good news I found out through the grapevine," Dr. Sterling said as she made her way over to Austin's bed.

"What's that?"

"Well, after what happened on Sunday the Feds have decided to commute your sentence. They're gonna let you out early."

Austin immediately screwed his face up. "Wait, what?!?"

"Yeah...You heard me right. You get out at the end of the week."

With tears damn near forming in his eyes, Austin lowered his head. "Shit, does my mom know?"

"Nope, because I wanted you to do the honors by telling her...in person..."

"Wait, is this a joke, Dr. Sterling? Please tell me you're joking!"

"No, not at all. I'll give Mrs. Watkins a call later on this evening and have her to come down tomorrow so you can tell her the good news. How does that sound?"

"That sounds great...You know Myyah is there with her now!"

"Really? How did that happen?"

"Fredquisha apparently got into some mess with child services. My mom is currently watching Myyah. I really hope this isn't a joke you're telling me, Dr. Sterling, 'cuz that means I get to go home to my baby girl!"

Dr. Sterling leaned over to Austin and pinched his arm. "You felt that?"

"Yeah…"

"Not a dream. It's very real. I'll give Mrs. Watkins soon. Enjoy the rest of your day!"

CHAPTER TWENTY-NINE

*W*ednesday afternoon. Chicago's South Side. The busy and relatively quiet 2nd floor of Illinois Department of Children and Family Services located right on 62nd and Emerald. The neighborhood: Englewood.

"Hahah! Yess, bissssh! James is a mothafuckin' trip, you hear me! That nigga is so nasty. He had his tongue all deep down my ass last night, you would've swore that nigga was looking for Waldo!"

Shirley McGill, mid-50s, a senior DCFS case manager on the cusp of retirement, made no qualms about talking about her freaky sex life with her close-knit group of co-workers. Between her, Geraldine, Theresa, and Juanita, Shirley was the only married social worker. The rest of the women were either divorced or in on-and-off relationships. Dick desperate they were, the three always huddled around Shirley during the afternoon to hear her rehash her nasty sex stories.

"Yesss girl, I want that done to me! I ain't never had my ass ate!" Geraldine roared and clapped her hands. "Ohhh, chile! I cain't even imagine! YESS GUHL! I SAID CAIN'T!" she barked sticking her tongue out. Geraldine was in her early 40s and resembled a voluptuous Anita Baker with a gap in between her two front teeth.

"Hahah! Hoe, you a trip! That's just nasty. I wouldn't dare have a nigga stick his tongue in my ass. That's doin' too much. Just give me some bomb ass head and dick and I'm good," Theresa remarked as she smacked on a Harold's wing. Fried extra hard. Doused in mild sauce. Salt and pepper. Just how Theresa liked it.

Theresa, approaching the age of fifty, was a solid four hundred pounds. Rumor had it her husband Darius left her...for another man. Her husband leaving her was one of the major reasons she spiraled into a depression and ended up developing an eating disorder. Although she was the heaviest in the group, ironically, she was the most stylish. Despite her size, when she wasn't blowing her money on fast food, she was blowing it at the MAC store, designer clothes, and shoes. Guess you can do that when you are making nearly $85,000 a year as a state-based social worker. Couldn't do that working for a private, nonprofit agency.

"Girl, that's why yo ass ain't got no man now. You too prissy. You better stop being prissy with that pussy!" Shirley jokingly spat back to her social worker-colleague smacking on the chicken wing.

Shirley was a tad voluptuous herself. Her skin tone radiated mahogany brown. Long, silky jet black hair she attributed to her "Indian" roots ran down her thick back. Despite her age, she didn't have a single strand of gray. James, her husband of over thirty years, was so madly in love with the woman, he showered her with gifts and flowers every day. And Shirley loved because every time an edible arrangement showed up to the office, she had to show off to all the women in her office. Pussy must taste like birthday cake because Shirley made it known James was eating it every night like a fat five-year-old.

Theresa rolled her eyes and produced a nasty yet nonserious scowl on her face. "Bitch, it's one thing to get my pussy ate," Theresa mumbled as she took another bite from the chicken wing and licked her mouth. "But it's another to let a man stick his tongue down in my ass. The fuck? He don't know what I ate for the day? What if I just took a big shit?"

"Girl, you overthinkin' it. I don't give a fuck what nobody says. I'm gon get my ass ate if a nigga offers it. And James offered. Shiit!" Shirley laughed. "Anyways, chile, what time is it?" she asked as she spun around in her seat and stared into her cubicle.

"Almost 2 PM…" Juanita commented as she caught a quick gaze of the time on the bottom right corner of her government-issued laptop's screen.

Shirley exhaled and rolled her eyes. She looked down at her desk and saw a mound of cases she had to work on today. Shirley knew she had to work on a few unannounced house visits today but was pussyfooting given she truly didn't care about her job anymore. A thirty year veteran with the Illinois Department of Children and Family Services, Shirley was less than a year away from retirement. With nearly four months of sick and vacation saved up in her PTO bank, she could've called off for the rest of the day. However, Charles, the director of the field office, needed her to help with some extra cases that recently came down the pipeline.

"Let's see which one of these 'outstanding' mothers I gotta go visit today," Shirley joked, sarcasm lacing her words. She picked up a manila folder and went over an intake form from the child abuse hotline. "Myyah Chennelle Watkins…mother Fredquisha Pierce…They don't live too far away from here. 63rd and Halsted…Intake scored her a 7 out of 10…Ughhh, I do not feel like dealing with these people today. Lord knows I don't!"

Shirley turned to Juanita, "Hey…Juanita. You ever heard of heffa? Fredquisha Pierce? Her mama must've been on crack when she named her this horrible ass name! She don't stay too far away from here."

"Nah, I ain't never heard that name," Juanita answered as she too fumbled through some paperwork.

Shirley fumbled through the file and went over details reported by Mrs. Watkins. "Apparently she got this girl living in filth. Grandma called in and said the girl gets hit and cursed out daily."

The senior-level social worker then powered on her laptop and click on the icon on the desktop taking her DCFS' case management software. The software was linked to a massive database that tracked all abuse hotline call-ins, prior child abuse cases that were either closed or under current investigation, as well as contemporaneous notes and documents of other social workers. Shirley typed in Fredquisha's full name in the search bar. The child abuse hotline case popped up. But that file was just a duplicate of the already printed file Shirley had in her possession. She scrolled down and saw that a section 8 program manager from Chicago Housing Authority had entered in some information in regards to Fredquisha's household. She opened the document and quickly skimmed it. Shirley learned that Fredquisha has been a section 8 voucher recipient for some years but had no prior complaints from landlords or from the housing authority. She didn't have a criminal record either. As she kept digging finally she stumbled upon a recently updated case entered into the system from the Chicago Police Department. She glanced over the police report and saw that Chicago PD had put in a request to have a social worker conduct an investigation based on the recent fight Fredquisha had with her two sons. Shirley absorbed all the details of the incident and then took notes in regards to possible questions she was going to as Fredquisha. She closed her laptop and packed her purse with her keys and cell phone. "Alright, ya'll. Lemme go do this quick check-up on this hussy. I'mma probably just head on home afterward. Give me a call if ya'll need anything."

"Alright, girl," Theresa mumbled as she slurped on a peach NeHi.

Shirley got up from her seat and slowly made her way out of the building and to her Ford Explorer in the building's parking lot. "Can't wait until I'm retired from this raggedy ass mothafucka…"

"**M**an, these bitches is just so basic! Couldn't be me! Why these hoes be postin' all this all their personal business on social media and shit?!?" Fredquisha mumbled to herself, puffing on a Newport.

Earlier while she was sitting down, wasting time, anticipating a social worker to arrive at her 'newly renovated apartment', she scrolled through her Facebook newsfeed and came across a video of some girl she went to high school with years ago. The chick was going off on Facebook live trying to expose her bestie for sleeping with her husband.

"I always knew Terrell was a lyin' ass dog anyways…"

KNOCK! KNOCK! KNOCK!

MooMoo jumped at the sound of thunderous knocks at her front door. Was that a social worker? "Coming!" she yelled, quickly changing the tone of her voice.

Earlier Fredquisha had taken a shower and put on a presentable outfit. A basic white tee. Jeans. Some flip-flops. Nothing that would make her look too "ratchet". The first impression was the best impression.

She spent most of her morning doing her best to tidy up a bit, ensuring the apartment still appeared in excellent shape. Then again, it had only been a good 24 hours since it was completely cleaned out, exterminated and revamped.

MooMoo lunged at the door, and just as she was about to open it, she quickly realized she still had the cigarette in her mouth. "Oh fuck, fuck, fuck!" she gasped as she dashed back over to her living room and put the cigarette out in an ashtray. A brand new one at that. She'd get back to the half-smoked square later. She picked up a bottle of air freshener on the coffee table, sprayed fervently all over and then threw the bottle back onto the table.

KNOCK! KNOCK!

"Sorry! Here I come!" Fredquisha barked as she literally threw herself at the door and opened it. She clutched her chest and tried to control her breathing, but her entire disposition suddenly changed once her eyes landed on the individual in front of her. It was her long-time caseworker from Chicago Housing Authority, Victoria Bivens.

"Hey...Vicky! What you doin' over here?" Fredquisha inquired in full-on surprise. She tried to act dumb but she now she assumed there was a possibility Mr. Garrison snaked her and went ahead and called Section 8 to get her kicked out. Guess it was his way of trying to cover his behind in case the State came after him and tried to then petition to get him removed from being a part of the Section 8 program.

"Nothing much, Fredquisha," Vicky nonchalantly smiled. "So, wassup with this call I got from DCFS?" the tall, slender dark-skinned housing program manager asked.

"What you mean?"

"Well, actually, can I come in?"

"Yeah, sure..."

Fredquisha opened the door more and led the caseworker in. Vicky slowly peered around the living room and then sniffed.

"Damn, it smells very nice in here! What kind of incense is that?" she asked, instantly turning her attention towards Fredquisha.

"Oh, it's some potpourri. I got it from the Dollar Store on Stony Island."

"Oh, damn, I need to get me some. Anyways, let's have a seat and talk for a second..."

"Ok, cool."

The two women strolled over to the couch. Television was blaring in the background. Fredquisha picked up the tv's remote control and turned it off. "So, wassup?" Fredquisha nervously asked as she scratched her bonnet-covered head.

"Well, I just got a call from a caseworker down at DCFS. Mrs. McGill. Actually, her and I used to work together years ago when I used to work for the State. She was on her way over here to do an unannounced visit to look into this child abuse call that came into the DCFS hotline over the weekend. Myyah's grandmother called in and said that you had been hurting the girl, abusing her and calling her names. Then, she also told me some days ago you got into a fight with your boys? What's really going on?"

Fredquisha lowered her gaze and shook her head. Suddenly she busted out in tears and began to wail. "Mrs. Watkins! Austin's mama is such a bully! She's doing everything in her power to get Myyah taking away from me! I do not be hitting that girl other than just discipline her when she act up around the house!"

"So, you haven't been hitting her or cursing her out?"

"NO!" Fredquisha sniffled and wiped her runny nose. "I mean, from time to time, I might give her a little tap on her ass, but I do not be punching her! That's my daughter. I love her! Why would I do all that?!?!"

"Ok, calm down, I get it. It looks like you're under a lot of stress..." Vicky then turned her attention deep into the apartment and looked around. "Another thing she said when she called into the abuse hotline was that the apartment was a complete disaster. But that seems to not be the case, so I can check that off my list of complaints."

"Right! See what I mean. That bitch is just fucking with me! FOR NO REASON! She just mad because Austin, Myyah's daddy, is in jail and she don't want me to have my baby! She really trying to get me all messed up!"

Fredquisha's tone became a lot more vicious and audible. Vicky was looking increasingly concerned by the aggressive body language MooMoo was projecting onto her.

"Ok, just calm down," Vicky consoled as she held hands up, palms facing Fredquisha, letting her know she need to stop and take and get a control of herself.

"Sorry, I'm just goin' through it right now. I've been trying to look for a job. Money is getting tight. My boys are getting grown and grown..."

"Yes, and about that...So you three got into a big fight?"

"Yes, unfortunately..."

"How'd that happen?"

Fredquisha paused for a moment. She couldn't dare confess and tell the woman Quimani got his damn babysitter pregnant. "I don't know. They just going through puberty. They got some anger management issues. I think it was because I threatened to take their PlayStation away."

"Ok, well. Where are they at now?"

"They with their grandma. Police told me to stay away until DCFS did an investigation or else I could into trouble."

"Ok, well...Hey, fights happen. I used to get into all the time with my mother, so I understand. Anyways, it seems as though the incident wasn't that big of a deal. And where is Myyah?"

Fredquisha once again lowered her head. "She...She never came back from her grandma's place. I let her stay with Mrs. Watkins for the weekend but Mrs. Watkins went behind my back and pulled that big ass stunt!"

"Oh...Ok. Yeah. She even called the local police station out there and had Myyah talk to a detective that works closely with child abuse cases. They can't do anything though until DCFS does an investigation and plus it's outside of their jurisdiction. They referred it over to Chicago Police Department. Really, it's all in Mrs. McGill's hands."

"Ok…" Fredquisha continued to sob.

"Just to let you know, I kind of talked Mrs. McGill from coming over here. She was literally on her way, but she started to feel a bit under the weather. So, she gave me a call to see if I could swing by and do a quick home visit and ask you some questions…She still has to do an interview though."

"Ok…"

"And by interview, I mean she's going to interview your sons and Myyah."

"How she gon do that if Myyah ain't here…"

"Well, first of all, technically if you have custody over Myyah and you haven't been found yet to do anything wrong, Myyah is supposed to be here. Has she been missing school?"

"YESS!" Fredquisha barked.

"Ok, well that's a big no-no. I'mma gonna go ahead and let Mrs. McGill know Myyah is still staying with the grandmother. Also, I'll go ahead and give the police department out where Mrs. Watkins lives a call to let them know Myyah needs to be back immediately or she could be charged with kidnapping."

"Ok, that's what I thought! I just don't understand why that lady is playing games with me!"

"Hey, look. It happens. Families get into these disputes. People make up false abuse claims to get revenge for this and that. I see it all the time. This just sounds like all one big mix-up. Anyways, let me get going so we can get Myyah back home. She might have to stay with your mother until Mrs. McGill completes her interviews and investigation. Ok?"

"Ok. I understand."

"Good. Anywho – girl – let me get going. I got a hair

appointment at 4 that I do not wanna miss! Traffic is already starting to get bad."

"Ok, thank you so much, Vicky. I promise you I ain't been hitting my kids. I love them too much."

"I hear you, lady. I understand. Anyways, let me get going. If you need anything, just give me a call. You still got my number, right?"

"Yeah."

"Ok, and on my way to my hair appointment I'll give Mrs. McGill a call and let her know what I observed. I gotta document this for CHA regulations though. It won't count against you, but we gotta just put this on our system. I'll also give the detective out in Matteson a call and let him know Mrs. Watkins needs to return Myyah ASAP."

"Ok, sounds great. Thank you so much!"

"No worries, girl! This is my job! I'm getting paid to help people!"

Vicky produced a light smile and stood up. She adjusted her outfit and made her way out the door. Fredquisha quickly locked the door, dashed over to her couch and picked up her phone. She pulled up her mother's phone number and hit dial.

Ring. Ring. Ring. Ring.

"Wassup, bitch? Social worker hoe came over yet?"

"Bitch! My case manager from Section 8 did! You know... that tall, black ass bitch Vicky with no edges?"

"Oh yeah. She nice! Don't say that about her!"

"That bitch ugly as fuck! Anyways! She stopped the social worker from coming over here. GIRL! SHE SAVED MY LIFE!"

"What you mean she stopped her?"

"Apparently the social worker lady and Vicky know each other. So she called her and asked her to do the home visit until she do an interview with Quimani, Zy'meer and Myyah! Then she gon tell me Mrs. Watkins need to return Myyah ASAP. She gon call the police too!"

"See, I told you! I don't know why that boujee bitch thought she was gonna keep my mothafuckin' granddaughter. Bitch had me fucked up."

"She said she might have to stay with you too!" Fredquisha, excited more than ever now, quickly changed her disposition. She picked up her pack of cigarette from off the coffee table, slapped a cig in her mouth and lit up as her mother continued to rant.

"Well, let me try to clean my shit up a bit before they try to come after me. You and yo children ain't gon fuck wit my program, hoe!".

"Anyways…How Quimani and Zy'meer doing?"

"Girl…Usual. Eating up all my food. Anyways, if that social worker lady finna come by to talk to them, I'mma need them to set them straight. 'Cuz the last thing you need is for their bad asses to spill ya business."

"Ok, well, tell them I said I'll do anything to make up for what I did to them. I'll take them to Universal Studios, Disney World, and shit. I'll take them to get some deep dish pizza in Downtown. Whatever…"

"Right. You better. 'Cuz you gon need them to lie their asses off. The only one I'm worried about is Myyah. How you gon get her straight?"

"Shit, I don't even know…"

"Don't worry about it. I'll take care of it when she get here later tonight."

CHAPTER THIRTY

*L*ate Wednesday afternoon. Almost evening. Suburban Matteson. The quiet, comfy Watkins Residence.

Myyah sat peacefully and rapt in front of Mrs. Watkins large flat screen television in the dimly lit living room.

"Do you wanna build a snowman? Come on, let's go and play!"

Princess Anna's soft and angelic lyrics from Disney movie "Frozen" boomed from the television's speakers. This was the first time ever Myyah had watched Frozen and she was wholly captivated. Nonetheless, despite Frozen being a cult classic for all children across the globe, nothing could dissuade Myyah from keeping The Princess And The Frog from being her all-time Disney fave.

Mrs. Watkins, still a bit nerve wrecked, strolled into the living room and smiled as she stared at her granddaughter. "Hey, baby girl! Guess what! I just got off the phone with your daddy and he has some exciting news to tell me tomorrow!"

Myyah twirled her attention briefly away from the television screen and beamed back at her granny. "What did daddy say, grandma?"

"I don't know! He said it's a surprise and he doesn't wanna tell me until tomorrow when I go visit him!"

"Oh, ok!"

Myyah without hesitation threw her attention back to the movie. She didn't want to miss a single second. With the biggest smile running from the Atlantic to the Pacific on her angelic brown face, the girl further surrendered her nubile doe eyes into the icy yet heavenly imagery of the Disney cartoon.

Sitting Indian style only a few feet away from the television, she held her head in her the palms of her hand and just kept smiling away. Despite all the relentless pain and horrid abuse she suffered at the hands of Fredquisha, nothing could still wipe this girl's incorruptibility away. Despite having to be forced to mature for her age, Myyah was still an endearing six-year-old to her core who enjoyed the simplicity of a cartoon.

So, baby girl just kept on smiling...

This was the life she'd always imagined she'd have one day. To be in the comfort of a loving home, away from the desolation and darkness of the violent ghetto and pervasive squalor her egg donor-birth canal better known as her 'mother' kept her imprisoned in.

This was if the life she'd always dreamt about during those dreadful, teary nights after a sadistic ass beating – to be around those who truly cared for her and let her be herself. Not always on guard. No paranoia or fear running through her limber body. Hopefully soon once daddy gets released from jail, her, Daddy, Granny, and Uncle Jonah could all live together in the spacious house and be a healthy, happy and wholesome family. Live, laugh and love into eternity. Was that too much too much for baby girl to ask for?

The way Myyah was so entranced with the film was refreshing for Mrs. Watkins to observe, but it was also gut-wrenching given for the grandmother. In her mind, no child should be so enthralled to the point of wanting to watch hours upon hours of television like this. The bitter reality though was that the cartoons were nothing more than animated escapism for the poor girl.

Jonah, still a bit hazy from a quick cat nap, slowly sauntered into the living room. "Hey, ya'll...What you watchin' there, princess?" Jonah let out a laugh as he asked his awe-struck niece.

"I'm watching Frozen! I ain't never seen this movie before, Uncle Jonah! It's so good!"

"Really? Every girl I know has seen this! You never saw this before?"

"Nope! Never"

Jonah quickly remembered who her mother was. His smile devolved into flatness. "Oh, well, I hope you like it. We can go out later tonight and get you some more movies if you like!"

"Ok!" Myyah chirped, not even giving Jonah eye contact. Her eyes were very much glued to the television.

Austin chuckled and moved closer to his mother. Mrs. Watkins was sitting on the couch observing baby girl. "So, any word yet from the police or DCFS?" Jonah quietly asked as he sat down.

"Nope...not yet..."

Buzz. Buzz. Buzz. Mrs. Watkins' phone vibrated in her pocket. She whipped it out and glared down at the unfamiliar 708 area code. Local to Chicago's south suburbs.

"Lemme see who this," Mrs. Watkins said as she got up from the couch and made her way deep into the kitchen. She didn't want to disturb Myyah from watching her movie.

Mrs. Watkins answered the phone, "Good evening..."

The man on the other end cleared his throat. "Hey, Mrs. Watkins? This is Detective Jackson with the Matteson Police Department. I have some updates to give you in regards to Myyah..."

"Oh, hey, good evening Detective. I wasn't expecting your

call at all! I hope it's good news." A tinge of nausea erupted from pits of Mrs. Watkins stomach.

"So, I was just informed by a case manager through Chicago Housing Authority and DCFS that you are currently keeping Myyah at your residence? Is this true?"

"Well, yes it is. I can't have that girl going back to her mother's place until I'm confident someone is going to keep her safe."

"Mrs. Watkins...." Detective Jackson exhaled. "Technically you can't do that. I am sure you are aware of this."

Mrs. Watkins closed her eyes and pursed her lips. "Yes, I know *technically* I wasn't supposed to do this, but I hadn't heard anything since the weekend in regards to my call. Why is it taking them so long for DCFS to do some sort of emergency investigation? Do they not think this is serious? Didn't you give them all the information Myyah told you?"

"Yes, I referred everything over to the Chicago Police Department. And yes, they have the case in their hands, Mrs. Watkins. DCFS is doing an investigation as we speak, but like I told you a few days ago, you have to let them do what they have to do before any serious moves are made. What you did is technically a felony and you could definitely serve jail time."

Fighting back tears, Mrs. Watkins slowly shook her head no. She couldn't fathom the sheer incompetence of the police department and DCFS, and deep down she just knew something bad, really bad, was bound to happen to Myyah.

"So, what exactly are you telling me, Detective Jackson?"

"Ma'am, what I'm telling you is that Myyah must immediately go back to her legal guardian or unfortunately I am going to have to arrest you and charge you with kidnapping and child endangerment..."

"Sir, please. This just isn't right. Can you all just not hol—"

Detective Jackson interrupted, "Mrs. Watkins. I have to be very clear with you. Myself, along with a Chicago police officer and a DCFS caseworker will be at your residence in the next thirty minutes to pick up Myyah."

"Ok..."

"Look, I'm sorry this has to happen, but this is just the law. We have to respect the process and let the investigators do their job."

"I understand..."

"Great. See you in thirty minutes."

"Ok," Mrs. Watkins then hung up her phone.

Jonah unbeknownst to Mrs. Watkins was standing off to the side listening to the exchange. "Mama...What's wrong?"

Mrs. Watkins slowly spun her head to Jonah and shone grief buried in the features of her narrow face. "Myyah has to go back. Or I'm going to get in trouble. Cops and a social worker will be here in thirty minutes to take her back to the city."

Jonah took in a deep breath and exhaled, "See, mama. I told you we should've never done this."

Mrs. Watkins got up from the seat and began to release tears of sorrow. "I know, I know. I just thought maybe perhaps something miraculous would happen. I guess not. Let me go get her bags packed."

"How are we going to tell her?" Jonah asked with a lowered gaze.

"Ughhh...I guess I'll have to tell her now."

Mrs. Watkins, nervous more than ever to deliver the devastating news, sauntered into the living room. Myyah's gaze was still glued to the television. A faint smile still present on her face.

"Hey, umm, Myyah, baby girl. Let's go upstairs right quick. Granny needs to talk to you, ok?"

"Granny, can we talk later 'cuz the movie is so good!"

"It's very important Myyah."

"Ok." Baby girl's light response was respectful. She stood up and walked over to grandma, instantly grabbing her hand.

Silent, once the duo made their way upstairs and into her 'room', Mrs. Watkins gently closed the door and escorted the girl to her bed. She sat her down and rubbed her back as she looked deep into her unassuming eyes.

This was going to be the hardest thing to tell the girl. Mrs. Watkins almost felt like she was about to reveal to the girl the death of a close relative. Grandma exhaled.

"Baby girl…I know I said you can stay here until your daddy gets out and you won't have to go back to live with Fredquisha. But unfortunately, until the police arrest her…"

Mrs. Watkins struggled with her tears. "…You're gonna have to go back home."

Myyah's mouth instantly hung open and her eyes widened in fear. "But Grandma, you said that I wouldn't have to go back to Fredquisha's place."

"I know. I'm so sorry Myyah. It's just that we have to follow the rules. I can't just take you just yet. I am going to fight to get you. You just might have to stay at Fredquisha's place until I can get you."

"But how long is that gonna take?"

Mrs. Watkins could see the sadness quickly overtake baby girl's face.

"I don't know, but I am going to pray it won't be too long. I swear to God, child, I'm gonna make sure you are safe."

"Grandma. I'll do whatever it takes to not have to go back. I can hide. I can go hide in the closet and you can say you lost me."

Mrs. Watkins let out a nervous chuckle, "Myyah, I can't hide you. I can get in trouble."

"Ok…" Myyah's eyes began to swell with an ocean of painful tears.

"Listen, baby girl. Do not cry. You're gonna make me cry. I don't want you to go either, but the policeman called me and said you have to go back to Fredquisha's place or I could go to jail. Do you want me to go to jail?"

"No..."

"Ok, well. Don't cry. You just need to be strong for Grandma. Strong for your daddy. Strong for yourself. I know this is not the news you wanna hear, but we just gotta keep praying and hoping God is going to change this situation for us. You understand?"

Myyah wiped the few tears that trickled down her face. Why was God forsaking her like this? she thought to herself.

"Here, let's get your stuff packed up..."

"Ok," baby girl replied nonchalantly. Death-like silence occupied the room that was now once again a guestroom.

"Grandma..."

"Yes, darling?"

"What will you all do if I die? I know I'm going to die if I go back."

Mrs. Watkins immediately grew terrified at hearing that question. She shivered, shocked Myyah would even bring her possible death into the equation.

"What? Why did you ask me that? Don't say that! You're not gonna die, ok?" Mrs. Watkin cried. She hugged Myyah and embraced her tightly. Although Mrs. Watkins didn't want to let the idea of Myyah's death flow through her head, it was very much a possibility if the situation of abuse was that grave.

Mrs. Watkins held the girl for a few more minutes and then let her go. She got up and began to pack up the girl's belongings. In less than fifteen minutes now the grieving grandmother expected the law to show up and do what they very much accused her of – kidnap her granddaughter and endanger her life by putting her back into the custody of Fredquisha.

A good fifteen minutes expired...

Ding-Dong. The doorbell rung, echoing all the way upstairs.

Myyah and Mrs. Watkins were still in the room, trying their best to appreciate every single, last second they had together.

Grandma's body shuddered at the sound of the sharp melodic doorbell. "That must be Detective Jackson. Come on. Let's go downstairs."

Myyah didn't say anything. Baby girl's face glowered. A pall of gloom occupied her childish facial features. She stood up from the bed and slowly trailed her grandmother downstairs. The moment the two entered the foyer, Jonah was already standing there attentive at the door. Detective Jackson, along with a Chicago Police Officer stood off to the side. A Latina-looking woman, presumably the DCFS social worker, stood idly anticipating the girl.

"Good evening, Mrs. Watkins. This is Officer Jiminewski from the Chicago Police Department and Ms. Gonzalez from DCFS."

"Evening, ma'am," the short and stubby white Chicago police officer smiled and nodded. "Good evening," Mrs. Watkins responded.

"Good evening, ma'am. Is this Ms. Myyah?" Ms. Gonzales grinned.

Bitch, who else would it be? Mrs. Watkins thought to herself just as a scowl entered her facial expression. Mrs. Watkins glanced down at Myyah and slowly rubbed her back.

"Yes, it is…" Mrs. Watkins replied.

"Myyah, they are going to take you back home, ok?" Ms. Gonzales said.

She grabbed Myyah's somewhat resistant soft hand and gently pulled her to the door.

"We will be in touch, ma'am," Ms. Gonzalez further stated, looking at Mrs. Watkins with her stern, judging eyes.

Detective Jackson walked up to Mrs. Watkins, "Is this her belongings?" he asked.

"Yes…"

"Great, I'll take those," Detective Jackson took Myyah's belongings and then regrouped with Officer Jiminewski and Ms. Gonzales, Myyah by her side.

"Everything is gonna be alright, Myyah. Don't worry. We are going to help you."

Myyah instantly screwed up her face and without hesitation, the tears fell down her face. She wailed, "GRANDMA, PLEASE NO!"

"Myyah, calm down. It's gonna be alright! I promise you, baby girl! Don't be afraid."

"NO! PLEASE!" Myyah attempted to run off, but before she could Ms. Gonzales held her back.

Mrs. Watkins clutched mouth. Tears swam down her cheeks. Jonah lowered his gaze as his own tears dropped down to the floor.

"Don't worry, Myyah. We are gonna make sure you are ok, but you have to go back to your other grandmother!" The social worker did her best to give the girl her assurance, but she didn't believe her. Her wailing intensified.

"Ok, let's go before this gets any worse," Detective Jackson demanded as he shuttled himself along with the Chicago officer, Ms. Gonzales, and Myyah out of the front door.

Mrs. Watkins and Jonah slowly trailed them and as Myyah slowly trekked away her wails became more and more distant. Officer Jiminewski opened up the back seat to his unmarked beige CPD-issued Crown Vic and put the innocent yet defiant abused girl in the backseat. Ms. Gonzales got in the front. Detective Jackson placed Myyah's belongings in the trunk.

Detective Jackson then made his way over to his black Matteson Police Department Crown Vic, hopped in the front and waited for the Chicago officer lead the way. Myyah looked out the back passenger seat of the car, continuing to cry. Her eyes wide open and reddened. Cheeks rosy. Her mouth slobbered. That was the last parting image Mrs. Watkins now had in her meek possession of her granddaughter as the two cop cars sailed off into the setting Chicago sun.

CHAPTER THIRTY-ONE

7:23 PM flashed on the CPD Crown Victoria's radio.
Partly cloudy lavender and bronze skies shone as the sun began to sink along the vast horizon, skyscrapers in the backdrop, making way for the moon. Fading orange sunlight glowed. Evening prepared to cast its shroud of darkness over the city. Perhaps the dimming sunlight gifted a window of opportunity; a small, glimmering chance of hope for poor Myyah to escape this looming, dreadful reality she was about to re-enter in Englewood. Was there a possibility somehow, some way Officer Jiminewski would suddenly turn the car around and take her back to Matteson to be with her grandmother, the girl wondered.

Myyah sat back in her seat, seatbelt locked across her tiny chest. Baby girl peered out of the tinted, guarded passenger window as the Crown Vic hit seventy-five on I-57. Her eyes weren't latched onto the constantly changing scenery. She was adrift in her own imagination, doing her best to subdue the tremoring fear growing in her abdomen. The trauma of having her emotions toyed with shut her down. Silent – she couldn't ponder on anything else other than the terror she was about to experience and how she could escape.

"So, Myyah…What do you like to do for fun?" Ms. Gonzales asked.

Myyah didn't respond. She kept gazing out the window.

Ms. Gonzales turned in her seat and scanned the motionless girl up and down.

"It's gonna be ok. We're gonna make sure you're ok."

Myyah still didn't respond.

"You want some candy? I have a Snicker's bar…" Ms. Gonzales created a nervy grin on her wide, tanned face.

"No," Myyah mumbled.

"Ok…" Ms. Gonzales turned back into her seat. No one else said anything for the remainder of the ride.

As the police car entered city limits, familiar Southside territory seeped into Myyah's eyes. She knew they weren't too far away from the apartment on 63rd street. Ten to fifteen minutes away she figured. Her breathing ticked up a bit.

The Crown Vic hit light yet steady traffic. Moments later, instead of getting off on 63rd street, the officer pulled off 71st and headed east. Myyah was now confused. Although she was six and still didn't have a solid grasp on a sense of direction, she didn't recognize the area they were trekking towards.

The city blocks now completely unfamiliar, the area wasn't ass teeming with dilapidation as her native Englewood. This area was a tad denser with storefronts, bungalows, apartment buildings and three flats. The Crown Vic came up to Bennett Avenue and made a quick right. Some apartment buildings down, the cop car stopped in the middle of the packed one-way street. The officer flicked on his police lights. No sirens blared. Flashing Chicago cop blue light bounced off the cars parked along the street. Light even bounced off the windows of the apartment buildings that lined the dark avenue.

"We're here," Officer Jiminewski said.

"Great...Myyah, this is your other grandmother's place. You have to temporarily stay here for a while, ok?"

"How long I gotta stay here?" Myyah inquired.

"It might be a for a few days. Maybe even a little bit longer. But it shouldn't be that long?"

"Well, why can't I just stay with my other grandma? This grandma don't like me..."

"What makes you say that?"

"'Cuz she just don't like me. She treat me differently than the other kids."

"Ok, well, you won't have to stay here that much longer. We are gonna see what problems are going on and if it turns out that your mother or grandmother can't keep you, there is a good chance you will go back to your other grandmother, ok?"

"Are you lying to me?"

Ms. Gonzales was caught by surprise by the stern, terse question coming from the six-year-old.

"No, I am not lying. I am telling you the truth. Don't worry, ok?"

Myyah didn't respond. Ms. Gonzales glanced over at the unfazed officer. He didn't care quite honestly. This was the end of his shift and he just wanted to make it back to his condo on the Northwest Side in time to crack a few beers and catch this Chicago White Sox documentary that was coming on ESPN at 10. "Ready?" he asked Ms. Gonzales. "Yeah," the social worker exhaled.

The officer got out followed by Ms. Gonzales. Once Myyah was helped out of the car, the officer grabbed her belongings from the trunk and the trio proceeded to make their way towards the entrance of the vast South Shore apartment building. Ms. Gonzales searched for Evelyn's apartment number on the large doorbell panel near the door. Buzzzzzz.

"HELLO?" Evelyn barked.

Ms. Gonzales leaned in a bit and spoke into the cruddy silver speaker slot. "Hey, Evelyn. This is Ms. Gonzales with DCFS. I have your granddaughter with me downstairs."

"OK!!!"

Buzzzzzzzzz. The front door opened. The trio strolled in. Myyah in front. They made their way to the fifth floor of the rank, piss and cigarette-smelling building.

Knock! Knock!

Myyah, Officer Jiminewski, and Ms. Gonzales stood idly awaiting Evelyn to open her front door. Within seconds it flew open.

"Heyyyyyyy! Wassup, Myyah!" Evelyn put on the biggest fake smile known to humanity exposing her dark, straight teeth – a sign she'd been a chain smoker all her life. Her lips purple and plump like her daughter's, Evelyn was an occasional weed smoker, but she could blow a carton of Newports away every day. Luckily for her cigs were fucking expensive in the city. She probably would've been in hospice by now, dying from lung cancer if cigs were as cheap as they were in Indiana.

Myyah didn't respond, let alone move at all to the sound of her so-called other grandmother's welcome. She just stood there, gawked at her, not even a smile could come across her face.

It was so hard for Myyah to understand she was even here, staring at this woman who was the complete antithesis to her other grandmother. Myyah barely interacted with this woman. Fredquisha barely let her mother babysit the girl. Shit, truth was Evelyn never ever offered to even volunteer. She too held some slight disdain for Austin and as a result his progeny, Myyah.

Besides that, Mrs. Watkins projected all-around positive vibes. She was fit. Endearing. Had a zestfulness to her that no one could deny.

Evelyn, on the other hand, looked like Shrek and Fredquisha had a secret love child. Shrek-quisha. This grandma was dumpy, looked like she hadn't bathed in days. Always wore some cheap Wal-Mart one-piece romper. Flip flops always were on her crusty, ashy, and pudgy feet. She was a tad lighter in complexion than her daughter, but the blackest thing on her body aside from her tobacco-stained lips were her elbows and ankles. Those muhfuckas were South Sudan black. And just like her daughter, her flabby, undefined arms were exposed to the world, revealing fading tattoos that were probably etched on by some unlicensed tattoo artist.

"WELL! Come on in! Don't be shy!"

Evelyn suddenly grabbed Myyah's wrist and pulled her into the hazy apartment.

"Where should I put these bags, ma'am?" Officer Jiminewski asked. He was averse to ambling inside the apartment.

"Hold on...DONTERIO! COME GET THESE BAGS FROM THIS OFFICER!" Grandma Evelyn growled to her youngest son, Fredquisha's youngest brother, Myyah's other uncle.

The tall, dark-skinned, dreadheaded uncle who had nothing on but a wife beater and some off-brand basketball shorts, strolled over and took the bags from the cop. "Wassup, Myyah, I ain't seent you in a minute! Damn guhl, you gettin' big as shit! What yo stupid mama been feeding you?"

Of course, Myyah didn't respond. She just tightened her lips and scanned the cluttered the apartment. It wasn't as viscerally nasty as her mother's, but it was cluttered enough to make her skin crawl and itch.

"Whatever, don't talk to me then..." Donterio threw the bags down near a kitchen counter and made his way back to his room.

Ms. Gonzales took mental notes too of just how a tad bit filthy the apartment was and wondered if this was a good idea, after all, to drop the girl off at the grandmother's apartment.

"HEY! QUIMANI AND ZY'MEER! YO SISTA IS HERE! COME OUT HERE!" Evelyn screamed at the top of her lungs. Within seconds the two bad ass brothers made their presence within the living room and laughed. "What she doin' here? Why she not at mama's house?!?" Zy'meer laughed.

Quimani playfully pushed the girl. She quickly stuck her hand out and pushed him back. "Don't touch me!"

"Girl, who you talkin' to! I'm yo older brother. You 'pose to respeck me!"

"I DON'T HAVE TO! YOU NOT FREDQUISHA AND YOU NOT MY DADDY!"

"Fuck yo daddy! He in jail! Dumb nigga!"

Evelyn gawked at the siblings and quickly intervened to dead the brewing fight. "HEY! YA'LL CUT THAT OUT! LEAVE MYYAH ALONE AND GO BACK TO YOUR ROOM! NOW!"

Zy'meer stuck his tongue out. "That's why you ain't got no room and we do!" he mocked as he and his brother took off running down the dimly lit apartment hallway.

"Sorry about that ya'll. You know these kids are something else…"

Ms. Gonzales looked a bit bothered. She glanced at Officer Jiminewski. He was unfazed. He yawned and rubbed his chest. "So, is there anything else we need to do Ms. Gonzales?" He asked. It was so evident by now to Ms. Gonzales that the uncaring cop was ready to get the fuck up out of there.

"Yeah, let me just talk to Myyah for a second…in private. If you don't mind, ok?"

"Ok…" the officer began to walk off, "I'll be downstairs wait-ing…Make it quick."

"Gotcha," Ms. Gonzales said back to the officer and then turned her attention to Myyah. "Come here, Myyah. Out in the hallway for a second."

"Why she gotta go out there?"

"Ma'am. I just need to have a word with her in private...if you don't mind, ok?"

"Ok...Fine..."

Myyah cautiously walked over to Ms. Gonzales. Evelyn's eyes turned to curious slits as she lightly tapped her right foot against the ground. "Whatever, I'mma get her straight when this Spanish bitch leaves," she whispered under her breath.

Ms. Gonzales pulled the girl away from the door and walked her some feet down to be out of sight and sound from the potentially nosey grandmother. The social worker leaned down to give the obviously nervous and concerned girl eye contact. It was her way of trying to ensure she was going be looking out for her.

"Listen to me, ok?" Ms. Gonzales looked around. "I'm gonna try to get you out of here ASAP. Hopefully, I'm gonna go talk to your other grandma and then go to court to see what we can do. We just gotta unfortunately follow the law." Ms. Gonzales tried her best to explain in such a simple way the complex reason as to why Myyah had to stay with this evidently trifling other grandmother of hers.

"Ok..." Myyah replied

"But, in the meantime, please, if anything bad happens to you. If your grandmother touches you. Hits you. Curses at you. Says mean things to you. Please, when the other social worker lady comes, you need to tell her everything. I already know you shouldn't be here, so I am gonna tell the other social worker lady what's going on, ok?"

"Ok..."

"Don't be afraid. Everything is gonna be alright. Just pray to God every night."

Myyah heard that before, and despite being six, she found herself leaning towards being an agnostic. Was God really there, listening to her pleas and cries? she wondered.

"Also, if anyone else tried to hurt you or do bad things to you, please say something. Do you know how to call 9-11?"

"Yes…"

"Ok then. Well. You're gonna go back to school tomorrow, so also let your teachers and principals know if something happens to you. But again, when the other lady comes to talk to you, tell her everything that happened to you, ok?"

"Ok…"

Ms. Gonzales smiled, leaned and hugged the girl. "Ayyy, pobrecita…" (poor child).

The social worker stood up and escorted the girl back into the living room of Evelyn's apartment. "Alright, Evelyn. I just had to have a little pep talk with Ms. Myyah here. She's all yours now."

Evelyn fake smiled. "Alrighty now! We gon have some fun while you over here!" Evelyn exclaimed.

"Yeah, have some fun Myyah…and remember what I told you."

"Ok, I will." Myyah's doe eyes widened; full fear and anxiety coming from innocent pupils shot the social worker's conscience. Fucckk, Ms. Gonzales thought to herself.

"You all have a good night!" Ms. Gonzales once again ran a nervous grin across her face and made her way out of the living room and out of the building.

Once she made back into the officer's squad car, she glanced at the unsympathetic officer. "Poor child," she exhaled and shook her head.

"Yeah, well. Can't save everybody. Anyways, let's get the hell up out of here. I am not trying to do a single extra hour of OT tonight."

The oblivious, emotionally numb officer and the heart-wrenched social worker sped off down the street and into the growing dark night.

CHAPTER THIRTY-TWO

$\mathcal{M}$yyah stood at the door, frozen. She couldn't move.

"Girl, come over here! Why you just standing there like that? Evelyn growled as she sat on the couch. She leaned her portly self towards her cluttered coffee table and snatched up her pack of cigs. She pulled out a square, slapped it in her mouth and lit it up. A rerun of Good Times lowly blared in the backdrop. From a distance, Quimani and Zy'meer could be heard playing all the way in the back in their room. Low, deep, and heavy bass rumbled from Donterio's room.

Evelyn too was a section 8 recipient. After the infamous Cabrini Green high rises were shut down back in the early 2000s, she moved to the South Shore neighborhood into a three bedroom, two bath rundown apartment. The 52-year-old grandmother was currently unemployed as well. Well, in actuality, she never held a real job in her life. For a brief moment she worked as a school security guard in her mid-30s, but that job only lasted for a good six months after she was fired for getting into an altercation with a parent. Aside from Donterio, her only son who was also the youngest, and Fredquisha, Evelyn had two other daughters. Shantasha, 29, lived all the way out in Rockford with her boyfriend. Her other daughter, Jazmine, 20, lived down in Carbondale, a college town about a good four hours south of Chicago. Jazmine was the only child of Evelyn's who seemed to be starkly different from the rest. She was currently working on her bachelor's degree in hospitality management, and after graduation, she planned on getting as far away from her family.

Myyah slowly and cautiously walked into the somewhat dark and now smoky living room. But rather than get in close proximity to her grandma, she stood off to the side near the couch and remained silent and motionless.

"Come on over here and sit down. We need to talk. I barely get a chance to see my other grandbaby...," Evelyn sneered as she took a long drag from the cigarette.

Myyah, with her hands behind her back, took small steps towards the unfamiliar woman and stood there, not even able to look the woman in her eyes. Her gaze was lowered. Her facial expression reeked of depression and frustration.

"Ahhh, girl. Don't be afraid of me. I know you been through a lot dealing with your crazy ass mama. Come on over here and let me talk to you for a second, baby...Don't be afraid of me," Evelyn smiled, blowing a steady stream of smoking from her nostrils.

Myyah sat down on an adjacent couch and held her arms as she watched the rerun of Good Times.

"So, tell me what's been going on? Your mother been putting your hands on you?"

Myyah glanced over at Evelyn and didn't respond. She kept quiet. She didn't know if this was some sort of trap question the woman was throwing at her to inevitably report back to Fredquisha what she confessed. Baby girl slowly shook her head no. She had to lie so she wouldn't dig herself deeper into another situation.

Evelyn smirked and didn't say anything. She took another puff from her cigarette and then whistled out a choo choo of smoke in another direction so the fumes wouldn't irritate the obviously scared granddaughter.

"Myyah, baby girl, I know the truth. I know what your mama been doing to you. I always told her she need to stop putting her hands on you and treating you all foul and what not. Don't be scared, baby girl. I tried to help so many times but your mama told me to back off."

Myyah was still quiet. Evelyn got up from her spot on the couch and walked over to her entertainment center. Despite living in a cruddy apartment building, Evelyn had some pretty high tech stuff adorning her living room. A massive 60-inch flatscreen TV sat off on the front wall of the living room. Two big bookshelves were on each side, both containing an array of DVDs and VHS tapes.

"You like movies? I got all types of cartoons!"

"Yeah, I do…" Myyah finally spoke.

"You know, remember that time your other grandma gave you Princess And the Frog? And then she took it away?"

Myyah's eyes widened in slight surprise. Suddenly her disposition changed a bit. "Yeah!"

Evelyn grinned and pulled out a copy of the DVD. "I had always been meaning to give you this for your birthday, but your mama told me no and that you didn't deserve it."

"For real?"

"Yeah! You wanna watch it?"

Bashful she now was, Myyah held her hands up to her face. She slowly nodded her head up and down, "Yeah," she mumbled. Her eyes reeked of meek innocence. Evelyn was playing her cards right. She knew the exact triggers to pull with the girl.

"Ok, well, before we watch the movie, did your other granny feed you?"

"We had somethin' to eat earlier. I had a peanut butter and jelly sandwich..."

"Oh, chile, you probably still hungry!"

Myyah nodded her head and her cute, bubbly eyes broadened. "Yeah."

Evelyn pulled out her phone from her back pocket and glared at the time. It was nearly 9 PM. "Well, I gotta take you to school in the morning..." She paused for a moment and then looked up at the ceiling as if she was contemplating on a hard decision. "But...I'll order you some food from Italian Fiesta. We can get a large pepperoni and sausage pizza. You like pizza?"

Myyah quickly nodded in agreement. She was becoming more and more elated at her grandmother's plans despite the fact that just moments ago she felt super-uncomfortable around the woman.

"I bet you your mama don't let you eat pizza, huh?"

"No, she doesn't. She say I'm too young to eat pizza. She let Quimani and Zy'meer eat all the food."

"Well, that ain't gonna happen in my house...You can eat all the food you wanna eat. I got some ice cream in the freezer too. All kinds. Chocolate. Strawberry. Vanilla. I can make you a sundae and we can sit up and watch the movie! I even bought you some new clothes for school and what not! I know school is almost over but I can't have my grandbaby lookin' all rough and shit out here."

Earlier that day, in preparation for Myyah's arrival, Evelyn went out and bought the girl a few outfits from Marshall's up in South Loop. Then she headed over to a Jewel-Osco not too far away from her apartment. She bought a smorgasbord of groceries to load up her fridge, freezer, and cabinets with an arrangement of desserts, snacks, chips, cereals, etc.

"Really?!?" Myyah exclaimed and smiled.

"See, there you go! I knew I could make you smile." Evelyn exhaled, "I just wish your mama wasn't so trifling. Anyways, I'm gonna pop this movie in. Make yourself comfortable. I'm gonna order this pizza too, ok?"

"Ok…"

"And don't be afraid to call me NaNa. You don't have to call me granny. Just don't call me by my first name, ok love? That's not respectful to call your elders by your first name."

"I know, it just that Fredquisha make me call her by her first name."

"Oh, I know. And that ain't right. That's your mama. I swear I don't know what I did with that no good daughter of mines…" Evelyn rolled her eyes and proceeded to dial up Italian Fiesta which was a local pizza parlor not too far away from her apartment.

As the movie began to play and Myyah made herself more and more comfortable in the apartment, she began to tune out her surroundings and get lost in her favorite animated film. Some minutes passed and once Evelyn got off the phone with the pizza restaurant, she sauntered over to the couch where Myyah was sitting and sat next to her. She looked down at her and lightly tugged her to sit closer to her. Myyah was nervous at first. It was the first time ever she'd been that closely snuggled up against the woman.

Evelyn began to run her hands through Myyah's hair and smirked, "Girl, you so beautiful. You look just like your daddy. You saw him at the dance the other night?"

"Yeah!"

"You had fun?"

"Yup…We got into a car accident and almost didn't make it, but we was still able to go."

"That's good! I'm so happy for you. You gotta have yo daddy in yo life…Anyways, so tell me, Myyah. Your mama been hitting you and calling you names?"

Myyah turned her face and gawked up at NaNa. "Yeah," she tearfully confessed.

"That's so bad. She call you names too?"

"Yes…"

"Like what kind of names?"

"Can I say them, NaNa?"

"Yeah, tell me the names…"

"She call me a hoe, bitch, slut. NaNa, what's a slut?"

"That's a bad word! She said all that to you?"

"Yes…"

"How does it make you feel? Are you scared?"

Myyah didn't respond. She just held her face. Her eyes watered. "It make me feel sad. I think sometimes she might try to kill me." Myyah began to sniffle and stutter, "I-I-I do-don't wanna die. I'm afraid to-to die…"

"Oh, poor baby! You not gonna die! Don't cry!"

Myyah by this point couldn't help it. Her face flooded with salty tears of grief and pain. Her cheeks soaked and glistened well enough to let Evelyn know just the amount of turmoil the girl had gone through living with her mother.

While the turbulent, young life experience shone through the eruption of tears running down Myyah's face, Evelyn was a tad unfazed. She knew exactly what she was doing. Psychology. Mending and twisting the girl's young, naïve mind to extract something from her necessary to advance an agenda she had all along.

"Awww, poor baby! It's gonna be alright," Evelyn consoled as she buried the girl in her chest and rubbed her back. "Shhh, shhh, shhh, come on now. I don't want you to miss the movie, ok?" Evelyn stated with softness defining her plea to the emotionally, physically and even spiritually battered girl.

"Ok-k-k," Myyah stammered, wiping her reddened watery eyes. She sniffled. Baby girl threw her gaze back onto the television. She allowed herself to get lost in the Disney fantasy, taking her mind off from the dismal, abusive reality that NaNa reminded her of on purpose.

Checkmate. Evelyn smiled as she kept consoling the girl. "Let me go get you some water, ok? Or do you want a pop? I got some scrawberry soda in the fridge. You want a can?"

"Yeah…"

"Ok, chile. Keep watching your movie. Let me go get your pop." Evelyn plopped herself up from the couch and meandered deep into her kitchen. She flicked on the light switch and walked over to the fridge. Before she opened it though, she gawked at her apartment lease renewal notice she had on the fridge's door being held up with some plumber's business card magnet. For months NaNa had been contemplating whether or not she wanted to move, but she didn't quite have the finances to go to the place she truly desired – a renovated high rise over in Hyde Park.

Some months ago Evelyn found out through her section 8 caseworker down at the Chicago Housing Authority that long-time voucher holders were going to get first dibs at moving into newly constructed mixed-income high rises popping up all over Hyde Park and parts of Bronzeville. This new building being built right off the Lake was speaking life into Evelyn. It was slated to be one of the largest luxury high rises on the South Side. In Chicago, the city council had passed a law some years ago that made it mandatory for multi-unit housing developers to offer a certain percentage of building units to low-income families who qualified for housing assistance. Evelyn was one of those who qualified. She was elated to find out that just in a few months the new luxury high-rise was slated to open and she wanted a four bedroom all to herself. The only drawback was that her current voucher would only cover up to 80% of the rent. This four bedroom apartment she wanted was $3,000, which meant she'd need to come up with an additional $600 plus the costs of utilities to afford the apartment. Right now Evelyn was paying no more than $200 for everything. However, now that she had some sort of 'temporary' custody over Myyah, deep down something was telling her she could finesse both her daughter and DCFS to make the custody permanent. If that happened Evelyn would get her claws onto Myyah's SSI and any future child support payments coming from Austin.

Although Evelyn and Fredquisha had some semblance of a "normal" mother-daughter relationship, deep down Evelyn always had some sort of weird envy of her daughter. For starters, she felt Fredquisha wasted her good looks and body on no good dope dealers who obviously didn't amount to shit. In Evelyn's mind, Fredquisha could've been someone...A prominent hairstylist. Owner of a nail salon. Maybe even a model. But she just chased dope dealer dick and got nothing in return. She just devolved into having a bad body, inconsistent under-the-table cash from her baby daddies, and a roach-infested apartment. Although Evelyn herself made somewhat of the same mistakes when it came to her choice in men when she was younger, mama always figured she'd set a good enough example for her daughters so they wouldn't go down the same road. Her two other daughters seemed to kind of get it, but not Fredquisha. MooMoo had always kind of been the rebellious one, but Evelyn never said or did anything. She just went along with the program because, at the end of the day, she had her own life to live. Nevertheless, Evelyn also thought her daughter was a tad reckless and couldn't manage her ratchetness. The fight Fredquisha had with her sons set Evelyn off even more into thinking that Fredquisha needed to get her ratchetry under control, especially now that that pregnancy bombshell was dropped on everyone. Evelyn knew it was just a matter of time before Paulette would go run her mouth and possibly create more drama for everyone. So, rather than be a bystander and possibly lose the opportunity to get her hands on Myyah, 'NaNa' now had to put in that work to make sure granddaughter was 'safe and secure'. Make sure them gubment funds were safe and secure...

Evelyn opened the fridge, grabbed two cans of strawberry soda and made her way back into the living room. Myyah was completely enraptured by the movie. "The pizza should be here in the next twenty minutes or so," Evelyn chimed in a soft voice so she wouldn't interrupt the girl's attention towards the cartoon.

"Ok, NaNa," baby girl obliviously responded.

Evelyn sneered. Cha-ching! Payday was coming.

Evelyn assumed at any moment a caseworker was going to swing by and interview Myyah, Quimani and Zy'meer. She didn't give a fuck about the two boys, truth be told. Hell, if anything she felt they needed to go stay with their fathers or their other grandmothers. The person who she was going to work hard on was Myyah. And the crazy thing was, she didn't need to coach the girl to lie. What she planned on doing was making baby girl comfortable and free enough to confess everything. EVERYTHING. And Evelyn was going to buttress up her testimony with her own. Throw her own daughter under the bus...

CHAPTER THIRTY-THREE

"*T*hat was such a cute movie! Tomorrow we can go to Wal-Mart and see if we can buy some more DVDs. You wanna do that after school tomorrow?"

"Yes, NaNa," Myyah slowly responded. Sleepiness took over her body. With the pizza, soda and ice cream swimming in her tiny stomach, she was ready to lay down and rest. Such a long, depressing day, but at least it ended on a somewhat good note for baby girl.

"Ohh, girl, you sleepy I can tell. Come on. Let's go get you situated in ya bed. You're gonna be sleeping in the room with me. I got you a little air mattress in the corner for now, but once we get situated I'mma get you a room all to yourself," Evelyn smiled as she picked the girl up from the couch and led her down the hallway.

Myyah wiped her sleepy eyes and mumbled, "Ok."

Once inside the bedroom, Evelyn helped baby girl change into some pajamas she bought for her as well. Although she had a twin-sized air mattress situated in the corner of the bed near the radiator, Evelyn made sure the air mattress was super-comfortable. NaNa even bought new blankets and some pillows for grandbaby.

Once Evelyn got the young girl into her sleep outfit, she laid her down onto the air mattress and tucked her in. Unfortunately, baby girl was too sleepy and exhausted to fully realize just the depth of the nastiness of NaNa's room. Clothes were everywhere. The room reeked of cigarettes, ass, and beer mixed in NaNa's favorite knock-off Chanel No.5 Perfume.

Like her daughter, Evelyn had a roach problem inside of her apartment, but the vermin issue wasn't as disgustingly horrid compared to Fredquisha's situation just days ago. Evelyn was a tad bit more proactive though in trying to rid the apartment of roaches. The critter problem was also another reason why she was so hell bent on trying to get out and move into a subsidized luxury unit up in Hyde Park. She knew living with white folks and boujee niggas would upgrade her living situation and roaches, rats nor mice wouldn't be a part of it either.

"Aiiight girl, you fast asleep. Time for NaNa to get some muhfuckin' z's too! Gotta wake my ass up early to drive you to that school." Evelyn meandered her way over to her bed. She slipped out of her flip-flops and picked up a bonnet cap sitting on her dresser. Once she got her hair tucked under the bonnet, she took her shirt off. Her big, hanging titties luckily were netted with a bra. She plopped herself in the bed and within seconds began to snore.

Five roach goons crawled out of the radiator next to deeply sleeping Myyah. The roach clique was on a 3 AM hunt for some food they sensed some moments ago. They were amped, ready to hit a lick so they could come up in the muhfuckin' vicious streets of pest city. One of them, the obvious leader of the gang, spotted an unknown stranger sleeping on his turf. She was a pretty, petite brown skin girl who from a million miles away smelled of spicy pepperoni grease.

Triple OG Chief of the roach gang waved his antennas in the direction of Myyah, letting his crew know they spotted their unaware, young victim. The five roaches then scurried closer to Myyah. They crawled on her limbs and slowly made their way up her torso and chest. Myyah didn't flinch at all. The roaches trekked closer and closer to her face. Once they landed on her neck, they scratched and sniffed at the pizza grease spots stained under her chin and upper neck.

Myyah continued to sleep, unaware that the roaches were literally camping out on her face and upper body. Triple OG Chief roach grew angered. This young bitch didn't have any food. He looked to his side and saw another one of his partners too was visibly upset. Four of the roaches looked at each other, giving themselves the "Fuck It" look. So, they took off, but Triple OG Chief roach was mad. This victim he assumed was holding something valuable and the lil hoe didn't have anything on her. What a waste of time and energy. So, without hesitation Triple OG Chief roach bit into the girl's left cheekbone.

"AHHH! AHHHHHH!" Suddenly Myyah woke up and scratched hard at her face. Triple OG Chief roach scampered away and off into the room's deep darkness to catch up with the rest of his team. Maybe they needed to go onto a larger excursion in the apartment and find the real source of the pizza grease – the box of leftovers still sitting on the coffee table in the living room.

"NaNa! NaNa!" Myyah stormed out of the air mattress and lunged towards the side of the bed where Evelyn was sleeping on; her snores though amplified the entire room not allowing Myyah's fearful pleas enter her ears.

"Ahhhh! NaNa!" Myyah screamed again hoping by now her amplified cry would wake the grandmother up.

Evelyn slowly opened her eyes and choked a bit on her tongue. NaNa had severe sleep apnea and truth be told should've been sleeping with her CPAP mask on her face. "What, girl?" Evelyn lowly growled, somewhat annoyed baby girl had awakened her out of her deep, dreamy sleep.

"A roach bit me on my face!" Myyah cried as she fervently wiped her cheekbone. She could feel slight stinging irritation spread across her face.

Evelyn smacked her teeth. "Girl, you just probably had a nightmare. Ain't no damn roaches gon bite you on your face." NaNa yawned and wiped slobber from the corners of her mouth. Her mouth a bit parched from the snoring and the two cigs she smoked after she got done eating her pizza and ice cream with baby girl.

Myyah knew for sure though that wasn't a nightmare. The roach bite was definitely a reality, and as she continued to scratch her face, tears welled in her eyes.

Evelyn huffed and yawned again. "Come on and get in the bed with me. I knew I should've never had you sleep by yourself anyways..." NaNa pulled back the blanket showering her plump body and invited the girl to sleep next to her.

Myyah had all-out reluctance and fear racing through her body. Baby girl stood there for a moment or two before she gave in and crawled into the bed and snuggled herself next to Evelyn. However, she kept scratching her face hoping the stinging would subside. As a few minutes passed and surely the pain dithered away. Myyah closed her eyes once more and fell asleep.

CHAPTER THIRTY-FOUR

BEEP! BEEP! BEEP! BEEP!

*E*velyn's alarm clock jolted her and Myyah out of sleep. It was 6 AM and Myyah needed to be to school in less than an hour and a half. NaNa slowly opened her eyes and yawned. She wiped the crust out of her eyes and patted her bonnet. "Damn, I ain't even get good sleep," Evelyn complained as she licked the corners of her mouth with her dry tongue.

Myyah slowly slid out of the bed and clasped her face. "NaNa, my face is still hurting! I'm telling you a roach bit me last night!" the girl sluggishly complained. Intense drowsiness bogged her body. Still feeling extremely exhausted from yesterday all she could focus now on was the insect bite on her face.

"Here, let me see what you talkin' 'bout 'cuz I just cain't believe a damn roach bit you on yo face. Girl, I grew up in the projects and lived with roaches all my life. Roaches don't bite, girl" Evelyn grabbed Myyah's face and examined it. She did see a visible red spot protruding from her cheek but figured it wasn't that much of a big deal at all.

"Well, it still itchin'?" Evelyn asked.

"Yeah, it kind of stings!" Myyah cried.

"Well, come on, let's go and put some ointment on it so it'll go away. You still gotta go to school today."

"Ok, NaNa..." Once Evelyn got out of the bed she led the still sluggish girl to the bathroom. "My stomach also hurt too, NaNa. I don't feel good..."

Evelyn turned around and looked down at baby girl. Beads of sweat began to race down Myyah's pale face. "Damn, you gotta throw up or somethin'?"

"Ye-yeah," Myyah stammered as she grabbed her stomach and leaned over a bit.

"Come on, let's go to the bathroom then so you can use the potty. You can't be throwing up on my floor and stuff."

"Ok," Myyah replied, but she grew increasingly confused. The room was spinning and she felt hazy more than ever. This wasn't just sluggishness still swamping the girl. Something else was going on.

They made it inside the bathroom inside Evelyn's room. NaNa grabbed some itch cream from her medicine cabinet and rubbed a dab into Myyah's sore cheek.

Suddenly, without hesitation, vomit erupted from Myyah's mouth, chunks landed all over Evelyn and the floor.

"GOD DAMN!" Evelyn barked as she stood back a bit and watched the girl throw up food she apparently still had marinating in the acidic pits of her tiny stomach. "Girl! You alright?"

"No...I feel sick, NaNa. Like really sick..."

"Ahhh, shit. I knew we should've never got you that pizza. Ate all that pizza and ice cream last night. That shit give me heartburn. Probably why I didn't sleep good last night either," Evelyn continued to complain. "DONTERIO! DONTERIO!"

"Whhhhhhaaaaat?!?!" Her son's voice could be faintly heard echoing from his room.

"GO GRAB ME SOME PAPERTOWELS FROM THE KITCHEN AND SOME FABULOSO! MYYAH DONE THREW UP ALL OVER THE PLACE! HURRY UP!"

Donterio's door could be heard swinging open. Evelyn sat Myyah down on the toilet and used one of her washcloths to wipe her face. By this point, Myyah was extremely dizzy and more nauseated than ever. Her hair was damp from intense sweating. Her face clammy. Her eyes sunken.

Donterio entered the room. He looked around before he noticed his mother hovering over Myyah in the bathroom. "Oh, there you are…What happened?"

"I'on know! She just started throwin' up all over the place!" Evelyn continued to examine her woozy-looking grand-daughter as she swayed side to side sitting on the toilet.

"Damn, she look fucked up. You smoked some green around her or some shit?" Donterio jokingly asked.

"Boy, shut the fuck up and get the fuck out of my room. I need to get her cleaned up and take her to school. She got tests and shit."

Donterio smacked his teeth. "Anyways, I'm finna head out. I got a job interview…"

"Good! 'Cuz you gon need a job soon so you can get the hell up outta my house wit cho sorry behind. Just like yo damn daddy. Ain't worth a damn!"

Donterio rolled his eyes and quickly departed the room.

Evelyn took the paper towel her son brought to her from the kitchen and doused it in Fabuloso. She began to wipe up the vomit from the ceramic tile floor as Myyah still sat on the toilet quiet and solemn like a Zen Buddhist monk meditating.

"Damn, girl…I can't believe you threw up all over my damn flo like this! Wheww, chile!"

Not bothering to pay attention to the gravely sick girl,

Evelyn continued to mop up the vomit into the paper towel. She worked quickly because she knew she needed to get the girl to school ASAP. There was also a real possibility that a social worker from DCFS was going to swing by later tonight to conduct an interview with Myyah. Evelyn needed Myyah to be in the best spirits, ready to spill all the mothafuckin' beans about her mother.

With her eyes barely open, Myyah continued to gaze around the bathroom. Everything was spinning faster and faster as if she was on a Six Flags roller coaster. Her breathing became shallow. Her blood pressure began a steady decline as her heart beat became slower and lighter.

Evelyn plopped herself up from the ground and threw away the vomit-riddled paper towel. She then glanced over at Myyah. "Let me give you some stomach medicine."

Myyah didn't respond. Her limp, tired body continued to sway in chaotic directions. All of sudden she lost control over her senses and blacked out. She collapsed to the floor and began to violently convulse, thick white foam erupted from her mouth.

"Myyah! MYYAH! WHAT'S WRONG?!?!?" Evelyn lunged down at the girl's tremoring body. She grabbed her and picked her up. She then barged back into her room and laid her on the bed as her tremoring ceased. Her body made one last tick, and her eyes opened. Darkness overcame the girl; a thick pall of numbing motionless covered her body.

"DONTERIO! DONTERIO! GET IN HERE!"

"WHAT?!? I GOTTA GO!" he screamed back, not realizing that now his mother's yell was more of a cry.

Donterio sauntered into the room with a scowl of annoyance on his face.

"What, mama!?!? Shit, I gotta go—"

Evelyn clasped her mouth! "Somethin' ain't' right with her! I think she had a seizure! CALL 9-11!"

"What happened!?!?" Donterio looked over at Myyah.

"I DON'T KNOW! SHE JUST FELL OFF THE DAMN TOILET AND STARTED HAVIN' A SEIZURE!"

"FUCK!" Donterio quickly whipped out his iPhone and dialed 9-11. Quimani and

Zy'meer, now awake, entered the room and gawked over to Myyah's motionless body and their frantic grandmother. "What's goin' on, grandma?" Zy'meer inquired.

"YOUR SISTER IS SICK! SHE AIN'T MOVING!"

Evelyn hovered over the girl and placed her head over the girl's chest. No heartbeat could be heard. She then ran her fingers across the girl's neck to feel a pulse. No pulse. She then Myyah wasn't breathing either.

"OH, FUCK! SHE AIN'T BREATHIN' AND HER HEART AIN'T BEATING! I THINK SHE MIGHT BE DEAD!"

"The ambulance should be here in a few minutes they said!" Donterio barked as he lunged towards Myyah to see if he could possibly help her out.

"I know CPR, mama! Move!"

"Please! Do something! HELP HER!"

Donterio began chest compressions on the girl. "Mama, open her mouth and breathe into it!"

"She still got throw up and shit in her mouth!"

"MAMA! PLEASE JUST DO IT! CPR WON'T WORK IF SHE DON'T GET OXYGEN TO HER BRAIN!"

"Fine!" Evelyn leaned over and wiped the girl's mouth with a shirt she picked up from the floor. She reluctantly placed her lips over the girl's mouth and lightly breathed in as Donterio kept pushing down on the girl's chest.

"MOVE, MAMA! YOU AIN'T DOIN' IT RIGHT!" Donterio commanded as he pushed his mother out of the way. "JUST GO CHECK DOWNSTAIRS TO SEE IF THE AMBULANCE IS HERE! QUIMANI AND ZY'MEER! GO WITH GRANDMA! NOW!"

Evelyn along with her grandsons stormed the room and made their way downstairs.

"Fuck, fuck, fuck," Donterio cried as he couldn't feel a heartbeat come back yet nor could he feel Myyah's breathing restart.

"Please, don't die on me, girl! PLEASE!"

To be continued...

CHAPTER THIRTY-FIVE

*B*uzz. Buzz. Buzz. "Ughhh, this dude just doesn't get it." Katina felt her phone buzzing in her back pocket. She already had an inkling it was Deontae once again sending her a text message from a different phone.

Since their little "encounter" earlier this week, it was obvious by the barrage of text messages he kept blasting her with that he wasn't over it. He'd be damned if Katina was just going to up and leave. This wasn't even just about the pussy. This was all about his control over her and his need for her to stabilize his lifestyle. Without her, everything around him would begin to crumble.

Katina though, strong more than ever, simply ignored his "idle" threats. But the more he persisted, the more she grew concerned that Deontae was really going to make good on his threats. What that threat would look like? Well, Katina didn't know.

But she had something for his ass though...

With their encounter coupled with the stream of threatening text messages, the first thing she was planning on doing was going down to the police station to file a temporary restraining order against him. Then she was going to go make sure her gun card was still up to date with the City of Chicago. She no longer trusted this fuck nigga since every day he was showing his true colors of desperation and insecurity. If he tried it with her on that level, she was ready to kill him if necessary.

Katina whipped out her phone, glanced down and saw the message from the blocked number…

"You betta get yo mind right before I do…" the text message read. The ICU nurse immediately deleted it and shook her head. She took a deep breath and rolled her eyes.

"Girl, you alright? You looked stressed? Margaret, another nurse in the ICU asked once she sensed Katina looked a bit shook. "Yeah, I'm cool. Just dealing with a no good ass nigga," she fake smiled and laughed. Deep down, she was a tad fearful but ready to defend herself at all cost if Deontae truly tried to put his hands on her or pull some other crazy shit. She had to. By any means necessary now was she going to defend herself and her kids. Crazy how niggas can quickly lose their cool even just after days of a breakup. Literally, days…It wasn't even a full week since Katina left her apartment she shared with the sorry ass nigga.

Katina waltzed over to Margaret. She yawned, "Girl, I'm so ready to leave. These overnights are really starting to get to me…"

"Hell, who you tellin? Shit, I just put in an application down at Mercy Medical in Aurora. I need me a regular 9-5 now. These overnights are killing my sex life and I'm gaining weight," Margarete complained.

"Hey, Katina and Margaret, go and get a room ready. We have a new patient coming in in the next hour or so!" Ophelia, the chief pediatric nurse, yelled from the central nurse's station.

From the stern and grave tone of the manager's voice, Katina and Margaret quickly killed their conversation and found the closest available room to prepare for a new patient. Once the two women prepared a bed, EKG machine and other relevant ICU room equipment, they sauntered back out of the room and prepared for the arrival of the patient.

Fifteen quick minutes transpired inside the cold and bright ICU floor...A long hospital bed escorted by two doctors and a nurse made its way down one of the corridors in the pediatric ICU unit. One of the doctors – a tall, lanky, baldheaded white man – turned his attention towards Ophelia sitting at the nurse's station and asked, "Do you all have the room set up for patient Myyah Watkins?"

"Yessir, Room 809...What are her vitals?" Ophelia asked as she got up from the nurse's station and escorted Myyah and the doctors towards the room.

"She's stable now. BP a tad low. 89/65. Heart rate around 75. She was code blue earlier, but the paramedics were able to get her heart started again. We are going to need to run some CT scans on her. Blood tests haven't come back yet."

"What happened?" Ophelia asked as they entered the room.

"Don't know. Grandmother said she may have gotten food poisoning, but the girl complained earlier about being bitten by a bug."

Ophelia screwed her face up, "What kind of bug?"

"A roach possibly..."

"Roaches bite?"

"Ehhh, apparently. But I don't know. I'm just thinking it's probably a really bad case of E. coli poisoning," the emergency room physician indicated. Guess he couldn't imagine that a bug would actually inflict this type of health disaster on the young girl, let alone something as simple as a common roach. "But I went ahead and contacted an infectious disease specialist and the chief neurologist to look into the case. Her brain activity is showing possible damage…"

"Ok," Ophelia responded. "Let me go get two of my other nurses to help out with the transition."

"Ok, perfect," the lead doctor responded.

Ophelia quickly stepped out of the room and gawked back at the nurse's station. "Hey, Katina, I'm assigning you this patient. Let's get her set up. Neurology and Infectious Disease are coming down at any moment to figure out what's going on…"

Katina got up from her seat at one of the other nurse's stations and made her way over to the room. "I can take it from here," Katina stated as she stepped deeper into the room and quickly began to help the nurse from the emergency room hook up additional equipment to Myyah to monitor her obviously frail condition.

Tina tightened her lips and shook her head. "Wow, she's such a pretty little girl…"

"Yeah, she's so adorable, hopefully, she'll be able to pull out of this one, but I don't know, things aren't looking good," the portly old white nurse murmured as she hooked up an additional breathing apparatus to Myyah's mouth.

With so many tubes running in and out of Myyah's body you would've thought she was a part of some elaborate science experiment. But this wasn't an experiment. This was a dark reality the girl succumbed to and here she was now fighting for her young life.

Once Katina observed the girl's vitals, she examined the IV bag running saline and medication into the Myyah's skinny brown arm.

"Poor little girl," Katina huffed. Despite being a mother of two, as a nurse, Katina saw so many children die over and over again the pediatric ICU. Incessant observation of seeing young children pass away made Katina very immune to the looming possibility of Myyah's death. Baby girl would just be another unfortunate victim of some tragic circumstance that cut her life too soon. Nonetheless, Katina had no time to enrapture her feelings into Myyah. Her job was to do everything in her power to make sure her vitals were stable enough for the doctors to perform their routine tests and diagnostics and then proceed with any type of medical procedure deemed necessary. But there was also the unfortunate possibility of consulting immediate family to make an end-of-life decision. Everyday ritual at the Downtown Children's hospital. Everyday ritual for Katina.

Nurse Katina made her way out of the room and back over to the nurse's station. She sat down next to Margaret and immediately began processing Myyah's intake paperwork for the next round of doctors to look at once they made their way to her room. "Ughh, this would be the way to end my day," Katina grumbled, shaking her head.

CHAPTER THIRTY-SIX

*A*nother usual Wednesday morning for Fredquisha. Not a damn thing was really on her agenda other than the anticipation and worry of having to deal with DCFS. By this point though she was so sure of herself that nothing would come of their investigation and eventually her kids would return to their "new" home. Still doing her best to keep the house as tidy as possible, Fredquisha carefully paced the apartment living room making sure her shit was still intact.

"Fuck!" Fredquisha growled once her eyes saw a roach scramble from underneath the couch. "Ughhh, I knew those muhfuckas weren't completely gone yet! I just knew it!"

MooMoo shook her head and huffed. She whipped out her phone and was just about to dial Mr. Garrison...now her somewhat sugar daddy. But just as she was about hit dial on the phone and curse the man out for getting his workers to do a piss poor job with the extermination, Fredquisha was suddenly distracted by three loud thuds on her door.

BOOM! BOOM! BOOM!

MooMoo threw her attention towards the door. She wasn't expecting any company and no one buzzed her doorbell from outside the building. Had to be either a neighbor, Glen or Mr. Garrison. And if it was Mr. Garrison she was about to give him a mouth full in regards to the roach she just saw moments ago. She stormed towards her front door and peeped out door's peephole. "Oh, fucking Deontae!"

A relieved MooMoo quickly unlocked her door. "Boy, whatchu want?!? I was gonna hit you up later tonight for some dro! You must've been reading my mind!"

Deontae nervously chuckled as he strolled right into the apartment without even allowing MooMoo to welcome him in.

"Damn, girl! This shit look different than a muhfucka! You got this place cleaned the fuck up!"

"Yeah…I gotta get a clean and shit 'cuz I got some peoples coming over later," MooMoo replied, scrunching her face up. She quickly noticed how dressed down Deontae was. Any other day Deontae would've been dressed to the nine, looking like the typically paid dope boy he claimed to be, but this morning he was looking a bit shaggy.

"So, umm, what's wrong? Wassup?" MooMoo asked.

"Man, I know this gon sound weird as shit, but I need a place to crash," Deontae explained as he sat down on the couch, edgy as shit.

MooMoo screwed her face up even more. Was this nigga really being serious right now? she wondered. "What the fuck you mean you need a place to stay?"

Deontae smacked his teeth and lowered his gaze. His body language emitted shame for what he was about to say. "Man, my baby moms Tina kicked me out. The apartment in her name and the landlord said I gotta go since my name ain't on the lease. I ain't got nowhere else to say 'cuz my mama'nem crib already packed to the brim."

"Damn, none of your homeboys can't even let you stay with them?"

"Nah, I already asked. None of they bitches wanna let me stay and shit."

"And you ain't got no cousins and what not you can stay with?"

Deontae smacked his teeth once more, "Nah, sis."

"So….." Fredquisha mumbled, tapping her foot against the floor, hands on her waist. "What you sayin' is you wanna stay with me?"

"I mean…I can't think of anyone else. Besides, I mean, I figure since we cool and all, and we kick it from time to time and shit, you know, hey," Deontae nervously grinned. Essentially what he was alluding to was the fact that since he'd already tagged the pussy several times, MooMoo shouldn't really have any qualms letting him stay.

"Boy, I got my kids livin' with me and then I got this social worker lady supposed to be comin' over my place at any moment now and shit. I don't know, Deontae. Besides, I'm kinda seein' someone right now…" She was lying about seeing someone. Trel had ghosted her ass.

"Fuck…." Deontae shook his head. "Shit, man, bro. Look, I just need like a week or two until I can get my shit together. I had to spend a night in my car and shit."

"Damn, for real? I mean…" MooMoo thought about it for a second. She could see Deontae was looking stressed the fuck out. Truth be told, Deontae, if he wasn't such a sheisty character, had a chance of being with MooMoo for the long-term. But to MooMoo, Deontae was nothing more than her source of weed, pills and occasional dick.

"Fine. A week. But you gon have to run me some cash and weed…"

Deontae hopped up from the couch and smiled. "Damn, I got you. I swear…"

Fredquisha held out and opened her right hand. She rolled

her neck and didn't say a word. But the look she gave Deontae let him instantly know he had to put down a deposit.

"Oh, you think I'm tweakin'. I got you, sis," he replied as he whipped out his wallet and handed Fredquisha a couple of twenties.

She quickly counted the money. $150. "Ok, and the weed?"

"It's downstairs in the car..."

"Ok, don't fuck with me. My head is already spinning 'cuz I ain't smoke some good ass weed in days. Anyways, I'm cleaning up my apartment. You can chill out if you want..."

"Oh, so you don't want wanna have a lil fun or some shit?" Deontae smiled, grabbing his crotch. "Boy, like I said, I'm seeing someone right now..."

"Man, ya'll ain't married!"

"And?!?! Nigga, once I'm loyal, I'm not sharing this lil pussy with nobody!"

"Lil pussy? Bihhhhh...." Deontae smacked his teeth extra hard this time.

"WHAT YOU SAY?!?!" Fredquisha rolled her neck. She gave Deontae that look that if he uttered one more smart thing she'd instantly renege on her offer to let him stay at her apartment.

"Nothin'. I'm just gonna watch a lil tv then until you get done."

"Good then. And when I'm done, then I'mma need you to run the store and get me some shit for my place. I need some candles, garbage bags, a new broom, and some Windex."

"Damn, you got me doin' shit thought like I'm yo nigga. Can a nigga at least get a taste of that pussy if I'm gon' be helpin' you out and some shit!"

"UGHHHH! Fine! One time! But later. I got real shit to do today!"

Deontae produced a wide Joker grin as he sat back down on the couch. "Ok, I'm game..."

Buzz. Buzz. Buzz. Fredquisha's phone vibrated in her back

pocket. She quickly pulled it out and glanced down at the screen. Evelyn was calling her. MooMoo swiped right and answered, "Wassup, ma?"

"Hey, Fredquisha…" Evelyn replied, sounding depressed and filled with angst.

"Damn, why you sound like that? You high or some shit?"

"Fredquisha, you need to get down to Northwestern Memorial ASAP. Myyah is in the ICU. Doctors saying she may not make it."

Fredquisha squeezed her face in shock. Maybe she misheard her mother so she had to have her repeat what she just dropped on her. "Wait, what you say? What are you talkin' about, ma?"

"MooMoo, it's serious. Just bring yo ass down here. The doctors are giving her possibly hours to live."

Fredquisha's disposition suddenly changed. The woman who was once a hardened ghetto vixen suddenly succumbed to deep grief and sorrow. "WHAT ARE YOU TALKIN' ABOUT, MA?!? WHAT HAPPENED?!?!"

"Baby, please, don't do this right now. Just get down here!"

Fredquisha didn't even bother to continue talking. She instantly hung up the phone and began to cry.

"Yo, damn, what's going on?" Deontae asked.

"Deontae, take me to Northwestern Children's Hospital! My baby is dying!"

"What!??! What you talkin' about?!?"

"PLEASE, JUST GET UP AND TAKE ME TO THE HOSPITAL!"

"Man, that's where my baby moms work at!?! You must know that bitch too! Ya'll tryin' to play games on me or some shit!?!?"

"NO! I DON'T KNOW THAT BITCH! MY MAMA JUST CALLED ME AND TOLD ME MY BABY GIRL IS IN THE HOSPITAL DYING!"

"Mannnn! What the fuck?!?" Deontae jumped from the

QUAN MILLZ

couch and kept shaking his head. He almost didn't want to believe Fredquisha. But now with tears streaming down her face and her entire body quivering he had no other choice to believe her.

"Come on, man. Let's go. What the fuck happened to her?!?"

"I don't know! My mama just called me and told me she's in the hospital and she ain't got long left to live!" With so much unexpected fretfulness and anguish overtaking Fredquisha, she almost collapsed to the floor.

Deontae lunged at his new roommate and grabbed her before she could fall. "Fuckkk! Come on, I got you, sis! Shhh, come on now. Everything is gonna be cool."

Once Fredquisha got a sense of herself again, she quickly scrambled the living room to grab her purse and keys. She, along with Deontae, then stormed the front door and made their way downstairs. Time was of the essence now. It was so crazy how suddenly Fredquisha found some sense of motherliness and concern for her only daughter. Was it front? No. Fredquisha truly was taken aback and couldn't fathom the idea of suddenly losing the girl. Then again, maybe it was the hormones from her current pregnancy kicking in, making her over-emotional.

CHAPTER THIRTY-SEVEN

*T*he moment frantic Fredquisha dashed inside the automatic double doors of Northwestern Children's hospital, she ran straight towards the receptionist's desk. "MY BABY! Myyah Watkins is in here! I NEED TO SEE HERE NOW!" MooMoo cried.

The older white woman, 'Nowalski', polish, as evident by the golden nameplate pinned to her upper right shirt, gawked at Fredquisha and immediately began to type away in her computer. "You said her name was Myyah Watkins?"

"Yes, bitch! Hurry up! MYYAH WATKINS!"

"Ma'am, you don't have to use that type of language, I am trying to help. Please help me spell her name."

"DAMN! M. Y. Y. A. H...LAST NAME WATKINS! Now hurry da fuck up!" Fredquisha once against proceeded to curse the woman who obviously was sincerely trying to help her.

The receptionist could tell just by Fredquisha's flustered body language that she was in distress and so she didn't want to further agitate her. "She's in the Intensive Care Unit. Room 809. Go to the elevators and go to the 8th floor, ma'am!"

MooMoo didn't bother to give the woman a thank you. She

just took off running towards the elevators and made her way up to the eighth floor. Once she'd arrived at the ICU, still in full-on manic mode, she quickly searched the long corridor, confused as to which direction where Myyah's room was at. She'd texted and called Evelyn earlier to let her know she was at the hospital but Evelyn wasn't responding. Perhaps NaNa had bad reception. Maybe the phone died. Maybe Myyah was already dead and Evelyn passed the fuck out. Who knows.

MooMoo, still confused and visibly angered, noticed a nurse walking towards her.

"Excuse me, I'm lookin' for my baby girl...Myyah Watkins. She in Room 809. Where is that?!?"

"Are you her mother?" The nurse was Margaret.

"YES!"

"Ok, come with me. Her grandmother is in the room with her right now talking to one of the doctors..." The two women then began to quickly make their way down the corridor and to Myyah's room. Each step Fredquisha made towards the room, her intense sorrow was matched with the heavy coldness of the ICU wing. Her body shivered and she held herself tightly, hoping she could provide some little warmth to her body. So many regrets ran through her mind. She just knew she should've been gave up custody of Myyah to Mrs. Watkins and perhaps now she wouldn't find herself into this position of having to see her only daughter laid up in the hospital bed on the cusp of death.

The moment Fredquisha entered the room and saw Myyah lying motionless with an overflowing abundance of tubes running throughout every single orifice in her body, she clung her mouth and began to weep. "Ohhhh, my baby girl. Ohhh noooo!" She walked closer to the bed and began to tremble uncontrollably.

Evelyn and Donterio were the only ones in the room with the doctor.

A short, brown tanned man, possibly Indian or Arab, saun-tered over to Fredquisha and produced a somewhat, flat smile. A smile that attempted to inject the mother with some sense of hope and consolation.

"Ma'am, I'm Dr. Swati. I'm the chief pediatric neurologist at Northwestern Hospital…"

Fredquisha didn't respond. She just looked the man up and down, her body still quivering in fear. She turned her attention back to Myyah and moved closer to her. The clashing sounds of the EKG machine mixing in with the respirator pumping oxygen into Myyah's small, frail lungs was a second-by-second beating reminder that at any moment Myyah's life would slip away. The angel of death was near…

"Is she gonna make it?!? What's wrong with her?" Fredquisha finally had the strength to ask her barrage of questions.

"Well, I am doing my best to make sure Myyah pulls through, but unfortunately things are not looking so great. We ran some blood tests. She suddenly came down with a severe case of bacterial meningitis. It's an infection of her brain. We have her on heavy rounds of antibiotics to ward off the infec-tion. We just conducted a cat scan earlier and her brain has sustained a good deal of damage."

"So, what you saying is she brain dead?"

Dr. Swati took a deep breath. "Almost…Not quite."

"So, I am so confused. Is what you doin' gonna work or not?!?"

"We don't know yet. We have her in an induced coma to see how well the therapies will work. It might take some hours to up to a day to know for sure. But it is probably best to be prepared to make final preparations…"

"NO! No! No! You gotta do somethin'! Ya'll got all of this damn equipment and shit and ya'll mean to tell me ya'll can't save my daughter?!? How did she even get the infection??!?"

Dr. Swati pursed his lips and slightly lowered his gaze. He

looked over at Evelyn. NaNa was visibly tired and upset. Couldn't even give her own daughter eye contact.

"Ma! What happened to her?!? What did you do?" Fredquisha strolled over to Evelyn and looked her up and down with a slightly annoyed and anxious gaze.

"I don't know, girl. She said last night she had got bitten by a roach on her face. I didn't believe it 'cuz how in the hell a roach gon bite her!"

"WHAT?!? You mean to tell me a muthafuckin' roach in yo apartment bit her?!?"

"That's what she said, but you and I know damn well ain't no goddamn roaches biting people like that. Bitch, we from the projects. We deal wit roaches all the time. I think she got sick at that other grandma's house! Ain't no damn roach gon give her meningitis!"

Fredquisha closed her eyes and rapidly tapped her foot against the cold ground. "This not even makin' no damn sense!"

"Uhummm," Dr. Swati cleared his throat. "Ladies, can I please ask you to lower your voice. We have other patients…"

"Fine, sorry Doctor," Evelyn apologized.

"I will be right back to do another round of checks. In the meantime, please I ask you to maintain your volume," Dr. Swati explained and then exited the room.

"Where is Quimani and Zy'meer?" Fredquisha asked.

"They downstairs with Ray'nem."

"Uncle Ray?"

"Yeah…" Evelyn coughed. "So, when you gon' call Mrs. Watkins and let her know what happened?"

"I don't know, I can't even think about that shit yet. I don't wanna call her just yet 'cuz then it's gon be all types of fuckin' bullshit and I already wanna fight that hoe!"

"Well, you better think about this, 'cuz umm, if you trying to get DCFS off your back, it's best you call her and let her know in case Myyah don't make it. Then, they gonna really take them boys away. You want that?"

"Ma, is that all you care about?!? My baby girl is sitting up here fucking dying and yo—"

"No! You ain't gon' do that to me! No, little girl!" Evelyn interrupted as she stood up from her seat. "Don't try to act like you care about the girl and what not now. I been told yo ass to let the other grandma take care of her since you always had an issue with her. Now that her ass is almost dead you suddenly wanna act like a mothafuckin' mother and shit. Bitch, you need to get real, get right and do what you gotta do to fix this shit. 'Cuz quite frankly I'm tired of mopping up yo shit!"

"You know what, Ma! Fuck you!"

"Bitch, FUCK ME?!?"

"Ay, come on, ya'll, the doctor said be quiet!" Donterio barked, quickly coming in between the two women who looked like they were on the verge of getting into an all-out physical brawl.

Katina, hearing the commotion, quickly entered the room and scanned the situation. She already knew from the faint expletives being dropped of what was going down in room 809.

"Excuse me, ya'll. I am sure the doctor already told ya'll to be quiet or else. Please lower your voice or we are going to have to ask you to leave and you won't be able to see Myyah until tomorrow!"

Crazy ain't it...Little did Fredquisha know she was being chastised by the very woman whose ex-nigga was now staying with her for the time being. Deontae was nowhere in sight. He actually took off. Told Fredquisha to give him a call once she got done and he would take her back to her crib.

The entire family didn't respond to Nurse Katina though. They just slightly nodded their head in agreement. Once Katina exited the room, Evelyn pushed her way past Fredquisha and said, "I need a cigarette."

Donterio stood his ground and then glared over at Fredquisha. "Sis, you gotta chill. It's gonna be alright. You just gotta be strong and be there for Myyah."

MooMoo just huffed, not responding. No time for the inspirational bullshit her younger brother loved spewing from time to time every time they interacted.

Younger bro, despite being as hood as they come, was always the more positive, upbeat sibling in his family. He wasn't aware of the extent of the emotional and occasional physical abuse wrought onto Myyah from his oldest sister, so he was extremely sympathetic.

"Just let me have some alone time with her, ok?" Fredquisha asked Donterio.

"Ok…" He respected her wish and quietly left the ICU room.

Fredquisha pulled a chair from the corner closer to Myyah's bed. She sat down and began to carefully observe her daughter's chest right with each pump of air going into her fragile chest. With each passing second, each passing minute, Fredquisha contemplated her next move. Evelyn was right though. Eventually, MooMoo needed to do the right thing and call Mrs. Watkins before the situation got even more grave. Reluctant, of course. But it had to be done. Fredquisha spent the next five minutes watching Myyah as the chirping of the EKG machine echoed throughout the room. From afar Fredquisha could sobs emanating from distant rooms. A child just died, and now a mother was locked into utter anguish, wailing to God to bring her baby back. That was not a state of emotion Fredquisha was prepared for at all. For the first time ever in her life, Fredquisha did something she never thought she'd do. She leaned forward, grabbed Myyah's delicate brown hand and rubbed it. She leaned down and kissed as tears fell from her eyes and onto the top of Myyah's soft hand. "Please, baby girl, don't die on me. Mommy is so sorry for everything I've done to you. If you make it, please, I promise I'll be the best mommy ever. I take back everything I've ever said to you. Every mean thing I've ever done to you." Fredquisha continued to plan kiss after kiss onto Myyah's hand.

"I'm back," Evelyn announced as she coolly and unapologetically strolled back into the room and made her way back to the other corner seat. Still no empathetic eye contact was given to her eldest. She was beyond frustrated because she felt this entire situation could've been avoided. A part of this was her fault, but also, she felt some blame should've gone to Fredquisha.

Fredquisha continued to sob holding Myyah's hand. Once she gathered herself she tucked her arm back to her side and stood up from the seat. "I'm finne go call Mrs. Watkins right now and let her know what's going on. Be right back," Fredquisha stammered and quickly jetted out of the room.

Once she made her way down the corridor and near the elevators, she whipped out her phone, pulled up Mrs. Watkins' number and hit dial.

Three rings later...

"Umm, what do you want?" Mrs. Watkins answered.

"Mrs. Watkins..." Fredquisha paused for a moment to contain herself. She was almost on the verge of tears again.

"Yesss?????" Fredquisha could hear Mrs. Watkins rolling her eyes through the phone.

"Myyah's in the hospital. It ain't lookin' too good..."

CHAPTER THIRTY-EIGHT

*M*rs. Watkins, up and energetic as usual, cheerfully strolled through the Cook County Jail visitor's parking lot. Austin had called her a day ago and told her he wanted her to come down so he could reveal a surprise to her. She didn't think much of it, just thought maybe he'd received an admissions letter in the mail from a college or university that he'd applied to.

The sun by the point in the day was manifesting its full glory, searing the back of Mrs. Watkins neck as she tried to diligently make her way through the vast parking lot. All of a sudden, she felt her phone go off inside her purse. She pulled it out and saw that Fredquisha was calling her.

Why was this bitch calling her? Grandma thought as she huffed and rolled her eyes. The phone kept ringing. She really didn't want to respond because if she did she had so much to lay onto the woman. "Fuck it, let me see what this scumbag whore wants..."

"Umm, what do you want?" Mrs. Watkins answered.

"Mrs. Watkins..."

Fredquisha then panned to silence.

"Yesss?????" Mrs. Watkins rolled her eyes through the phone as she steadily made her way closer and closer to the entrance of the jail.

"Myyah's in the hospital. It ain't lookin' too good…"

"What? Wait, what the fuck are you talking about?!? Are you bullshitting me and playing games on my phone, little ass girl?!?"

"No, Mrs. Watkins. I'm for real. Look, just come down to the hospital as soon as possible. Myyah is in the ICU at Northwestern Children's Hospital in Downtown."

Mrs. Watkins paused for a moment and seriously gave credence to what Fredquisha just mumbled. Damn, was she really serious? Mrs. Watkins could sense by the depressed and dark tone of Fredquisha's voice that something was seriously wrong with baby girl. Tears began to form in her eyes.

"Wait, Fredquisha, please, tell me you are not playing games with me…"

"Mrs. Watkins…I'm not. Myyah is in a coma. The doctors saying she got meningitis from a bug bite. I don't know what happened. The social workers dropped her off at my mama's place last night. I was at my place when my mama called me. I didn't even know what happened 'cuz I just got to the hospital myself not too long ago," Fredquisha cried.

"Ohmygod, ohmygod, Lord Jesus. Please tell me she's going to make it! Meningitis! Please, no, God, no! This is all your fault Fredquisha! ALL YOUR FUCKING FAULT"

"Mrs. Watkins, please, I ain't got time for all that right now! We need to be here for Myyah!"

"BITCH, FUCK YOU! YOU NEVER WAS THERE FOR MYYAH IN THE FIRST PLACE! BITCH, I SWEAR TO GOD WHEN I GET UP TO THAT HOSPITAL I'M GONNA FUCK YOU UP AND THAT STUPID, FAT ASS GHETTO MAMA OF YOURS! JUST WATCH, BITCH!"

"Bitch, you ain't gon do shit to me! Put your hands on me

and see I'll mop the floors with yo old ass! Lookin' like a busted ass Jada Pinkett on crack! Bitch, me and my mama will fuck you up if you try us!"

Mrs. Watkins couldn't hear anymore. Suddenly angered and ready to explode she hung up the phone and threw it back into her purse. She picked up her steps and dashed her way into the visitor's center of the massive jail complex. Once inside and checked in, she made her way straight to the hospital.

"So, take this once a day for the pain, but no more than twice a day because this is a very powerful anti-pain medication…" One of the nurses who worked inside the jail hospital was explaining to Austin instructions on how to take anti-pain meds once he was released.

Knock. Knock.

The conversation was suddenly interrupted by the loud knocks at the room door. The nurse, a plump young Latina, somewhat around Austin's age, as well as Austin himself turned their attention towards the door. Once it creaked open, Mrs. Watkins, visibly disturbed and angered, walked in and produced a nervous, somewhat fake smile. Her eyes were reddened. Her cheeks rosy.

"Hey, ma!" Austin smiled yet could immediately tell something was wrong. "What's going on? Allergies or something?"

"Excuse me, ma'am, can I talk to my son in private for a second?"

"Sure…" The nurse proceeded to walk out of the room.

"What's wrong, mama? Why you look like that?"

"Austin…" Mrs. Watkins got closer to Austin. "It's about Myyah. I just got a phone call from Fredquisha. Myyah is in the hospital and apparently things aren't looking too good."

The concerned father screwed his face up and gawked at his mother strangely. "Wait, what are you talking about, mama? Why is she in the hospital?"

"She came down with meningitis. I don't know! I just literally got the call about twenty minutes ago from that bitch! We gotta get you out of here to see what's going on!"

"Mama, please, don't do this to me. No," Austin began to weep.

"I don't know Austin what's really going on! I gotta get to the hospital as soon as possible. This shit just ain't right! I just knew something bad was gonna happen to her! I just knew it!"

Austin lowered his gaze and sobbed uncontrollably.

"Shhh, shhh, shhh, come on now, we don't know the full facts yet. I'm gonna get down there and see what's going on. What did you have to tell me though?"

"Shit, man, I was gonna say the feds letting me out early because of what happened! But now this shit! Come on, bro!"

"Ohhhh my God!" Mrs. Watkins shook her head and wept even more.

"Just go, mama. Go see what's going on."

"Ok..." Mrs. Watkins quickly gathered herself and gave her son a tight hug. She kissed him on his forehead and then proceeded to make her way out of the hospital. Once she made it to the parking lot, she called for a Lyft and went straight to the hospital.

"Good afternoon, ma'am. I'm here to see a patient by the name of Myyah Watkins."

The same receptionist, Ms. Nowalski, glanced up at Mrs. Watkins and let out a slight smile. "Is it spelled M, Y, Y, A, H?" she asked.

"Yes. Exactly. Thank you so much."

"Gotcha. Some of the other relatives were here visiting. She's in the intensive care unit. Room 809. Go to the elevators and then shoot straight up to the 8ᵗʰ floor. Enjoy the rest of your day, ma'am."

"Thank you," Mrs. Watkins responded and then swiftly made her way to the elevators and then up to the ICU.

Grandma got off the elevator and was immediately slapped with confusion as to which way she should go to get to Myyah's room. But wasn't even a full thirty seconds once Mrs. Watkins turned her head to the right and saw down a corridor Fredquisha coming out of a room. Fredquisha spotted her as well and stood her ground.

As Mrs. Watkins got closer and closer to the room, Mrs. Watkins didn't say a word. She paused, clenched her fists and looked MooMoo up and down.

"Move out of my way..." Mrs. Watkins took deep, heavy breaths – almost as if she was gearing up to go box the bitch if she dared tried to block her from entering the room.

MooMoo obliged. She simply rolled her eyes and silently moved to the side. Mrs. Watkins entered the room. Instantly taken aback by the dismal site of her granddaughter cling to her life, Grandma suddenly clasped her mouth in surprise and angst. This was all too real and raw for her, but it was almost as if it was destined to come. Mrs. Watkins' heart shattered to pieces as her eyes carefully scanned her precious granddaughter laying in deep sleep with several tubes running in and out of her small, slender body.

"Myyyah, no, baby girl, nooooooo," Mrs. Watkins sobbed as she made her way closer to the bed and began to massage Myyah's left arm. She then ran her hand across Myyah's chest, closed her eyes and tried to pray away this was not reality.

"Where's the doctor? I need to speak to the doctor!" Mrs.

Watkins announced, now ready to confront those responsible for Myyah's deteriorated condition.

"I'ono," Evelyn mumbled, still not bothering to give anyone any type of eye contact. She too was a bit still disturbed by everything. Guilt was a motherfucker. But Evelyn was more tripped up by the sudden craziness given this was now a stumbling block, big boulder really, in her plans to come up and get out of South Shore and move to that Hyde Park luxury building.

"What even happened!?!? How in the hell did she get bit?!?"

"Shit, I don't know. You tell me. You had her for the entire weekend. She only spent one night at my house."

"No, no, no, no, don't try to spin this shit on me, bitch! How dare you!"

"Then, how else she get meningitis?!? She said she got bit by a roach at my house, but ain't no damn roaches biting no damn body! She came down with that shit at your place! I had her for one night. Bought the girl pizza and ice cream. We watched movies and she was all fine until the next morning!"

"Oh, fuck no! BITCH, I see what you all got planned! This is exactly why I called DCFS on your low life ass daughter!"

"Bitch, you called DCFS on me too?!?" Fredquisha growled from behind.

Evelyn stood up from her seat and made her way close to Mrs. Watkins.

"Bitch, get out of my face unless you wanna see the other side of me."

Katina, once again hearing the commotion, stormed the room. "That's it. Everyone needs to leave NOW before I call the hospital police."

"I just got here! This isn't fair!"

"BUT YOU STARTED IT WITH US!" Evelyn yelled back, still ready to use her hands if she had to. Katina recognized Evelyn's combativeness and eyed her down. "Ma'am, I'm gonna have to ask you and your family to leave to let the other relatives have time with Myyah," Katina demanded.

"But she my damn daughter!" Fredquisha spat.

"Ma'am, please do not make this more difficult than what it needs to be…"

Fredquisha huffed, rolled her eyes and then made her way out of the door along with Evelyn and Donterio. Before Donterio made it out the door, he stopped and turned his attention towards Mrs. Watkins. "I'm sorry about everything, Mrs. Watkins. I truly am. I apologize for my family."

"BOY, BRING YO ASS OUT HERE! YOU TALKIN' TO THE OPPS AND SHIT. FUCK WRONG WITCHU?!?" Evelyn growled under her breath and yanked Donterio out of the room.

Mrs. Watkins didn't respond. Katina escorted MooMoo, Evelyn, and Donterio out of the ICU wing and to a visitor's room allowing Mrs. Watkins to have some alone time with her granddaughter. Now that there was nothing more than serenity and calm inside the room, Mrs. Watkins, still sobbing, pulled a chair close to Myyah's bed and buried her head into the bed next to the girl's side.

"Oh, baby girl, I'm so sorry. I should've hidden you. I should've listened to you and now look at you. Please do not die on me baby girl, Do not let go. I need you. Your daddy needs you the most. Please, Father God, don't do this to her. She didn't' ask for this lot in life."

Mrs. Watkins began to pray over her granddaughter. Her overflowing tears of sorrow dampened the hospital bed.

Some moments later, as Mrs. Watkins was still enraptured in her prayer, asking God to bring total healing and recovery to Myyah, Dr. Swati entered the room.

"Ma'am…"

Mrs. Watkins opened her praying eyes, turned around and looked at the doctor.

"Are you the doctor?"

"Yes..."

"Hi, I'm Mrs. Watkins...Myyah's other grandmother. Is she going to pull through?"

Dr. Swati took a deep breath and exhaled. He pursed his lips and stood solemnly.

"It's not looking too good, ma'am. She's sustained a serious brain injury from the infection. She had eighty-percent brain damage since she went into cardiac arrest. Right now she has enough function to maintain vitals, but in a situation like this, because she's so young, eventually once we pull back the respirator and the meds, more than likely she will be gone in hours unless we come up with another solution..."

"Oh, noooo, please, no. This cannot be real. Please, doctor," Mrs. Watkins lowered and shook her head. More tears raced down her cheeks.

"I'm sorry, ma'am. Is the father aware of what's going on?"

"Yes, and no...He's currently incarcerated."

"Oh...I am...sorry to hear that."

"No worries."

"Well, it's best to consult with him as soon as possible. However, after speaking with my nurses, if an end-of-life decision has to be made, I was informed that the mother, Fredquisha, is the sole guardian and will have the right to take Myyah of life support."

"Wait, what?!?"

"Yes..."

"I'm sorry. I know it's unfortunate, but it's the law."

Mrs. Watkins didn't respond. She just turned her attention away from the doctor and dug her face back into the bed. As the whooshing sound of the ventilator clashed with chirps of the EKG machine, Mrs. Watkins returned to her prayer.

"...Oh, Father God, I absolutely believe you have the power to heal. You demonstrated that on earth, and you still heal in miraculous ways today. Even when my faith is weak, you say it is enough, and my love for you is strong. And I know you already hold my heart and life in your hands. It's up to you. If I can bring you more glory through Myyah's healing, then that's what I ask for. That's what I desire. But if your answer is no, or not now, I know that your grace is sufficient for me."

CHAPTER THIRTY-NINE

1:01 AM danced on the massive electronic clock inside the stuffy Illinois DCFS office.

Something just wasn't sitting right with her.

Nausea grew in her stomach. A tension headache throbbed her temples.

Since dropping Myyah off at her other grandmother's house, Ms. Gonzales just knew she was making the wrong decision. That night after she left Myyah in the custody of a woman who she just sensed wasn't equipped to take proper care of her, Ms. Gonzales intuition kept screaming at her to do something. Do whatever was necessary to save that girl. Before it was too late…

Sitting at her desk, pondering over a mound of paperwork, Ms. Gonzales needed to work quickly to fix the situation. She didn't know how she was going to do it but it had to be done. She picked up her belongings, dashed outside, hopped in her car and sped off to Daley Elementary over in the neighboring Englewood.

M s. Gonzales took serious strides inside of the elementary school and quickly made her way straight to the front office. "Good Morning, ma'am," she announced in front of the receptionist sitting at a desk listening to the radio blaring Luther Vandross.

"Good Morning," Cassandra, the school's front office secretary and attendance clerk looked up at the social worker and produced a somewhat flat smile. "How can I help you?"

Ms. Gonzales proceeded to pull out her official Illinois DCFS badge and flashed to the tanned, voluptuous attendance clerk. "My name is Victoria Gonzales and I am a case manager with Illinois DCFS. I am trying to do an attendance check-in for a student currently enrolled at the school."

"Oh, ok. What's the name of the student?"

"Myyah Watkins..."

"Oh..." Cassandra's disposition suddenly changed. "Yeah, I just got a call from Evelyn, her grandmother. Apparently, she's in the hospital. She's really sick."

"What?!? I just saw her last night..."

"Yeah, I don't know. Apparently, she was sick earlier this week too. That's what her mother told us why she missed school. We have no idea what's going."

"Did they tell what hospital she's currently in?"

"No..."

"Damn it..." Ms. Gonzales threw her hands in the air and held her hand. "Sorry, I am currently conducting an investigation and it's important I try to track down the girl."

"I wish I could be of more service to you, but there isn't any more information I have. All I know is her grandmother called in crying, saying Myyah was terribly sick in the hospital. It sounded really serious."

"Ok, thank you so much..." Ms. Gonzales smiled. "Have a good day, ma'am." Once she ended the conversation she dashed out of the door and back to the parking lot. Once she hopped inside the car she sped off back to her office to figure out exactly where Myyah was at.

1 2:15 PM. Another day, another dollar for Ms. McGill and her bubbly DCFS case manager social worker colleagues. Among the smacking of rib tips and strawberry sodas procured from I-57 BBQ restaurant, the women were huddled in their area of the office floor, talking, joking and gossiping about the usual topics.

As usual Ms. McGill's sex life became the eventual subject of the lunch conversation. "Girl, yesss! Bitch, let me tell you what James did. He took some of that good ass Wing Stop ranch and dripped all down my coochie. Nigga slopped it all up," Shirley laughed as she wiped bbq sauce from around her greasy lips.

"Bitch, you gon get a nasty yeast infection if you keep engaging in this freaky shit. Watch and see. Yo pussy gon be out of commission for a good two months!" Theresa joked.

"Ahumm, Ms. McGill, can I talk to you for a second?"

Ms. Gonzales' stern announcement interrupted the live conversation between the gregarious black women.

"Hey, chica! What's going on?" Ms. McGill chuckled as she took a swig from her soda can.

"It's about one of the cases currently assigned to you. I was on call last night to do an emergency pick up for a child by the name of Myyah Chennelle Watkins. Sounds familiar?"

"Yeah, what's going on? I already had the mother's caseworker down at section 8 to do a home visit since that's also in their jurisdiction. I'm about to turn in a report."

"No, don't do that yet. The girl is in the hospital. I just spent the last hour or so trying to find out where she's at. I don't know what's wrong with her, but I did an attendance check-in at the school. The grandmother called in and said Myyah is gravely ill. I just called about three hospitals. I was able to track her down to Northwestern."

"Huh?!? So, wait…what made you do all of this if you had no real motive?" Ms. McGill asked, her tone suddenly becoming serious and a tad condescending.

"Because when I dropped her off last night with a police escort, the grandmother's apartment didn't look, well, it didn't look right to me."

"What are you trying to say? I mean, was it dilapidated? Roaches and rats running all over the place?"

"Ms. McGill – why didn't you do the home visit?"

"I got sick. Like I said, I had one of my girls down at Section 8 do it."

"But Ms. McGill, if you read the original report coming in from the hotline as well as the recent police report filed when the mother got into a fight with her two sons, you should've at least got someone else in our office to do a home visit. Now, this girl could be having a serious health issue because it seems like you didn't care too much…"

"Excuse me?" Ms. McGill's voice became very audible, loud enough to make the women around her turn around in her seats and mind their business. "Let me talk to you for a second in the conference room," Ms. McGill commanded.

The two women made their way inside of the conference room a few feet away. Ms. McGill slammed the door. Instantly Ms. Gonzales became shaken. "Ms. McGill, all of that isn't even necessary."

"Listen, let me tell you something. You are a rookie around here. I been doing this for thirty years. I'd be damned if you are gonna come in here and tell me how I am not doing my job. You gon respect me or else—"

"Or else what? Ms. McGill. You violated protocol. You didn't technically do the home visit. You are submitting potentially false information based on the testimony of someone not in our department, but from the city. How do we even know this case manager down at CHA even did a thorough inspection?"

Suddenly Ms. McGill got up into the younger girl's face. "You just don't get it, do you?" Ms. Gonzales didn't back down. "You think just because you some ole young white girl with a degree from the University of Chicago and shit, you can come in here and tell us black people what to do? I know my people. I know my community. Nothing happened to that girl according to the CHA caseworker. And I trust her advice. So, if you don't mind, I'm gonna go back and finish my lunch. Just mind your own damn business and work on your assigned cases. Thank you for last night, but I don't need any more of your assistance. Just drop it."

"Ms. McGill, I am going to have to go to the director about this. This isn't right. You aren't even showing the urgency to even drop what you are doing now to check up on the girl.... And for the record, I'm half black and grew up in Gary."

Ms. McGill couldn't say anything to rebut Ms. Gonzales. Hearing that her "colleague" was not only half-Black but grew up in a predominantly black Gary, Indiana was a jab at her ignorance and there was just no way she could come back. She just pushed past the young Hispanic social worker and went back to her desk.

Ms. Gonzales, however, wasn't going to back down. She was going to take things into her hands now. By any means necessary. Even if it meant she had to clash with the veteran social worker. Ms. McGill thought her clout and power inside the office was going to shut Ms. Gonzales down, but that wasn't the case. Right is right. Wrong is Wrong. DCFS wronged Myyah – otherwise possibly she wouldn't be in the position she was now in.

The young, mission-oriented social worker hurried back to her seat. She grabbed her belongings, laptop, issued cell phone and car keys. She once again made her way outside and made her way to her car. Off to Northwestern, she went in order to see about Myyah.

Ms. Gonzales strolled through the automatic double doors of the hospital and made her way straight to the receptionist's desk. "Good afternoon, ma'am. I'm here to check on a patient by the name of Myyah Watkins." Ms. Gonzales pulled out her DCFS badge and showed it to the woman. "I'm a state clinical social worker with DCFS. It's very important I see her."

Once again, the same receptionist. Ms. Nowalski glanced up at the social worker and let out a light smile. "Is it spelled M, Y, Y, A, H?"

"Yes…."

Already familiar with where Myyah was at, the receptionist didn't need to look up any of her info. "She's in the intensive care unit. Room 809. Go to the elevators and then shoot straight up to the 8th floor. Enjoy the rest of your day, ma'am."

"Thank you," Ms. Gonzales politely responded and then promptly made her way to the elevators and then up to the ICU. She got off the elevator, and like so many before her, was immediately slapped with confusion as to which way she should go to get to Myyah's room.

No one was around to ask for directions. The social worker just made a right and proceeded down the bright, cold, and quiet corridor of the ICU wing. She approached the nurse's station. "Good afternoon, ma'am. My name is Victoria Gonzales. I'm a state clinical social worker with the Illinois Department of Children and Family Services. I'm here to check up on a patient by the name of Myyah Watkins?"

Katina, sitting idly at the nurse's station going through

some paperwork, gawked up at the social worker. Returning a light smile, she got up and walked over to Ms. Gonzales. "Come with me, she's in room 809. Her grandmother is in there."

"Which one?"

"I believe she's the paternal grandmother."

Butterflies instantly formed in the hungry pits of Ms. Gonzales' stomach. "Oh, ok." Fuck, she thought to herself. This wasn't going to be a good look. How was she going to be able to look this woman in her face – the woman who should've rightfully cared for the girl all along – and tell her she essentially along with her agency fucked up big time.

Katina and Ms. Gonzales made their way towards the room.

Knock. Knock. Two light taps Katina gave the frame of the door to grab Mrs. Watkins' attention. Still disconcerted, Mrs. Watkins turned in her seat. Her sobbing face instantly grew into one of anger. "What are you doing here?"

Ms. Gonzales couldn't hold back though. Her eyes instantly watered and she clasped her face. Katina looked at the two women and then quietly took off.

"I'm so sorry, Mrs. Watkins. I...I was just doing my job."

"Well, look at what your job did."

"What happened to her? What's going on?"

"Meningitis...She's on life support. Most of her brain is damaged from her heart-stopping, the doctor said. They are hoping she might recover, but it ain't looking good."

"How in the hell did she get it?!? She was just fine when I dropped her off..."

"I don't know. Her other grandmother said she got bit by a roach. But they wanna blame it on me and say she got it from somewhere else."

"I'm, I'mmm, soo-ssorry, Mrs. Watkins," Ms. Gonzales wept as she wiped tears from her face. Although in her tenure she's seen some pretty nasty situations, this one was incredibly heartbreaking. Heartbreaking because she felt one-hundred percent responsible for all of this.

Mrs. Watkins though wasn't feeling the empathy or sympathy. Truth be told, she just wanted to continue to be alone with the girl and continue her prayer. No interruptions. She needed God to show up now.

Ms. Gonzales just stood there, now quiet, yet visibly disturbed seeing all of the tubes running in and out of Myyah's limp, motionless body.

"Mrs. Watkins..."

"What?" Grandma rudely responded.

"I don't know about you, but I believe in prayer...Can I pray for her?"

Mrs. Watkins turned in her seat once more, but this time with widened, watery eyes. Hearing those words made her give in. "Yes, if you want to. We can pray together. The more the better..."

"Ok..." Ms. Gonzales made her way closer kneeled down next to Mrs. Watkins. Grandma extended her left hand. Ms. Gonzales grabbed it. Both women then closed their eyes, and the social worker, this time needed to be proactive. It was her time to go to God and plead for his divine intervention.

"Lord Jesus, thank you for your continued mercy and blessings and showering your love on this precious, innocent girl named Myyah. I know that you hate what their illness is doing to them I ask, in the name of Jesus, that you would heal this disease, that you would have compassion and bring healing from all sickness. Your word says that when we call out to you the Eternal one you will give the order, heal and rescue us from certain death. In the Bible, I have read of miraculous healing and I believe that you still heal the same way today. I believe that there is no illness you cannot heal after all the bible tells of you raising people from the dead so I ask for your healing in this situation. I also know from my experience of life on earth that not everyone is healed if that happens here than keep my heart soft towards you, help me, help us, to understand your plan. Lord Jesus, thank you that our hope for healing is in you. If there are doctors or treatments that you would want to use to heal this disease I pray that you would guide the doctors to them. I ask for wisdom and discernment about which treatments to pursue. God, I thank you that Myyah belongs to you and that you are in control of everything that happens from our first breath to our last sigh. Amen."

CHAPTER FORTY

BEEP...BEEP...BEEP...BEEP...

*W*hoosh. *Whoosh. Whoosh.*
The sustaining sounds of Myyah's tiny heart beating, still clinging to life. Air continued to pump into her lungs through the life support machine.

It was around 3 PM and Mrs. Watkins was still in the room, closely snuggled against Myyah. Still in a deep prayerful, quiet trance, Ms. Watkins was just assured Myyah would be delivered from this tribulation. This was just a test of everyone's faith she wholeheartedly believed. With her faith unwavering Mrs. Watkins just knew once Myyah came out of this situation she was going to fight hard more than ever to get custody of her.

Knock. Knock. Katina was standing at the door.

"Mrs. Watkins...Dr. Swati and his team need to do some tests on Myyah. Can you please go to the visitor's area? When he is done, I will come get you and you can spend more time with Myyah," the nurse politely and calmly instructed.

"Ok," Mrs. Watkins responded as she got up from her seat.

She leaned over and planted a delicate kiss on top of Myyah's forehead and then rubbed the top of her hand. "I love you, baby girl. Pull through for me. Pull through for your daddy. He loves and misses you."

Grandma then exited the room. Following Katina's instructions, she made her way to the visitor's area. The room was somewhat crowded. And from the aura, Mrs. Watkins knew most of the people in the waiting area were Fredquisha and Evelyn's relatives. Evelyn glanced up at Mrs. Watkins, huffed and rolled her eyes. MooMoo willfully ignored her.

Grandma Watkins felt a tad uncomfortable being in the visitor's area, so she decided to head to another visitor's area so she can have real solace to herself. Besides, she also wanted to go ahead and see if she could get in touch with someone down at the jail and figure out a way to inform Austin about the state of his only daughter. Despite Austin being on the cusp of getting released and still being in the hospital, inmates could only make phone calls from approved personnel phones or from heavily monitor collect phones. Mrs. Watkins hopped on the elevator and made her way to the seventh floor. She found the visitor's area, sat in the corner and pulled out her cell phone. She immediately pulled up Dr. Sterling's contact info and dialed her number.

K nock. Knock. Knock.
Austin, reeling in slight pain, was anxiously awaiting any information he could get about his daughter. His mind was heavy. Soul in turmoil. The three thuds at the door temporarily took his mind away. "Come in," Austin barked.

Dr. Sterling walked with a serious look on her face. Her cell phone was glued in her hand. "Hey, Austin. I have your mother on the line. She has some information about Myyah..."

"Ok," Austin responded. Grief beginning to overtake the tone of his voice.

The jail-based social worker sauntered next to the bed and handed Austin the phone. "Hey, mama. What's the good news?" Austin nervously grinned.

"Austin...." Mrs. Watkins then let out a sigh. "I'm praying. I'm praying hard. However, things aren't looking good. I spoke to the doctor and Myyah did come down with a bad case of meningitis. She sustained some pretty serious brain damage and now she's on life support."

"What? No, please, mama. Please, no. This can't be real. Please tell me this can't be real." Long tears began to drizzle from the skies of his white eyes now turning red.

"Yes, Austin. This is real, unfortunately. But we gotta keep on praying and believing this is just a test."

Austin took the phone away from his ear for a second and clutched his mouth. His face tightened as more tears streamed down his dark brown chiseled face. Sobs poured from his mouth. Dr. Sterling, doing her best to console Austin, massaged his shoulder. Austin placed the phone back to his ear. "I'm gonna keep praying, mama."

"Do that, son. Do that. I'm gonna go back up in a few and see what the doctors said. They are performing some more tests on her."

"Ok. I love you, mama."

"I love you too, son. Myyah loves you too. Just know that. She loves you."

Austin didn't respond. He couldn't take it anymore. He handed the phone back to Dr. Sterling and immediately began to weep. His tears were plentiful and his aching sobs filled the room.

Dr. Sterling leaned over and hugged Austin. She rocked him back and forth and did her best to console him.

"Why? Why?!? Why did this have to happen to her, God?!? She didn't deserve this shit, bro!"

"Shh, shhh, everything happens for a reason, Austin. You have to believe that."

"Dr. Sterling, I gotta see her before it's too late. Is there a way I can see her?"

"Ughh, I don't know. Usually, it has to be extenuating circumstances. I'll see what I can do. I'll talk to some people right now and see what can be done."

"Ok," Austin mumbled.

"Stay strong, Austin. Myyah needs you when she pulls out of this. I'm going to be praying for you all as well. Let me go and see what can be done, ok?"

"Ok..."

Dr. Sterling exited the room and gently closed the door on her way out. Austin just knew deep in his heart his baby girl wasn't going to make it. He couldn't shake the feeling despite wanting to be positive. But something just told him all along something like this was bound to happen to Myyah. He just knew it, which was why he tried so hard before he got locked up to get his baby girl out of Fredquisha's custody. If Myyah pulled through though, he was going to war. He was going to get his baby girl at any cost.

CHAPTER FORTY-ONE

"*H*ey, Patricia. Can you go grab the mother and grandmothers of Myyah?" Dr. Swati announced towards the nurse's station as he coolly and sternly strolled out of Myyah's room.

"Yessir. I'll go get them now," the young blonde nurse responded as she stood up from her seat at the nurse's station and began her journey to the visitor's area to go grab Fredquisha and Evelyn.

Katina's overtime shift ended and she made her way back home so she can go straight to the police station and file the protective order against Deontae.

Once the young, slender blonde nurse made her way into the visitor's area, she gawped at Fredquisha and Evelyn. A few cousins, siblings and other relatives were in the visitor's area with Evelyn and MooMoo.

"Hey, you guys. Dr. Swati would like to speak to the mother and grandmothers of Myyah," Patricia announced.

"Ok," Evelyn mumbled as both she and Fredquisha stood up from their seats.

"Where's the other grandmother?" Patricia asked.

"I don't know. She left," MooMoo spat. A tad rude she was.

"Ok..."

The white nurse led Evelyn and Fredquisha down the corridor and into Myyah's room. Dr. Swati was in the room along with another doctor – a medium, dark-skinned man with a shiny bald head.

"Good evening, ladies..."

"Evenin'," Evelyn mumbled and cleared her throat. She had a cigarette earlier and her mouth was a bit dry.

"Well, this is my colleague, Dr. Obasanjo. We've done some more tests on Myyah and unfortunately, her brain has gone through some more decline. I believe it is the right thing to begin terminating life support. With the type of brain damage, she's sustained she may not fully recover. It appears that Myyah is in an extreme vegetative state and at this point, only a miracle will reverse everything..."

MooMoo began to choke up and lowered her head. Evelyn grabbed her and held her. "Shh, shh, don't cry, baby girl. Don't cry."

"I'm so sorry about this. Have you all be in contact with the biological father?" Dr. Swati inquired.

"No...He's in jail."

"Where is the other grandmother?"

"I don't know where she at..."

"Patricia, can you please go locate the other grandmother."

"Ok, sir..." Patrice quickly exited the room to go locate Mrs. Watkins.

Dr. Swati gently approached the two grieving women. He held tightly to a thick clipboard in his hand. Dr. Obasanjo came to his side. "We have a counselor on site to help you all plan for this decision. We will still be monitoring Myyah's condition closely. I will perform another final test in a few hours and then I will let you know what your next decision should be..."

"Ok," Fredquisha moaned as she wiped her damp face free of tears.

"Come on, let's go and talk about out this in private," Evelyn muttered.

"No worries...Dr. Obasanjo and I will leave you all to have privacy. I will consult with the other grandmother to let her know what's going on. I believe it is important to allow the biological father to also see his daughter before a final decision is made. Although you are the legal guardian, I would not recommend removal of the ventilation system until all relatives have had their chance to say goodbye."

"I understand," Fredquisha mumbled.

"Ok. I will leave you two in peace now. Once again, I'm so sorry that there isn't more we can do at this time..."

Dr. Swati and Dr. Obasanjo made their way out of the room leaving Fredquisha and Evelyn in solace with baby girl.

Evelyn waited for a few moments until she felt she had the quiet and privacy to say what she was about to say. The shady grandmother looked around and got into close proximity to her daughter. "So what you gon do?" she asked in a serious, demanding manner.

"What you mean what I'm gon do?"

"About Myyah...Are you gonna let them pull the plug?"

"I mean, that's what they saying we should do...I mean, what else we gonna do?"

Evelyn shut her eyes and shook it. Damn, was her daughter this fucking stupid, she thought to herself. "You not thinkin' long term. Fuck these doctors. What the fuck that short ass Indian man know? We need to get a second opinion. Besides, I don't believe in just lettin' people die like that. Damn doctors did yo granddaddy the same fuckin' way. Told mama to just pull the plug. Nah, fuck that. We need to get her to a different hospital to get a second opinion..."

"Mama, what?!? You talkin' crazy. Why would the doctors

just be makin' shit up like this? Besides, I just need to let Myyah go. Let her go on in peace. It just wasn't meant for me to have her."

Evelyn rolled her eyes and exhaled. "Look, I know you stress the fuck out right now, but again, you not thinkin' long-term. While we was in the visitor's area I was doin' some research on my phone. There was this girl out in San Francisco who had somethin' similar happen to her. They got her transferred to a rehab facility. We can still collect her government assistance and everything and what not..."

"Bitch, is that what you thinkin' about right now? A motha-fuckin' check?!?"

Evelyn paused. Couldn't say anything. She didn't think he'd get that type of visceral reaction from MooMoo. Thought she would've been somewhat game at least.

"Hey, look bitch, I'm just tryin' to look out for you..."

"Ma, just leave me alone. Go back to the visitor's area..."

Evelyn rolled her eyes again and huffed. "Ok, fine. But just remember, this is all your fault."

"Fuck you bitch..." MooMoo shoved her mother out of the way and made her way close to Myyah's bed. She had enough of her mother for the day.

Evelyn's eyes turned to vengeful slits as she made her way out of the room. She might lose Myyah, but those boys...They were hers now. She was going to do everything in her power to get them taken away from Fredquisha now that she saw her daughter was definitely not down for the program.

MooMoo sat next to the bed and held Myyah's hand.

"I'm sorry, baby girl. I'm sorry...God, please, I'm so sorry..."

CHAPTER FORTY-TWO

WEDNESDAY NIGHT

*S*tarry Chicago skies glistened over the vast Cook County Jail Complex. A few clouds filled the dark expanse, setting the gloomy tone.

Knock! Knock!

Two loud thuds pounced on Austin's hospital room door.

"Come in," Austin lowly mumbled. Dr. Sterling walked in with one of the jail guards.

"Hey, Dr. Sterling. What's going on?"

"Your mother is here to take you to go see Myyah. We talked to the Feds. They are going to grant you an earlier release given Myyah's condition. Get your belongings ready. I also have a bag of clothes you can change out of," Dr. Sterling said as she walked into the room and put the bag of clothes next to Austin's bed. "We'll be waiting outside…"

"Did you get any updates?"

"I am not too sure," Dr. Sterling responded. A neutral face projected her uncertainty although moments ago she did learn from Mrs. Watkins that Myyah's condition was deteriorating quickly. She didn't want to relay that information to Austin given she felt like it wasn't her place to do that and rightfully so.

"Ok..." Despite his side being in pain, Austin attempted his best to get up from the bed. He was wearing a long hospital-issued gown. Slippers covered his semi-ashy feet. Dr. Sterling left the room to give Austin some privacy.

As he opened up the bag filled with a change of clothes his anxiety ran high. A myriad of emotions began to crowd out his mind. Although he was still holding onto the belief that everything inevitably was going to be alright with Myyah, deep down his intuition kept informing him otherwise. He just sensed something was wrong. Terribly wrong. It was a dark feeling he simply couldn't shake. He knew his baby girl despite not really being able to be around her for the last two years.

Once Austin got changed, he made his way out of the room with his belongings in his hand. Dr. Sterling and the same jail guard then escorted Austin out of the hospital. Before he left he signed release paperwork, officially freeing him from the confines of the jail. While a part of him was elated to be finally free after two long, arduous years of being locked up, a part of him – his heart – was still imprisoned to unrelenting darkness. The whole purpose of his freedom was to renew his life. Renew his commitment to stop running in the streets and do better for not just his sake, but for Myyah's sake. It was a dream he visualized every day – but now it seemed as though the dream was slowly fading away.

The night's darkness grew in pitch. Austin, along with Dr. Sterling and the jail guard made their way out of the Cook County Jail complex and approached a black Honda Accord. A Lyft ride Mrs. Watkins ordered to get here. Grandma was waiting idly and solemn. As she looked off from a distance and saw Austin make his way closer and closer to her in the relatively empty visitor's parking lot, her arms wrapped around her frame doing her best to keep herself warm from the cold, night-time vicious Lake Michigan winds cutting through the air. A smile crept on her face, but it wasn't a smile of joy. It was a smile to help mask her deep apprehension.

"Hey, mama," Austin smiled. His eyes became watery as he lowered his gaze and went in to give her a hug.

"Austin…" Mrs. Watkins exhaled and closed her eyes.

"How is she doing? Is she any better?"

Mrs. Watkins pulled herself away from Austin and looked him his eyes. "No…"

Austin shut his eyes as he tried his best to contain his urge to bawl.

"So…What's happening now?"

"Fredquisha is discussing ending life support for Myyah. They haven't made a decision yet until you get a chance to see her."

Austin didn't respond.

Dr. Sterling, observing and hearing everything Mrs. Watkins just said, strode over Austin and placed her delicate hand on his shoulders. "Austin, I'm so sorry about everything. Don't stop believing in miracles though. Be encouraged. I have to get going. Austin, don't let this deter you from making the best of your life, ok?"

"Thank you, Dr. Sterling. Thank you for everything. I appreciate it."

"You're welcome…You all have a goodnight." Dr. Sterling grinned and went in to give Austin a hug, hopefully injecting him with the hope he needed to go through this trying time. Once she released herself from the hug she spun on her feet and coolly walked off with the jail guard to her side.

"Come on, let's get to the hospital as soon as possible," Mrs. Watkins muttered. The two of them hopped into the backseat and took off to make it as quickly to Northwestern Children's Hospital.

The elevator doors opened. Austin and Mrs. Watkins walked onto ICU floor and slowly made their way to Myyah's room. With each step Austin took, his stomach tightened and he almost became dizzy. Everything around him suddenly slowed down.

The moment they entered the room, the vibe and energy of everyone inside immediately shifted. Fredquisha was sitting down next to Myyah. Evelyn was sitting off in the corner with this scowl covering her face. Donterio was leaning up against the window.

"Well, well, well, look who it is...Thought you wasn't getting out for a few more months," Evelyn arrogantly spat.

Fredquisha turned around. Her face went from one of grief to one of annoyance. She said, "Hey," and then turned her attention back to Myyah.

"Oh my god! My baby girl...No, no, no, no, no, no! Please God, this is all just a dream...Please!" Austin cried as he strolled over to the bed. Niagra water falls tell down his dark brown cheeks. Can I have some alone time with her?" Austin politely asked, still weeping. He didn't have the time or the mental capacity to get into it with any of these trifling bitches. All his mind could think of was spending as much time he could with the girl. Seeing all of those tubes run in and out of her body was tearing him to shreds.

"Come on, mama. Let's give the man some space," Donterio said.

"Nah, I ain't goin' nowhere. Shut cho ass up," she barked at Donterio. She then looked at Austin and said, "This my granddaughter and you need to be even thankful we even let you in the room!"

"You know what you fat low life ass bitch, I'm ready to fuck you up! I'm tired of this shit!" Mrs. Watkins growled and suddenly tightened her fists, ready to go to war. She had enough of this pettiness.

"Come on, mama! Don't do that!" Austin cried.

Evelyn hopped on her feet and made a dash for Mrs. Watkins, but before she could get into the woman's face, Donterio lunged behind his mother and held her back. "Mama! STOP! What the hell are you doing?!? You foul as fuck!"

"LET ME THE FUCK GO!" Evelyn growled, ready to match Mrs. Watkins' energy.

"Ladies and gentlemen! This is unacceptable and Dr. Swati has given you all several warnings about this," Patricia, the white nurse, suddenly caught everyone's attention. "I am going to have ask everyone to leave the room or I will call the police."

"BITCH, CALL THE POLICE! WHITE BITCH!" Evelyn screamed.

Austin, very much still emotional yet trying to diffuse the situation, held onto his mother. "Fredquisha, how did this shit even happen? What did you do to her?"

"I ain't do shit," Fredquisha responded no even giving Austin eye contact.

Dr. Swati suddenly made his entrance into the room. "Everyone must leave. The police are on their way," he announced.

"Are you the doctor?" Austin turned around and asked the short Indian man.

"Yes, I am. Are you the father?"

"Yes..."

"What's going on?!? I just got here and they won't even tell me anything!" Austin cried.

Dr. Swati pursed his lips... "It's not looking too good. From the bite, she got she now has a severe case of meningitis. Her brain is barely registering any activity."

"Wait, what?! What do you mean by bites? I'm so confused right now!"

Dr. Swati fell silent and tightened his lips up again. He took a deep breath and then exhaled. He looked over at a tense Evelyn as she knew the truth of how the bite got there in the first place.

"It looks like Myyah was bitten by some critters in the house. Although extremely rare, based on the tests we ran from the lab, Myyah has been bitten by a few cockroaches. Cockroaches are known for carrying viruses and other bacteria. Unfortunately, Myyah got a bad viral infection that spread to her brain."

"WHAT!?!? You mean by daughter got fuckin' sick because of fuckin' roaches!?! I DON'T BELIEVE THIS SHIT! I'm going to KILL THAT BITCH!"

"FUCK NIGGA, YOU AIN'T GON DO SHIT TO MY DAUGHTER!"

"Nah, fuck all that you fat ass old bitch! All them dope boy dicks she suckin' and fuckin' she could've been had a better place! Your daughter is just a nasty, trifling ass bitch who never did shit for my daughter!" Austin continued to scream.

Before a potential brawl ensued, hospital police stormed the room and shouted,

"Police! Everyone needs to leave the room now per the orders of the doctor! Visiting hours OVER! EVERYONE!"

"Nah, I'm staying here with my baby!" Fredquisha cried.

"BITCH YOU NEVER TOOK CARE OF HER!" Austin yelled.

"Ma'am, you have to leave too. EVERYONE," the police officer looked at Fredquisha who suddenly was putting on some sobbing motherly front.

As more police officers flooded the ICU room, everyone was escorted out of the room and out of the intensive care unit. "Come on, let's just get the fuck away from those ghetto ass niggas," Mrs. Watkins grumbled as one group of police officers separated Austin and his mother as another group of officers pulled Fredquisha's family away. "You all need to stay far away from them or we're going to ban you all from the hospital, and might just even take you all to jail," one of the officers warned. The same officer then looked at Austin and Mrs. Watkins and said, "I suggest you all go down to the cafeteria. I'll tell the other officers to make sure the other family stays far away from you all."

"Officer, this just isn't fair. I barely even had a chance to see her," Austin groaned as tears poured from heavy red eyes. "Man, I just got out of jail and found out she was on life support!"

The brute policeman was a tad unsympathetic to Austin's plea. He shook his head and said, "I'm sorry guy, but this is still a hospital and once the doctor gives an order, we have to enforce it. If the doctor restores visitation rights, then we will work out an arrangement to make sure chaos doesn't happen again, ok?"

"He can actually stay. Everyone else must leave..." Dr. Swati intervened as he approached the menacing policeman.

Mrs. Watkins pulled out a napkin from her purse and wiped Austin's face free of tears.

"Everyone else has to leave though, including you ma'am," the officer said to Mrs. Watkins.

"Ok...I'll be down in the cafeteria, Austin. Jonah and his girl-friend are on their way." Mrs. Watkins then quickly left the room with police escort to her side.

Dr. Swati then led Austin back into the room. "You can stay here for the next hour or so," the doctor chirped then quickly made his way out of the room to give Austin much needed space.

As more tears kept running down Austin's face, he sat in the chair next to Myyah's bed and scanned her up and down. This shit was just still so unbelievable to him. Why God, why put my baby through all of this? She didn't deserve this, Austin silently begged to his sense of a higher power. He grabbed Myyah's hand and slowly massaged it. "Baby girl, please, you gotta get better for me and granny. I love you so much. Please don't do this to me. I will do anything to make sure you come back to me."

As the EKG machine kept chirping, monitoring Myyah's low pulse and the ventilator kept pumping air into her lungs, Austin was so immobilized in pain and grief that all he could do was just cry and cry. His sobs were so intense that they ached his head. After a few minutes passed and he was able to collect himself, all Austin could do at this point was to pray. Pray as hard as he could hoping God would send some sort of miracle.

An hour passed and just like he instructed, Dr. Swati made his way back into the room to end Austin's short visitation. It wasn't fair but given the precarious and tense situation between everyone, it had to be done.

"I'm so sorry about this, sir. I plan on running a few more tests with another colleague of mines from the University of Chicago Hospital. We are going to see if another treatment could work. I will let you know in the next few hours. I will also consult with the mother to let her know about my update."

"Ok, doctor. I appreciate it. Please, save my daughter. I am asking you to do everything you can."

"I will...If you need someone to talk to, we have counselors on site."

"I appreciate it." Austin made his way up from the bedside seat, leaned down and planted a kiss on top of Myyah's forehead. "Please, baby girl. Pull through from daddy. I love you. If you get better, I am going to do everything in my power to get you back and I promise 'til the day I die I will never let anyone harm you ever again."

CHAPTER FORTY-THREE

"*Mama*, do you need anything from the store? I'm gonna go to the Jewel to get some deli meat so I can pack my lunch for tomorrow," Katina asked her mother as she sat in the living room watching a rerun of Blackish.

"Nah, I'm good. But you sure you wanna go out this late? It's not safe, and besides, I don't know how I feel about you being out there with Deontae threatening you and shit."

Earlier that day, after getting off her shift, the first thing Katina did was go straight to the local police station in her mother' s neighborhood to see what she needed to do in order to get a protective order against Deontae. Unfortunately for her, she was informed that the process took place by going to the Cook County Court in Downtown and she'd need to do that first thing in the morning given they were already closed. In the meantime though, the police informed her that if Deontae continued to harass her, she could file a police report with them and they would possibly go out to look for him.

With all that in mind Katina still couldn't let Deontae's antics deter her from living life. The show still had to go on regardless if Deontae was going to act out. All Katina knew though was that if Deontae was going to pull the blickie on her again, she was going to pull hers out and use it.

"Mama, don't worry about me. I'm fine. Deontae ain't gon do shit. He's too much of a lazy ass to really take things there. He thought he could just ruffle my feathers, but baby I'm not bothered."

"You want me to go with you?"

"Nah, just stay here with the kids. I'm not gonna be gone for that long anyways…"

"Ok, well, take my car. The keys are on the table."

"Ok. Thanks!" Katina made towards the dining room table and grabbed her mother's car keys.

Despite it being summer, tonight was a tad chilly, so Katina had on a light denim jacket. It was also a way to conceal the heavy black gloc tucked on her side. A full clip was loaded inside the pistol. One was in the chamber.

Katina strode through the dining room and then into the dark living room, the television's luminosity filled the room. The kids were in the living room too with their eyes glued to the television. "Alright ya'll, be right back. I got my cell on me in case you need anything, mama."

"Ok, just be safe and watch your surroundings."

"Don't worry. I won't be gone that long."

Katina made her way outside and to the driveway. She pressed the car alarm and opened the driver's side door to her mother's Toyota Camry.

POW! POW!

Two loud gunshots blasted out nowhere. Their echoes filled the dark Southside street.

Katina instantly froze for a second. Everything around her became still. The sharpness of the sound was so piercing to her ears the only thing she could hear was her own scattered thoughts scrimmaging in her mind.

She looked down and saw the right side of her denim jacket

had a huge, growing plot of of her own blood. Was she shot? She pulled the jacket back and touch her side. Suddenly she collapsed to the ground. She pulled her hand up to her face and gawked at the sight of her own thick crimson blood covering her fingers. Her face, moments ago neutral and unconcerned, now was frightened and painful. The stinging pain of the gunshot wound spread to her side. As a trained nurse she now knew timing was everything. She could still breath. Her body was still in possession of energy – enough to quickly prop herself up against the car door.

"Tina! TINA!" Mama stormed out of the house with the kids to her side.

"I'm...I'm over here, mama," Tina cried out. "Hurry up, I've been shot!"

Mama, only wearing nothing but her nightgown and some slippers, scurried to the driver's side of the car and saw Katina trying her best to get up and stand up.

"Ohmygod! HE SHOT YOU!"

"I...I don't know, I need to get to the hospital quick, mama!"

The kids began to cry uncontrollably once they saw the condition their mother was in. Mattie, bawling herself, did her best to help Katina stand up straight. The nurse still clenched her side to contain the bleeding, but by the vast lake of blood evident on the driveway, it was just a matter of time before she was about to pass out.

"Ya'll go close the door and then get in the car! We gotta get to the hospital quick! Come on, Katina! Stay with me! Stay with me!" Mattie commanded as she could tell Katina was now slowly slipping into unconsciousness.

Katina tried to fight the urge to close her eyes. Her body grew increasingly weak by the second. She thought just a moment ago she could hang in there, but now that the initial round of adrenaline that injected her with a faux sense of life began to wane away, her destiny was looking dark and grave.

She just knew herself she was losing a good amount of blood and it was just a matter of time before she would succumb to darkness.

Mattie helped Katina over to the front passenger side and got her comfortably inside. "Please, baby, hang in there. Do not close your eyes, baby. Please do not die on me!"

"I'm tryin', mama. I'm tryin'. Let's go! Please!" Katina muttered as a few tears escaped the ducts of her heavy eyes.

The kids were now in the back seat – their attention completely throwing to what appeared to be their dying mother. "Mom, please don't die on us. Please do not die on us!" Desiree begged her mother.

"I won't…I won't. Ya'll just sit back and pray for me, ok?"

"Ok," both children responded with sadness and anxiety laced in their cracking, shrieking voices.

As Mattie sped out of the driveway and headed towards the closest hospital, Holy Cross on 68th, Katina fought and fought. Mattie kept begging her to keep her eyes closed. Her children did the same. As much as she resisted, she couldn't go on. Her pulse dropped. Her body began to grow limp and cold. Her breaths were light and shallow like feathers blowing in the wind. She closed her eyes and saw a great light beckoning her. Her head tilted the side and her breathing was no more.

An hour earlier...

"Yeah, suck that shit, bitch," Deontae moaned as he sat back in his Monte Carlo, getting the sloppiest head from some Popeye's drive-thru worker scalawag he met some few weeks ago.

Since dropping Fredquisha off at the hospital, he needed to clear his mind and get away from all of the drama that was happening. Although he knew he was pushing the limits by continuously threatening Katina, he was getting to the point where he was simply over her. Ready to move the fuck on and enjoy the newfound freedom of fucking as much as he could without worrying about having a baby mama-girlfriend staring down his back.

The 19-year-old girl went up and down his shaft, covering it up with the thickest, gooiest saliva she could form in her mouth (hours of watching PornHub videos helped her perfect her head techniques), she tickled Deontae's balls and taint. Sure fire way to make a nigga bust the biggest nut.

As he toked a blunt, Deontae stared down at his lap, admiring the girl's dick sucking skills. "Shit, where the fuck you learn that shit from?"

The girl chuckled as she released the dick from out of her mouth. "This shit is all natural. Dick suckin' run in my DNA," she continued to laugh. She stuffed the dick back in her mouth and continued to glide up and down, but this time faster, ready to extract the nut out of Deontae's hardened, veiny pipe.

"AHHHHH! Shit!" Deontae screamed as his nut blasted all up in the girl's mouth.

The girl didn't even hesitate in swallowing buddy's nut. His sperm was zesty and refreshing like licking on two scoops of mint chocolate ice cream. She wiped her mouth and sat back in the seat. "So, when you gon fuck me? I'm ready to ride the dick!" she demanded.

"Shiiit, we can fuck in here too!" Deontae replied, dick still a bit hard, wafting it in his hand.

"Why we can't go back to your place?" the Popeye's THOT asked.

Deontae smacked his teeth. "Man, I'm still stayin' with my mama'nem…"

"Oh…Well, shit, let's just go over to my crib. I just got my section 8!"

Deontae looked over at the girl, eyes widened. Fuck Fredquisha, he thought.

"Ok, shit. Where you stay at?"

"On 47th and Drexel!"

"Shiiit, let's go! Can't wait 'til I eat that pussy!"

CHAPTER FORTY-FOUR

10:31 tick tocked on the clock inside of Myyah's room as Austin made his way out. Taking his time to make it down the cold and bright corridor of the ICU floor, Austin still couldn't fathom how this was his reality. This was the day he longed for…To be free and be united with his daughter and change his life for her sake alone. But now there she was, alone, slowly dying in a hospital room with no one to her side other than a team of doctors trying to pull off one last miracle.

Austin strolled onto the elevator to make his way down to the cafeteria on the 2nd floor where his mother and his brother was at. "FUCK, FUCK, FUCK, FUCK!" Austin cried and roared as he punched one of the walls in the elevator. He shook his head and wiped his face free of tears. Although completely frustrated, Austin now realized there was nothing more he could do other than wait things out and hope God would somehow, someway pour down and gift him a miracle in the form of Myyah's recovery.

Once the elevator arrived on the second floor, Austin its sole occupant, he depressingly strode through the relatively quiet and somewhat empty cafeteria looking for his family. He scanned the floor. Over near a distant corner next to a Jimmy John's sub shop, the only restaurant that seemed open, there he spotted his mother along with his brother, Jonah, and his apparent girlfriend. He took slow, deliberate steps to them. Once he arrived, everyone stared at him, sensing he was so emotionally distraught. Austin couldn't hold it in anymore. He just broke down into more screams and tears.

"Son, please, just calm down. It's gonna be alright, it's gonna be alright, ok?" A crying Mrs. Watkins got up from her seat then wrapped her endearing arms around her emotionally wrecked son. Jonah, along with Miley, his girlfriend, wept as well as they encircled Austin and Mrs. Watkins. They all tightly hugged each other. "Come on bro, stay strong. We gotta be strong for Myyah. She can't see you breaking down like this, ok?"

Mrs. Watkins pulled out a napkin from her purse and wiped Austin's face free of tears. Jonah and Miley, sniffling, wiped their faces and gave Austin some space.

"I just can't believe this. This is just too much. This is so fucked up on so many levels," Austin groaned as he sat in a seat next to his mother.

"I know, baby. I know. But our weeping will endure for a night, but we gotta believe joy will come in the morning. We gotta just keep praying and hoping something good is going to happen out of all of this, ok?"

"Ok," Austin solemnly replied. A part of him didn't believe anything good was going to happen. That was just wishful thinking that he now found himself guilty of being in possession of now that his only daughter was knocking at death's door. He just knew Myyah's passing was inevitable.

Although Austin sensed everyone around him seemed to be somewhat in denial, he wasn't. Being involved in the streets, seeing so many people get caught up, knowing of so many people who got killed, hardened Austin into always expecting the worse. Having hope is nothing more than a way to placate the inevitable.

"You want anything to drink or eat, Austin?" Mrs. Watkins asked.

"Nah, I'm good, mama…"

"Ok…"

"We're gonna go check out what they have, you sure you don't want anything bro. This has to be far better than that jail food," Jonah tried to somewhat joke to lighten up the tense, somber mood.

"It's whatever, bro."

"Ok," Jonah replied as he took Miley's hand and led them off to the cafeteria line to see what was available.

Mrs. Watkins pulled her seat closer to her son as he held his head against the window and stared out of it, absorbing the dark skies, trying to subdue the millions of emotions and crazed thoughts overwhelming him. *Breathe in, breathe out,* he thought to himself, trying to use his mediation skills to control his explosive anger. Mrs. Watkins, not saying a word, rubbed Austin's back in a circular motion and then leaned her head onto Austin's shoulder. "I know you've expressed before in the past that sometimes you have issues with God, Austin, but this is the time we need to really to go to him to see us through this trial."

A few tears trickled out of Austin's eyes hearing his mother's request. "I don't know, mama, I don't know where to even begin with that."

"Here, let me help you…That's why I am here." Mrs. Watkins then took her head off Austin's shoulder and then grabbed Austin's right hand with both her hands. "Look at me…"

Austin slowly turned his face towards his mother's. His reddened eyes beamed into hers that were just as lava red. She closed her eyes, and Austin hesitantly followed suit.

"Heavenly father, we come before you right now in a dark

and trying situation, asking that you come and bring total healing to Myyah's body, oh father God. We ask that you ward off that demon of sickness and infection, oh Father God. Restore her to full health and bring peace and clarity to Austin and everyone else, oh heavenly Father. Father God, we ask that you also forgive those who have done wrong to our baby girl, but we also ask that you give us justice for the wrong being done to our precious Myyah. We know that all things are possible through Christ Jesus. In his name we pray, Amen…"

"Amen," Austin mumbled and then wiped his face free of tears.

"See, that wasn't too bad, now was it?" Mrs. Watkins smiled.

"No…

"See there, I told you praying isn't that bad. You should do it more often. We need it. It's the only thing that helps you get a sense of peace and tranquility, son."

"I meditate from time to time. Learned it in my anger management and conflict resolution class."

"That helps too. Meditate and pray. Anyways, I need to go use the bathroom."

"Ok," Austin replied.

Mrs. Watkins smiled and then got up from her seat. Seconds later Jonah and Miley walked back over. They had two bags of Jimmy John's in their hand along with some fountain cups. "I got you an Italian sub, bruh. And some sweet tea. Oh, and I also got you some chips and a chocolate chip cookie." Jonah sat down at an adjacent table. He opened up the bag and handed Austin a sub along with a bag of jalapeno flavored chips and a big chocolate chip cookie. Miley, still standing, handed Austin a medium-sized, ice-chilled cup and then sat down adjacent to Jonah. "Thanks, man, I really appreciate it."

As the two brothers and girlfriend began to eat, Mrs. Watkins moments later reappeared.

"What a bittersweet reunion. Oh well," Mrs. Watkins exhaled. "Do they have veggie subs, Jonah?" Mrs. Watkins asked.

"That's what I got Mrs. Watkins!" Miley smiled. "Cucumber, tomato, alfalfa sprouts, peppers, lettuce, seasoning, etc."

"Yeah, I can't eat all that pork like these boys do. I'm gonna get me something too," Mrs. Watkins smiled and then made her way over to the Jimmy John's restaurant inside the cafeteria.

After Mrs. Watkins got her veggie sub and the rest of the family finished eating, the entire Watkins tribe spent the rest of the evening huddled away in the vast cafeteria. Not getting any updates yet from the medical staff about Myyah's condition, Mrs. Watkins and Austin talked about the entire situation and how they planned on trying to seriously wrestle custody away from Fredquisha hopefully if Myyah recuperated. Although everyone knew that Myyah's condition wasn't looking good, Mrs. Watkins was hesitant to succumb to believing in a negative outcome and just had faith in knowing God was going to show up and restore Myyah's body.

Two hours passed. Austin sat back and just stared out of the window, taking in the light traffic that rumbled down the street next to the hospital. He was hoping any second someone would come and give them the greenlight to allow him to go back upstairs to be at Myyah's bedside. Shit, he at least wanted someone to give him updates about Myyah's condition.

"Damn man, like I am so confused...How in the hell is we supposed to get word on Myyah's condition?" Austin asked his mother. "I know...You know what, I'm gonna go find out myself. This is just wrong on so many levels." Mrs. Watkins got up from her seat. "You just stay here. I just don't want any trouble if I run into Fredquisha's family."

"Ok," Austin replied.

"Well, bro. I gotta take Miley back to her crib 'cuz she gotta get to work early in the AM."

"Austin, I'm praying for you and Myyah. I know God is

going to pull her through. Just stay positive, ok?" Miley said.
Austin stood up and dapped Jonah up and then gave a hug.

"Aiight bro, I'll be right back."

"Ok," Austin said.

As time seemed to slip away, and more thoughts continued to flood Austin's mind, the stress of dealing with the situation was tiring him out. When he was back in jail he was so used to going to bed at around 9:30 PM given his days usually started around 5 AM. His body was getting weary and drowsy, and all he needed right now was just to lay his body down and get some much-needed rest. Although he was still somewhat amped up with anxiety, as more time passed, and his mother still hadn't come down to report on any possible news of Myyah's condition, Austin laid his head down on the table, closed his eyes, and just allowed the drowsiness invading his body to give him some sleep. Hopefully, his mother would come down in a few more minutes to alert of what was going on.

CHAPTER FORTY-FIVE

"Fredquisha, Dr. Swati would like to speak to you in private. He has some more updates…" Patricia, the nurse, instantly grabbed Fredquisha's attention in the visitor's area, waking her out of a deep nap she very much needed to relieve herself from a tension headache pounding on the side of her head.

"Can I come?" Evelyn inquired, ready to jump out of her seat.

"I guess," Patricia responded.

Fredquisha and Evelyn got up and the both of them together followed Patricia back into Myyah's room. There she glanced at Dr. Swati and another doctor – a tall and slender white doctor with a semi-curly afro – hovering over Myyah engaging in light discussion.

Dr. Swati paused his conversation. "Fredquisha, I want you to meet Dr. Rosenberg. He's the chief pediatric neurologist from the University of Chicago. He and his team are working on an experimental treatment for child patients with significant amounts of brain damage," Dr. Swati explained.

Still numb and confused about the entirety of today's events,

Fredquisha just lightly smiled at the older and slender Jewish doctor. Dr. Rosenberg made his way over to Fredquisha and then stuck his hand out to shake her hand.

"Nice to meet you, Fredquisha. As Dr. Swati explained, given the severity of Myyah's condition, there is another possible experimental treatment option we are currently looking at. It involves the placement of embryonic neural stem cells into Myyah's brain."

"Wait, what does all of that even mean?" Evelyn interjected as she inquired with a raised brow standing next to Fredquisha.

Dr. Rosenberg continued, "Well, we would be taking nerve cells from fetuses and then transplanting them inside of areas of Myyah's brain that have accumulated significant damage."

Evelyn scrunched her face up and spat, "Well, how much it gon cost? I mean, we ain't even got the money like that. Will Medicaid even cover it?" Evelyn continued to gripe, "Besides, it's just an experiment. How you even know for sure it's gonna work? My grandbaby ain't no damn lab rat. We want real results."

Evelyn held her arms by their elbows as she rapidly tapped her left foot against the ground. Her somewhat defiant attitude was really beginning to rub Fredquisha the wrong way. MooMoo turned and looked at her mother, "Mama, just leave. Let me talk to the doctors alone. In fact, just go home. You've done enough already today. I'll call you when I get back home..."

"Girl, I ain't goin' nowhere! She my grandbaby too."

"Mama, not now. Please. You're just doin' the most. Just leave."

"Fine. I'm just tryin' to help..." Evelyn looked her daughter up and down with a slight scowl written on her face. She quietly exited Myyah's room thinking of her next game plan since her 'daughter' suddenly wanted to start to act like a mother and shit.

"Sorry about that, doctor…Please, tell me though. Will it work?"

"I can't guarantee anything. It's all experimental. However, if you are willing to give it a try, we just need your permission to begin the treatment as soon as possible."

"Ok. I'll do it. At this point, what else can be done? I mean, if she's almost completely brain dead, I might as well go ahead and do it."

"Exactly. We just need you to sign this release paperwork given us your permission to go ahead and begin the experimental treatments…"

"Ok…"

Dr. Swati handed Fredquisha a clipboard and a pen. She quickly scribbled her signature down at the bottom line without even bothering to read all of the terms and conditions. It didn't matter at this point though – this was God answering her prayer to help Myyah pull through.

"Ok, so we are going to begin treatment as soon as possible. We are going to start the procedure as soon as possible. We are going to get her prepared for surgery now."

"Can I say one last thing to her?"

"Sure," Dr. Swati responded as he stepped out of MooMoo's way and allowed her to saunter over to Myyah's bed. Fredquisha glanced at her daughter and smiled as a tear escaped her eye. She wiped her face and sniffled. She leaned down and planted a kiss on the side of her face. "Please, pull through my baby. Don't die on me. I promise I'm gonna change everything and do better by you. Please don't go…I promise I'm gonna be a better mama." MooMoo then lifted her face up, spun on her feet and quickly made her way out of the room so the doctors could go ahead and scuttle Myyah to surgery.

As she walked slowly down the long, cold corridor she suddenly felt her phone vibrating in her back pocket. Buzz. Buzz. Buzz. She figured it was probably her mother sending her a barrage of text messages. Come to find out once she pulled the phone out of her pocket and looked at the number, it was Mr. Garrison.

"Hey, Mr. Garrison. Now is not a good time to talk—"

"Why? Where you at? I miss you already. I got some good ass bud from one of my guys…"

"My daughter is in the hospital. Things ain't lookin' too great…"

"Ohhh, damn. I'm so sorry to hear that. You need somethin' from me?"

"Nah, I'm good, Mr. Garrison."

"Well, I need somethin' from you…"

"I'm tied up right now, Mr. Garrison. I can't go nowhere."

"You know I got a meeting on Friday with Section 8."

"Ok, and?"

"Well, the doctors are operating on your doctor, I'mma need you to come operate on me."

"Mr. Garrison, fuck that shit! You taking things too far!" Fredquisha growled in a whisper-like manner as she made her way next to the visitor's area. She didn't want to go back in and sit down given she didn't want everyone in her business.

"Sounds like you wanna be a homeless bitch," Mr. Garrison chuckled.

"Mr. Garrison, please! Can't you understand I'm going through some things?"

"And? We all go through some things. It's called life, bitch. I told yo ass that if I helped you, you gon help me. Besides, I'm going back to the DR in a few weeks anyways. When I leave you can go back to doin' what you were doin'."

Fredquisha paused for a moment, closed her watery eyes and just pondered about once again she found herself in a compromising situation with Nate. She huffed, "Fine, fine, fine." MooMoo opened her eyes and exhaled. "We can't do nothin' at my place 'cuz I got company."

319

"Shit, well, you need to come slide over to my place then."

"Well, can you order me a ride? I don't want none of my peoples to know where I'm going..."

"Yeah, I got you. Where you at?"

"Northwestern. The Children's Hospital in Downtown."

"Goddamn, that ride gon cost me $30. Pussy better be worth it."

Fredquisha didn't respond.

"Anyways, I'll order this Uber right now. Have yo ass ready in the next five minutes."

"Ok..."

"Call me zaddy..."

"What?" Fredquisha retorted with a scrunched up face.

"Yeah, bitch. Call me zaddy..."

Fredquisha still didn't respond.

"Alright nah...Keep fuckin' with me..."

"Ok, zaddy."

"Good. Seen you soon, you nasty slut." Mr. Garrison, crude more than ever, hung up the phone.

Fredquisha stuffed the phone back into her back pocket and strolled coolly into the visitor's area. "Hey, ya'll. I'm finne head out for a few. Myyah is about to go into surgery and I can't just be here in this hospital anymore."

Donterio, who was chopping it up with one of his cousins, stood up and walked over to Fredquisha. "What you mean, sis? You finne just bail? How long is the surgery gonna even last for?"

"I don't know. They preppin' her right now. It could be a few hours. I just...I just gotta get out of this depressin' mothafucka."

"But damn, sis. What if something happens and the docs need to see you?"

"I'm just gonna be right back. Just stay here for me in case ya'll find out something..."

"I guess," Donterio replied, confused. Why was his sister

acting this way all of suddenly? Why was it that important for her to dip out?

Fredquisha suddenly took off and quickly paced herself out of the hospital to await her ride to Mr. Garrison's place.

Some of Fredquisha's remaining family members looked a bit confused, but they took that as their cue that it wasn't even all that necessary to stay behind either. It was already damn near midnight and many of them had shit to do in the morning. Evelyn had already dipped out. Most of them were just there to support Fredquisha.

"You need a ride back home, cuz?" One of the cousins asked Donterio.

"Nah, I'm good, bruh. I'm gonna stay behind 'cuz Myyah about to go into surgery."

"Aiight, boy. Stay prayed up."

"Bet…"

As Donterio said his goodbyes to the remaining family members, he sat down and picked up a magazine. Although a tad tired himself, his care and concern for Myyah was keeping him up. Although it seemed as if now Fredquisha was slowly beginning to turn a new leaf by wanting to change her disposition for Myyah (for what reasons nobody still doesn't know yet), Donterio was the only person from MooMoo's family who seemed genuinely concerned. Evelyn was just worried about her plans getting squandered, and now that Myyah was on the cusp of death, she was onto her back-up plan – getting custody of Zy'meer and Quimani.

CHAPTER FORTY-SIX

*M*rs. Watkins anxiously stepped onto the ICU floor from the elevator, ready to get the latest updates into Myyah's condition. Making her way down the long corridor, she passed the nurse's station looking for Dr. Swati.

"Excuse me, ma'am...Can I help you?" Patricia, the white nurse, asked Mrs. Watkins.

Grandma turned her attention towards the young blonde nurse and smiled.

"Yes, I am looking to get an update on my granddaughter's condition. No one has contacted me to give me and my son an update. What's going on?"

"Oh, well, he just got done consulting with the mother and the other grandmother. Do you want to speak to him?"

"Sure..."

"Ok, let me page him." Patricia then picked up the beige phone next to her and dialed for Dr. Swati to come to the nurse's station to speak with Mrs. Watkins. As the anxious grandmother stood idle at the nurse's station, Donterio bumbled his way towards the station.

"Oh, hey...," Donterio uttered as he gawked at the grandmother he barely knew. They'd met before on a few occasions here and there, but never had a meaningful, serious conversation.

"Hey..."

"Don't worry. Everyone else went home. I'm just stayin' here until Myyah gets out of her surgery."

Patricia's eyes widened that Donterio revealed the news. Mrs. Watkins suddenly grew angry. What fuckin' surgery? she thought. The now visibly distraught grandmother looked at the nurse and growled, "Why didn't you just tell me that?"

"It was best the doctor told you those details, ma'am. I'm sorry..."

Donterio interjected, "Look, Mrs. Watkins. I know you ain't gettin' along with my mama'nem, but I just wanna let you know that it was me who tried my best to save Myyah this morning."

Mrs. Watkins wasn't feeling Donterio's vibe. She was thoroughly annoyed – why couldn't this white bitch just tell her the truth? Also, why was Donterio just standing next to her being somewhat a nuisance? She just wobbled her head and kept staring at Patricia.

"What kind of surgery is she even having?"

"Mrs. Watkins..." Dr. Swati called the grandmother's name, instantly catching her attention.

Mrs. Watkins spun on her heels and scanned the short Indian doctor up and down. "Doctor. Why wasn't I nor my son informed about Myyah's surgery? What's going on?"

"I do apologize. We only consulted with the mother since she is technically her legal guardian. One of my colleagues from the University of Chicago is performing a last minute surgery on Myyah to see if he could help reverse some of the brain damage."

"Wait, what?!? How could you all make such an important life decision for my granddaughter without even at least talking to my son?!?"

"I understand, and I do apologize, Mrs. Watkins. Time was of the essence and we didn't know exactly where you folks were at."

"Ughhh, whatever! What are you all doing to my grand-daughter? What kind of surgery is this?"

"Well, we are going to be transplanting some fetal neural stem cells into Myyah's brain. These are cells derived from fetuses. It will hopefully help reverse some if not all of the brain damage done to Myyah's brain. It's an experimental treatment but we are positive it may work."

Mrs. Watkins grumbled. "Well, let me go tell my son. When did Myyah go into surgery."

"We got her prepped about thirty minutes ago. She's currently on the operating table as we speak."

"Oh my god...ok, let me go get my son."

"Mrs. Watkins..." Donterio said.

"Yes," she replied looking at him.

"Just wanna let you know I've been praying for her. Anyways, nurse, where is the bathroom?"

"Down the hall and to your right..."

"Donterio...I'm sorry. I'm just stressed out," Mrs. Watkins apologized, producing a light smile on her face.

"I understand, Mrs. Watkins. I understand. Anyways, my bladder is about to explode. We can talk in the visitor's area if you like..."

"Ok."

"Austin! Austin! Wake up!"

Gasp! Austin suddenly opened his eyes and peered at his mother hovering over him. He wiped his face of slob. "What happened? Is there something wrong with Myyah?"

"No! She's in surgery right now. I just spoke with the doctor!

They are trying a last minute operation. Fredquisha and her crazy ass mama left already. The only person still here is Donterio."

"Donterio…Why is he hanging out here?"

"I don't know. I guess he just wants to stay to make sure everything is alright with Myyah." She grabbed her son's arm and yanked him out of the seat. "Come on, let's go up to the visitor's area! We need to be there to get any updates."

Grandma and Austin quickly paced their way through the relatively empty cafeteria and made their way to the elevators. Once they got to the ICU floor they went straight for the visitor's area.

"Sup, bruh," Donterio said once he saw Austin enter.

"What's good, homie?"

"Man, praying…I'm so sorry about everything, my dude. I tried my best to help save Myyah this morning. I'm the one who gave her CPR."

"I appreciate it, bro. I appreciate it."

"Anyways, look ya'll. I just wanna let ya'll know that whatever happens, I'm down to ride for ya'll. My mama and my sister ain't on shit. To be honest with you, I should've been cut them off, but hey, it is what it is. If ya'll need anything from me, just let me know. I really wanna stay as long as I can but I got this job interview in the morning. I told Fredquisha I'd stay behind until she got back, but she tweakin'."

"Where she even go?"

"Man, I don't know. She just dipped out."

"Alright, bruh. Don't wanna hold you up. Go handle ya business and good luck with the interview."

Donterio stood up from his seat and sauntered over to Austin and his mother. Austin stood up and dapped up with Donterio. Truth be told, Austin kind of liked Donterio, but obviously because there was animosity between him and Fredquisha, for years he kind of had to keep his distance.

"I'm praying for Myyah, for real for real. Ya'll stay blessed." Donterio made his way out of the visitor's area.

Austin sat back down and clasped his hands.

Mrs. Watkins shook her head. "Crazy. I always thought he was a no good ass nigga. Turns out he's the only one who seems to give a shit about anything from that family."

"I know," Austin said. "I know…"

CHAPTER FORTY-SEVEN

"*A*hhhhhh! AHHHHHHH!" Mr. Garrison screamed in carnal bliss as he blasted his old, thick nut all up in Fredquisha's lubed ass.

Not the pussy. Yes, the ass.

"God damn! FUCK!" the shady and perverted landlord panted, his hard dick still throbbing deep up in Fredquisha's tight anus.

"Damn, nigga. Could you have at least pulled the fuck out?"

Mr. Garrison snickered. "Girl, whatever…" He coughed and then rubbed his chest. "You wanna make a few extra dollars?"

Fredquisha, still on her knees, ass tooted in the air, turned over on her back and looked at Mr. Garrison with curiosity. She was vexed. What the fuck was he talking about?

"What you mean if I wanna make a few extra dollars?"

"Yeah…You heard me…" Mr. Garrison signed with his hands, "DO. YOU. WANT. TO. MAKE. A. FEW. EXTRA. DOLLARS?!? You fuckin' retarded or some shit?"

Fredquisha rolled her eyes. "No. I'm good. I heard you the first time. I'm going back to the hospital. I already told you I got a lot on my plate. My daughter is in surgery right now."

"Stop actin' like you a real mother and what not. I know you don't give a damn 'bout that girl. Yo ass just tryin' to put on a front and shit. You black bitches are so damn predictable, I swear. One day ya'll careless and reckless. Don't know how to raise kids. Next thing you know some shit happens, ya'll wanna act like ya'll motherfuckin' the best mamas on the planet. Maybe if yo lazy nigga ass wasn't runnin' around in the streets yo daughter wouldn't be in the predicament she in now."

Fredquisha's somewhat look of irritation devolved into a look of outright shock and outrage. Mr. Garrison saw her scowl too but he was completely unbothered by the fact he went low and got deep in her skin.

"YO, what the fuck is you talkin' about dude? My damn daughter is almost dead and the doctors tryin' to save her and shit!"

Mr. Garrison smacked his teeth and didn't relent.

"Bitch, shut up. If you were that concerned about ya damn nappy headed ass daughter you wouldn't be here lettin' me dick you down. Obviously, your priorities are all the way fucked up. Now, stop actin' stupid and make this extra cash. You know you need the loot."

Fredquisha abruptly hopped out of the bed, naked, cum swimming out of her asshole and down her cheeks. She lunged into Mr. Garrison's face, her fists balled up ready to fight, and screamed, "FUCK YOU AND FUCK YO MONEY! I DON'T NEED YOUR MONEY, YOU OLD ASS SLIMEY NIGGA!"

Mr. Garrison was unfazed. He chuckled and licked his lips. "You done?"

"MAN! FUCK YOU! I'M OUT! FUCK THE APARTMENT TOO! I DON'T CARE IF YOU CALL SECTION 8! I CAN ALWAYS GO STAY WITH MY MAMA! BETTER YET! I GOT PLENTY OF NIGGAS THAT WILL TAKE CARE OF ME!"

Fredquisha scrimmaged Mr. Garrison's bedroom looking for her clothes. She picked her pink pair of panties up off the ground and tried to quickly put them back on. Mr. Garrison moved adjacent to her as she quickly put her pants on. A half-drank bottle of Peach Ciroc was sitting on the nightstand next to his bed. He picked it up and took a huge swig. "Ahhh," he exhaled as the fruit-flavored alcohol swam down his dry throat.

"So, you don't wanna make this cash, huh?" Mr. Garrison said as he held the bottle in his hand. Fredquisha wasn't paying attention. She leaned down to pick her bra off the ground as Mr. Garrison quickly hovered over with the neck of the bottle in his hand.

"NO! SO STOP ASK—"

PLOW!

Mr. Garrison whipped the bottle across the back of Fredquisha's head. Shards and bits of glass flew all over the place. Unaware of what Mr. Garrison had up his sleeves, MooMoo suddenly grabbed the back of her head and then stumbled.

"What the, what the fuck?!?" she muttered and then fell the floor. She used her right hand to cover up the protrusion of blood flowing from the fleshy wound visible in the back of her head.

Mr. Garrison then punted Fredquisha in her stomach with his huge right foot.

"AHHHH!" MooMoo gasped and began to cough.

"Bitch, you think I'm playing games with you?!?" He continued to yell, "I was tryin' to play nice. But I see you must've really forgot who the fuck you dealin' with." Mr. Garrison then swung his fist right in the back of Fredquisha's head, further intensifying the stinging wound.

As MooMoo cried and tried to minimize the pain spreading through her abdomen, it was no match to the intense and agonizing pounding Mr. Garrison then commenced onto her body, delivering blow after blow. "GET UP BITCH! FIGHT BACK! YOU SUPPOSED TO BE BAD!"

Fredquisha tried her best to stand up to defender herself, but before she could fully erect herself, Mr. Garrison threw another mountainous hard blow into her stomach with his tightened fist. He grabbed her by her shoulders (she had no shirt on) and slammed her into the bed and began to batter her some more to subdue her defense. The crazed landlord quickly scanned the room to locate his pants. He yanked them off the floor, pulled the heavy black belt out of the pants' belt loops. Forming a makeshift whip, Mr. Garrison lashed MooMoo left and right all over. Her legs. Her back. Even her face. Any part of her body that was exposed received a lashing.

By this point, MooMoo wanted to pass the fuck out. Her head was in spinning, throbbing pain. The wound, still fresh, oozed blood onto the sheetless queen-sized mattress. You'd think given Mr. Garrison lived in a nice condo in suburban Elmhurst he'd at least keep fresh linen on his bed. Nope. He barely called the place home. His real den of luxury he called his residence was his time share in Punta Cana. There he'd deal with no-lip giving, submissive Dominican prostitutes who would've been more than glad to make an extra $20 to do whatever he pleased.

With sweat glistening down his face and stubbly chest, Mr. Garrison finished his beating and threw the belt onto the ground. "Now, I'm gon ask you again. Do you want this extra cash?"

"Ye-yeah," Fredquisha muttered as she wailed.

"Good. Don't fuck with me ever again. I got this Polish cracka comin' over who wants a taste of some black pussy. He's helpin' me do some work on some of my properties. I promised to pay him fifty percent cash, fifty percent ass. Now, he's gonna come in here at any minute. I want you to do what you gotta do to make him happy. Suck his balls. Eat his ass. Make that cracka realize nigga pussy is the best thing since Popeye's Fried Chicken butter biscuits with honey. I'll slide you an extra $100."

"Ok," MooMoo replied.

"Good. We got an understanding. Now go get yourself cleaned up. He should be here in the next fifteen minutes. And go wipe yo ass. You got some shit on my dick..." Mr. Garrison sniggered as he moved his sweaty, naked fat body towards his dresser. "Oh yeah, and fuck yo daughter."

CHAPTER FORTY-EIGHT

THURSDAY MORNING. 6:45 AM.

*P*igeons chirped outside the bedroom window of Deontae's new THOTiana. In actuality, her name was Tatiana – a nineteen-year-old mother of two, veteran Popeye's drive-thru window worker and cosmetology student. Her biggest accomplishment to date that she loved bragging about was being able to secure section 8 housing in a newly constructed building on the South Side.

After a night of fucking, the two were nestled away in her queen-sized bed, naked, recuperating from eight orgasms.

Buzz. Buzz. Buzz.

Deontae slowly opened his eyes and looked around. God damn, this is a nice ass muhfuckin' place, he thought to himself, admiring the sheik section 8 apartment his new boo acquired thanks to Chicago Housing Authority. He rolled over and rumbled through his pockets as he heard his phone continue to buzz. He whipped it out of his pants' right pocket and saw an unfamiliar 708 number. Scrunching his face up, he quickly tried to figure out who was calling him. Fuck it. He answered – "Hello?"

Tatiana awakened from her deep sleep and wiped her eyes.

"I did it..." a female voice on the other end declared.

"Did what? Who is this?"

"It's me...Tish."

Deontae's eyes widened. It was Tisha – some chick he got pregnant a while back and had a secret baby with.

"Why you callin' me this early and shit? I already slid you the $300 you said you needed. What the fuck is you talkin' 'bout?"

"I popped that hoe. You said the only way you'd come back to me is if you got rid of the bitch. So, I did it."

Deontae was still very much confused. Two years ago, when him and Tish were deep into their fling, Deontae had expressed to her that the only way he could be with her was if he got Katina out of his life. He said he had too much baggage (long history plus kids) with her and somewhat depended on her for a lot of shit. She retorted and always told him she could take care of her if need be, but truth be told, Deontae just wanted the pussy from Tisha. Nothing more, nothing less. When she got pregnant, her odd "devotion" to Deontae amped up even more. Every time they'd meet up so he could visit his secret two-year-old son, Deontae Jr., Tisha would beg Deontae to just move in with her out in Romeoville, the far southwestern suburbs of the city. Of course, Deontae didn't want to be tied down to another bitch, so he'd throw every excuse in the book to not take her up on the offer.

"Look, I ain't got time for this right now—"

"I shot the bitch. Gave her two rounds last night. I know that bitch is dead now. So what you gon do?"

Deontae's eyes grew even wider in surprise and anxiety.

"You shot who?!?"

"Katina. That fat bitch you said you was tired of. I got rid of her finally, boo."

Deontae threw the sheets of his naked body and manically paced the floor. "Yo, you got to be fuckin' kidding me right now?!?!?"

"No...I've been following that bitch for a hot minute. I've been watching everything. The night she left. The night you ended up leaving to go over that dirty yellow bitch's crib in Englewood. I even know where you at right now. I told you I was a ride or die."

"Yo, you got to be fuckin' kidding me!" Everything around Deontae was spinning a million miles per hour. The walls were caving in. The lunatic shit he was hearing come out of Tish's mouth was crashing into ears like an asteroid smacking against earth, causing an apocalyptic cataclysm.

"No, I'm not kidding. So, what you gon' do?"

"Man, you crazy as fuck! I ain't down with this shit at all. I know I said I ain't wanna fuck with her no more, but you with the shits. BITCH, GET OFF MY LINE! I DON'T KNOW YOU!"

"Don't hang up on me, Deontae!"

"Man, fuck you bitch! You crazy as fuck!" Deontae hung the phone up and threw it on the pile of his clothes nuzzled next to the bed.

"What's wrong??!?" Tatiana asked, looking concerned like a muhfucka.

"Man, this crazy ass bitch I used to deal with back in the day talkin' 'bout she popped my baby mama. She crazy as fuh. My BM at work right now. I hate it when bitches be playin' games and shit," Deontae growled as he jumped back into the bed and threw the covers back over his naked body.

Buzz. Buzz. Buzz. Deontae's phone went off again.

"This better not be her crazy ass callin' me again." He rolled over and picked it up. The phone number he glanced at was recognizable – it was his nigga Pac from the set. "Ay yo, waddup, G?"

"Yo, my dude, you heard about your baby moms?"

Deontae's pupils widened and the whites of his eyes shown fretful redness.

"Nah, what the fuck happened!?!?"

"Yo, someone popped her ass last night in front of her mama's crib, joe!" Joe is a term Chicago niggas used to refer to one another.

"WHAT?!?!?" Damn, Tisha wasn't lying. This psycho bitch really laid his baby mama out, he manically thought as he bounced out of the bed again.

"Yeah, bro! She ain't dead though. Word out in the streets is they sayin' you had somethin' to do with it! Everybody been tryin' to hit yo other line, but you wasn't answerin!" Pac was referring to Deontae's other cell phone he used more so to communicate with regular folks. The phone he was on now, a burner, was used to cell dope and he also used it to talk to his side bitches, so only a few had the number. His "main" phone was left downstairs in his car.

"Fuck, fuck! What hospital she at?!? You know?"

"Man, I don't even know. But from what I heard she in serious condition. Shit, they probably moved her to a different hospital and shit."

"FUCK!" Deontae screamed. "I need to find her! I ain't have shit to do with this!"

"Man, you sure bro?"

Deontae scrunched his face up. "Nigga, am I sure?!? NIGGA, YES I AM SURE! WHY THE FUCK WOULD I WANNA POP MY BABY MAMA AND SHIT?!?!"

Tatiana, staring at Deontae, shook at every word that came out of his mouth.

"Aiight, damn, just calm down broski. I just wanted to see what the fuck is up! I knew you ain't do that shit."

335

"Man, whatever. Let me hit you back…"

"Aiight, bet. Hit my line." Pac hung up.

"Yo, shorty. I gotta go. I'm holla…"

Tatiana, a bit scared, looked at Deontae and mumbled, "Ok, just call me later…I hope everything is alright."

"Yeah, I'm cool. Just some crazy shit."

CHAPTER FORTY-NINE

THURSDAY MORNING. 6:57 AM.

*B*eep. Beep. Beep. Beep.

The non-stop chirping of the EKG machine inside of a University of Chicago Hospital ICU room blared. Air flowing from the ventilator pumped life-giving oxygen into Katina's lungs as she lay in a medically induced coma. Tubes ran through her nostrils. And IV bag slowly dripped the strongest dosage of morphine to subside the pain that overtook her body.

Streams of cold air blowing from the AC vent inside the room wrapped around Mattie, Katina's mother, making her mood all the more somber as she stared onward at her motionless daughter fighting for her life.

Dr. Rampsarard, the emergency room physician, closely examined Katina's vitals. With his lips pursed on his dark brown slender Indian face, he turned his attention towards Mattie as she sat in the corner silent. He exhaled and gave her the look. The all-too familiar look that registered the possibility of hopelessness. It was good to have a glimmer of hope, but by the heavy and low look on the doctor's face, Mattie just knew things weren't looking too good.

"Well, ma'am, we are still keeping her in a coma, but Katina lost a lot of blood. She has some reduced kidney function. Also, one of the bullets pierced her liver. There is the possibility she might need a transplant."

"Oh, my, god..." Mattie lowered her head as tears swam in her eyes. Luckily, the kids weren't in the room to hear the somewhat dreadful prognosis. "So, what are the next steps?"

"Well, we are searching for a donor as we speak. But with the way things are looking, if we don't get a donor by the end of the week, there is a great chance that Katina won't make it," Dr. Rampsarard explained.

Mattie couldn't fight holding back her tears and screams anymore. Her cries of angst filled with the room, echoing even outside the doors and onto the already depressingly cold and grief-stricken soundless ICU floor.

"Don't give up hope though, ma'am. I am gonna fight hard to make sure we find a donor in time. I am gonna do my best to make sure she gets that transplant."

"Ok...," Mattie replied. She propped herself up from her seat and made her way out of the room. She needed the space and the warmth of sunlight to inject her with some energy. The last twenty four hours was beyond tiring and now that she was on the verge of losing her only child, she needed to quickly come up with solutions. But not just solutions to figure out how Katina was going to find a liver transplant. But solutions on how she was going to get justice for her daughter.

Earlier she had spoken with a detective from the Chicago Police Department about possible suspects. She had told Detective McNulty that Deontae was probably the prime perpetrator behind the attempted murder. She told him the very reason why Katina was staying with her was because she grew tired of Deontae's incessant infidelities coupled with his tiring, low lifeish ways. The icing on the cake was when Deontae threatened her at gunpoint, which inevitably prompted her to go seek a protective order against him. But to no avail, that didn't happen. However, so far, with no real evidence implicating Deontae in the possible murder plot and so far no sign of his whereabouts, the police were taking their diligent time to make moves against him.

Detective McNulty said he was going to send some of his guys out to go look for Deontae and bring him in for questioning. But with scant circumstantial evidence and the possibility, of course, Deontae would deny any involvement once they interrogated him, the Detective told Mattie to prepare for a protracted investigation.

This, of course, is not what Mattie wanted to hear. Deep down in the base of her motherly soul, she just knew Deontae was the one. Who else would it be? Katina had no other significant spouse in her life. No bitter or jealous ex-friends. As far as she knew, Katina wasn't sleeping around with another woman's man. All signs definitely pointed to Deontae. Detective McNulty assured her he somewhat felt the same, but the 'system' needed to work in order to verify and already presumed conclusion. Again though, this isn't something no parent wanted to hear. Mattie wanted immediate justice – Deontae needed to be got already. Even if he didn't necessarily pull the trigger, his antics led to this fate.

Making her way outside while a few relatives looked after the kids in the visitor's area, Mattie found an empty shaded corner. She needed a cigarette. She scrambled through her pursue, pulled out a pack of Virginia Slims and slapped a square into her mouth. Once she lit up the cigarette, she took two long pulls and blew the smoke from her nostrils. She then pulled out her cell phone and dialed up her cousin Terry.

Terry, aka, Fat Terry, was a triple OG Four Corner Hustler gang chief from back in the day. Although he wasn't as heavily involved in the gang anymore, he still had a clout and pull on the West side city streets.

The phone rang. Seconds later – "Hey, cuzzo! I ain't heard from you a minute! What's good chica?!?" Terry laughed, not knowing what had went down over the last twenty-four hours.

"Terry…" Mattie replied somberly. "Katina got shot."

"What?!?" Terry's somewhat elated disposition turned into volcanic anger. "Is she ok?!?"

"Well, yeah, for right now. She's in a coma. She need a liver transplant."

"You've got to be fuckin' kidding me!?! Who the FUCK tried to kill my kinfolk?"

"Her baby daddy. This no good ass nigga named Deontae?!?"

"WHAT!?!? That clown ass nigga!?!? I told her ass years ago to drop that fool!"

"I know, but that foolish part of her was too afraid to let go of garbage and now she gotta pay for this shit."

"Nah, fuck that. I'm gonna make his ass pay for this shit. So what you want me to do?"

"Do what you gotta do."

"Don't say a fuckin' word, kinfolk. I'm on it. That nigga fucked with the wrong family."

"Thanks, blood. I'll have to pay you back."

"Don't even worry about it. This what family supposed to do. Go back and look after my baby cousin and let her know I got her back. Give me a call if anything changes and if she gets better."

"Ok, I will."

"Aiight, cuzzo."

Mattie hung up the phone and finished her cigarette. Her eyes turned to vengeful slits, fully aware of what was going to ensue now that she got her family deeply involved in this drama.

She put her cigarette out and blew the remaining smoke out

of her mouth. Once she made her way back into the hospital and to the visitor's area of the hospital, she informed her grandchildren and a few relatives of Katina's need for a transplant. They prayed, but as they prayed, Mattie plotted and anxiously waited for Deontae's assumed inevitable demise. This fuck nigga had to pay.

CHAPTER FIFTY

"*A*ustin! Wake up!"

Austin's eyes widened and glanced over at his mother who had her attention thrown straight ahead at Dr. Swati standing solemnly in the visitor's area.

"Oh, damn, I'm sorry," Austin apologized. He didn't know how long his mother had been trying to wake him up or how long Dr. Swati had been standing there.

Dr. Swati didn't say anything in response. He was quiet. Ghastly quiet and his eyes locked onto Austin.

"Is the entire family here? Myyah's mother?" Dr. Swati asked.

"Nah, she ain't come back yet," Donterio replied. He too was now awake.

"Any news?" Austin asked, wiping his eyes free of sleep. Since Myyah was in surgery all the family could do was anxiously wait, pray and then hopefully get some sleep in the visitor's area.

Dr. Swati made his way close to Austin and Ms. Watkins. He

closed his apparently heavy eyes, took a small inhale of breath and then and huffed, "Myyah's gone, Austin..."

"What?" Austin's eyes widened and he stood up from his seat.

"I'm so sorry Austin...She passed away at the tail end of the procedure."

"Wait, what the fuck do you mean she passed away? My daughter is dead? My baby girl is dead?"

"Yes, I am so sorry Austin..."

"HOW THE FUCK DID THIS EVEN HAPPEN?!?!?" Austin cried, his shrieking filling the entire visitor's room.

"Shhh, shhh, Austin, calm down, son, it's gonna be ok!" Mrs. Watkins quickly stood on her feet to quickly console her son. Although she was overwhelmed with grief herself, she could tell by the growing violent tone of Austin's voice that he was about to break down and possibly go crazy. And the last thing she wanted Austin to do was to make a sudden move against the doctor.

Doing her best to hold Austin back Mrs. Watkins clutched her mouth and her eyes turned to squints as tears streamed down her face.

The doctor took a step back and continued to explain, "During the procedure, no matter what we tried, Myyah's condition just kept getting worse and worse. We tried everything in the books to stabilize her vitals, but nothing worked. It seemed as if her body couldn't handle the stress of surgery given she was already in such bad shape. Once again, I'm so sorry. I'll alert our grief counselors to come and speak with you all..."

"That won't be necessary, Dr. Swati. I appreciate it, but it won't be necessary."

"Ok, well, as I said, I truly apologize. If you all like, you can go to her room to go be with her until her funeral arrangements are made."

"Ok..."

Donterio, silent, with a few tears streaming down his face, walked over to Austin and leaned in to give him a hug. "Sorry, bruh. I'm so sorry for all of this. I wish I could reverse time. This shit is fucked up, bruh."

Austin closed his eyes and rocked back and forth. "NOOOO! NOO!" he screamed.

Mrs. Watkins tightened her embrace around Austin as he continued to scream. "Come on son, we gotta be strong. Baby girl would want that, ok? Let's go see her now. I know this is painful, but we gotta keep strong."

"Mama, I can't. I can't live. My baby is gone. My baby is gone. I can't get it together," Austin stammered as his frame quivered.

"Shh, shh, shh, I know, son. But please, don't say that. You gotta be strong for everyone else, including me," Mrs. Watkins cried as she dragged Austin out of the visitor's area.

As Austin and Mrs. Watkins left the visitor's area and made a slow, long and painful journey to Myyah's room, he couldn't bring himself to see his baby girl lying motionless in the bed, her life quickly snuffed away from her.

Feet away from the room, Austin damn near collapsed.

"Come on, son. Please, don't do this..."

Once they got to the door of Myyah's room, Austin's eyes were blinded by a flood of tears. A myriad of emotions oppressed his soul. Mrs. Watkins and Austin entered the room and intensely stared at the now lifeless Myyah. Austin once again damn near collapsed to the ground but Mrs. Watkins managed to keep him up.

One of the nurses who was in the room preparing Myyah's body and decommissioning all of the machines in the room looked over at Mrs. Watkins and Austin and said, "I'm so sorry about all of this. My condolences go out to you and your family. I believe a grief counselor on site is on their way if you need someone to talk to. Other than that, I will leave you all to have your time. Again, I am truly sorry and may God give you peace in this trying time." The Latina-looking nurse then pursed her lips and patted Austin on his back and then proceeded to make her way out of the room.

"Ohhh, baby girl," Austin muttered as he made his way closer to Myyah. With no more pipes or tubes running in and out of her mouth or nostrils, she looked like she was sleeping peacefully.

Austin picked her small, brown hand up and gently rubbed it. Mrs. Watkins then walked over and rubbed the side of her face. "Oh, my precious granddaughter. I cannot believe this happened to you..."

CHAPTER FIFTY-ONE

A WEEK LATER...

*T*he Watkins family was slowly escorted into the vast, relatively filled Church by one of the funeral home directors. As everyone in the congregation took to their feet to welcome in the family in mourning, the organist and church pianist played a typical black gospel melody to hopefully damped the mood a bit.

Numb, confused, bitter and angry, Austin still couldn't wrap his mind around how he everything just suddenly got to this point. This didn't have to happen. He kept telling himself that over and over again since her passing. Her death did not have to happen. Had the State did a timely investigation, Myyah would be very much alive right now, in his arms, playing at a park or going to get ice cream on this beautiful Saturday mid-morning. Instead, here he was, a father grieving over a daughter he never really had a thorough chance to develop a relationship with.

As Austin, dressed in a black suit, held firm onto his grief-stricken mother, they slowly sauntered down closer and closer to the lilac and blue mist colored open casket. It was the perfect color to match the custom lavender princess dress Myyah had on.

Each footstep Austin took, the closer he got to the casket, the more he couldn't handle seeing his baby girl lay up in that casket. From afar he could see her soft yet stiff brown face along with her slender torso with her hands resting delicately on top.

Austin gawked over to his right and already saw that Fredquisha and his overly large family's presence were nestled comfortably inside the church. Fredquisha herself, instead of being dressed in normal and usual conservative funeral attire, was wearing a basic white blouse, some business casual pants, and some run-down pumps. You would've sworn the bitch was going to a job interview at a local mall, not the funeral of her own damn fucking daughter.

Seeing her and just how drab she looked intensified Austin's rage. But instead of letting cavalier attire and presence keep him dismayed, he continued to meditate in his head, allowing the young gospel soloist now softly humming Yolanda Adams' "The Battle Is Not Yours" to carry his mind away. He had to because truth be told, Austin for the last few days was on the absolute get on the verge of killing somebody. Myyah didn't need to be in that casket, Fredquisha's ass belonged in there he reasoned. The bitch was absolutely worthless – her and her entire family. The only exception was Donterio because unlike the rest of the ratchet family, Donterio was the only who seemed to operate with decency and common sense.

It was completely fucked up too because after Myyah passed away, Fredquisha never showed up to the hospital to be by her bedside until the funeral home took in her body. She stayed away from the hospital – her and the rest of the family...Except for Donterio of course. Donterio also acted as an emissary between his family and Austin's. What made Austin even more enraged was that Fredquisha didn't even have the decency or respect to offer to help cover the funeral expenses. She told Donterio to go back and tell Austin and Mrs. Watkins she was absolutely broke and couldn't afford nothing more than a simple funeral home service and cremation. The Watkins family, of course, refused to let Myyah be funeralized in such a cheap manner, so, without hesitation Mrs. Watkins offered to cover the entire funeral expense. She felt as though her baby girl, her one and only precious granddaughter Myyah, deserved a princess-like homegoing.

As Austin and his mother got close to Myyah's casket, they both broke down in synchrony, their wails filling the church. Jonah and the rest of the other siblings surrounded Austin and Mrs. Watkins and did their best to console them. Austin took one last glance at his beautiful daughter, leaned down and planted a kiss on her forehead and rubbed her cheek. "I love you, Myyah. You're gonna be alright, ok? You're gonna be alright. God's got you now. Oh, my baby. My beautiful baby... You look so beautiful," Austin cried as he continued to delicately rub the side of her face.

Austin's breathing picked up and his heart raced. Out of the corner of his eye, he could see Fredquisha staring off into nothing in particular. Some knock-off Gucci shades adorned her face as she held a funeral program in her hand. Her legs were crisscrossed and her just sat there, silent, motionless, in her seat as if she were attending the funeral of someone else's child. Her nonchalance and indifferent state of emotion were driving Austin even more crazy. But again, nonetheless, he had to do his best to make sure that on this day he can remember his baby girl and do away the sickening thoughts of murdering his child's mother. Finally, the Watkins clan was escorted to their pews inside the church and the service began.

New Faith Baptist Church was a medium-sized megachurch located right in the heart of Matteson with a congregation of about a thousand people. However today, no more than two hundred people were in attendance for Myyah's funeral. Most of the people here with family members, friends, and a few church congregants. As the Pastor of the church began to officiate the funeral, one by one, people were invited to the podium to give their remarks about Myyah's life. Teachers, neighbors and a few other people got up and said kind remarks about the girl and how much she meant to everyone. Towards the latter half the ceremony, right before her casket was to be closed, another song was going to be sung by the church's soloist to coincide with the 'crowning' of Princess Myyah.

The soloist, a young light-skinned girl with microbraids closed her eyes and began to pour out her heartful lyrics to the slow melody emanating from the church organ and piano.

"...I shall wear a crown
When it's all over
I'm going to put on my robe
Tell the story how I made it over
Soon as I get home
I shall see His face
When it's all over..."

One of the funeral home workers slowly made his way down the aisle towards Myyah's casket. Taking his time, taking deliberate step after step, he held firmly onto a pillow in which Myyah's princess crown, the same one Austin and Mrs. Watkins gifted her just over a week ago, rested on. Everyone in the congregation stood to their feet, shouting, holding their hands up in their air as they knew that fateful moment arrived. Baby girl would be crowned the heavenly, angelic princess she now was and her casket would be closed forever. As the funeral home worker made his way to the casket, Austin, Mrs. Watkins, Donterio and a few other stood to their feet and made their way to the casket. Austin, tears streaming down his face, observed the funeral home worker delicately fix the crown onto Myyah's head. As the soloist intensified her singing, Austin's heart pounded ferociously because he just knew at any second the lid to the casket would be closed and this would be the last time he would ever see his baby girl ever again. Mrs. Watkins then stood to her feet and held Austin, just knowing he was on the verge of collapsing.

Now was that time...The funeral home director sauntered over to the casket, pulled out a device used to lower the inside panel of the casket holding the body. He inserted the screwdriver like device into a tiny hole on the side of the casket and lowered Myyah's body deep into the casket. Another funeral home director then took a few pink roses adorning the casket and inserted them in between Myyah's hand. That same funeral director then took the outside linen and carefully tucked it into the inside of the casket. She then gave Austin, Jonah, and Donterio a slight nod. That was her signal that they should then lean in, place their hands on the side of the top-half casket lid and slowly lower it until it sealed shut. The three men followed suit and as the casket lid inched closer and closer, Austin trembled and let out a huge wail.

"NOOOO! GOD! PLEASE, GOD! NO! PLEEASE!" he screamed.

Mrs. Watkins tightened her embrace around Austin and rubbed his back. "I know, son. I know. God's got her now. God is in control."

After leaving the church, a solemn procession of about thirty cars made their way from the church out in the south suburbs to Oak Woods Cemetery on the City's south side. With three police motorcycle escorts leading the way, the long caravan of mourners banded together as they flowed through traffic, slowly journeying to the vast historic cemetery located right in the heart of the Greater Grand Crossing neighborhood.

After thirty minutes of trekking through light traffic on the expressway, the entourage arrived at the vast gates of the cemetery. With two local Chicago police motorcycle escorts first pulling in, the cream-colored Cadillac hearse pulled in and made its way in as the rest of the entourage followed. Once they arrived at the burial site covered in a green tent, Austin along with his brothers and another cousin, got out of the family limousine and then made their way to the hearse so they could carry Myyah's casket towards the plot.

Mr. Barrett, the funeral director, got out of the passenger side of the hearse and then opened the back of the hearse. Mr. Barrett leaned into the back of the hearse, slid Myyah's casket out and from there Austin and his family carried the tiny casket over to the plot's lowering setup.

Family members, relatives, friends and others who knew Myyah drizzled their grief-stricken bodies into the tent, crowding around each other. Austin and his immediately family sat down on the seats as more mourners surrounded the family to begin the burial's last rites and rituals.

Mr. Barrett, the tall, elderly and incredibly dark-skinned funeral director who had a full head of curly white hair, scanned the entire group of mourners and began to recite the last rites before the lowering of Myyah's casket.

"Well, Beloved, we have come literally to the last mile of the way. You can't go any further than this when you are made of flesh and blood. We were with Myyah when she breathed, and we were with her when she took her final breath. But you know, the concern isn't with our departed young sister. The concern is with us – the living. Our young sister is now in another world, a world much larger than what we can imagine. A divine world. God's world. But for those of us who remain, the living, we have a task not to be concerned with those who have left us but to be concerned with those who are still among us. All of us, from the youngest to the oldest still here today, should stop hurting one another and love one another. We are family. And if we can make that commitment today then Myyah's living has meant something even beyond herself. Let's remember the grieving families now. Their days will be filled with sorrow. We must understand they have given up a portion of themselves. Anybody can stand with them today, but days from now, we must be reminded of their grief, and pick up the phone, call them up and say, 'I just called you up to say I love you and I am still here with you, and I mean it from the bottom of my heart'. And now, FOR AS MUCH as it hath pleased Almighty God, in his wise providence, to take out of this world the soul of our deceased sister, we therefore commit her body to the ground; earth to earth, ashes to ashes, dust to dust; looking for the general Resurrection in the last day, and the life of the world to come, through our Lord Jesus Christ; at whose second coming in glorious majesty to judge the world, the earth, and the sea shall give up their dead; and the corruptible bodies of those who sleep in him shall be changed, and made like unto his own glorious body; according to the mighty working whereby he is able to subdue all things unto himself. Amen..."

"Amen," everyone lowly responded at the close of Mr. Barrett's recitation.

The same funeral home attendant who passed out flowers to the family moments ago then leaned into Mrs. Watkins' left ear and instructed her they can now proceed to place the roses on top of Myyah's casket. Mrs. Watkins got up from her seat and placed the rose in her hand onto the casket. Austin and the rest of the family did the same.

Three Mexican cemetery workers then proceeded over to the plot and began to unhinge the casket so it could make its slow six-feet passage down into the freshly dug grave. Sobs within those in attendance intensified. The reality of Myyah's death sunk deeper into Austin's mind and he couldn't hold back anymore. "My baby girl is gone!" he uncontrollably sobbed, throwing his fists in the air, fighting the invisible demons that were trying to devour his newly found redemption.

"It's gonna be ok, baby...She's watching over us now. She's now our angel...," Mrs. Watkins consoled as she rubbed Austin's back. As much as Austin wanted to believe everything his mother was saying, he couldn't. He just continued to shake his head. The total shock and disbelief of Myyah's death was just still very overwhelming and rupturing to his soul. A part of him was now slowly getting covered with dirt. From that moment as the cemetery workers began the process of enclosing the casket into its vault, Austin's soul was no more. A blank cloud of darkness inoculated him and all he could think about was inflicting pain. Murder. Once again, he looked out the corner of his eye and observed just how fucking nonchalant and cavalier Fredquisha was. This bitch had to die he reasoned. She had to go sooner rather than later.

Richard, one of Jonah's best friends, days ago had agreed to sing one last song before everyone left the grave. He made his way from the crowd and greeted everyone. "To the Watkins family, you have my deepest condolences. At the request of my best friend and brother, Jonah, this is for our angel, our princess..."

CHAPTER FIFTY-TWO

THREE WEEKS LATER...

*U*sually Sunday evenings after church, Mrs. Watkins would make a huge southern dinner for her and her kids. Everyone would come over, sometimes even friends and distant cousins, just to laugh it up and have a good time around some good home cooked food. Mrs. Watkins tirelessly and studiously slaved away in the kitchen, wanting to make sure all of her cooking was perfected. A huge black cauldron of collards boiled on the gas stove. In fact, collard greens were her fave to cook every Sunday. She had a special recipe she got from her grandmother. The recipe made Mrs. Watkins leave her house every Friday and go into Downtown to get fresh pork neckbones along with spicy hot sausage from a butchery in Fulton Market. The sausage was used to cook jambalaya or dirty rice. This afternoon, aside from the collard greens, Mrs. Watkins had four cheese macaroni and cheese baking in the oven. On a counter top, a spread of crispy pieces of fried chicken cooled off on a pan. Three buttery pound cakes cooled off on an adjacent counter.

Despite the aromas of southern comfort floating in the air, Mrs. Watkins was still grieving from Myyah's loss and she was slowly doing her best to get over the sudden and unexpected death.

"Hey, Austin! Dinner's ready!" Mrs. Watkins beckoned Austin to come downstairs and eat supper. "Everyone is gonna be on their way soon," she continued.

Austin, hearing his mother's call from his room upstairs, didn't suddenly bust a move to get ready to get his grub on. He himself was still frozen and bitter knowing his baby girl was gone forever. It is said that time heals all wounds, but it was going to take an eternity to heal the one gaping in Austin's heart and mind. And that wound, well, he was at the point where he felt there was going to be nothing to heal it.

Actually...

He did have his mindset on what could be therapeutic, but he was deliberating back and forth as to whether or not it would be the right healing for his broken soul.

Since Myyah's death, he had been fighting hard not to breakdown and succumb back to his dark ways. Every second, minute and hour was an intense struggle, and as time progressed Austin found himself conjuring up thoughts of homicide.

Austin, laying in his bed, eyes glued to the slowly moving ceiling fan blades, slowly rubbed his abs. While he was in jail he learned the art of meditation by a yoga instructor who volunteered her services to the detention center. It was a part of teaching inmates anger management and conflict resolution. But fuck all of that anger management bullshit. Austin's baby girl was gone out of his life, and the person who he knew was completely responsible for her death was her no good, trifling ass bitch of a mother, Fredquisha.

Not responding to his mother's call, Austin slowly got up from the bed and made his way to his closet. He slipped on a pair of jeans, his Jordans and then threw a black hoodie on. He quickly dashed into his bedroom's bathroom, washed his face and hands and then dashed downstairs.

"Mama, I'm finne head out for a few…I'll give you a call later, ok?"

"Damn, son! I just made all of this food and you just about to bounce? Everyone is literally coming over any second now!"

"Yeah, sorry mama, I just need to just clear my mind, that's all. I'll be back soon, I promise!" Austin then reached in, planted a kiss on Mrs. Watkins' cheek and quickly made his way out of the house.

CHAPTER FIFTY-THREE

*S*ad but seemingly encouraging lyrics from a gospel song lowly blared from the car's radio. With salty rivers of tears still pouring from his reddened eyes, Austin took swigs from a bottle of E&J. He'd already smoked three big ass blunts back to back. Completely gone and numb, deep down he just knew there was no other real reason to keep living. Myyah was his reason. And now that she was gone he truly wanted to be dead too.

As the slow and somewhat melancholic gospel music continued to play, he stared down at a picture of him and Myyah the night of the Daddy-Daughter dance. He continued to weep as more and more tears streamed down his face, mixing in with the sweat gushing from his wide brown brow. "Oh, Myyah. I can't keep living. You were my only reason for trying to change. Why God? Why?!?" Austin slurred and then took another swig from his drink.

The sun was beginning to set. Mrs. Watkins sent Austin a few text messages back to back asking him if everything was alright and if he'd planned on coming back home. He lied and assured her that he was, but the reality was that he was ready to kill Fredquisha. That bitch had to die. Her blood needed to be poured out into the streets.

Austin opened up the glove compartment and whipped out a gloc. He loaded it with a full clip and then tucked it into his waist. His eyes turned to slits, and he wiped his nose free of sweat and running snot.

For the last hour or so, Austin had been parked on a street right across from Fredquisha's apartment. He had spent so much time debating what he was about to do, but now that his mind was made up, he was ready to go guns a blazing and kill everything in his sight. He got out of the car and slowly meandered across the street. Just as he was about to reach the main entrance, a cream-colored Cadillac pulled up to the side. Two big ass goonish niggas, both wearing doo rags and leather jackets, plopped themselves out the car and looked around. It was like these niggas were double-checking to make sure their surroundings were safe of anyone who might be nosey. One of them spotted Austin and scanned him up and down. He opened up his jacket and pulled out a big ass Desert Eagle. His eyes turned to those familiar slits, easily suggesting to Austin he better mind his business and move the fuck on.

"I suggest you get lost, partnah," the big goonish nigga growled, showing off the gun that obviously was loaded and ready to be used.

Austin didn't say a word, he just quickly spun on his feet. Despite alcohol and weed mixed in with rage and confusing running through his system, Austin sobered the fuck up and made his way back to his car. Actually his mother's whip.

"Fuckkk," Austin mumbled as he quickly hopped back into the car, started it up and sped off. "Who the fuck them niggas was??!?" he said to himself as he barreled down the street and around the corner. He pulled over to a side parking spot. He thought to himself for a second and couldn't help but think those niggas were going into the apartment building to fuck someone up. The street nigga inside of Austin said, "Nigga, mind ya business and go back home." But the inquisitive and investigative nigga retorted with, "Go check this shit out. Just stay in the cut."

Austin swung the car right around the corner and rather than parking directly across the street from Fredquisha's apartment entrance, he parked a few cars down, still able to have clear sight of the two goonish niggas standing idly. They were still scanning the area. Probably waiting for someone Austin presumed. Then Austin saw a familiar face...His mama's cousin's ex-husband -- that crackhead Glen.

Glen quickly strolled up to the two dudes, looked around and then dapped up with one of them. Austin then observed one of the dudes slide Glen a manila envelope. The crackhead maintenance man then quickly opened the door and three them disappeared.

Austin continued inside the car to wait to see what was about to go down next. Some moments later he heard loud screams emanating from the building. He couldn't immediately discern who was screaming, but it sounded like a mix of a man and a woman. The screams got louder, and by the raspiness of the screaming woman's voice, he could it tell it was Fredquisha.

Austin got out the car and ran towards the side of a car closer to the entrance of the building. He ducked and peered up towards Fredquisha's apartment. His anxiety ran high. His hands quivered as he held his composure leaning against the car.

POW! POW! POW!

Fredquisha screamed again, this time louder and more pronounced. Austin could hear her beg for her life.

POW! POW!

The screams were no more.

A minute later the two men came bursting through the

entrance, looked around and then quickly hopped in the Cadillac and sped off down the street.

Hyperventilating and trying to get a control of his rapid heartbeat, Austin still ducked himself behind the car waiting for the crazy scene to clear. He then stood up and quickly ran back to his car, started it up and took off. He didn't want to be on the scene if and when cops arrived.

EPILOGUE

A YEAR LATER...

*T*ime, as it was said before, surely does begin to heal all things. For Austin, since Myyah's death and oddly enough the murder of Fredquisha, he was able to slowly move on with his life. Not a day went by where he didn't think about his daughter. He missed her every day. Her smile. Her laugh. Just her very presence, although two years went by where he barely saw her.

But as time moved on, and his spirituality and sense of life's purpose deepened, he realized that things happened for a reason. As tragic as things may be when they happen in our lives, indeed they happen for reason. Sometimes we are given the privilege to understand the reasons, sometimes not. But when we don't understand, at least at that moment in time, we have to just lean on God's understanding since he is the one who ordains all things to happen. That was the way Austin saw it and now believed it. With that being said, Austin, after getting released from jail, started school and set his eyes on getting his degree in construction and real estate development.

It's funny how Karma, divine intervention, etc., (whatever you want to call it) has a way of showing you your purpose and what God has in store for you. The day when he went to go possibly kill Deontae and then kill himself, had not those two men been there to stop Austin dead in his tracks and making him leave, God knows what his suicide would've triggered. Just more heartache, more pain, more devastation for so many people who deep down Austin truly loved. And for that, that was a huge lesson for Austin to learn. Yeah, bad shit happens, but bad shit happens to everyone. And just because bad shit happens to you doesn't give you the right to then make more bad shit happen for everyone else.

That early evening when Fredquisha was killed, she had been helping Deontae to hide out from both the police as well as the rumored hittas who were after him. Unfortunately for Fredquisha, she didn't know Deontae was also hiding out from the hittas and had she known that she probably would've never kept him in her apartment. However, keeping Deontae there served her well for the time being. She still got good dick, good weed and most importantly, she was able to use Deontae as a deterrent to stop Mr. Garrison from taking advantage of her.

Nonetheless, the two unidentified men, with the assistance of Glen the crackhead, killed Fredquisha and Deontae in retaliation for trying to kill Katina. Fredquisha, unfortunately, had to go because she was collateral damage and the two men didn't want any identifying witnesses. They couldn't risk it and didn't any anything to come back and get Katina nor Katina's mother in trouble.

Speaking of Katina – within days of getting shot, she was able to get her transplant. Within three months she was fully rehabilitated and back to working and finally was making the courage to enroll in school. The same school as Austin...

"Yes, can I get a spicy chicken sandwich, extra pickles, and a large fry?"

Austin was standing in line, ordering a chicken sandwich from the Chick-Fil-A restaurant inside the student cafeteria. It was ritual for him to come here right after his 2 PM class to grab a bite to eat and then spend the next two or three hours studying.

After getting his food and sitting down, he went straight into his books and spent the next hour or so studying real estate finance. He took a sip from peach lemonade ice tea and slapped a fry in his mouth. With his eyes glued to the complex mathematical formulas, he steadily took notes.

"Fuck!"

Suddenly looked up and saw a woman, Katina, slip on her ass and spill her food tray all over the place. She too had gone to Chick-Fil-A and ordered a meal. Food and drink spilled everywhere. Katina, slightly moaning and looking disappointed, was still on the ground trying to pull herself up and minimize the embarrassment.

Austin closed his book and quickly went to go help Katina off the ground.

"Damn, let me help you up. You look like you took a huge fall there," Austin said and smiled as he helped Katina off the ground.

"Shit, damn it…I was looking forward to that too. I just spent my last $10 on that meal and can't eat until later tonight when I go to work!" Katina complained and shook her head. "Oh, well. Thank you, sir."

"No worries…Sorry about that," Austin responded.

"Oh, don't worry about me. I'm pretty sure you have enough worries in the world. The last thing you need to do is worry about me."

Austin paused for a moment and took in Katina's humble and infectious smile. There was something about her, something inviting. Something angelic. He couldn't quite put his finger on it, but he wanted to probe deeper.

"Well, let me get on my way. I probably didn't need that chicken anyways," Katina laughed.

"Here, let me treat you. I'm not trying to flirt with you or anything, I swear. But I feel bad seeing as how you wanna eat something and you gotta jet off to work soon."

"No. No, you don't have to do that."

"Listen...I don't mind. Besides, I can use another chicken sandwich myself. I can take down five of those."

"Hahaha, really? You got an appetite!" Katina snickered. Seeing Austin's smile and his desire to help her was really messing with her head. It had been a while since someone had shown genuine non-sexual interest in her, especially a black man.

The nurse and now student thought about it for a second. "Sure, I don't mind. What's your name anyways?"

"Austin...You?"

"Katina."

"Nice to meet you," Austin said as he extended his hand.

"Nice to meet you as well." Katina extended hers, and the two shook hands. They walked over to the Chick-Fil-A counter and they proceeded to order their food. After they got their meals they walked back over to the table where Austin still had his stuff. They chopped it up for a few moments, exchanged numbers and went their separate ways.

"Hey mama," Austin said as he made his way into the living room. Mrs. Watkins, as usual, was in her living room doing yoga to a DVD she had popped in moments earlier.

"Oh, hey son! How was school?"

"It was good...Same ole, same ole. Getting ready for this big exam."

"Oh, well that's good. When you get a chance, you got some letter from some law office."

"Ok," Austin replied and then went into the kitchen and saw his mail neatly stacked on a counter.

He rummaged through a few letters, throwing away mostly junk mail in an adjacent trash can. Finally, once he got to the letter his mother was talking about, he opened it and scanned it.

Reading it word by word, his heart almost came to a complete screeching halt.

"WHAT THE FUCK!?!?! ARE YOU FUCKING KIDDING ME?!?!?"

Mrs. Watkins stopped her yoga poses and quickly ran into the kitchen. "What's wrong? What happened?" she asked, somewhat out of breath.

"This has to be some sort of goddamn fucking joke!"

"Austin, baby, please, tell me what's going on?"

"Fredquisha's mama got a fuckin' lawsuit going against the hospital for medical malpractice. She's suing them for $10 million, talkin' 'bout they botched the surgery and shit with that experimental drug or whatever. She won the mothafuckin' lawsuit, but I am next of kin, the courts were about to give me half of the judgment. BUT, this bitch is challenging my paternity, stating that I am not Myyah's biological father!"

"WHAT?!?!?" Mrs. Watkins' screamed.

"YES! READ THIS SHIT!" Austin handed his mother the paper. She quickly scanned its content and immediately clutched her chest in surprise. She gasped and looked up at Austin, and her look of surprise suddenly turned into a look of disgust.

"Austin, wait, I am so confused. What the fuck does she mean you are not the biological father?!?!? Didn't you all take a DNA test to even prove paternity from the get go?!?!"

Austin paused for a moment.

He never did a DNA test. He never challenged paternity over Myyah from the get. He'd always assumed she was his biological daughter, no questions asked.

Mrs. Watkins closed her eyes and exhaled. She lowered her head and shook it. "Austin, please, baby, please tell me you took a paternity test."

"No, mama. I just assumed she was mines. I mean, she looked just like me. What the fuck!?!?"

"Oh, God!" Mrs. Watkins kept shaking her head as she held the letter from the law firm that was coordinating the medical malpractice lawsuit. She glanced back down at it again and saw that they were requesting Austin to come to court next week and submit to a court-ordered posthumous paternity test.

"This is so fucking unreal. Austin, please, this cannot be real. I am just. This is just too much. I don't feel well, call 9-11. I think I'm gonna pass out," Mrs. Watkins screeched as she held her head and damn near collapsed to her knees.

THE FOLLOWING WEEK...

"In the case of The Estate of Fredquisha Pierce vs. Northwestern Children's Memorial Hospital, will the plaintiffs and defendants please rise. The Honorable Gary Truman is presiding," the burly black court bailiff announced.

On one side of the small courtroom were attorneys representing the hospital. On the other side were attorneys representing Evelyn.

Evelyn and the rest of her family were attendance in the courtroom, quietly awaiting what the judge was about to say. Donterio wasn't present. After Myyah's passing, he had enough of dealing with his mother and decided to move out of Chicago for good. He met his now fiancée and was attending vocational school down in Orlando while working as a mechanic at an Enterprise Rent-A-Car at the airport. Fredquisha's two boys weren't present either. Both of them were staying with their fathers. As for Quantaysia, right before Fredquisha was murdered, she paid the girl to get an abortion behind her mother's back.

Austin, Mrs. Watkins and the rest of the family were huddled away in the courtroom too. With his eyes concentrated on the Judge, he just knew at any moment the judge was going to summon him forward to do a DNA test right then and there. Austin and his mom had hired a lawyer to represent them. One of the things they were confused about was how the court was going to conduct some sort of paternity test given that Myyah was long gone. Turns out, the hospital still had fresh blood samples from Myyah that had been refrigerated for experimental purposes. It was also one of the reasons too why the University of Chicago along with Northwestern were found liable for medical malpractice. They used Myyah as a guinea pig for an experimental stem cell treatment that had not been FDA-approved.

"Is Mr. Austin Watkins present today?"

"Yes, your honor," Austin proudly stated as he stood up.

All eyes were on him.

"Can you please approach my bench?"

"Yes, your honor."

Austin, decked out in a grey Armani suit, made his way towards the front. He could feel the gawks coming from

Evelyn's family crawling down the back of his head and neck. He approached the judge, no smile was present on his face.

"As you understand, Mr. Watkins, the Estate of Fredquisha Pierce is making a paternity challenge. They dispute you are the biological father of Myyah Watkins. Although you were listed as the biological father on the birth certificate, if indeed it does turn out true, based on a court-mandated paternity test, that you are not the biological father, you understand that you will not be entitled to half of the judgment awarded to the estate of Myyah Watkins, correct?"

"Yes, your honor. I am completely aware. My attorney informed me of everything."

"Ok, good. Bailiff, can you please hand me the results of the DNA test?"

The bailiff handed the judge a manila envelope, and he quickly scanned the results. With his lips pursed, he got to the end of the document and then looked at Austin.

"Well, unfortunately, sir, you are not the biological father of Myyah Watkins. According to the test conducted by LabCorp, there is 100% chance you are not the father."

Light oohs poured from the people sitting inside the courtroom.

Austin lowered his head and shook it. A few tears trickled down his eyes as he tried to fight back rage.

"I'm so sorry, sir. I know this is devastating news. I know there is nothing the court can do in order to provide solace in this situation."

Mrs. Watkins and the rest of the family were in total shock and disbelief. Mrs. Watkins was crying her eyes out in silence, absolutely shocked at the news. The girl, who for so many years was her precious granddaughter, after all, wasn't hers at all. It was all one big lie that Fredquisha probably knew of but was too arrogant and deceitful to let Austin know the truth.

Evelyn, on the other hand, had a look of joy plastered across her face. The bitch looked like she was ready to run out the room and announce to the world she had just won the lottery, and indeed she did now that the judge was on the cusp of handing over $10 million to her.

Light chatter and laughs filled the room, obviously coming from Evelyn's family members and friends.

"Can I please ask the conversations and laughs to cease. This is an important matter," the judge explained. "A matter in which I am on the verge of handing over a $10 million judgment to a family that seems more concerned with receiving a large amount of money than the emotional state of this man who was lied to for years. While in any other circumstance I would've ended this case right here and signed over the judgment, I cannot in good conscience do that. Ms. Gonzales, can you please approach the witness stand?"

"Yes, your honor…"

Suddenly, deep from within the crowded courthouse, Ms. Gonzales, the social worker who dealt firsthand with Myyah's DCFS case rose from her seat and quickly made her way to the witness stand.

"Thank you, Ms. Gonzales. I am going to ask you a series of questions in regards to the DCFS investigation you conducted last year when Myyah Watkins was still in custody of Fredquisha Pierce, along with the grandmother on a temporary basis. Please, thoroughly recount all of which you witnessed along with a summary of findings DCFS found before Myyah Watkins' passing…"

"Yes, your honor."

Austin, who by now, was back in his seat, looked very confused as to what was going on. However, on the other side, the look on Evelyn's face wasn't that of confusion. It was one of shock and disgust. Was this judge about to play her for a fool?

Ms. Gonzales laid it all out. She gave a thorough recount of the entire investigation that was conducted last year. She talked about the living conditions of Evelyn's apartment, the negligence of now the retire DCFS caseworker Shirley McGill and the initial police report filed by Mrs. Watkins at the Matteson Police Station. She testified that before Myyah's death, she convinced her director to go ahead with giving Mrs. Watkins court-ordered temporary custody over Myyah but by then it was too late. She rolled out an extensive case and based on her research on Fredquisha's past, along with written testimony from her former landlord, Mr. Garrison, that Fredquisha was unequipped to be a mother. After she spilled the tea, laying out a case against Evelyn and Fredquisha, she made her way back to her seat.

"Well, it is the decision of the court based on the findings of DCFS that I cannot in good faith erase the assumed paternity of Mr. Watkins. Although based on the paternity test it is well established that Mr. Watkins was not the biological father, the fact remains that DCFS was on the verge of pushing custody to her grandmother, Mrs. Watkins. I should also note that even if Mr. Watkins was the biological father, I would still transfer the judgment to him and his family rather than the Pierce family. DCFS and the State of Illinois clearly didn't do their jobs and in this instance, the State and DCFS would be facing serious litigation. Therefore, I hereby award the entire $10 million judgment to Austin Watkins and his family. That is all."

Austin's eyes widened even absolute surprise. Mrs. Watkins and the rest of the family looked at each other. What in the fuck just happened, Austin thought to himself.

"Austin, baby, Austin! Did you hear that?!?!?"

"Wait, so I'm confused…They are giving me $10 million??!?"

"YES!"

"AHHHHHHHHHHHH!" Mrs. Watkins screamed. "BUT GOD! BUT GOD!"

❄

A YEAR LATER...

"Baby girl, seems like you had a big purpose. A much bigger purpose than all of us could see. I miss you so much. You are on my mind all the time. Although it turns out you were never mine from the get-go, none of that matters. I still love you like my own, and you will always be near and dear to me in my heart."

Austin, standing directly in the front of Myyah's headstone, leaned down and dropped a single pink rose on her grave. He kissed the tips of his hands and then planted his fingertips onto the top of the headstone. He looked to the open blue skies and smiled.

"Everything has a reason, I guess. I hope you are watching all the cartoons you want in Heaven," Austin laughed as he wiped some tears from his cheek.

"I'm sure she is," Katina said as she wrapped her arms around Austin. "I'm sure she is watching them all, over and over again."

Austin looked over at Katina, now his wife and then looked down at her belly. She was five months pregnant. Austin and Katina had hit off big time, and it only took Austin ninety-three days to realize Katina was god-sent. So, he proposed.

"It's so crazy how you were the same nurse that tended to her bedside. Man, God is crazy yet awesome."

"Life is strange like that."

"Strange and beautiful."

The two of them embraced, kissed and then walked away from the grave holding hands. They approached Austin's black Rolls Royce, hopped in and quietly took off.

After graduating from college, Austin used a portion of the judgment to immediately start his own real estate empire. He poured his money into rehabbing dilapidated houses and apartment buildings all throughout the South and West sides of the city. He also started his own nonprofit foundation, setting up basketball camps, mentoring programs and other afterschool activities for troubled youth. Katina decided not to continue on with getting her master's in nursing. Instead, Austin gave her money to help start and manage a low-income clinic all throughout Chicago. Out of the kindness of his heart, Austin, who forgave Fredquisha and Evelyn for all they did, and also realize his complicity in the situation, did give some money to Evelyn to help her move into the apartment building in Hyde Park. He also hired her to help manage a few properties throughout the neighborhood. She forgave Austin, stopped smoking, lost weight and eventually started attending church services with Mrs. Watkins.

Austin's ordeal, his quest to save his baby girl, taught him one valuable lesson. A lesson anyone, regardless of race, socioeconomic status, gender, culture, sexual orientation, etc., should learn. Love thy neighbor. He couldn't in good faith take the judgment and not at least help Evelyn and the rest of Fredquisha's family. He didn't have it in his heart to be that crude and one-dimensional. And so, for Austin's forgiveness of everything that transpired and his desire to move forward, for Austin's pulsing desire to see beyond everyone's flaws as so many people saw beyond his, he did his best to make sure everyone had a chance to get things right before it was too late. Too late before another girl, or even boy ended up like Myyah. She was an example, and all we need is one sacrificing example to know we should learn to love one another.

-THE END-

Made in the USA
Las Vegas, NV
14 April 2022

47482688R00219